# *In The Roar Of The Sea*

## Sabine Baring-Gould

Baring-Gould, Sa

In the roar of
the sea : a tale
of the Cornish
          FT Pbk

1823734

British Library Cataloguing In Publication Data
A Record of this Publication is available
from the British Library

ISBN 1846853354
978-1-84685-335-7

First published April 1892
This edition published 2006 by

Diggory Press Ltd
Three Rivers, Minions, Liskeard, Cornwall, PL14 5LE, UK
WWW.DIGGORYPRESS.COM

# CHAPTER I
## OVER AND DONE

SITTING in the parsonage garden, in a white frock, with a pale green sash about her waist, leaning back against the red-brick wall, her glowing copper hair lit by the evening sun, was Judith Trevisa.

She was tossing guelder-roses into the air; some dozens were strewn about her feet on the gravel, but one remained of the many she had plucked and thrown and caught, and thrown and caught again for a sunny afternoon hour. As each greenish-white ball of flowers went up into the air, it diffused a faint but pleasant fragrance.

"When I have done with you, my beauty, I have done altogether," said Judith.

"With what?"

Her father spoke. He had come up unperceived by the girl, burdened with a shovel in one hand and a bucket in the other, looking pale, weary, and worn.

"Papa, you nearly spoiled my game. Let me finish, and I will speak."

"Is it a very serious matter, Judith, and engrossing?"

"Engrossing, but not serious, Je m'amuse."

The old rector seated himself on the bench beside her, and he also leaned back against the red-brick, gold-and-grey-lichen-spotted wall, and looked into the distance before him, waiting till his daughter was ready to speak, not, perhaps, sorry to have a little rest first, for he was over-tired. Had Judith not been absorbed in her ball-play with the guelder-rose bunch, she would have noticed his haggard appearance, the green hue about his mouth, the sunken eyes, the beaded brow. But she was counting the rebounds of her ball, bent on sustaining her play as long as was possible to her.

She formed a charming picture, fresh and pure, and had the old man not been over-tired, he would have thought so with a throb of parental pride.

She was a child in size, slender in build, delicate in bone, with face and hands of porcelain transparency and whiteness, with, moreover, that incomparable complexion only seen in the British Isles, and then only with red-gold hair.

Her bronze leather shoes were the hue of some large flies that basked and frisked on the warm wall, only slightly disturbed by the girl's play, to return again and run and preen themselves again, and glitter jewel-like as studs on that sun-baked, lichen-enamelled wall. Her eyes, moreover, were lustrous as the backs of these flies, iridescent with the changing lights of the declining sun, and the changed direction of her glance following the dancing ball of guelder-rose. Her long fingers might have been of china, but that when raised so that the sun struck their backs they were turned to a translucent rose. There was no colour in her cheek, only the faintest suffusion of pink on the temples below where the hair was rolled back in waves of luminous molten copper dashing against the brick wall.

"I have done my work," said the rector.

"And I my play," responded the girl, letting the ball drop into her lap and rock there from one knee to the other. "Papa! this fellow is the conqueror; I have made him dance thirty-five great leaps, and he has not yet fallen—wilfully. I let him go down and get breath just now. There lie all my dancers dead about me. They failed very speedily."

"You cannot be for ever playing, Ju."

"That is why I play now, papa. When playtime is over I shall be in earnest indeed."

"Indeed?" the old man sighed.

Judith looked round, and was shocked to see how ill her father appeared to be.

"Are you very tired, darling papa?"

"Yes—over-tired."

"Have you been at your usual task?"

3

"Yes, Ju—an unprofitable task."

"Oh, papa!"

"Yes, unprofitable. The next wind from the sea that blows—one will blow in an hour—and all my work is undone."

"But, my dear papa!" Judith stooped and looked into the bucket. "Why!—what has made you bring a load of sand up here? We want none in the garden. And such a distance too!—from the church. No wonder you are tired."

"Have I brought it?" he asked, without looking at the bucket.

"You have, indeed. That, if you please, is unprofitable work, not the digging of the church out of the sand-heaps that swallow it."

"My dear, I did not know that I had not emptied the pail outside the churchyard gate. I am very tired; perhaps that explains it."

"No doubt about it, papa. It was work quite as unprofitable, but much more exhausting, than my ball-play. Now, papa, whilst you have been digging your church out of the sand, which will blow over it again to-night, you say, I have been pitching and tossing guelder-roses. We have been both wasting time, one as much as the other."

"One as much as the other," repeated the old man.

"Yes, dear, one as much as the other, and I have been doing it all my time here—morally, spiritually, as well as materially, digging the church out of the smothering sands, and all in vain—all profitless work. You are right, Ju."

"Papa," said Judith hastily, seeing his discouragement and knowing his tendency to depression, "papa, do you hear the sea how it roars? I have stood on the bench, more than once, to look out seaward, and find a reason for it; but there is none—all blue, blue as a larkspur; and not a cloud in the sky—all blue, blue there too. No wind either, and that is why I have done well with my ball-play. Do you hear the roar of the sea, papa?" she repeated.

"Yes, Ju. There will be a storm shortly. The sea is thrown into great swells or rollers, a sure token that something is coming. Before night a gale will be on us."

Then ensued silence. Judith with one finger trifled with the guelder-rose bunch in her lap musingly, not desirous to resume her play with it. Something in her father's manner was unusual, and made her uneasy.

"My dear!" he began, after a pause, "one must look out to sea—into the vast mysterious sea of the future—and prepare for what is coming from it. Just now the air is still, and we sit in this sweet, sunny garden, and lean our backs against the warm wall, and smell the fragrance of the flowers; but we hear the beating of the sea, and know that a mighty tempest with clouds and darkness is coming. So in other matters we must look out and be ready—count the time till it comes. My dear—when I am gone—"

"Papa!"

"We are looking out to sea and listening. That must come at some time—it may come sooner than you anticipate." He paused, heaved a sigh, and said, "Oh! Jamie! What are we to do about Jamie?"

"Papa, I will always take care of Jamie."

"But who will take care of you?"

"Of me? Oh, papa, surely I can take care of myself!"

He shook his head doubtfully.

"Papa, you know how strong I am in will—how firm I can be with Jamie."

"But all mankind are not Jamies. It is not for you I fear, as much as for you and him together. He is a trouble and a difficulty."

"Jamie is not so silly and troublesome as you think. All he needs is application. He cannot screw his mind down to his books—to any serious occupation. But that will come. I have heard say that the stupidest children make the sharpest men. Little by little it will come, but it will come certainly. I will set myself as my task to make Jamie apply his mind and become a useful man, and I shall succeed, papa." She caught her father's hand between hers, and slapped it joyously, confidently. "How cold your hand is, papa! and yet you look warm."

"You were always Jamie's champion," said her father, not noticing her remark relative to himself.

"He is my twin brother, so of course I am his champion. Who else would be that, were not I?"

"No—no one else. He is mischievous and trouble-some—poor, poor fellow. You will always be to Jamie what you are now, Ju—his protector or champion? He is weak and foolish, and if he were to fall into bad hands—I shudder to think what might become of him."

"Rely on me, dearest father."

Then he lifted the hand of his daughter, and looked at it with a faint smile. "It is very small, it is very weak, to fight for self alone, let alone yourself encumbered with Jamie."

"I will do it, papa, do not fear."

"Judith, I must talk gravely with you, for the future is very dark to me; and I am unable with hand or brain to provide anything against the evil day. Numbness is on me, and I have been hampered on every side. For one thing, the living has been so poor, and my parishioners so difficult to deal with, that I have been able to lay by but a trifle. I believe I have not a relative in the world—none, at all events, near enough and known to me that I dare ask him to care for you—"

"Papa, there is Aunt Dionysia."

"Aunt Dionysia," he repeated, with a hesitating voice. "Yes; but Aunt Dionysia is—is not herself capable of taking charge of you. She has nothing but what she earns, and then—Aunt Dionysia is—is—well—Aunt Dionysia. I don't think you could be happy with her, even if, in the event of my departure, she were able to take care of you. Then—and that chiefly—she has chosen, against my express wishes—I may say, in defiance of me—to go as housekeeper into the service of the man, of all others, who has been a thorn in my side, a hinderer of God's work, a—but I will say no more."

"What! Cruel Coppinger?"

"Yes, Cruel Coppinger. I might have been the means of doing a little good in this place, God knows! I only think I might; but I have been thwarted, defied, insulted by that man. As I have striven to dig my buried church out of the overwhelming sands, so have I striven to lift the souls of my poor parishioners out of the dead engulfing sands of savagery, brutality, very heathenism of their mode of life, and I have been frustrated. The winds have blown the sands back with every gale over my work with spade, and that stormblast Coppinger has devastated every trace of good that I have done, or tried to do, in spiritual matters. The Lord reward him according to his works."

Judith felt her father's hand tremble in hers.

"Never mind Coppinger now," she said, soothingly.

"I must mind him," said the old man, with severe vehemence. "And—that my own sister should go, go—out of defiance, into his house and serve him! That was too much. I might well say, I have none to whom to look as your protector." He paused awhile and wiped his brow. His pale lips were quivering. "I do not mean to say," said he, "that I acted with judgment, when first I came to S. Enodoc, when I spoke against smuggling. I did not understand it then. I though with the thoughts of an inlander. Here—the sands sweep over the fields, and agriculture is in a measure impossible. The bays and creeks seem to invite—will—I leave it an open question. But with regard to wrecking—" His voice, which had quavered in feebleness, according with the feebleness of his judgment relative to smuggling, now gained sonorousness.

"Wrecking, deliberate wrecking, is quite another matter. I do not say that our people are not justified in gathering the harvest the sea casts up. There always must be, there will be wrecks on this terrible coast: but there has been—I know there has been, though I have not been able to prove it—deliberate provocation of wrecks,—and that is the sin of Cain. Had I been able to prove—"

"Never mind that now, dear papa. Neither I nor Jamie are, or will be, wreckers. Talk of something else. You over-excite yourself."

Judith was accustomed to hear her father talk in an open manner to her. She had been his sole companion for several years, since his wife's death, and she had become the confidant of his inmost thoughts, his vacillations, his discouragements, not of his hopes—for he had none, nor of his schemes—for he formed none.

"I do not think I have been of any use in this world," said the old parson, relapsing into his tone of discouragement, the temporary flame of anger having died away. "My sowing has produced no harvest. I have brought light, help, strength to none. I have dug all day in the vineyard, and not a vine is the better for it; all cankered and fruitless."

"Papa—and me? Have you done nothing for me?"

"You!"

He had not thought of his child.

"Papa! Do you think that I have gained naught from you? No strength, no resolution from seeing you toil on in your thankless work, without apparent result? If I have any energy and principle to carry me through —I owe it to you."

He was moved, and raised his trembling hand and laid it on her golden head.

He said no more, and was very still.

Presently she spoke. His hand weighed heavily on her head.

"Papa, you are listening to the roar of the sea?" He made no reply.

"Papa, I felt a cold breath; and see, the sun has a film over it. Surely the sea is roaring louder!"

His hand slipped from her head and struck her shoulder—roughly, she thought. She turned, startled, and looked at him. His eyes were open, he was leaning back, almost fallen against the wall, and was deadly pale.

"Papa, are you listening to the roar?"

Then a thought struck her like a bullet in the heart.

"Papa! Papa! My papa!—speak—speak!"

She sprang from the bench—was before him. Her last guelder-rose had rolled, had bounded from her lap, and had fallen on the sand the old man had listlessly brought up from the church. His work, her play, were for ever over.

# CHAPTER II
## A PASSAGE OF ARMS

THE stillness preceding the storm had yielded. A gale had broken over the coast, raged against the cliffs of Pentyre, and battered the walls of the parsonage, without disturbing the old rector, whom no storm would trouble again, soon to be laid under the sands of his buried churchyard, his very mound to be heaped over in a few years, and obliterated by waves of additional encroaching sand. Judith had not slept all night. She —she, a mere child, had to consider and arrange everything consequent on the death of the master of the house. The servants—cook and housemaid—had been of little, if any, assistance to her. When Jane, the housemaid, rushed into the kitchen with the tidings that the old parson was dead, cook, in her agitation, upset the kettle and scalded her foot. The gardener's wife had come in on hearing the news, and had volunteered help. Judith had given her the closet-key to fetch from the stores something needed; and Jamie, finding access to the closet, had taken possession of a pot of raspberry jam, carried it to bed with him, and spilled it over the sheets, besides making himself ill. The housemaid, Jane, had forgotten in her distraction to shut the best bedroom casement, and the gale during the night had wrenched it from its hinges, flung it into the garden on the roof of the small conservatory, and smashed both. Moreover, the casement being open, the rain had driven into the room unchecked, had swamped the floor, run through and stained the drawing-room ceiling underneath, the drips had fallen on the mahogany table and blistered the veneer. A messenger was sent to Pentyre Glaze for Miss Dionysia Trevisa, and she would probably arrive in an hour or two.

Mr. Trevisa, as he had told Judith, was solitary; singularly so. He was of a good Cornish family, but it was one that had dwindled till it had ceased to have other representative than himself. Once well estated, at Crockadon, in S. Mellion, all the lands of the family had been lost; once with merchants in the family, all the fortunes of these merchants industriously gathered had been dissipated, and nothing had remained to the Reverend Peter Trevisa but his family name and family coat, a garb or, on a field gules. It really seemed as though the tinctures of the shield had been fixed in the crown of splendour that covered the head of Judith. But she did not derive this wealth of red-gold hair from her Cornish ancestors, but from a Scottish mother, a poor governess whom Mr. Peter Trevisa had married, thereby exciting the wrath of his only sister and relative, Miss Dionysia, who had hitherto kept house for him, and vexed his soul with her high-handed proceedings. It was owing to some insolent words used by her to Mrs. Trevisa, that Peter had quarrelled with his sister at first. Then when his wife died, she had forced herself on him as housekeeper, but again her presence in the house had become irksome to him, and when she treated his children—his delicate and dearlyloved Judith with roughness, and his timid, silly Jamie with harshness, amounting in his view to cruelty —sharp words had passed between them; sharp is, however, hardly the expression to use for the carefully worded remonstrances of the mild rector, though appropriate enough to her rejoinders. Then she had taken herself off, and had become housekeeper to Curll Coppinger—Cruel Coppinger, as he was usually called, who occupied Pentyre Glaze, and was a fairly well-to- do single man.

Mr. Trevisa had not been a person of energy, but one of culture and refinement; a dispirited, timid man. Finding no neighbours of the same mental texture, nor sympathetic, he had been driven to make of Judith, though a child, his companion, and he had poured into her ear all his troubles, which largely concerned the future of his children. In his feebleness he took comfort from her sanguine confidence, though he was well aware that it was bred of ignorance, and he derived a weak satisfaction from the thought that he had prepared her morally, at all events, if in no other fashion, for the crisis that must come when he was withdrawn.

Mr. Peter Trevisa—Peter was a family Christian name—was for twenty-five years rector of S. Enodoc, on the north coast of Cornwall at the mouth of the Camel. The sand dunes had encroached on the church of S. Enodoc, and had enveloped the sacred structure. A hole was broken through a window, through which the interior could be reached, where divine service was performed occasionally in the presence of the churchwardens, so as to establish the right of the rector, and through this same hole bridal parties entered to be coupled, with their feet ankle-deep in sand that filled the interior to above the pew-tops.

But Mr. Trevisa was not the man to endure such a condition of affairs without a protest and an effort to remedy it. He had endeavoured to stimulate the farmers and landowners of the parish to excavate the buried church, but his endeavours had proved futile. There were several reasons for this. In the first place, and certainly foremost, stood this reason: as long as the church was choked with sand and could not be employed for regular divine service, the tithe-payers could make a grievance of it, and excuse themselves from paying their tithe in full, because, as they argued, "Parson don't give us sarvice, so us ain't obliged to pay'n." They knew their man, that he was tenderconscienced, and would not bring the law to bear upon them; he would see that there was a certain measure of justness in the argument, and would therefore not demand of them a tithe for which he did not give them the quid pro quo. But they had sufficient shrewdness to pay a portion of their tithes, so as not to drive him to extremities and exhaust his patience. It will be seen, therefore, that in the interests of their pockets, the tithe-payers did not want to have their parish church excavated. Excavation meant weekly service regularly performed, and weekly service regularly performed would be followed by exaction of the full amount of rent-charge. Then, again, in the second place, should divine service be resumed in the church of S. Enodoc, the parishioners would feel a certain uneasiness in their consciences if they disregarded the summons of the bell; it might not be a very lively uneasiness, but just such an irritation as might be caused by a fly crawling over the face. So long as there was no service they could soothe their consciences with the thought that there was no call to make an effort to pull on Sunday breeches and assume a Sunday hat, and trudge to the church. Therefore, secondly, for the ease of their own consciences, it was undesirable that S. Enodoc should be dug out of the sand.

Then lastly, and thirdly, the engulfment of the church gave them a cherished opportunity for being nasty to the rector, and retaliating upon him for his incaution in condemning smuggling and launching out into anathema against wrecking. As he had made matters disagreeable to them—tried, as they put it, to take the bread out of their mouths, they saw no reason why they should spend money to please him.

Mr. Trevisa had made very little provision for his children, principally, if not wholly, because he could not. He had received from the farmers and landowners a portion of tithe, and had been contented with that rather than raise angry feelings by demanding the whole. Out of that portion he was able to put aside but little.

Aunt Dionysia arrived, a tall, bony woman, with hair turing grey, light eyes and an aquiline nose, a hard, self-seeking woman, who congratulated herself that she did not give way to feelings.

"I feel," said she, "as do others, but I don't show my feelings as beggars expose their bad legs."

She went into the kitchen. "Hoity-toity!" she said to the cook, "fine story this— scalding yourself. Mind this; you cook meals, or no wage for you." To Jane, "The mischief you have done shall be valued and deducted from any little trifle my brother may have left you in his will. Where is Jamie? Give me that joint of fishing-rod; I'll beat him for stealing raspberry jam."

Jamie, however, on catching a glimpse of his aunt had escaped into the garden and concealed himself. The cook, offended, began to clatter the saucepans.

"Now, then," said Mrs. Trevisa—she bore the brevet-rank—"in a house of mourning, what do you mean by making this noise, it is impertinent to me."

The housemaid swung out of the kitchen, muttering.

Mrs. Trevisa now betook herself upstairs in quest of her niece, and found her with red eyes.

"I call it rank felo-de-se," said Aunt Dionysia. "Every one knew—he knew, that he had a feeble heart, and ought not to be digging and delving in the old church. Who sent the sand upon it? Why, Providence, I presume. Not man. Then it was a-flying in the face of Providence to try to dig it out. Who wanted the church? He might have waited till the parishioners asked for it. But there—where is Jamie? I shall teach him a lesson for stealing raspberry jam."

"Oh, aunt, not now—not now!"

Mrs. Trevisa considered a moment, then laid aside the fishing-rod.

"Perhaps you are right. I am not up to it after my walk from Pentyre Glaze. Now, then, what about mourning? I do not suppose Jamie can be measured by guess-work. You must bring him here. Tell him the whipping is put off till another day. Of course you have seen to black things for yourself. Not? Why, gracious heavens! is everything to be thrown on my shoulders? Am I to be made a beast of burden of? Now, no mewling and pewking. There is no time for that. Whatever your time may be, mine is valuable. I can't be here for ever. Of course every responsibility has been put on me. Just like Peter— no consideration. And what can I do with a set of babies? I have to work hard enough to keep myself. Peter did not want my services at one time; now I am put upon. Have you sent for the undertaker? What about clothing again? I suppose you know that you must have mourning? Bless my heart! what a lot of trouble you give me."

Mrs. Trevisa was in a very bad temper, which even the knowledge that it was seemly that she should veil it, could not make her restrain. She was, no doubt, to a certain extent fond of her brother—not much, because he had not been of any advantage to her; and no doubt she was shocked at his death, but chiefly because it entailed on herself responsibilities and trouble that she grudged. She would be obliged to do something for her nephew and niece; she would have to provide a home for them somewhere. She could not take them with her to Coppinger's house, as she was there as a salaried servant, and not entitled to invite thither her young relatives. Moreover, she did not want to have them near her. She disliked young people; they gave trouble, they had to be looked after, they entailed expenses. What was she to do with them? Where was she to put them? What would they have to live upon? Would they call on her to part-maintain them? Miss Dionysia had a small sum put away, and she had no intention of breaking into it for them. It was a nest-egg, and was laid by against an evil day that might come on herself. She had put the money away for herself, in her old age, not for the children of her feeble brother and his lack-penny wife to consume as moth and rust. As these thoughts and questions passed through her mind, Aunt Dionysia pulled open drawers, examined cupboards, pried into closets, and searched chests and wardrobes.

"I wonder now what he has put by for them," she said aloud.

"Do you mean my dear papa?" asked Judith, whose troubled heart and shaken spirits were becoming angry and restless under the behaviour of the hard, unfeeling woman.

"Yes, I do," answered Mrs. Trevisa, facing round, and glaring malevolently at her niece. "It is early days to talk of this, but it must be done sooner or later, and if so, the sooner the better. There is money in the house, I suppose?"

"I do not know."

"I must know. You will want it—bills must be paid. You will eat and drink, I suppose? You must be clothed. I'll tell you what: I'll put the whole case into the hands of Lawyer Jenkyns, and he shall demand arrears of tithe. I know what quixotish conduct Peter—"

"Aunt, I will not allow this." A light flush came into the girl's cheek.

"It is all very well talking," said Aunt Dionysia; "but black is not white, and no power on earth can make me say that it is so. Money must be found. Money must be paid for expenses, and it is hard that I should have to find it; so I think. What money is there in the house for present necessities? I must know."

Suddenly a loud voice was heard shouting through the house—.

"Mother Dunes! old Dunes! I want you."

Judith turned cold and white. Who was this that dared to bellow in the house of death, when her dear, dear father lay upstairs with the blinds down, asleep? It was an insult, an outrage. Her nerves had already been thrilled, and her heart roused into angry revolt by the cold, unfeeling conduct of the woman who was her sole relative in the world. And now, as she was thus quivering, there came this boisterous shout.

"It is the master!" said Mrs. Trevisa, in an awestruck voice, lowered as much as was possible to her.

To Coppinger alone was she submissive, cringing, obsequious.

"What does he mean by this—this conduct?" asked Judith, trembling with wrath.

"He wants me."

Again a shout. "Dunes! old fool! the keys!"

Then Judith started forward, and went through the door to the head of the staircase. At the foot stood a middle-sized, strongly-built, firmly-knit man, in a dress half belonging to the land and half to the sea, with high boots on his legs, and a slouched hat on his head. His complexion was olive, his hair abundant and black, covering cheeks and chin and upper lip. His eyes were hard and dark. He had one brown hand on the banister, and a foot on the first step, as though about to ascend when arrested by seeing the girl at the head of the stairs before him. The house was low, and the steps led without a break directly from the hall to the landing which gave communication to the bedrooms. There was a skylight in the roof over the staircase, through which a brilliant flood of pure white light fell over Judith, whereas every window had been darkened by drawn blinds. The girl had found no sombre dress suitable to wear, and had been forced to assume the same white gown as the day before, but she had discarded the green sash and had bound a black ribbon about her waist, and another about her abundant hair. A black lace kerchief was drawn over her shoulders across her breast and tied at her back. She wore long black mittens.

Judith stood motionless, her bosom rising and falling quickly, her lips set, the breath racing through her nostrils, and one hand resting on the banister at the stair-head.

In a moment her eyes met those of Coppinger, and it was at once as though a thrill of electric force had passed between them.

He desisted from his attempt to ascend, and said, without moving his eyes from hers, in a subdued tone, "She has taken the keys," but he said no more. He drew his foot from the step hesitatingly, and loosened his hand from the banister, down which went a thrill from Judith's quivering nerves, and he stepped back.

At the same moment she descended a step. Still looking steadily into the dark, threatening pupils, without blinking or lowering her orbs. Emboldened by her boiling indignation, she stood on the step she had reached with both feet firmly planted there, and finding that the banister rattled under her hand she withdrew it, and folded her arms. Coppinger raised his hand to his head and took off his hat. He had a profusion of dark, curly, flowing hair, that fell and encircled his saturnine face.

Then Judith descended another step, and as she did so he retreated a step backwards. Behind him was the hall door, open; the light lay wan and white there on the gravel, for no sunshine had succeeded the gale. At every step that Judith took down the stair Coppinger retreated. Neither spoke; the hall was still, save for the sound of their breath, and his came as fast as hers. When Judith had reached the bottom, she turned —Coppinger stood in the doorway now—and signed to her aunt to come down with the keys.

"Take them to him—Do not give them here—outside."

Mrs. Trevisa, surprised, confounded, descended the stair, went by her, and out through the door. Then Judith stepped after her, shut the door to exclude both Aunt Dionysia and that man Coppinger, who had dared, uninvited, on such a day to invade the house.

She turned now to remount the stairs, but her strength failed her, her knees yielded, and she sank upon a step, and burst into a flood of tears and convulsive sobs.

# CHAPTER III
# CAPTAIN CRUEL

CAPTAIN COPPINGER occupied an old farmhouse, roomy, low built, granite quoined and mullioned, called Pentyre Glaze, in a slight dip of the hills near the cliffs above the thundering Atlantic. One ash shivered at the end of the house—that was the only tree to be seen near Pentyre Glaze. And—who was Coppinger? That is more than can be told. He had come—no one knew whence. His arrival on the north coast of Cornwall was mysterious. There had been haze over the sea for three days. When it lifted, a strange vessel of foreign rig was seen lying off the coast. Had she got there in the fog, not knowing her course; or had she come there knowingly, and was making for the mouth of the Camel? A boat was seen to leave the ship, and in it a man came ashore; the boat returned to the vessel, that thereupon spread sail and disappeared in the fog that re-descended over the water. The man gave his name as Coppinger—his Christian name, he said, was Curll, and he was a Dane; but though his intonation was not that of the Cornish, it was not foreign. He took up his residence in S. Enodoc at a farm, and suddenly, to the surprise of every one, became by purchase the possessor of Pentyre Glaze, then vacant and for sale. Had he known that the estate was obtainable, when he had come suddenly out of the clouds into the place to secure it? Nobody knew, and Coppinger was silent.

Thenceforth Pentyre Glaze became a harbour and den of every lawless character along the coast. All kinds of wild uproar and reckless revelry appalled the neighbourhood day and night. It was discovered that an organized band of smugglers, wreckers, and poachers made this house the centre of their operations, and that "Cruel Coppinger" was their captain. There were at that time—just a century ago—no resident magistrates or gentry in the immediate neighbourhood. The yeomen were bribed, by kegs of spirits left at their doors, to acquiesce in a traffic in illicit goods, and in the matter of exchange they took their shares. It was said that on one occasion a preventive man named Ewan Wyvill, who had pursued Coppinger in his boat, was taken by him, and his head chopped off by the captain with his boat axe, on the gunwale. Such was the story. It was never proved. Wyvill had disappeared, and the body was recovered headless on the Doom Bar. That violence had been used was undoubted, but who had committed the crime was not known, though suspicion pointed to Coppinger. Thenceforth, none ever called him Curll; by one consent he was named Cruel. In the West of England every one is given his Christian name. An old man is Uncle, and an old woman Aunt, and any one in command is a Captain. So Coppinger was known as Captain Cruel, or as Cruel Coppinger.

Strange vessels were often seen appearing at regular intervals on the coast, and signals were flashed from the one window of Pentyre Glaze that looked out to sea.

Amongst these vessels, one, a full-rigged schooner, soon became ominously conspicuous. She was for long the terror of the Cornish coast. Her name was The Black Prince. Once, with Coppinger on board, she led a revenue cutter into an intricate channel among the rocks, where, from knowledge of the bearings, The Black Prince escaped scathless, while the king's vessel perished with all on board.

Immunity increased Coppinger's daring. There were certain bridle-roads along the fields over which he exercised exclusive control. He issued orders that no man should pass over them by night, and accordingly from that hour none ever did.

Moreover, if report spoke true—and reports do not arise without cause—Coppinger was not averse from taking advantage, and that unlawful advantage, of a wreck. By "lawful" and "unlawful" two categories of acts are distinguished, not by the laws of the land, but by common consent of the Cornish conscience. That same Cornish conscience distinguished wrecking into two classes, as it distinguished then, and distinguishes still, witchcraft into two classes. The one, white witchcraft, is legitimate and profitable, and to be upheld; the other, black witchcraft, is reprehensible, unlawful, and to be put down. So with wrecking. The Bristol Channel teemed with shipping, flights of white sails passed in the offing, and these vessels were, when inward bound, laden with sugars and spices from the Indies, or with spirits and wines from France. If outward bound, they were deep in the water with a cargo of the riches of England.

Now, should a gale spring up suddenly and catch any of these vessels, and should the gale be—as it usually is, and to the Cornish folk, favourably is—from the north-west, then there was no harbour of refuge along that rock-bound coast, and a ship that could not make for the open was bound inevitably to be pounded to pieces against the precipitous walls of the peninsula. If such were the case, it was perfectly legitimate for every householder in the district to come down on the wreck, and strip it of everything it contained.

But, on the other hand, there was wrecking that was disapproved of, though practised by a few, so rumour said, and that consisted in luring a vessel that was in doubt as to her course, by false signals, upon a reef or bar, and then, having made a wreck of her, to pillage her. When on a morning after a night in which there had been no gale, a ship was found on the rocks, and picked as clean as the carcase of a camel in the desert, it was open to suspicion that this ship had not been driven there by wind or current; and when the survivors, if they reached the shore, told that they had been led to steer in the direction where they had been cast away by certain lights that had wholly deceived them, then it was also open to suspicion that these lights had been purposely exhibited for the sake of bringing that vessel to destruction; and when, further, it was proved that a certain set or gang of men had garnered all the profits, or almost all the profits, that accrued from a wreck, before the countryside was aware that a wreck had occurred, then it was certainly no very random conjecture that the wreck had been contrived in some fashion by those who profited by it. There were atrocious tales of murder of shipwrecked men circulating, but these were probably wholly, or at all events in part, untrue. If, when a vessel ran upon the rocks, she was deserted by her crew, if they took to the boats and made for shore, then there remained no impediment to the wreckers taking possession; it was only in the event of their finding a skipper on board to maintain right over the grounded vessel, or the mariners still on her engaged in getting her off, that any temptation to violence could arise. But it was improbable that a crew would cling to a ship on such a coast when once she was on the breakers. It was a moral certainty that they would desert her, and leave the wreck to be pillaged by the rats from shore, without offer of resistance. The character of the coastwreckers was known to seamen, or rather a legend full of horror circulated relative to their remorseless savagery. The fear of wreckers added to the fear of the sea, would combine to drive a crew, to the last man, into the boats. Consequently, though it is possible that in some cases murder of castaway men may have occurred, such cases must have been most exceptional. The wreckers were only too glad to build a golden bridge by which the wrecked might escape. Morally, without a question, those who lured a hapless merchantman upon the rocks were guilty of the deaths of those sailors who were upset in their boats in escaping from the vessel, or were dashed against the cliffs in their attempts to land, but there was no direct blood guiltiness felt in such cases; and those who had reaped a harvest from the sea counted their gains individually, and made no estimate of the misery accruing thereby to others.

# CHAPTER IV
## HOP O' MY THUMB

"Listen to me," said Judith.

"Yes, Ju!"

The orphans were together in the room that had been their father's, the room in which for some days he had lain with the blind down, the atmosphere heavy with the perfume of flowers, and that indescribable, unmistakable scent of death. Often, every day, almost every hour, had Judith stolen into the room whilst he lay there, to wonder with infinite reverence and admiration at the purity and dignity of the dead face. It was that of the dear, dear father, but sublimed beyond her imagination. All the old vacillation was gone, the expression of distress and discouragement had passed away, and in their place had come a fixity and a calm, such as one sees in the busts of the ancient Roman Cæsars, but with a superadded etheriality—if such a word can be used—that a piece of pagan statuary never reached. Marvellous, past finding out, it is that death which takes from man the spiritual element, should give to the mere clay a look of angelic spirituality, yet so it is—so it was with the dead Peter Trevisa; and Judith, with eyes filling as fast as dried, stood, her hands folded, looking into his face, felt that she had never loved, never admired him half enough when he was alive. Life had been the simmer in which all the scum of trivialities, of infirmities, of sordidness had come to and shown itself on the surface. Now Death had cleared these all away, and in the peaceful face of the dead was seen the real man, the nobility, sanctity, delicacy that formed the texture of his soul, and which had impressed the very clay wrapped about that volatile essence.

As long as the dear father's body lay in the house, Judith had not realized her utter desolation. But now the funeral was over, and she had returned with her brother to the parsonage, to draw up the blinds, and let the light once more enter, and search out, and revivify the dead rooms.

She was very pale, with reddened eyes, and looking more fragile and transparent than ever she did before, worn and exhausted by tearful, wakeful nights, and by days of alternating gusts of sorrow and busy preparation for the funeral, of painful recollections of joyous days that were past, and of doubtful searchings into a future that was full of cloud.

Her black frock served to enhance her pallor, and to make her look thinner, smaller than when in white or in colour.

She had taken her place in her father's high-backed leather chair, studded thick with brass nails, the leather dulled and fretted by constant use, but the nail-heads burnished by the same treatment.

Her brother was in the same chair with her; both his arms were round her neck, and his head was on her shoulder. She had her right arm about his waist, her left was bowed, the elbow leaning on the chair arm, her hand folded inwards, and her weary head resting on its back.

The fine weather broken in upon by the gale had returned; the sun shone in unhindered at the window, and blazed on the children's hair; the brass nails, polished by friction, twinkled as little suns, but were naught in lustre to the gorgeous red of the hair of the twins, for the first were but brass, and the other of living gold.

Two more lonely beings could hardly be discovered on the face of the earth—at all events in the peninsula of Cornwall,—but the sense of this loneliness was summed in the heart of Judith, and was there articulate; Jamie was but dimly conscious of discomfort and bereavement. She knew what her father's death entailed on her, or knew in part, and conjectured more. Had she been left absolutely alone in the world, her condition would have been less difficult than it was actually, encumbered with her helpless brother. Swimming alone in the tossing sea, she might have struck out with confidence that she could keep her head above water, but it was quite otherwise when clinging to her was a poor half-witted boy, incapable of doing anything to save himself, and all whose movements tended only to embarrass her. Not that she regretted for an instant having to care for Jamie, for she loved him with sisterly and motherly love combined, intensified in force by fusion; if to her a future seemed inconceivable without Jamie, a future without him would be one without ambition, pleasure, or interest.

The twin brother was very like her, with the same beautiful and abundant hair, delicate in build, and with the same refined face, but without the flashes of alternating mood that lightened and darkened her face. His had a searching, bewildered, distressed expression on it—the only expression it ever bore except when he was out of temper, and then it mirrored on its surface his inward ill-humour. His was an appealing face, a face that told of a spirit infantile, innocent, and ignorant, that would never grow stronger, but which could deteriorate by loss of innocence— the only change of which it was capable. The boy had no inherent naughtiness in him, but was constantly falling into mischief through thoughtlessness, and he was difficult to manage, because incapable of reasoning.

What every one saw—that he never would be other than what he was—Judith would not admit. She acknowledged his inaptitude at his books, his frivolity, his restlessness, but believed that these were infirmities to be overcome, and that when overcome, the boy would be as other boys are.

Now these children—they were aged eighteen, but Jamie looked four years younger—sat in their father's chair, clinging to each other, all in all to one another, for they had no one else to love, and who loved them.

"Listen to me, Jamie."

"Yes, Ju, I be—"

"Don't say 'I be'—say 'I am.'"

"Yes, Ju."

"Jamie, dear!" she drew her arm tighter about him; her heart was bounding, and every beat caused her pain. "Jamie, dear, you know that, now dear papa is gone, and you will never see him in this world again, that—"

"Yes, Ju."

"That I have to look to you, my brother, to stand up for me like a man, to think and do for me as well as for yourself—a brave, stout, industrious fellow."

"Yes, Ju."

"I am a girl, and you will soon be a man, and must work for both of us. You must earn the money, and I will spend it frugally as we both require it. Then we shall be happy again, and dear papa in Paradise will be glad and smile on us. You will make an effort, will you not, Jamie? Hitherto you have been able to run about and play and squander your time, but now serious days have come upon us, and you must fix your mind on work and determine—Jamie—mind, screw your heart to a strong determination to put away childish things and be a man, and a strength and a comfort to me."

He put up his lips to kiss her cheek, but could not reach it, as her head was leaning on her hand away from him.

"What are you fidgeting at, my dear?" she asked, without stirring, feeling his body restless under her arm.

"A nail is coming out," he answered.

It was so; whilst she had been speaking to him he was working at one of the brass studs, and had loosened its bite in the chair.

"Oh, Jamie! you are making work by thus drawing out a nail. Can you not help me a little, and reduce the amount one has to think of and do? You have not been attending to what I said, and I was so much in earnest." She spoke in a tone of discouragement, and the tone, more than the words, impressed the susceptible heart of the boy. He began to cry.

"You are cross."

"I am not cross, my pet; I am never cross with you, I love you too dearly; but you try my patience sometimes, and just now I am overstrained—and then I did want to make you understand."

"Now papa's dead I'll do no more lessons, shall I?" asked Jamie, coaxingly.

"You must, indeed, and with me instead of papa."

"Not rosa, rosæ?"

"Yes, rosa, rosæ."

Then he sulked.

"I don't love you a bit. It is not fair. Papa is dead, so I ought not to have any more lessons. I hate rosa, rosæ!" He kicked the legs of the chair peevishly with his heels. As his sister said nothing, seemed to be inattentive—for she was weary and dispirited—he slapped her cheek by raising his hand over his head.

"What, Jamie? strike me, your only friend?"

Then he threw his arms round her again, and kissed her. "I'll love you; only, Ju, say I am not to do rosa, rosæ!"

"How long have you been working at the first declension in the Latin Grammar, Jamie?"

He tried for an instant to think, gave up the effort, laid his head on her shoulder, and said—

"I don't know and don't care. Say I am not to do rosa, rosæ!"

"What! not if papa wished it?"

"I hate the Latin Grammar!"

For a while both remained silent. Judith felt the tension to which her mind and nerves had been subjected, and lapsed momentarily into a condition of something like unconsciousness, in which she was dimly sensible of a certain satisfaction rising out of the pause in thought and effort. The boy lay quiet, with his head on her shoulder, for a while, then withdrew his arms, folded his hands on his lap, and began to make a noise by compressing the air between the palms.

"There's a finch out there going 'Chink! chink!' and listen, Ju! I can make 'chink! chink!' too."

Judith recovered herself from her distraction, and said—

"Never mind the finch now. Think of what I say. We shall have to leave this house."

"Why?"

"Of course we must, sooner or later, and the sooner the better. It is no more ours."

"Yes, it is ours. I have my rabbits here."

"Now that papa is dead, it is no longer ours."

"It's a wicked shame."

"Not at all, Jamie. This house was given to papa for his life only; now it will go to a new rector, and Aunt Dunes is going to fetch us away to another house."

"When?"

"To-day."

"I won't go," said the boy. "I swear I won't."

"Hush, hush, Jamie! Don't use such expressions. I do not know where you have picked them up. We must go."

"And my rabbits, are they to go too?"

"The rabbits? We'll see about them. Aunt—"

"I hate Aunt Dunce!"

"You really must not call her that; if she hears you she will be very angry. And consider, she has been taking a great deal of trouble about us."

"I don't care."

"My dear, she is dear papa's sister."

"Why didn't papa get a nicer sister—like you?"

"Because he had to take what God gave him."

The boy pouted, and began to kick his heels against the chair legs once more.

"Jamie, we must leave this house to-day. Aunt is coming to take us both away."

"I won't go."

"But, Jamie, I am going, and the cook is going, and so is Jane."

"Are cook and Jane coming with us?"

"No, dear."

"Why not?"

"We shall not want them. We cannot afford to keep them any more, to pay their wages; and then we shall not go into a house of our own. You must come with me, and be a joy and rest to me, dear Jamie."

She turned her head over, and leaned it on his head. The sun glowed in their mingled hair—all of one tinge and lustre. It sparkled in the tears on her cheek.

"Ju! may I have these buttons?"

"What buttons?"

"Look!"

He shook himself free from his sister, slid his feet to the ground, went to a bureau, and brought to his sister a large open basket that had been standing on the top of the bureau. It had been turned out of a closet by Aunt Dionysia, and contained an accumulation of those most profitless of collected remnants—odd buttons, coat buttons, brass, smoked mother-of-pearl, shirt buttons, steel clasps—buttons of all kinds, the gathering together made during twenty-five years. Why the basket, after having been turned out of a lumber-closet, had been left in the room of death, or why, if turned out elsewhere, it had been brought there, is more than even the novelist can tell. Suffice it that there it was, and by whom put there could not be said.

"Oh! what a store of pretty buttons!" exclaimed the boy. "Do look, Ju! these great big ones are just like those on Cheap Jack's red waistcoat. Here is a brass one with a horse on it. Do see! Oh, Ju! please get your needle and thread and sew this one on to my black dress."

Judith sighed. It was in vain for her to impress the realities of the situation on his wandering mind.

"Hark!" she exclaimed. "There is Aunt Dunes. I hear her voice—how loud she speaks! She has come to fetch us away."

"Where is she going to take us to?"

"I do not know, Jamie."

"She will take us into the forest and lose us, like as did Hop-o'-my-Thumb's father."

"There are no forests here—hardly any trees."

"She will leave us in the forest, and run away."

"Nonsense, Jamie!"

"I am sure she will. She doesn't like us. She wants to get rid of us. I don't care. May I have the basket of buttons?"

"Yes, Jamie."

"Then I'll be Hop-o'-my-Thumb."

# CHAPTER V
# THE BUTTONS

IT WAS as Judith surmised. Mrs. Dionysia Trevisa had come to remove her nephew and niece from the rectory. She was a woman decided in character, especially in all that concerned her interests. She had made up her mind that the children could not be left unprotected in the parsonage, and she could not be with them. Therefore they must go. The servants must leave; they would be paid their month's wage, but by dismissing them their keep would be economised. There was a factotum living in a cottage near, who did the gardening, the cinder-sifting, and boot-cleaning for the rectory inmates, he would look after the empty house, and wait on in hopes of being engaged to garden, sift cinders, and clean boots for the new rector.

As it was settled that the children must leave the house, the next thing to consider was where they were to be placed. The aunt could not take them to Pentyre Glaze; that was not to be thought of. They must be disposed of in some other way.

Mrs. Trevisa had determined on a sale of her brother's effects: his furniture, bedding, curtains, carpets, books, plate, and old sermons. She was anxious to realize as soon as possible, so as to know for certain what she could calculate upon as being left for the support of Judith and the brother. To herself the rector had left only a ring and five guineas. She had not expected more. His decease was not likely to be a benefit, but, on the contrary, an embarrassment to her. He had left about a thousand pounds, but then Mrs. Trevisa did not yet know how large a bite out of this thousand pounds would be taken by the dilapidations on rectory, glebe, and chancel. The chancel of the church was in that condition that it afforded a wide margin for the adjudication of dilapidations. They might be set down at ten shillings or a thousand pounds, and no one could say which was the fairest sum, as the chancel was deep in sand and invisible. The imagination of the valuer might declare it to be sound or to be rotten, and till dug out no one could impeach his judgment.

In those days, when an incumbent died, the widow and orphans of the deceased appointed a valuer, and the in-coming rector nominated his valuer, and these two cormorants looked each other in the eyes—said to each other, "Brother, what pickings?" And as less resistance to being lacerated and cleaned to the bone was to be anticipated from a broken-hearted widow and helpless children than from a robust, red-faced rector, the cormorants contrived to rob the widow and the fatherless. Then that cormorant who had been paid to look after the interest of the widow and children and had not done it said to the other cormorant, "Brother, I've done you a turn this time; do me the like when the chance falls to you." Now, although nominally the money picked off the sufferers was to go to the account of the in-comer, it was not allowed to pass till the cormorants had taken toll of it. Moreover, these cormorants were architects, builders, solicitors, or contractors of some sort, and looked to get something further out of the in-coming man they favoured, whereas they knew they could get nothing at all out of the departed man who was buried. Now we have pretended to change all this; let us persuade ourselves we have made the conduct of these matters more honest and just.

Aunt Dionysia did not know by experience what valuers for dilapidations were, but she had always heard that valuation for dilapidations materially diminished the property of a deceased incumbent. She was consequently uneasy, and anxious to know the worst, and make the best of the circumstances that she could. She saw clearly enough that the sum that would remain when debts and valuation were paid would be insufficient to support the orphans, and she saw also with painful clearness that there would be a necessity for her to supplement their reduced income from her own earnings. This conviction did not sweeten her temper and increase the cordiality with which she treated her nephew and niece.

"Now, hoity-toity!" said Aunt Dionysia; "I'm not one of your mewlers and pewkers. I have my work to do, and can't afford to waste time in the luxury of tears. You children shall come with me. I will see you settled in, and then Balhachet shall wheel over your boxes and whatever we want for the night. I have been away from my duties longer than I ought, and the maids are running wild, are after every one who comes near the place, like horse-flies round the cattle on a sultry day. I will see you to your quarters, and then you must shift for yourselves. Balhachet can come and go between the rectory and Zachie Menaida as much as you want."

"Are we going to Mr. Menaida's, aunt?" asked Judith.

"Did not I say Zachie Menaida? If I said Zachie Menaida I suppose I meant what I said, or are you hard of hearing? Come—time to me is precious. Bustle—bustle—don't keep me waiting whilst you gape."

After a while Mrs. Trevisa succeeded in getting her nephew and niece to start. Judith, indeed, was ready at the first suggestion to go with her aunt, glad to get over the pang of leaving the house as quickly as might be. It was to be the rupture of one thread of the tie that bound her to the past, but an important thread. She was to leave the house as a home, though she would return to it again and again to carry away from it such of her possessions as she required and could find a place for at Zachary Menaida's. But with Jamie it was other. He had run away, and had to be sought, and when found coaxed and cajoled into following his aunt and sister.

Judith had found him, for she knew his nooks and dens. He was seated in a laurel-bush playing with the buttons.

"Look, Ju! there is some broken mirror among the buttons. Stand still, and I will make the sun jump into your eyes. Open your mouth, and I will send him down your throat. Won't it be fun; I'll tease old Dunes with it."

"Then come along with me."

He obeyed.

The distance to Zachary Menaida's cottage was about a mile and a quarter, partly through parish roads, partly through lanes, the way in parts walled and hedged up against the winds, in others completely exposed to every breath of air, where it traversed a down.

Judith walked forward with her aunt, and Jamie lagged. Occasionally his sister turned her head to reassure herself that he had not given them the slip; otherwise she attended as closely as she was able to the instructions and exhortations of her aunt. She and her brother were to be lodged temporarily at Uncle Zachie's, that is to say, with Mr. Menaida, an elderly, somewhat eccentric man, who occupied a double cottage at the little hamlet of Polzeath. No final arrangement as to the destination of the orphans could be made till Aunt Dunes knew the result of the sale, and how much remained to the children after the father's trifling debts had been paid, and the considerable slice had been cut out of it by the valuers for dilapidations. Mrs. Trevisa talked fast in her harsh tones, and in a loud voice, without undulation or softness in it, and expected her niece to hear and give account for everything she told her, goading her to attention with a sharp reminder when she deemed that her mind was relaxed, and whipping her thoughts together when she found them wandering. But, indeed, it was not possible to forget for one moment the presence and personality of Dionysia, though the subject of her discourse might be unnoticed.

Every fibre of Judith's heart was strung and strained to the uttermost, to acutest feeling, and a sympathetic hand drawn across them would have produced a soft, thrilling, musical wail. Her bosom was so full to overflow that a single word of kindness, a look even that told of love, would have sufficed to make the child cast herself in a convulsion of grief into her aunt's arms, bury her face in her bosom, and weep out her pent-up tears. Then, after perhaps half an hour, she would have looked up through the rain into her aunt's face, and have smiled, and have loved that aunt passionately, self-sacrificingly, to her dying day. She was disposed to love her—for was not Dionysia the only relative she had; and was she not the very sister of that father who had been to her so much? But Mrs. Trevisa was not the woman to touch the taught chords with a light hand, or to speak or look in love. She was hard, angular, unsympathetic; and her manner, the intonations of her voice, her mode of address, the very movements of her body, acted on the strained nerves as a rasping file, that would fret-till it had torn them through.

Suddenly, round a corner where the narrow road turned, two hundred yards ahead, dashed a rider on a black steed, and Judith immediately recognized Coppinger, on his famous mare, Black Bess: a mare much talked of, named after the horse ridden by Dick Turpin. The recognition was mutual. He knew her instantly; with a jerk of the rein and a set of the brows he showed that he was not indifferent.

Coppinger wore his slouched hat, tied under his chin and beard, a necessary precaution in that gale-swept country; on his feet to his knees were high boots. He wore a blue knitted jersey, and a red kerchief about his throat.

Captain Cruel slightly slackened his pace, as the lane was narrow; and as he rode past, his dark brow was knit, and his eyes flashed angrily at Judith. He deigned neither a glance nor a word to his housekeeper, who curtseyed and assumed a fawning expression.

When he had passed the two women he dug his spurs into Black Bess and muttered some words they did not hear.

Judith, who had stood aside, now came forward into the midst of the roadway and rejoined her aunt, who began to say something, when her words and Judith's attention were arrested by shouts, oaths, and cries in their rear.

Judith and her aunt turned to discover the occasion of this disturbance, and saw that Coppinger was off his horse, on his feet, dragging the brute by the rein, and was whirling his crop, or hunting-whip, as he pursued Jamie flying from him with cries of terror. But that he held the horse and could not keep up with the boy, Jamie would have suffered severely, for Coppinger was in a livid fury.

Jamie flew to his sister.

"Save me, Ju! he wants to kill me."

"What have you done?"

"It is only the buttons."

"Buttons, dear?"

But the boy was too frightened to explain.

Then Judith drew her brother behind her, took from him the basket he was carrying, and stepped to encounter the angry man, who came on, now struggling with his horse, cursing Bess because she drew back, then plunging forward with his whip above his head brandished menacingly, and by this conduct further alarming Black Bess.

Judith met Coppinger, and he was forced to stay his forward course.

"What has he done?" asked the girl. "Why do you threaten?"

"The cursed idiot has strewn bits of glass and buttons along the road," answered the captain, angrily. "Stand aside that I may lash him, and teach him to frighten horses and endanger men's lives."

"I am sorry for what Jamie has done. I will pick up the things he has thrown down."

Cruel Coppinger's eyes glistened with wrath. He gathered the lash of his whip into his palm along with the handle, and gripped them passionately.

"Curse the fool! My Bess was frightened, dashed up the bank, and all but rolled over. Do you know he might have killed me?"

"You must excuse him; he is a very child."

"I will not excuse him. I will cut the flesh off his back if I catch him."

He put the end of the crop handle into his mouth, and, putting his right hand behind him, gathered the reins up shorter and wound them more securely about his left hand.

Judith walked backward, facing him, and he turned with his horse and went after her. She stooped and gathered up a splinter of glass. The sun striking through the gaps in the hedge had flashed on these scraps of broken mirror and of white bone, or burnished brass buttons, and the horse had been frightened at them. As Judith stooped and took up now a buckle, then a button, and then some other shining trifle, she hardly for an instant withdrew her eyes from Coppinger; they had in them the same dauntless defiance as when she encountered him on the stairs of the rectory. But now it was she who retreated, step by step, and he who advanced, and yet he could not flatter himself that he was repelling her. She maintained her strength and mastery unbroken as she retreated.

"Why do you look at me so? Why do you walk backwards?"

"Because I mistrust you. I do not know what you might do were I not to confront you."

"What I might do? What do you think I would do?"

"I cannot tell. I mistrust you."

"Do you think me capable of lashing at you with my crop?"

"I think you capable of anything."

"Flattering that!" he shouted, angrily.

"You would have lashed at Jamie."

"And why not? He might have killed me."

"He might have killed you, but you should not have touched him—not have thought of touching him."

"Indeed! Why not?"

"Why not?" She raised herself upright and looked him straight into his eyes, in which fire flickered, flared, then decayed, then flared again.

"You are no Dane, or you would not have asked Why not?' twice. Nay, you would not have asked it once."

"Not a Dane?" His beard and moustache were quivering, and he snorted with anger.

"A Dane, I have read in history, is too noble and brave to threaten women, and to strike children."

He uttered an oath, and ground his teeth.

"No; a Dane would never have thought of asking 'Why not?—why not lash a poor little silly boy?'"

"You insult me! You dare to do it?"

Her blood was surging in her heart. As she looked into this man's dark and evil face she thought of all the distress he had caused her father, and a wave of loathing swept over her, nerved her to defy him to the uttermost, and to proclaim all the counts she had against him.

"I dare do it," she said, "because you made my own dear papa's life full of bitterness and pain—"

"I! I never touched him, hardly spoke to him. I don't care to have to do with parsons."

"You made his life one of sorrow through your godless, lawless ways, leading his poor flock astray, and bidding them mock at his warnings and despise his teachings. Almost with his last breath he spoke of you, and the wretchedness of heart you had caused him. And then you dared—yes—you dared—you dared to burst into our house where he lay dead, with shameful insolence to disturb its peace. And now—" she gasped, "and now, ah! you lie when you say you are a Dane, and talk of cutting and lashing the dead father's little boy on his father's burial day. You are but one thing I can name—a coward!"

Did he mean it? No! But blinded, stung to madness by her words, especially that last, he raised his right arm with the crop.

Did she mean it? No! But in the instinct of self-preservation, thinking he was about to strike her, she dashed the basket of buttons in his face, and they flew right and left over him, against the head of Black Bess, a rain of fragments of mirror, brass, steel, mother-of-pearl, and bone.

The effect was instantaneous. The mare plunged, reared, threw Coppinger backwards from off his feet, dashed him to the ground, dragged him this way, that way, bounded, still drawing him about by the twisted reins, into the hedge, then back, with his hoofs upon him, near, if not on, his head, his chest—then, released by the snap of the rein, or through its becoming disengaged, Bess darted down the lane, was again brought to a standstill by the glittering fragments on the ground, turned, rushed back in the direction whence she had come, and disappeared.

Judith stood panting, paralyzed with fear and dismay. Was he dead, broken to pieces, pounded by those strong hoofs?

He was not dead. He was rolling himself on the ground, struggling clumsily to his knees.

"Are you satisfied?" he shouted, glaring at her like a wild beast through his tangled black hair that had fallen over his face. "I cannot strike you nor your brother now. My arm and the Lord knows what other bones are broken. You have done that—and I owe you something for it."

# CHAPTER VI
## UNCLE ZACHIE

THE astonishment, the consternation of Mrs. Trevisa at what had occurred, which she could not fully comprehend, took from her the power to speak. She had seen her niece in conversation with Cruel Coppinger, and had caught snatches of what had passed between them. All his words had reached her, and some of Judith's. When, suddenly, she saw the girl dash the basket of buttons in the face of the Captain, saw him thrown to the ground, drawn about by his frantic horse, and left, as she thought, half dead, her dismay was unbounded. It might have been that Coppinger threatened Judith with his whip, but nothing could excuse her temerity in resisting him, in resisting him and protecting herself in the way she did. The consequences of that resistance she could not measure. Coppinger was bruised, bones were broken, and Aunt Dionysia knew the nature of the man too well not to expect his deadly animosity, and to feel sure of implacable revenge against the girl who had injured him—a revenge that would envelop all who belonged to her, and would therefore strike herself.

The elderly spinster had naturally plenty of strength and hardness that would bear her through most shocks without discomposure, but such an incident as that which had just taken place before her eyes entirely unnerved and dismayed her.

Coppinger was conveyed home by men called to the spot, and Mrs. Trevisa walked on with her niece and nephew in silence to the house of Mr. Zachary Menaida. Jamie had escaped over the hedge, to put a stone and earth barrier between himself and his assailant directly Judith interposed between him and Coppinger. Now that the latter was gone, he came, laughing, over the hedge again. To him what had occurred was fun.

At Menaida's the aunt departed, leaving her nephew and niece with the old man, that she might hurry to Pentyre Glaze and provide what was needed for Coppinger. She took no leave of Judith. In the haze of apprehension that enveloped her mind glowed anger against the girl for having increased her difficulties and jeopardized her position with Coppinger.

Mr. Zachary Menaida was an old man, or rather a man who had passed middle age, with grizzled hair that stood up above his brow, projecting like the beak of a ship or the horn of an unicorn. He had a big nose inclined to redness, and kindly, watery eyes, was close shaven, and had lips that, whenever he was in perplexity, or worried with work or thought, he thrust forward and curled. He was a middle-statured man, inclined to stoop.

Uncle Zachie, as he was commonly called behind his back, was a gentleman by birth. In the Roman Catholic Church there is a religious order called that of Minims. In England we have, perhaps, the most widely-diffused of orders, not confined to religion—it is that of Crochets. To this order Mr. Menaida certainly belonged. He was made up of hobbies and prejudices, but they were hobbies and prejudices that might bore, but never hurt others.

Probably the most difficult achievement one can conceive for a man to execute is to stand in his own light; yet Mr. Menaida had succeeded in doing this all through his life. In the first place, he had been bred up for the law, but had never applied himself to the duties of the profession to which he had been articled. As he had manifested as a boy a love of music, his mother and sister had endeavoured to make him learn to play on an instrument; but, because so urged, he had refused to qualify himself to play decently on pianoforte, violin, or flute, till his fingers had stiffened, whereupon he set to work zealously to practise, when it was no longer possible for him to acquire even tolerable proficiency.

As he had been set by his father to work on skins of parchment, he turned his mind to skins of another sort, became an eager naturalist and taxidermist.

That he had genius, or rather a few scattered sparks of talent in his muddled brain, was certain. Every one who knew him said he was clever, but pitied his inability to turn his cleverness to purpose. But one must take into consideration, before accepting the general verdict that he was clever, the intellectual abilities of those who formed this judgment. When we do this, we doubt much whether their opinion is worth much. Mr. Menaida was not clever. He had flashes of wit, no steady light of understanding. Above all, he had no application, a little of which might have made him a useful member of society.

When his articleship was over, he set up as a solicitor, but what business was offered him he neglected or mismanaged, till business ceased to be offered. He would have starved had not a small annuity of fifty pounds been left him to keep the wolf from the door, and that he was able to supplement this small income with money made by the sale of his stuffed specimens of sea-fowl. Taxidermy was the only art in which he was able to do anything profitable. He loved to observe the birds, to wander on the cliffs, listening to their cries, watching their flight, their positions when at rest, the undulations in their feathers under the movement of the muscles as they turned their heads or raised their feet; and when he set himself to stuff the skins he was able to imitate the postures and appearance of living birds with rare fidelity. Consequently, his specimens were in request, and ornithologists and country gentlemen whose gamekeepers had shot rare birds desired to have the skins dealt with, and set in cases, by the dexterous fingers of Mr. Zachary Menaida. He might have done more work of the same kind, but that his ingrained inactivity and distaste for work limited his output. In certain cases Mr. Menaida would not do what was desired of him till coaxed and flattered, and then he did it grumblingly and with sighs at being subjected to killing toil.

Mr. Menaida was a widower; his married life had not been long; he had been left with a son, now grown to manhood, who was no longer at home. He was abroad, in Portugal, in the service of a Bristol merchant, an importer of wines.

As already said, Uncle Zachie did not begin the drudgery of music till it was too late for him to acquire skill on any instrument. His passion for music grew with his inability to give himself pleasure from it. He occupied a double cottage at Polzeath, and a hole knocked through the wall that had separated the lower rooms enabled him to keep his piano in one room and his bird-stuffing apparatus in the other, and to run from one to the other in his favourite desultory way, that never permitted him to stick to one thing at a time.

Into this house Judith and her brother were introduced. Mr. Menaida had been attached to the late rector, the only other gentleman in culture, as in birth, that lived in the place, and when he was told by Miss, or, as she was usually called, Mrs. Trevisa, that the children must leave the parsonage and be put temporarily with some one suitable, and that no other suitable house was available, he consented without making much objection to receive them into his cottage. He was a kindly man, gentle at heart, and he was touched at the bereavement of the children whom he had known since they were infants.

After the first salutation, Mr. Menaida led Judith and the boy into his parlour, the room opening out of his workshop.

"Look here," said he, "what is that?" He pointed to his piano.

"A piano, sir," answered Judith.

"Yes—and mind you, I hate strumming, though I love music. When I am in, engaged at my labours, no strumming. I come in here now and then as relaxation, and run over this and that; then, refreshed, go back to my work, but, if there is any strumming, I shall be put out. I shall run my knife or needle into my hand, and it will upset me for the day. You understand—no strumming. When I am out, then you may touch the keys, but only when I am out. You understand clearly? Say the words after me: 'I allow no strumming.'"

Judith did as required. The same was exacted of Jamie. Then Mr. Menaida said—

"Very well; now we will have a dish of tea. I daresay you are tired. Dear me, you look so. Goodness bless me! indeed you do. What has tired you has been the trial you have gone through. Poor things, poor things! There, go to your rooms; my maid Jump will show you where they are, and I will see about making tea. It will do you good. You want it. I see it."

The kind-hearted man ran about.

"Bless my soul! where have I put the key of the caddy? And—really—my fingers are all over arsenical soap. I think I will leave Jump to make the tea. Jump, have you seen where I put the key? Bless my soul! where did I have it last? Never mind; I will break open the caddy."

"Please, Mr. Menaida, do not do that for us. We can very well wait till the key is found."

"Oh! I don't know when that will be. I shall have forgotten about it if I do not find the key at once, or break open the caddy. But, if you prefer it, I have some cherry brandy, or I would give you some milk punch."

"No—no, indeed, Mr. Menaida."

"But Jamie—I am sure he looks tired. A little cherry brandy to draw the threads in him together. And suffer me, though not a doctor, to recommend it to you. Bless my soul! my fingers are all over arsenical soap. If I don't have some cherry brandy myself I shall have the arsenic get into my system. I hope you have no cuts or scratches on your hand. I forgot the arsenic when I shook hands with you. Now, look here, Jump, bring in the saffron cake, and I will cut them each a good hunch. It will do you good, on my word it will. I have not spared either figs or saffron, and then—I will help you, as I love you. Come and see my birds. That is a cormorant— a splendid fellow—looks as if run out of metal, all his plumage, you know, and in the attitude as if swallowing a fish. Do you see?—the morsel is going down his throat. And—how much luggage have you? Jump! show the young lady where she can put away her gowns and all that sort of thing. Oh, not come yet? All right—a lady and her dresses are not long parted. They will be here soon. Now, then. What will you have?—some cold beef—and cider? Upon my soul! you must excuse me. I was just wiring that kittiwake. Excuse me—I shall be ready in a moment. In the meantime, there are books—Rollin's 'Ancient History,' a very reliable book. No—upon my word, my mind is distracted. I cannot get that kittiwake right without a glass of port. I have some good port. Oliver guarantees it—from Portugal, you know. He is there—first-rate business, and will make his fortune, which is more than his father ever did."

Mr. Menaida went to a closet, and produced a bottle.

"Come here, Jamie. I know what is good for you."

"No—please, Mr. Menaida, do not. He has not been accustomed to anything of the sort. Please not, sir."

"Fudge!" said Uncle Zachie, holding up a glass and pouring cherry brandy into it. "What is your age?—seventeen or eighteen, and I am fifty-two. I have over thirty years more experience of the world than you. Jamie, don't be tied to your sister's apron-string. I know what is best for you. Girls drink water, men something better. Come here, Jamie!"

"No, sir—I beseech you."

"Bless my soul! I know what is good for him. Come to me, Jamie. Look the other way, Judith, if I cannot persuade you."

Judith sighed, and covered her face with her hands. There was to be no help, no support in Uncle Zachie. On the contrary, he would break down her power over Jamie.

"Jamie," she said, "if you love me, go upstairs."

"Presently, Ju. I want that first." And he took it, ran to his sister, and said—

"It is good, Ju!"

"You have disobeyed me, Jamie—that is bad."

She stood on the threshold of further trouble, and she knew it.

# CHAPTER VII
# A VISIT

NO SLEEP visited Judith's eyes that night till the first streaks of dawn appeared, though she was weary, and her frail body and over-exerted brain needed the refreshment of sleep. But sleep she could not, for cares were gathering upon her.

She had often heard her father, when speaking of Mr. Menaida, lament that he was not a little more self-controlled in his drinking. It was not that the old fellow ever became inebriated, but that he hankered after the bottle, and was wont to take a nip continually to strengthen his nerves, steady his hand, or clear his brain. There was ever ready some excuse satisfactory to his own conscience; and it was due to these incessant applications to the bottle that his hand shook, his eyes became watery, and his nose red. It was a danger Judith must guard against, lest this trick should be picked up by the childish Jamie, always apt to imitate what he should not, and acquire habits easily gained, hardly broken, that were harmful to-himself. Uncle Zachie, in his good nature, would lead the boy after him into the same habits that marred his own life.

This was one thought that worked like a mole all night in Judith's brain; but she had other troubles as well to keep her awake. She was alarmed at the consequences of her conduct in the lane. She wondered whether Coppinger were more seriously hurt than had at first appeared. She asked herself whether she had not acted wrongly when she acted inconsiderately, whether in her precipitation to protect herself she had not misjudged Coppinger, whether, if he had attempted to strike her, it would not have been a lesser evil to receive the blow, than to ward it off in such a manner as to break his bones. Knowing by report the character of the man, she feared that she had incurred his deadly animosity. He could not, that she could see, hurt herself in the execution of his resentment, but he might turn her aunt out of his house. That she had affronted her aunt she was aware; Mrs. Trevisa's manner in parting with her had shown that with sufficient plainness.

A strange jumble of sounds on the piano startled Judith. Her first thought and fear was that her brother had gone to the instrument, and were amusing himself on the keys. But on listening attentively she was aware that there was sufficient sequence in the notes to make it certain that the performer was a musician, though lacking in facility of execution. She descended the stairs and entered the little sitting-room. Uncle Zachie was seated on the music-stool, and was endeavouring to play a sonata of Beethoven that was vastly beyond the capacity of his stiff-jointed fingers. Whenever he made a false note he uttered a little grunt and screwed up his eyes, endeavoured to play the bar again, and perhaps accomplish it only to break down in the next.

Judith did not venture to interrupt him. She took up some knitting, and seated herself near the piano, where he might see her without her disturbing him. He raised his brows, grunted, floundered into false harmony, and exclaimed, "Bless me! how badly they do print music now-a-days. Who, without the miraculous powers of a prophet, could tell that B should be natural?" Then, turning his head over his shoulder, addressed Judith, "Good-morning, missie. Are you fond of music?"

"Yes, sir, very."

"So you think. Every one says he or she is fond of music, because that person can hammer out a psalm tune or play the 'Rogues' March.' I hate to hear those who call themselves musical strum on a piano. They can't feel; they only execute."

"But they can play their notes correctly," said Judith, and then flushed with vexation at having made this pointed and cutting remark. But it did not cause Mr. Menaida to wince.

"What of that? I give not a thank-you for mere literal music-reading. Call Jump, set 'Shakespeare' before her, and she will hammer out a scene—correctly as to words; but where is the sense? Where the life? You must play with the spirit and play with the understanding also, as you must read with the spirit and read with the understanding also. It is the same thing with bird-stuffing. Any fool can ram tow into a skin and thrust wires into the neck, but what is the result? You must stuff birds with the spirit and stuff with the understanding also—or it is naught."

"I suppose it is the same with everything one does— one must do it heartily and intelligently."

"Exactly! Now you should see my boy Oliver. Have you ever met him?"

"I think I have; but, to be truthful, I do not recollect him, sir."

"I will bring you his likeness—in miniature. It is in the next room." Up jumped Mr. Menaida, and ran through the opening in the wall, and returned in another moment with the portrait, and gave it into Judith's hands.

"A fine fellow is Oliver! Look at his nose how straight it is. Not like mine—that is a pump-handle. He got his good looks from his mother, not from me. Ah!" He reseated himself at the piano, and ran— incorrectly—over a scale. "It is all the pleasure I have in life, to think of my boy, and to look at his picture, and read his letters, and drink the port he sends me—first-rate stuff. He writes admirable letters, and never a month passes but I receive one. It would come expensive if he wrote direct, so his letter is enclosed in the business papers sent to the house at Bristol, and they forward to me. You shall read his last—out loud. It will give me a pleasure to hear it read by you."

"If I read properly, Mr. Menaida—with the spirit and with the understanding."

"Exactly! But you could not fail to do that, looking at the cheerful face in the miniature, and reading his words—pleasant and bright as himself. Pity you have not seen him; well, that makes something to live for. He has dark hair and blue eyes—not often met together, and when associated, very refreshing. Wait! I'll go after the letter; only, bless my soul! where is it? What coat did I have on when I read it? I'll call Jump. She may remember. Wait! do you recall this?"

He stumbled over something on the keys which might have been anything.

"It is Haydn. I will tell you what I think: Mozart I delight in as a companion; Beethoven I revere as a master; but Haydn I love as a friend. You were about to say something?"

Judith had set an elbow on the piano and put her hand to her head, her fingers through the hair, and was looking into Uncle Zachie's face with an earnestness he could not mistake. She did desire to say something to him; but if she waited till he gave her an opportunity she might wait a long time. He jumped from one subject to another with alacrity, and with rapid forgetfulness of what he was last speaking about.

"Oh, sir, I am so very, very greateful to you for having received us into your snug little house—"

"You like it? Well, I only pay seven pounds for it. Cheap, is it not? Two cottages— labourers' cottages— thrown together. Well, I might go farther and fare worse."

"And, Mr. Menaida, I venture to ask you another favour, which, if you will grant me, you will lay me under an eternal obligation."

"You may command me, my dear."

"It is only this—not to let Jamie have anything stronger than a glass of cider. I do not mind his having that; but a boy like him does not need what is, no doubt, wanted by you who are getting old. I am so afraid of the habit growing on him of looking for and liking what is too strong for him. He is such a child, so easily led, and so unable to control himself. It may be a fancy, a prejudice of mine"—she passed her nervous hand over her face—"I do hope I am not offending you, dear Mr. Menaida; but I know Jamie so well, and I know how carefully he must be watched and checked. If it be a silly fancy of mine—and perhaps it is only a silly fancy—yet," she put on a pleading tone, "you will humour me in this, will you not, Mr. Menaida?"

"Bless my soul! you have only to express a wish, and I will fulfil it. For myself, you must know, I am a little weak; I feel a chill when the wind turns north or east, and am always relaxed when it is in the south or west; that forces me to take something just to save me from serious inconvenience, you understand."

"Oh quite, sir."

"And then—confound it!—I am goaded on to work when disinclined. Why, there's a letter come to me now from Plymouth—a naturalist there, asking for more birds; and what can I do? I slave, I am at it all day, half the night; I have no time to eat or sleep. I was not born to stuff birds. I take it as an amusement, a pastime, and it is converted into a toil. I must brace up my exhausted frame; it is necessary to my health, you understand?"

"Oh yes, Mr. Menaida. And you really will humour my childish whim?"

"Certainly; you may rely on me."

"That is one thing I wanted to say. You see, sir, we have but just come into your house, and already, last night, Jamie was tempted to disobey me, and take what I thought unadvisable, so—I have been turning it over and over in my head—I thought I would like to come to a clear understanding with you, Mr. Menaida. It seems ungracious in me, but you must pity me. I have now all responsibility for Jamie on my head, and I have to do what my conscience tells me I should do; only, I pray you, do not take offence at what I have said."

"Fudge! my dear; you are right, I dare say."

"And now that I have your promise—I have that, have I not?"

"Yes, certainly."

"Now I want your opinion, if you will kindly give it me. I have no father, no mother, to go to for advice; and so I venture to appeal to you—it is about Captain Coppinger."

"Captain Coppinger!" repeated Uncle Zachie, screwing up his brows and mouth. "Umph! He is a bold man who can give help against Captain Coppinger, and a strong man as well as bold. How has he wronged you?"

"Oh! he has not wronged me. It is I who have hurt him."

"You—you?" Uncle Zachie laughed. "A little creature such as you could not hurt Captain Cruel!"

"But, indeed, I have; I have thrown him down and broken his arm and some of his bones."

"You!" Uncle Zachie's face of astonishment and dismay was so comical that Judith, in spite of her anxiety and exhaustion, smiled; but the smile was without brightness.

"And pray, how in the name of wonder did you do that? Upon my word, you will deserve the thanks of the Preventive men. They have no love for him; they have old scores they would gladly wipe off with a broken arm, or, better still, a cracked skull. And pray, how did you do this? With the flour-roller?"

"No, sir; I will tell you the whole story."

Then, in its true sequence, with great clearness, she related the entire narrative of events. She told how her father, even with his last breath, had spoken of Coppinger as the man who had troubled his life by marring his work; how that the Captain had entered the parsonage without ceremony when her dear father was lying dead upstairs, and how he had called there boisterously for Aunt Dionysia because he wanted something of her. She told the old man how that her own feelings had been wrought, by this affront, into anger against Coppinger. Then she related the incident in the lane, and how that, when he raised his arm against her, she had dashed the buttons into his face, frightened the horse, and so produced an accident that might have cost the Captain his life.

"Bless my soul!" exclaimed Mr. Menaida, "and what do you want? Is it an assault? I will run to my law-books and find out; I don't know that it can quite be made out a case of misadventure."

"It is not that, sir."

"Then what do you want?"

"I have been racking my head to think what I ought to do under the circumstances. There can be no doubt that I aggravated him. I was very angry, both because he had been a trouble to my darling papa, and then because he had been so insolent as to enter our house and shout for Aunt Dunes; but there was something more—he had tried to beat Jamie, and it was my father's day of burial. All that roused a bad spirit in me, and I did say very bad words to him— words a man of metal would not bear from even a child, and I suppose I really did lash him to madness, and he would have struck me—but perhaps not, he might have thought better of it. I provoked him, and then I brought about what happened. I have been considering what I ought to do. If I remain here and take no notice, then he will think me very unfeeling, and that I do not care that I have hurt him in mind and body. It came into my head last night that I would ask aunt to apologize to him for what I had done, or, better still, should aunt not come here to-day, which is very likely, that I might walk with Jamie to Pentyre and inquire how Captain Coppinger is, and send in word by my aunt that I am sorry—very sorry."

"Upon my soul, I don't know what to say. I would not have done this to Coppinger myself for a good deal of money. I think if I had, I would get out of the place as quickly as possible, whilst he was crippled by his broken bones. But then, you are a girl, and he may take it better from you than from me. Well—yes; I think it would be advisable to allay his anger if you can. Upon my word, you have put yourself into a difficult position. I'll go and look at my law books, just for my own satisfaction."

A heavy blow on the door, and without waiting for a response and invitation to enter, it was thrown open, and there entered Cruel Coppinger, his arm bandaged, tied in splints, and bound to his body, with his heavy walking-stick brandished by the uninjured hand. He stood for a moment glowering in, searching the room with his keen eyes till they rested on Judith. Then he made an attempt to raise his hand to his head, but ineffectually.

"Curse it!" said he, "I cannot do it; don't tear it off my head with your eyes, girl. Here, you Menaida, come here and take my hat off. Come instantly, or she—she will do—the devil knows what she will not do to me."

He turned, and with his stick beat the door back, that it slammed behind him.

# CHAPTER VIII
## A PATCHED PEACE

"Look at her!" cried Coppinger, with his back against the house door, and pointing to Judith with his stick.

She was standing near the piano, with one hand on it, and was half turned towards him. She was in black, but had a white kerchief about her neck. The absence of all colour in her dress heightened the lustre of her abundant and glowing hair.

Coppinger remained for a moment pointing, with a half-sneer on his dark face. Mr. Menaida had nervously complied with his demand, and had removed the hat from the smuggler, and his dark hair fell about his face. That face was livid and pale; he had evidently suffered much, and now every movement was attended with pain. Not only had some of his bones been broken, but he was bruised and strained.

"Look at her!" he shouted again, in his deep commanding tones, and he fixed his fierce eyes on her and knitted his brows. She remained immoveable, awaiting what he had to say. Though there was a flutter in her bosom, her hand on the piano did not shake.

"I am very sorry, Captain Coppinger," said Judith, in a low, sweet voice, in which there was but a slight tremulousness. "I profess that I believe I acted wrongly yesterday, and I repeat that I am sorry—very sorry, Captain Coppinger."

He made no reply. He lowered the stick that had pointed at her, and he leaned on it. His hand shook because he was in pain.

"I acted wrongly yesterday," continued Judith; "but I acted under provocation that, if it does not justify what I did, palliates the wrong. I can say no more—that is the exact truth."

"Is that all?"

"I am sorry for what was wrong in my conduct— frankly sorry that you are hurt."

"You hear her?" laughed Coppinger, bitterly. "A little chit like that to speak to me thus"—then turning sharply on her, "Are you not afraid?"

"No, I am not afraid; why should I be?"

"Why? Ask any one in S. Enodoc—any one in Cornwall—who has heard my name."

"I beg your pardon. I do not want to ask any one else in S. Enodoc, any one else in Cornwall. I ask you."

"Me? You ask me why you should be afraid of me?" He paused, drew his thick brows together till they formed a band across his forehead. "I tell you that none has ever wronged me by a blade of grass or a flock of wool but has paid for it a thousand fold. And none has ever hurt me as you have done—none has ever dared to attempt it."

"I have said that I am sorry."

"You talk like one cold as a mermaid. I do not believe in your fearlessness. Why do you lean on the piano. There, touch the wires with the very tips of your fingers, and let me hear if they give a sound—and sound they will if you tremble."

Judith exposed some of the wires by raising the top of the piano. Then she smiled, and stood with the tips of her delicate fingers just touching the chords. Coppinger listened, so did Uncle Zachie, and not a vibration could they detect.

Presently she withdrew her hand, and said, "Is not that enough? When a girl says, 'I am sorry,' I supposed the chapter was done and the book closed."

"You have strange ideas."

"I have those in which I was brought up by the best of fathers."

Coppinger thrust his stick along the floor.

"Is it due to the ideas in which you have been brought up that you are not afraid—when you have reduced me to a wreck?"

"And you?—are you afraid of the wreck that you have made?"

The dark blood sprang into and suffused his whole face. Uncle Zachie drew back against the wall and made signs to Judith not to provoke their self-invited visitor; but she was looking steadily at the Captain, and did not observe the signals. In Coppinger's presence she felt nerved to stand on the defensive, and more, to attack. A threat in his whole bearing, in his manner of addressing her, roused every energy she possessed.

"I tell you," said he harshly, "if any man had used the word you threw at me yesterday, I would have murdered him; I would have split his skull with the handle of my crop."

"You raised your hand to do it to me," said Judith.

"No!" he exclaimed violently. "It is false; come here, and let me see if you have the courage, the fearlessness you affect. You women are past-masters of dissembling. Come here; kneel before me and let me raise my stick over you. See; there is lead in the handle, and with one blow I can split your skull and dash the brains over the floor."

Judith remained immoveable.

"I thought it—you are afraid."

She shook her head.

He let himself, with some pain, slowly into a chair.

"You are afraid. You know what to expect. Ah! I could fell you and trample on you and break your bones, as I was cast down, trampled on, and broken in my bones yesterday—by you, or through you. Are you afraid?"

She took a step towards him. Then Uncle Zachie waved her back, in great alarm. He caught Judith's attention, and she answered him, "I am not afraid. I gave him a word I should not have given him yesterday. I will show him that I retract it fully." Then she stepped up to Coppinger and sank on her knees before him. He raised his whip, with the loaded handle, brandishing it over her.

"Now I am here," she said, "I again ask you forgiveness, but I protest an apology is due to me."

He threw his stick away. "By heaven, it is!" Then in an altered tone, "Take it so, that I ask your forgiveness. Get up; do not kneel to me. I could not have struck you down had I willed, my arm is stiff. Perhaps you knew it."

He rose with effort to his feet again. Judith drew back to her former position by the piano, two hectic spots of flame were in her cheek, and her eyes were preternaturally bright.

Coppinger looked steadily at her for awhile, then he said, "Are you ill? You look as if you were."

"I have had much to go through of late."

"True."

He remained looking at her, brooding over something in his mind. She perplexed him; he wondered at her. He could not comprehend the spirit that was in her, that sustained a delicate little frame, and made her defy him.

His eyes wandered round the room, and he signed to Uncle Zachie to give him his stick again.

"What is that?" said he, pointing to the miniature on the stand for music, where Mr. Menaida had put it, over a sheet of the music he had been playing, or attempting to play.

"It is my son, Oliver," said Uncle Zachie.

"Why is it there? Has she been looking at it. Let me see it."

Mr. Menaida hesitated, but presently handed it to the redoubted Captain, with nervous twitches in his face. "I value it highly—my only child."

Coppinger looked at it, with a curl of his lips; then handed it back to Mr. Menaida.

"Why is it here?"

"I brought it here to show it her. I am very proud of my son," said Uncle Zachie.

Coppinger was in an irritable mood, captious about trifles. Why did he ask questions about this little picture? Why look suspiciously at Judith as he did so—suspiciously and threateningly?

"Do you play on the piano?" asked Coppinger. "When the evil spirit was on Saul, David struck the harp and sent the spirit away. Let me hear how you can touch the notes. It may do me good. Heaven knows it is not often I have the leisure or the occasion or am in the humour for music. I would hear what you can do."

Judith looked at Uncle Zachie.

"I cannot play," she said; "that is to say, I can play, but not now, and on this piano."

But Mr. Menaida interfered and urged her to play. He was afraid of Coppinger.

She seated herself on the music-stool and considered for a moment. The miniature was again on the stand. Coppinger put out his stick and thrust it off, and it would have fallen had not Judith caught it. She gave it to Mr. Menaida, who hastily carried it into the adjoining room, where the sight of it might no longer irritate the Captain.

"What shall I play?—I mean, strum?" asked Judith, looking at Uncle Zachie. "Beethoven? No—Haydn. Here are his 'Seasons.' I can play 'Spring.'"

She had a light but firm touch. Her father had been a man of great musical taste, and he had instructed her. But she had, moreover, the musical faculty in her, and she played with the spirit and with the understanding also. Wondrous is the power of music, passing that of fabled necromancy. It takes a man up out of his most sordid surroundings, and sets him in heavenly places. It touches fibres of the inner nature lost, forgotten, ignored, and makes them thrill with a new life. It seals the eyes to outward sights, and unfurls new vistas full of transcendental beauty; it breathes over hot wounds and heals them; it calls to the surface springs of pure delight, and bids them gush forth in an arid desert.

It was so now, as, under the sympathetic fingers of Judith, Haydn's song of the "Spring" was sung. A May world arose in that little dingy room: the walls fell back and disclosed green woods thick with red robin and bursting bluebells, fields golden with buttercups, hawthorns clothed in flower, from which sang the blackbird, thrush, the finch, and the ouzel. The low ceiling rose and overarched as the speed-well blue vault of heaven, the close atmosphere was dispelled by a waft of crisp, pure air; shepherds piped, Boy Bluet blew his horn, and milkmaids rattled their pails and danced a ballet on the turf; and over all, down into every corner of the soul, streamed the glorious, golden sun, filling the heart with gladness.

Uncle Zachie had been standing at the door leading into his workshop, hesitating whether to remain, with a Pish! and a Pshaw! or to fly away beyond hearing. But he was arrested, then drawn lightly, irresistibly, step by step, towards the piano, and he noiselessly sank upon a chair, with his eyes fixed on Judith's fingers as they danced over the keys. His features assumed a more refined character as he listened; the water rose into his eyes, his lips quivered, and when, before reaching the end of the piece, Judith faltered and stopped, he laid his hand on her wrist and said: "My dear—you play, you do not strum. Play when you will— never can it be too long, too much for me. It may steady my hand, it may dispel the chill and the damp better than—but never mind—never mind."

Why had Judith failed to accomplish the piece? Whilst engaged on the notes she had felt that the searching, beaming eyes of the smuggler were on her, fixed with fierce intensity. She could meet them, looking straight at him, without shrinking, and without confusion, but to be searched by them whilst off her guard, her attention engaged on her music, was what she could not endure.

Coppinger made no remark on what he had heard, but his face gave token that the music had not swept across him without stirring and softening his hard nature.

"How long is she to be here—with you?" he asked, turning to Uncle Zachie.

"Captain, I cannot tell. She and her brother had to leave the rectory. They could not remain in that house alone. Mrs. Trevisa asked me to lodge them there, and I consented. I knew their father."

"She did not ask me. I would have taken them in."

"Perhaps she was diffident of doing that," said Uncle Zachie. "But really, on my word, it is no inconvenience to me. I have room in this house, and my maid Jump has not enough to do to attend on me."

"When you are tired of them send them to me."

"I am not likely to be tired of Judith, now that I have heard her play."

"Judith—is that her name?"

"Yes—Judith."

"Judith!" he repeated, and thrust his stick along the floor meditatively. "Judith!" Then, after a pause, with his eyes on the ground, "Why did not your aunt speak to me? Why does she not love you? —she does not, I know. Why did she not go to see you when your father was alive? Why did you not come to the Glaze?"

"My dear papa did not wish me to go to your house," said Judith, answering one of his many questions, the last, and perhaps the easiest to reply to.

"Why not?" he glanced up at her, then down on the floor again.

"Papa was not very pleased with Aunt Dunes—it was no fault on either side, only a misunderstanding," said Judith.

"Why did he not let you come to my house to salute your aunt?"

Judith hesitated. He again looked up at her searchingly.

"If you really must know the truth, Captain Coppinger, papa thought your house was hardly one to which to send two children—it was said to harbour such wild folk."

"And he did not know how fiercely and successfully you could defend yourself against wild folk," said Coppinger, with a harsh laugh. "It is we wild men that must fear you, for you dash us about and bruise and break us when displeased with our ways. We are not so bad at the Glaze as we are painted, not by a half— here is my hand on it."

Judith was still seated on the music-stool, her hands resting in her lap. Coppinger came towards her, walking stiffly, and extending his palm.

She looked down in her lap. What did this fierce, strange man, mean?

"Will you give me your hand?" he asked. "Is there peace between us?"

She was doubtful what to say. He remained, awaiting her answer.

"I really do not know what reply to make," she said, after awhile. "Of course, so far as I am concerned, it is peace. I have myself no quarrel with you, and you are good enough to say that you forgive me."

"Then, why not peace?"

Again she let him wait before answering. She was uneasy and unhappy. She wanted neither his goodwill nor his hostility.

"In all that affects me, I bear you no ill-will," she said, in a low, tremulous voice; "but in that you were a grief to my dear, dear father, discouraging his heart, I cannot be forgetful, and so full of charity as to blot it out as though it had not been."

"Then let it be a patched peace—a peace with evasions and reservations. Better that than none. Give me your hand."

"On that understanding," said Judith, and laid her hand in his. His iron fingers closed round it, and he drew her up from the stool on which she sat, drew her forward near the window, and thrust her in front of him. Then he raised her hand, held it by the wrist, and looked at it.

"It is very small, very weak," he said, musingly. Then there rushed over her mind the recollection of her last conversation with her father. He, too, had taken and looked at her hand, and had made the same remark.

Coppinger lowered her hand and his, and, looking at her, said—

"You are very wonderful to me."

"I—why so?"

He did not answer, but let go his hold of her, and turned away to the door.

Judith saw that he was leaving, and she hastened to bring him his stick, and she opened the door for him.

"I thank you," he said, turned, pointed his stick at her, and added, "It is peace— though a patched one."

# CHAPTER IX
## C. C

DAYS ensued, not of rest to body, but of relaxation to mind. Judith's overstrained nerves had now given them a period of numbness, a sleep of sensibility with occasional turnings and wakenings, in which they recovered their strength. She and Jamie were settled into their rooms at Mr. Menaida's, and the hours were spent in going to and from the rectory removing their little treasures to the new home—if a temporary place of lodging could be called a home—and in arranging them there.

There were a good many farewells to be taken, and Judith marvelled sometimes at the insensibility with which she said them—farewells to a thousand nooks and corners of the house and garden, the shrubbery, and the glebe farm, all endeared by happy recollections, now having their brightness dashed with rain.

To Judith this was a first revelation of the mutability of things on earth. Hitherto, as a child, with a child's eyes and a child's confidence, she had regarded the rectory, the glebe, the contents of the house, the flowers in the garden, as belonging inalienably to her father and brother and herself. They belonged to them together. There was nothing that was her father's that did not belong to Jamie and to her, nothing of her brother's or her own that was not likewise the property of papa. There was no mine or thine in that little family of love—save only a few birthday presents given from one to the other, and these only special property by a playful concession. But now the dear father was gone, and every right seemed to dissolve. From the moment that he leaned back against the brick, lichenstained wall, and sighed—and was dead, house and land had been snatched from them. And though the contents of the rectory, the books, and the furniture, and the china belonged to them, it was but for a little while; these things must be parted with also, turned into silver.

Not because the money was needed, but because Judith had no settled home, and no prospect of one. Therefore she must not encumber herself with many belongings. For a little while she would lodge with Mr. Menaida, but she could not live there for ever; she must remove elsewhere, and she must consider, in the first place, that there was not room in Uncle Zachie's cottage for accumulations of furniture, and that, in the next place, she would probably have to part with them on her next remove, even if she did retain them for a while.

If these things were to be parted with, it would be advisable to part with them at once. But to this determination Judith could not bring herself at first. Though she had put aside, to be kept, things too sacred to her, too much part of her past life, to be allowed to go into the sale, after a few days she relinquished even these. Those six delightful old coloured prints, in frames, of a fox-hunt—how Jamie had laughed at them, and followed the incidents in them, and never wearied of them—must they go—perhaps for a song? It must be so. That work-table of her mother's, of dark rosewood, with a crimson bag beneath it to contain wools and silks, one of the few remembrances she had of that mother whom she but dimly recalled—must that go?—what, and all those skeins in it of coloured floss silk, and the piece of embroidery half finished? the work of her mother, broken off by death—that also? It must be so. And that rusty leather chair in which papa had sat, with one golden-headed child on each knee cuddled into his breast, with the flaps of his coat drawn over their heads, which listened to the tick-tick of his great watch, and to the tale of Little Snowflake, or Gracieuse and Percinet?—must that go also? It must be so.

Every day showed to Judith some fresh link that had to be broken. She could not bear to think that the mother's work-table should be contended for at a vulgar auction, and struck down to a blousy farmer's wife; that her father's chair should go to some village inn to be occupied by sots. She would rather have seen them destroyed; but to destroy them would not be right.

After a while she longed for the sale; she desired to have it over, that an entirely new page of life might be opened, and her thoughts might not be carried back to the past by everything she saw.

Of Coppinger nothing further was seen. Nor did Aunt Dionysia appear at the rectory to superintend the assortment of the furniture, nor at Mr. Menaida's to inquire into the welfare of her nephew and niece. To Judith it was a relief not to have her aunt in the parsonage whilst she was there; that hard voice and unsympathetic manner would have kept her nerves on the quiver. It was best as it was, that she should have time, by herself, with no interference from any one, to select what was to be kept and put away, what was to be sold;—to put away gently, with her own trembling hand, and with eyes full of tears, the old black gown and the Oxford hood that papa had worn in church, and to burn his old sermons and bundles of letters, unread and uncommented on by Aunt Dunes.

In these days Judith did not think much of Coppinger. Uncle Zachie informed her that he was worse, he was confined to his bed, he had done himself harm by coming over to Polzeath the day after his accident, and the doctor had ordered him not to stir from Pentyre Glaze for some time—not till his bones were set. Nothing was known of the occasion of Coppinger's injuries, so Uncle Zachie said; it was reported in the place that he had been thrown from his horse. Judith entreated the old man not to enlighten the ignorance of the public; she was convinced that naught would transpire through Jamie, who could not tell a story intelligibly; and Miss Dionysia Trevisa was not likely to publish what she knew.

Judith had a pleasant little chamber at Mr. Menaida's; it was small, low, plastered against the roof, the rafters showing, and whitewashed like the walls and ceiling. The light entered from a dormer in the roof, a low window glazed with diamond quarries set in lead that clickered incessantly in the wind. It faced the south, and let the sun flow in. A scrap of carpet was on the floor, and white curtains to the window. In this chamber Judith ranged such of her goods as she had resolved on retaining, either as indispensable, or as being too dear to her to part with unnecessarily, and which, as being of small size, she might keep without difficulty.

Her father's old travelling trunk, covered with hide with the hair on, and his initials in brass nails—a trunk he had taken with him to college—was there, thrust against the wall; it contained her clothes.

Suspended above it was her little bookcase, with the shelves laden with "The Travels of Rolando," Dr. Aitkin's "Evenings at Home," Magnal's "Questions," a French dictionary, "Paul and Virginia," and a few other works such as were the delight of children from ninety to a hundred years ago.

Books for children were rare in those days, and such as were produced were read and re-read till they were woven into the very fibre of the mind, never more to be extricated and cast aside. Now it is otherwise. A child reads a story-book every week, and each new story-book effaces the impression produced by the book that went before. The result of much reading is the same as the result of no reading—the production of a blank.

How Judith and Jamie had sat together perched up in a sycamore, in what they called their nest, and had revelled in the adventures of Rolando, she reading aloud, he listening a little, then lapsing into observation of the birds that flew and hopped about, or the insects that spun and crept, or dropped on silky lines, or fluttered humming about the nest, then returned to attention to the book again! Rolando would remain through life the friend and companion of Judith. She could not part with the four-volumed, red-leather-backed book.

For the first day or two Jamie had accompanied his sister to the rectory, and had somewhat incommoded her by his restlessness and his mischief, but on the third day, and thenceforth, he no further attended her. He had made fast friends with Uncle

Zachie. He was amused with watching the process of bird-stuffing, and the old man made use of the boy by giving him tow to pick to pieces and wires to straighten.

Mr. Menaida was pleased to have some one by him in his workshop to whom he could talk. It was unimportant to him whether the listener followed the thread of his conversation or not, so long as he was a listener. Mr. Menaida, in his solitude, had been wont to talk to himself, to grumble to himself at the impatience of his customers, to lament to himself the excess of work that pressed upon him and deprived him of time for relaxation. He was wont to criticise, to himself, his success or want of success in the setting up of a bird. It was far more satisfactory to him to be able to address all these remarks to a second party.

He was, moreover, surprised to find how keen and just had been Jamie's observation of birds, their ways, their attitudes. Judith was delighted to think that Jamie had discovered talent of some sort, and he had, so Uncle Zachie assured her, that imitative ability which is often found to exist alongside with low intellectual power, and this enabled him to assist Mr. Menaida in giving a natural posture to his birds.

It flattered the boy to find that he was appreciated, that he was consulted, and asked to assist in a kind of work that exacted nothing of his mind.

When Uncle Zachie was tired of his task, which was every ten minutes or quarter of an hour, and that was the extreme limit to which he could continue regular work, he lit his pipe, left his bench, and sat in his armchair. Then Jamie also left his tow picking or wire punching, and listened, or seemed to listen, to Mr. Menaida's talk. When the old man had finished his pipe, and, with a sigh, went back to his task, Jamie was tired of hearing him talk, and was glad to resume his work. Thus the two desultory creatures suited each other admirably, and became attached friends.

"Jamie! what is the meaning of this?" asked Judith, with a start, and a rush of blood to her heart.

She had returned in the twilight from the parsonage. There was something in the look of her brother, something in his manner that was unusual.

"Jamie! What have you been taking? who gave it you?"

She caught the boy by the arm. Distress and shame were in her face, in the tones of her voice.

Mr. Menaida grunted.

"I'm sorry, but it can't be helped—really it can't," said he, apologetically. "But Captain Coppinger has sent me down a present of a keg of cognac—real cognac, splendid, amber-like—and, you know, it was uncommonly kind. He never did it before. So there was no avoidance; we had to tap it and taste it, and give a sup to the fellow who brought us the keg, and drink the health of the Captain. One could not be churlish; and, naturally, I could not abstain from letting Jamie try the spirit. Perfectly pure—quite wholesome—first-rate quality. Upon my word, he had not more than a fly could dip his legs in and feel the bottom; but he is unaccustomed to anything stronger than cider, and this is stronger than I supposed."

"Mr. Menaida, you promised me—"

"Bless me! There are contingencies, you know. I never for a moment thought that Captain Coppinger would show me such a favour, would have such courtesy. But, upon my honour, I think it is your doing, my dear! You shook hands and made peace with him, and he has sent this in token of the cessation of hostilities and the ratification of the agreement."

"Mr. Menaida, I trusted you. I did believe, when you passed your word to me, that you would hold to it."

"Now—there, don't take it in that way. Jamie, you rascal, hop off to bed. He'll be right as a trivet tomorrow morning, I stake my reputation on that. There, there, I will help him upstairs."

Judith suffered Mr. Menaida to do as he proposed. When he had left the room with Jamie, who was reluctant to go, and struggled to remain, she seated herself on the sofa, and covering her face with her hands, burst into tears. Whom could she trust? No one.

Had she been alone in the world she would have been more confident of the future, been able to look forward with a good courage; but she had to carry Jamie with her, who must be defended from himself, and from the weak good nature of those he was with.

When Uncle Zachie came downstairs, he slunk into his work-room, and was very quiet. No lamp or candle was lighted, and it was too dark for him to continue his employment on the birds. What was he doing? Nothing. He was ashamed of himself, and keeping out of Judith's way.

But Judith would not let him escape so easily; she went to him, as he avoided her, and found him seated in a corner turning his pipe about. He had been afraid of striking a light, lest he should call her attention to his presence.

"Oh, my dear, come in here into the workshop to me! This is an honour, an unexpected pleasure. Jamie and I have been drudging like slaves all day, and we're fagged—fagged to the ends of our fingers and toes."

"Mr. Menaida, I am sorry to say it, but if such a thing happens again as has taken place this evening, Jamie and I must leave your house. I thank you with an overflowing heart for your goodness to us; but I must consider Jamie above everything else, and I must see that he be not exposed to temptation."

"Where will you take him?"

"I cannot tell; but I must shield him."

"There, there, not a word! It shall never happen again. Now let bye-gones be bye-gones, and play me something of Beethoven, whilst I sit here and listen in the twilight."

"No, Mr. Menaida, I cannot. I have not the spirit to do it. I can think only of Jamie."

"So you punish me!"

"Take it so. I am sorry; but I cannot do otherwise."

"Now, look here! Bless my soul! I had almost forgotten it. Here is a note for you, from the Captain, I believe." He went to the chimney-piece and took down a scrap of paper, folded and sealed.

Judith looked at it, then went to the window, broke the seal, and opened the paper. She read—

"Why do you not come and see me? You do not care for what you have done. They call me cruel; but you are that.—C. C."

# CHAPTER X
## EGO ET REGINA MEA

THE strange, curt note from Cruel Coppinger served in a measure to divert the current of Judith's thoughts from her trouble about Jamie. It was perhaps as well, or she would have fretted over that throughout the night, not only because of Jamie, but because she felt that her father had left his solemn injunction on her to protect and guide her twin brother, and she knew that whatsoever harm, physical or moral, came to him, argued a lack of attention to her duty. Her father had not been dead many days, and already Jamie had been led from the path she had undertaken to keep him in.

But when she began to worry herself about Jamie, the bold characters, "C. C.," with which the letter was signed, rose before her, and glowed in the dark as characters of fire.

She had gone to her bedroom, and had retired for the night, but could not sleep. The moon shone through the lattice into her chamber, and on the stool by the window lay the letter, where she had cast it. Her mind turned to it.

Why did Coppinger call her cruel? Was she cruel? Not intentionally so. She had not wilfully injured him. He did not suppose that. He meant that she was heartless and indifferent in letting him suffer without making any inquiry concerning him.

He had injured himself by coming to Polzeath to see her the day following his accident. Uncle Zachie had assured her of that.

She went on in her busy mind to ask why he had come to see her? Surely there had been no need for him to do so! His motive—the only motive she could imagine—was a desire to relieve her from anxiety and distress of mind; a desire to show her that he bore no ill-will towards her for what she had done. That was generous and considerate of him. Had he not come she certainly would have been unhappy and in unrest, would have imagined all kinds of evil as likely to ensue through his hostility—for one thing, her aunt's dismissal from her post might have been expected.

But Coppinger, though in pain, and at a risk to his health, had walked to where she was lodging to disabuse her of any such impression. She was grateful to him for so doing. She felt that such a man could not be utterly abandoned by God, entirely void of good qualities, as she had supposed, viewing him only through the representations of his character and the tales circulating relative to his conduct that had reached her.

A child divides mankind into two classes—the good and the bad, and supposes that there is no debatable land between them, where light and shade are blended into neutral tint; certainly not that there are blots on the white leaf of the lives of the good, and luminous glimpses in the darkness of the histories of the bad. As they grow older they rectify their judgments, and such a rectification Judith had now to make.

She was assisted in this by compassion for Coppinger, who was in suffering, and by self-reproach, because she was the occasion of this suffering.

What were the exact words Captain Cruel had employed? She was not certain; she turned the letter over and over in her mind, and could not recall every expression, and she could not sleep till she was satisfied.

Therefore she rose from bed, stole to the window, took up the letter, seated herself on the stool, and conned it in the moonlight. "Why do you not come and see me? You do not care for what you have done." That was not true; she was greatly troubled at what she had done. She was sick at heart when she thought of that scene in the lane, when the black mare was leaping and pounding with her hoofs, and Coppinger lay on the ground. One kick of the hoof on his head, and he would have been dead. His blood would have rested on her conscience never to be wiped off. Horrible was the recollection now, in the stillness of the night. It was marvellous that life had not been beaten out of the prostrate man, that, dragged about by the arm, he had not been torn to pieces, that every bone had not been shattered, that his face had not been battered out of recognition. Judith felt the perspiration stand on her brow at the thought. God had been very good to her in sending His angel to save Coppinger from death and her from bloodguiltiness. She slid to her knees at the window, and held up her hands, the moonlight illuminating her white upturned face, as she gave thanks to Heaven that no greater evil had ensued from her inconsidered act with the button-basket, than a couple of broken bones.

Oh! it was very far indeed from true that she did not care for what she had done. Coppinger must have been blind indeed not to have seen how she felt her conduct. His letter concluded: "They call me cruel; but you are that." He meant that she was cruel in not coming to the Glaze to inquire after him. He had thought of her trouble of mind, and had gone to Polzeath to relieve her of anxiety, and she had shown no consideration for him—or not in like manner.

She had been very busy at the rectory. Her mind had been concerned with her own affairs, that was her excuse. Cruel she was not. She took no pleasure in his pain. But she hesitated about going to see him. That was more than was to be expected of a young girl. She would go on the morrow to Coppinger's house, and ask to speak to her aunt; that she might do, and from Aunt Dionysia she would learn in what condition Captain Cruel was, and might send him her respects and wishes for his speedy recovery.

As she still knelt in her window, looking up through the diamond panes into the clear, grey-blue night sky, she heard a sound without, and, looking down, saw a convoy of horses pass, laden with bales and kegs, and followed or accompanied by men wearing slouched hats. So little noise did the beasts make in traversing the road, that Judith was convinced their hoofs must be muffled in felt. She had heard that this was done by the smugglers. It was said that all Coppinger's horses had their boots drawn on when engaged in conveying run goods from the place where stored to their destination.

These were Coppinger's men, this his convoy, doubtless. Judith thrust the letter from her. He was a bad man, a very bad man; and if he had met with an accident, it was his due, a judgment on his sins. She rose from her knees, turned away, and went back to her bed.

Next day, after a morning spent at the rectory, in the hopes that her aunt might arrive, and obviate the need of her going in quest of her, Judith, disappointed in this hope, prepared to walk to Pentyre. Mrs. Dionysia had not acted with kindness towards her. Judith felt this, without allowing herself to give to the feeling articulate expression. She made what excuses she could for Aunt Dunes: she was hindered by duties that had crowded upon her, she had been forbidden going by Captain Cruel; but none of these excuses satisfied Judith.

Judith must go herself to the Glaze, and she had reasons of her own for wishing to see her aunt, independent of the sense of obligation on her, more or less acknowledged, that she must obey the summons of C. C. There were matters connected with the rectory, with the furniture there, the cow, and the china, that Mrs. Trevisa must give her judgment upon. There were bills that had come in, which Mrs. Trevisa must pay, as Judith had been left without any money in her pocket.

As the girl walked through the lanes she turned over in her mind the stories she had heard of the smuggler Captain, the wild tales of his wrecking ships, of his contests with the Preventive men, and the ghastly tragedy of Wyvill, who had been washed up headless on Doom Bar. In former days she had accepted all these stories as true, had not thought of questioning them; but now that she had looked Coppinger in the face, had spoken with him, experienced his consideration, she could not believe that they were to be accepted without question. That story of Wyvill—that Captain Cruel had hacked off his head on the gunwale with his axe—seemed to her now utterly incredible. But if true! She shuddered to think that her hand had been held in that stained with so hideous a crime.

Thus musing, Judith arrived at Pentyre Glaze, and entering the porch, turned from the sea, knocked at the door.

A loud voice bade her enter. She knew that the voice proceeded from Coppinger, and her heart fluttered with fear and uncertainty. She halted, with her hand on the door, inclined to retreat without entering; but again the voice summoned her to come in, and gathering up her courage she opened the door, and, still holding the latch, took a few steps forward into the hall or kitchen, into which it opened.

A fire was smouldering in the great open fire-place, and beside it, in a carved oak armchair, sat Cruel Coppinger, with a small table at his side, on which were a bottle and glass, a canister of tobacco and a pipe. His arm was strapped across his breast as she had seen it a few days before. Entering from the brilliant light of day, Judith could not at first observe his face, but, as her eyes became accustomed to the twilight of the smoke-blackened and gloomy hall, she saw that he looked more worn and pale than he had seemed the day after the accident. Nor could she understand the expression on his countenance when he was aware who was his visitor.

"I beg your pardon," said Judith; "I am sorry to have intruded; but I wished to speak to my aunt."

"Your aunt? Old mother Dunes? Come in. Let go your hold of the door and shut it. Your aunt started a quarter of an hour ago for the rectory."

"And I came along the lane from Polzeath."

"Then no wonder you did not meet her. She went by the church path, of course, and over the down."

"I am sorry to have missed her. Thank you, Captain Coppinger, for telling me."

"Stay!" he roared, as he observed her draw back into the porch. "You are not going yet?"

"I cannot stay for more than a moment in which to ask how you do, and whether you are somewhat better? I was sorry to hear you had been worse."

"I have been worse, yes. Come in. You shall not go. I am mewed in as a prisoner, and have none to speak to, and no one to look at but old Dunes. Come in, and take that stool by the fire, and let me hear you speak, and let me rest my eyes a while on your golden hair—gold, more golden than that of the Indies."

"I hope you are better, sir," said Judith, ignoring the compliment.

"I am better now I have seen you. I shall be worse if you do not come in."

She refused to do this by a light shake of the head.

"I suppose you are afraid. We are wild and lawless men here, ogres that eat children! Come, child, I have something to show you."

"Thank you for your kindness; but I must run to the parsonage; I really must see my aunt."

"Then I will send her to Polzeath to you when she returns. She will keep; she's stale enough."

"I would spare her the trouble."

"Pshaw! She shall do what I will. Now see—I am wearied to death with solitude and sickness. Come, amuse yourself, if you will, with insulting me—calling me what you like; I do not mind, so long as you remain."

"I have no desire whatever, Captain Coppinger, to insult you and call you names."

"You insult me by standing there holding the latch— standing on one foot, as if afraid to sully the soles by treading my tainted floor. Is it not an insult that you refuse to come in? Is it not so much as saying to me, 'You are false, cruel, not to be trusted; you are not worthy that I should be under the same roof with you, and breathe the same air'?"

"Oh, Captain Coppinger, I do not mean that!"

"Then let go the latch and come in. Stand, if you will not sit, opposite me. How can I see you there, in the doorway?"

"There is not much to see when I am visible," said Judith, laughing.

"Oh no! not much! Only a little creature who has more daring than any man in Cornwall—who will stand up to, and cast at her feet, Cruel Coppinger, at whose name men tremble."

Judith let go her hold on the door, and moved timidly into the hall; but she let the door remain half open, that the light and air flowed in.

"And now," said Captain Coppinger, "here is a key on this table by me. Do you see a small door by the clock case. Unlock that door with the key."

"You want something from thence?"

"I want you to unlock the door. There are beautiful and costly things within that you shall see."

"Thank you; but I would rather look at them some other day, when my aunt is here, and I have more time."

"Will you refuse me even the pleasure of letting you see what is there?"

"If you particularly desire it, Captain Coppinger, I will peep in—but only peep."

She took the key from his table, and crossed the hall to the door. The lock was large and clumsy, but she turned the key by putting both hands to it. Then, swinging open the door, she looked inside. The door opened into an apartment crowded with a collection of sundry articles of value: bales of silk from Italy, Genoa laces, Spanish silver-inlaid weapons, Chinese porcelain, bronzes from Japan, gold and silver ornaments, bracelets, brooches, watches, inlaid mother-of-pearl cabinets—an amazing congeries of valuables heaped together.

"Well, now!" shouted Cruel Coppinger. "What say you to the gay things there? Choose—take what you will. I care not for them one rush. What do you most admire, most covet? Put out both hands and take—take all you would have, fill your lap, carry off all you can. It is yours."

Judith drew hastily back and re-locked the door.

"What have you taken?"

"Nothing."

"Nothing? Take what you will; I give it freely."

"I cannot take anything, though I thank you, Captain Coppinger, for your kind and generous offer."

"You will accept nothing?"

She shook her head.

"That is like you. You do it to anger me. As you throw hard words at me—coward, wrecker, robber— and as you dash broken glass, buttons, buckles, in my face, so do you throw back my offers."

"It is not through ingratitude—"

"I care not through what it is! You seek to anger, and not to please me. Why will you take nothing? There are beautiful things there to charm a woman."

"I am not a woman; I am a little girl."

"Why do you refuse me?"

"For one thing, because I want none of the things there, beautiful and costly though they be."

"And for the other thing—?"

"For the other thing—excuse my plain speaking— I do not think they have been honestly got."

"By heavens!" shouted Coppinger. "There you attack and stab at me again. I like your plainness of speech. You do not spare me. I would not have you false and double like old Dunes."

"Oh, Captain Coppinger! I give you thanks from the depths of my heart. It is kindly intended, and it is so good and noble of you, I feel that; for I have hurt you and reduced you to the state in which you now are, and yet you offer me the best things in your house —things of priceless value. I acknowledge your goodness; but just because I know I do not deserve this goodness I must decline what you offer."

"Then come here and give me the key."

She stepped lightly over the floor to him and handed him the great iron key to his store chamber. As she did so he caught her hand, bowed his dark head, and kissed her fingers.

"Captain Coppinger!" She started back, trembling, and snatched her hand from him.

"What! have I offended you again? Why not? A subject kisses the hand of his queen; and I am a subject, and you—you my queen."

# CHAPTER XI
## JESSAMINE

"How are you, old man?"

"Middlin', thanky'; and how be you, gov'nor?"

"Middlin' also; and your missus?"

"Only sadly. I fear she's goin' slow but sure the way of all flesh."

"Bless us! 'Tis a trouble and expense them sort o' things. Now to work, shall we? What do you figure up?"

"And you?"

"Oh well, I'm not here on reg'lar business. Huntin' on my own score to-day."

"Oh, aye! Nice port this."

"Best the old fellow had in his cellar. I told the executrix I should like to taste of it, and advise thereon."

The valuers for dilapidations, vulgarly termed delapidators, were met in the dining-room of the deserted parsonage. Mr. Scantlebray was on one side, Mr. Cargreen on the other. Mr. Scantlebray was on that of the "orphings," as he termed his clients, and Mr. Cargreen on that of the Rev. Mr. Mules, the recently-nominated rector to S. Enodoc.

Mr. Scantlebray was a tall, lean man, with light grey eyes, a red face, and legs and arms that he shook every now and then as though they were encumbrances to his trunk, and he was going to shake them off, as a poodle issuing from a bath shakes the water out of his locks. Mr. Cargreen was a bullet-headed man, with a white neckcloth, grey whiskers, a solemn face, and a sort of perpetual "Let-us-pray" expression on his lips and in his eyes—a composing of his interior faculties and abstraction from worldly concerns.

"I am here," said Mr. Scantlebray, "as adviser and friend—you understand, old man—of the orphings and their haunt."

"And I," said Mr. Cargreen, "am ditto to the incoming rector."

"And what do you get out of this visit?" asked Mr. Scantlebray, who was a frank man.

"Only three guineas as a fee," said Mr. Cargreen. "And you?"

"Ditto, old man—three guineas. You understand, I am not here as valuer to-day."

"Nor I—only as adviser."

"Exactly! Taste this port. 'Taint bad—out of the cellar of the old chap. Told auntie I must have it, to taste and give opinion on."

"And what are you going to do to-day?"

"I'm going to have one or two little things pulled down, and other little things put to rights."

"Humph! I'm here to see nothing is pulled down."

"We won't quarrel. There's the conservatory, and the linney in Willa Park."

"I don't know," said Cargreen, shaking his head.

"Now, look here, old man," said Mr. Scantlebray.

"You let me tear the linney down, and I'll let the conservatory stand."

"The conservatory—"

"I know; the casement of the best bedroom went through the roof of it. I'll mend the roof and repaint it. You can try the timber, and find it rotten, and lay on dilapidations enough to cover a new conservatory. Pass the linney; I want to make pickings out of that."

It may perhaps be well to let the reader understand the exact situation of the two men engaged in sipping port. Directly it was known that a rector had been nominated to S. Enodoc, Mr. Cargreen, a Bodmin valuer, agent, and auctioneer, had written to the happy nominee, Mr. Mules, of Birmingham, inclosing his card in the letter, to state that he was a member of an old established firm, enjoying the confidence, not to say the esteem, of the principal county families in the north of Cornwall, that he was a sincere Churchman, that, deploring as a true son of the Church, the prevalence of Dissent, he felt it his duty to call the attention of the reverend gentleman to certain facts that concerned him, but especially the CHURCH, and facts that he himself, as a devoted son of the Church on conviction, after mature study of its tenets, felt called upon, in the interests of that Church he so had at heart, to notice. He had heard, said Mr. Cargreen, that the outgoing parties from S. Enodoc were removing, or causing to be removed, or were proposing to remove, certain fixtures in the parsonage, and certain outbuildings, barns, tenements, sheds, and linneys on the glebe and parsonage premises, to the detriment of its value, inasmuch as that such removal would be prejudicial to the letting of the land, and render it impossible for the incoming rector to farm it himself without re-erecting the very buildings now in course of destruction, or which were purposed to be destroyed: to wit, certain out-buildings, barns, cattle-sheds, and linneys, together with other tenements that need not be specified. Mr. Cargreen added that, roughly speaking, the dilapidations of these buildings, if allowed to stand, might be assessed at £300; but that, if pulled down, it would cost the new rector about £700 to re-erect them, and their re-erection would be an imperative necessity. Mr. Cargreen had himself, personally, no interest in the matter; but, as a true son of the Church, &c., &c.

By return of post Mr. Cargreen received an urgent request from the Rev. Mr. Mules to act as his agent, and to act with precipitation in the protection of his interests.

In the meantime Mr. Scantlebray had not been neglectful of other people's interest. He had written to Miss Dionysia Trevisa to inform her that, though he did not enjoy a present acquaintance, it was the solace and joy of his heart to remember that some years ago, before that infelicitous marriage of Mr. Trevisa, which had led to Miss Dionysia's leaving the rectory, it had been his happiness to meet her at the house of a mutual acquaintance, Mrs. Scaddon, where he had respectfully, and, at this distance of time, he ventured to add, humbly and hopelessly admired her; that, as he was riding past the rectory, he had chanced to observe the condition of dilapidation certain tenements, pig-styes, cattle-sheds, and other outbuildings were in, and that, though it in no way concerned him, yet, for auld lang syne's sake, and a desire to assist one whom he had always venerated and, at this distance of time might add, had admired, he ventured to offer a suggestion: to wit, That a number of unnecessary outbuildings should be torn down and utterly effaced before a new rector was nominated, and had appointed a valuer; also that certain obvious repairs should be undertaken and done at once, so as to give to the parsonage the appearance of being in excellent order, and cut away all excuse for piling up dilapidations. Mr. Scantlebray ventured humbly to state that he had had a good deal of experience with those gentlemen who acted as valuers for dilapidations, and with pain he was obliged to add that a more unscrupulous set of men it had never been his bad fortune to come into contact with. He ventured to assert that, were he to tell all that he knew, or only half of what he knew, as to their proceedings in valuing for dilapidations, he would make both of Miss Trevisa's ears tingle.

At once Miss Dionysia entreated Mr. Scantlebray to superintend and carry out with expedition such repairs and such demolitions as he deemed expedient, so as to forestall the other party.

"Chicken!" said Mr. Cargreen. "That's what I've brought for my lunch."

"And 'am is what I've got," said Mr. Scantlebray. "They'll go lovely together." Then, in a loud tone— "Come in!"

The door opened, and a carpenter entered with a piece of deal board in his hand.

"You won't mind looking out of the winder, Mr. Cargreen?" said Mr. Scantlebray. "Some business that's partick'ler my own. You'll find the jessamine— the white jessamine—smells beautiful."

Mr. Cargreen rose, and went to the dining-room window that was embowered in white jessamine, then in full flower and fragrance.

"What is it, Davy?"

"Well, sir, I ain't got no dry old board for the floor where it be rotten, nor for the panelling of the doors where broken through."

"No board at all?"

"No, sir—all is green. Only cut last winter."

"Won't it take paint?"

"Well, sir, not well. I've dried this piece by the kitchen fire, and I find it'll take the paint for a time."

"Run, dry all the panels at the kitchen fire, and then paint 'em."

"Thanky', sir; but how about the boarding of the floor? The boards 'll warp and start."

"Look here, Davy, that gentleman who's at the winder a-smelling to the jessamine is the surveyor and valuer to t'other party. I fancy you'd best go round outside and have a word with him, and coax him to pass the boards."

"Come in!" in a loud voice. Then there entered a man in a cloth coat, with very bushy whiskers. "How d'y' do, Spargo? What do you want?" "Well, Mr. Scantlebray, I understand the linney and cowshed is to be pulled down."

"So it is, Spargo."

"Well, sir!" Mr. Spargo drew his sleeve across his mouth. "There's a lot of very fine oak timber in it— beams, and such like—that I don't mind buying. As a timber merchant, I could find a use for it."

"Say ten pound."

"Ten pun'! That's a long figure!"

"Not a pound too much; but come—we'll say eight."

"I reckon I'd thought five."

"Five!—pshaw! It's dirt cheap to you at eight."

"Why to me, sir?"

"Why, because the new rector will want to rebuild both cattleshed and linney, and he'll have to go to you for timber."

"But suppose he don't, and cuts down some on the glebe?"

"No, Spargo—not a bit. There at the winder, smelling to the jessamine, is the new rector's adviser and agent. Go round by the front door into the garding, and say a word to him—you understand, and—" Mr. Scantlebray tapped his palm. "Do now go round and have a sniff of the jessamine, Mr. Spargo; and I don't fancy Mr. Cargreen will advise the rector to use home-grown timber. He'll tell him it sleeps away, gets the rot, comes more expensive in the long run."

The valuer took a wing of chicken and a little ham, and then shouted, with his mouth full—"Come in!"

The door opened, and admitted a farmer.

"How 'do, Mr. Joshua? middlin'?"

"Middlin', sir, thanky'."

"And what have you come about, sir?"

"Well—Mr. Scantlebray, sir, I fancy you ha'n't offered me quite enough for carting away of all the rummage from them buildings as is coming down. 'Tis a terrible lot of stone, and I'm to take 'em so far away."

"Why not?"

"Well, sir, it's such a lot of work for the hosses, and the pay so poor."

"Not a morsel, Joshua—not a morsel."

"Well, sir, I can't do it at the price."

"Oh, Joshua! Joshua! I thought you'd a better eye to the future. Don't you see that the new rector will have to build up all these outbuildings again, and where else is he to get stone except out of your quarry, or some of the old stone you have carted away, which you will have the labour of carting back?"

"Well, sir, I don't know."

"But I do, Joshua."

"The new rector might go elsewhere for stone."

"Not he. Look there, at the winder is Mr. Cargreen, and he's in with the new parson, like a brother —knows his very soul. The new parson comes from Birmingham. What can he tell about building-stone here? Mr. Cargreen will tell him yours is the only stuff that ain't powder."

"But, sir, he may not rebuild."

"He must. Mr. Cargreen will tell him that he can't let the glebe without buildings; and he can't build without your quarry stone: and if he has your quarry stone—why, you will be given the carting also. Are you satisfied?"

"Yes—if Mr. Cargreen would be sure—"

"He's there at the winder, a-smelling to the jessamine. You go round and have a talk to him, and make him understand—you know. He's a little hard o' hearing; but the drum o' his ear is here," said Scantlebray, tapping his palm.

Mr. Scantlebray was now left to himself to discuss the chicken wing—the liver wing he had taken—and sip the port; a conversation was going on in an undertone at the window; but that concerned Mr. Cargreen and not himself, so he paid no attention to it.

After a while, however, when this hum ceased, he turned his head, and called out—

"Old man! how about your lunch?"

"I'm coming."

"And you found the jessamine very sweet?"

"Beautiful! beautiful!"

"Taste this port. It is not what it should be: some the old fellow laid in when he could afford it—before he married. It is passed, and going back; should have been drunk five years ago."

Mr. Cargreen came to the table, and seated himself. Then Mr. Scantlebray flapped his arms, shook out his legs, and settled himself to the enjoyment of the lunch, in the society of Mr. Cargreen.

"The merry-thought! Pull with me, old man?"

"Certainly!"

Mr. Scantlebray and Mr. Cargreen were engaged on the merry-thought, each endeavouring to steal an advantage on the other, by working the fingers up the bone unduly—when the window was darkened.

Without desisting from pulling at the merry-thought each turned his head, and Scantlebray at once let go his end of the bone. At the window stood Captain Coppinger looking in at the couple, with his elbow resting on the window-sill.

Mr. Scantlebray flattered himself that he was on good terms with all the world, and he at once with hilarity saluted the Captain by raising the fingers greased by the bone to his brow.

"Didn't reckon on seeing you here, Cap'n."

"I suppose not."

"Come and pick a bone with us?"

Coppinger laughed a short snort through his nostrils.

"I have a bone to pick with you already."

"Never! no, never!"

"You have forced yourself on Miss Trevisa to act as her agent and valuer in the matter of dilapidations."

"Not forced, Captain. She asked me to give her friendly counsel. We are old acquaintances."

"I will not waste words. Give me her letter. She no longer requires your advice and counsel. I am going to act for her."

"You, Cap'n! Lor' bless me! You don't mean to say so!"

"Yes. I will protect her against being pillaged. She is my housekeeper."

"But see! she is only executrix. She gets nothing out of the property."

"No—but her niece and nephew do. Take it that I act for them. Give me up her letter."

Mr. Scantlebray hesitated.

"But, Cap'n, I've been to vast expense. I've entered into agreements—"

"With whom?"

"With carpenter and mason about the repairs."

"Give me the agreements."

"Not agreements exactly. They sent me in their estimates, and I accepted them, and set them to work."

"Give me the estimates."

Mr. Scantlebray flapped all his limbs, and shook his head.

"You don't suppose I carry these sort of things about with me?"

"I have no doubt whatever they are in your pocket." Scantlebray fidgeted.

"Cap'n, try this port—a little going back, but not to be sneezed at."

Coppinger leaned forward through the window.

"Who is that man with you?"

"Mr. Cargreen."

"What is he here for?"

"I am agent for the Reverend Mules, the newly appointed rector," said Mr. Cargreen, with some dignity.

"Then I request you both to step to the window to me."

The two men looked at each other. Scantlebray jumped up, and Cargreen followed. They stood in the window-bay at a respectful distance from Cruel Coppinger.

"I suppose you know who I am?" said the latter, fixing his eyes on Cargreen.

"I believe I can form a guess."

"And your duty to your client is to make out as bad a case as you can against the two children. They have had just one thousand pounds left them. You are going to get as much of that away from them as you are permitted."

"My good sir—allow me to explain—"

"There is no need," said Coppinger. "Suffice it that you are one side. I—Cruel Coppinger—on the other. Do you understand what that means?"

Mr. Cargreen became alarmed, his face became very blank.

"I am not a man to waste words. I am not a man that many in Cornwall would care to have as an adversary. Do you ever travel at night, Mr. Cargreen?"

"Yes, sir, sometimes."

"Through the lanes and along the lonely roads?"

"Perhaps, sir—now and then."

"So do I," said Coppinger. He drew a pistol from his pocket, and played with it. The two "dilapidators" shrank back. "So do I," said Coppinger; "but I never go unarmed. I would advise you to do the same —if you are my adversary."

"I hope, Captain, that—that—"

"If those children suffer through you more than what I allow"—Coppinger drew up his one shoulder that he could move—"I should advise you to consider what Mrs.

Cargreen will have to live on when a widow." Then he turned to Scantlebray, who was sneaking behind the window-curtain.

"Miss Trevisa's letter, authorizing you to act for her?"

Scantlebray, with shaking hand, groped for his pocket-book.

"And the two agreements or estimates you signed."

Scantlebray gave him the letter.

"The agreements also."

Nervously, the surveyor groped again, and reluctantly produced them. Captain Coppinger opened them with his available hand.

"What is this? Five pounds in pencil added to each, and then summed up in the total? What is the meaning of that, pray?"

Mr. Scantlebray again endeavoured to disappear behind the curtain.

"Come forward!" shouted Captain Cruel, striking the window-sill with the pistol.

Scantlebray jumped out of his retreat at once.

"What is the meaning of these two five pounds?"

"Well, Sir—Captain—it is usual; every one does it. It is my—what d'y' call it?—consideration for accepting the estimates."

"And added to each, and then charged to the orphans, who pay you to act in their interest—so they pay wittingly, directly, and unwittingly, indirectly. Well for you and for Mrs. Scantlebray that I release you of your obligation to act for Mother Dunes—I mean Miss Trevisa."

"Sir," said Cargreen, "under the circumstances, under intimidation, I decline to sully my fingers with the business. I shall withdraw."

"No, you shall not," said Cruel Coppinger, resolutely. "You shall act, and act as I approve; and in the end it shall not be to your disadvantage."

Then, without a word of farewell, he stood up, slipped the pistol back into his pocket, and strode away.

Mr. Cargreen had become white, or rather, the colour of dough. After a moment he recovered himself somewhat, and, turning to Scantlebray, with a sarcastic air, said—

"I hope you enjoy the jessamine. They don't smell particularly sweet to me."

"Orful!" groaned Scantlebray. He shook himself —almost shaking off all his limbs in the convulsion— "Old man—them jessamines is orful!"

## CHAPTER XII
## THE CAVE

SOME weeks slipped by without bringing to Judith any accession of anxiety. She did not go again to Pentyre Glaze, but her aunt came once or twice in the week to Polzeath to see her. Moreover, Miss Dionysia's manner towards her was somewhat less contrary and vexatious, and she seemed to put on a conciliatory manner, as far as was possible for one so angular and crabbed. Gracious she could not be; nature had made it as impossible for her to be gracious in manner as to be lovely in face and graceful in movement.

Moreover, Judith observed that her aunt looked at her with an expression of perplexity, as though seeking in her to find an answer to a riddle that vexed her brain. And so it was. Aunt Dunes could not understand the conduct of Coppinger towards Judith and her brother. Nor could she understand how a child like her niece could have faced and defied a man of whom she herself stood in abject fear. Judith had behaved to the smuggler in a way that no man in the whole country-side would have ventured to behave. She had thrown him at her feet, half killed him, and yet Cruel Coppinger did not resent what had been done; on the contrary, he went out of his way to interfere in the interest of the orphans. He was not the man to concern himself in other people's affairs; why should he take trouble on behalf of Judith and her brother? That he did it out of consideration for herself, Miss Trevisa had not the assurance to believe.

Aunt Dunes put a few searching questions to Judith, but drew from her nothing that explained the mystery. The girl frankly told her of her visit to the Glaze and interview with the crippled smuggler, of his offer to her of some of his spoil, and of her refusal to receive a present from him. Miss Trevisa approved of her niece's conduct in this respect. It would not have befitted her to accept anything. Judith, however, did not communicate to her aunt the closing scene in that interview. She did not tell her that Coppinger had kissed her hand, nor his excuse for having done so, that he was rendering homage to a queen.

For one thing, Judith did not attach any importance to this incident. She had always heard that Coppinger was a wild and insolent man, wild and insolent in his dealings with his fellow-men, therefore doubtless still more so in his treatment of defenceless women. He had behaved to her in the rude manner in which he would behave to any peasant girl or sailor's daughter who caught his fancy, and she resented his act as an indignity, and his excuse for it as a prevarication. And, precisely, because he had offended her maidenly dignity, she blushed to mention it, even to her aunt, resolving in her own mind not to subject herself to the like again.

Miss Trevisa, on several occasions, invited Judith to come and see her at Pentyre Glaze, but the girl always declined the invitation.

Judith's estimate of Cruel Coppinger was modified. He could not be the utter reprobate she had always held him to be. She fully acknowledged that there was an element of good in the man, otherwise he would not have forgiven the injury done him, nor would he have interfered to protect her and Jamie from the fraud and extortion of the "dilapidators." She trusted that the stories she had heard of Coppinger's wild and savage acts were false, or over-coloured. Her dear father had been mislead by reports, as she had been, and it was possible that Coppinger had not really been the impediment in her father's way that the late rector had supposed.

Jamie was happy. He was even, in a fashion, making himself useful. He helped Mr. Menaida in his bird-stuffing on rainy days; he did more, he ran about the cliffs, learned the haunts of the wild-fowl, ascertained where they nested, made friends with Preventive men, and some of those fellows living on shore, without any very fixed business, who rambled over the country with their guns, and from these he was able to obtain birds that he believed Mr. Menaida wanted. Judith was glad that the boy should be content, and enjoy the fresh air and some freedom. She would have been less pleased had she seen the companions Jamie made. But the men had rough good humour, and were willing to oblige the half-witted boy, and they encouraged him to go with them shooting, or to sit with them in their huts.

Jamie manifested so strong a distaste for books, and lesson time being one of resistance, pouting, tears, and failures, that Judith thought it not amiss to put off the resumption of these irksome tasks for a little while, and to let the boy have his run of holidays. She fancied that the loss of his father and of his old home preyed on him more than was actually the case, and believed that by giving him freedom till the first pangs were over, he might not suffer in the way that she had done.

For a fortnight or three weeks Judith's time had been so fully engaged at the parsonage, that she could not have devoted much of it to Jamie, even had she thought it desirable to keep him to his lessons; nor could she be with him much. She did not press him to accompany her to the rectory, there to spend the time that she was engaged sorting her father's letters and memoranda, his account books and collection of extracts made from volumes he had borrowed, as not only would it be tedious to him, but he would distract her mind. She must see that he was amused, and must also provide that he was not at mischief. She did take him with her on one or two occasions, and found that he had occupied himself in disarranging much that she had put together for the sale.

But she would not allow him wholly to get out of the way of looking to her as his companion, and she abandoned an afternoon to him now and then, as her work became less arduous, to walk with him on the cliffs or in the lanes, to listen to his childish prattle, and throw herself into his new pursuits. The link between them must not be allowed to become relaxed, and, so far as in her lay, she did her utmost to maintain it in its former security. But, with his father's death, and his removal to Mr. Menaida's cottage, a new world had opened to Jamie; he was brought into association with men and boys whom he had hardly known by sight previously, and without any wish to disengage himself from his sister's authority, he was led to look to others as comrades, and to listen to and follow their promptings.

"Come, Jamie," said Judith, one day. "Now I really have some hours free, and I will go a stroll with you on the downs."

The boy jumped with pleasure, and caught her hand.

"I may take Tib with me?"

"Oh yes, certainly, dear."

Tib was a puppy that had been given to Jamie by one of his new acquaintances.

The day was fresh. Clouds driving before the wind, now obscuring the sun, and threatening rain, then clearing and allowing the sun to turn the sea green and gild the land. Owing to the breeze, the sea was ruffled and strewn with breakers shaking their white foam.

"I am going to show you something I have found, Ju," said the boy. "You will follow, will you not?"

"Lead the way. What is it?"

"Come and see. I found it by myself. I shan't tell any one but you."

He conducted his sister down the cliffs to the beach of a cove. Judith halted a moment to look along the coast with its mighty, sombre cliffs, and the sea glancing with sun or dulled by shadow to Tintagel Head standing up at the extreme point to the north-east, with the white surf lashing and heaving around it. Then she drew her skirts together, and descended by the narrow path along which, with the lightness and confidence of a kid, Jamie was skipping.

"Jamie!" she said. "Have you seen?—there is a ship standing in the offing."

"Yes; she has been there all the morning."

Then she went further.

The cove was small, with precipitous cliffs rising from the sand to the height of two to three hundred feet. The seagulls screamed and flashed to and fro, and the waves foamed and threw up their waters lashed into froth as white and light as the feathers on the gulls. In the concave bay the roar of the plunging tide reverberated from every side. Neither the voice of Jamie, when he shouted to his sister from some feet below, nor the barking of his little dog that ran with him, could be distinguished by her.

The descent was rapid and rugged, yet not so precipitous but that it could be gone over by asses or mules. Evidence that these creatures had passed that way remained in the impression of their hoofs in the soil, wherever a soft stratum intervened between the harder shelves of the rock, and had crumbled on the path into clay.

Judith observed that several paths—not all mulepaths —converged lower down at intervals in the way by which she descended, so that it would be possible, apparently, to reach the sand from various points in the down, as well as by the main track by which she was stepping to the beach.

"Jamie!" called Judith, as she stood on the last shoulder of rock before reaching the beach over a wave-washed and smoothed surface. "Jamie! I can see that same ship from here."

But her brother could not hear her. He was throwing stones for the dog to run after, and meet a wave as it rushed in.

The tide was going out; it had marked its highest elevation by a bow of foam and strips of dark seaweed and broken shells. Judith stepped along this line, and picked out the largest ribbon of weed she could find. She would hang it in her bedroom to tell her the weather. The piece that had been wont to act as barometer was old, and, besides, it had been lost in the recent shift and confusion.

Jamie came up to her.

"Now, Ju, mind and watch me, or you will lose me altogether."

Then he ran forward, with Tib dancing and yelping round him. Presently he scrambled up a shelf of rock inclined from the sea, and up after him, yelping, scrambled Tib. In a moment both disappeared over the crest.

Judith went up to the ridge and called to her brother.

"I cannot climb this, Jamie."

But in another moment, a hundred yards to her right, round the extremity of the reef, came Tib and his master, the boy dancing and laughing, the dog ducking his head, shaking his ears, and, all but laughing also, evidently enjoying the fun as much as Jamie.

"This way, Ju!" shouted the boy, and signed to his sister. She could not hear his voice, but obeyed his gestures. The reef ran athwart the top of the bay, like the dorsal, jagged ridge of a crocodile half buried in the sand.

Judith drew her skirts higher and closer, as the sand was wet, and there were pools by the rock. Then, holding her ribbon of seaweed by the harsh, knotted root, torn up along with the leaf, and trailing it behind her, she followed her brother, reached the end of the rock, turned and went in the traces of Jamie and Tib in the sand parallel to her former course.

Suddenly, and quite unexpectedly, on the right hand there opened before her, in the face of the cliff, a cave, the entrance to which was completely masked by the ridge she had turned. Into this cave went Jamie with his dog.

"I am not obliged to follow you there!" protested Judith; but he made such vehement signs to her to follow him that she good-humouredly obeyed.

The cave ran in a long way, at first at no great incline, then it became low overhead, and immediately after the floor inclined rapidly upward, and the vault took a like direction. Moreover, light appeared in front. Here, to Judith's surprise, she saw a large boat, painted grey, furnished with oars and boat-hook. She was attached by a chain to a staple in the rock. Judith examined her with a little uneasiness. No name was on her.

The sides of the cave at this point formed shelves, not altogether natural, and that these were made use of was evident, because on them lay staves of broken casks a four-flanged boat anchor, and some oars. Out of the main trunk cave branched another that was quite dark, and smaller; in this Judith, whose eyes were becoming accustomed to the twilight, thought she saw the bows of a smaller boat, also painted grey.

"Jamie!" said Judith, now in serious alarm; "we ought not to be here. It is not safe. Do—do come away at once."

"Why, what is there to harm us?"

"My dear, do come away." She turned to retrace her steps, but Jamie stopped her.

"Not that way, Ju! I have another by which to get out. Follow me still."

He led the way up the steep rubble slope, and the light fell fuller from above. The cave was one of those into which when the sea rolls and chokes the entrance, the compressed air is driven out by a second orifice.

They reached a sort of well or shaft, at the bottom of which they stood, but it did not open vertically but bent over somewhat, so that from below the sky could not be seen, though the light entered. A narrow path was traced in the side, and up this Jamie and the dog scrambled, followed by Judith, who was most anxious to escape from a place which she had no doubt was one of the shelter caves of the smugglers—perhaps of Cruel Coppinger, whose house was not a mile distant.

The ascent was steep, the path slippery in places, and therefore dangerous. Jamie made nothing of it, nor did the little dog, but Judith picked her way with care; she had a good steady head, and did not feel giddy, but she was not sure that her feet might not slide in the clay where wet with water that dripped from the sides. As she neared the entrance she saw that hartstongue and maidenhair fern had rooted themselves in the sheltered nooks of this tunnel.

After a climb of a hundred feet she came out on a ledge in the face of the cliff above the bay, to see, with a gasp of dismay, her brother in the hand of Cruel Coppinger, the boy paralyzed with fear so that he could neither stir nor cry out.

"What!" exclaimed the Captain, "you here?" as he saw Judith stand before him.

The puppy was barking and snapping at his boots. Coppinger let go Jamie, stooped and caught the dog by the neck. "Look at me," said the smuggler sternly, addressing the frightened boy. Then he swung the dog above his head and dashed it down the cliffs; it caught, then rolled, and fell out of sight —certainly with the life beaten out of it.

"This will be done to you," said he; "I do not say that I would do it. She"—he waved his hand towards Judith—"stands between us. But if any of the fifteen to twenty men who know this place and come here should chance to meet you as I have met you, he would treat you without compunction as I have treated that dog. And if he were to catch you below—you have heard of Wyvill, the Preventive man?—you would fare as did he. Thank your sister that you are alive now. Go on—that way—up the cliff." He pointed with a telescope he held.

Jamie fled up the steep path like the wind.

"Judith," said Coppinger, "will you stand surety that he does not tell tales?"

"I do not believe he will say anything."

"I do not ask you to be silent. I know you will not speak. But if you mistrust his power to hold his tongue, send him away—send him out of the country—as you love him."

"He shall never come here again," said Judith, earnestly.

"That is well; he owes his life to you."

Judith noticed that Cruel Coppinger's left arm was no more in a sling, nor in bands.

He saw that she observed this, and smiled grimly. "I have my freedom with this arm once more—for the first time to-day."

## CHAPTER XIII
## IN THE DUSK

"Kicking along, Mr. Menaida, old man?" asked Mr. Scantlebray, in his loud, harsh voice, as he shook himself inside the door of Uncle Zachie's workshop. "And the little 'uns? Late in life to become nurse and keep the bottle and pap-bowl going, eh, old man? How's the orphings? Eating their own weight of victuals at twopence-ha'penny a head, eh? My experience of orphings isn't such as would make a man hilarious, and feel that he was filling his pockets."

"Sit you down, sir; you'll find a chair. Not that one, there's a dab of arsenical paste got on to that. Sit you down, sir, over against me. Glad to see you and have some one to talk to. Here am I slaving all day, worn to fiddlestrings. There's Squire Rashleigh, of Menabilly, must have a glaucous gull stuffed at once that he has shot; and there's Sir John St. Aubyn, of Clowance, must have a case of kittiwakes by a certain day; and an institution in London wants a genuine specimen of a Cornish chough. Do they think I'm a tradesman to be ordered about? That I've not an income of my own, and that I am dependent on my customers? I'll do no more. I'll smoke and play the piano. I've no time to exchange a word with any one. Come, sit down. What's the news?"

"It's a bad world," said Mr. Scantlebray, settling himself into a chair. "That's to say, the world is well enough if it warn't for there being too many rascals in it. I consider it's a duty on all right-thinking men to clear them off."

"Well, the world would be better if we had the making of it," acquiesced Mr. Menaida. "Bless you! I've no time for anything. I like to do a bit of bird-stuffing just as a sort of relaxation after smoking, but to be forced to work more than one cares—I won't do it! Besides, it is not wholesome. I shall be poisoned with arsenic. I must have some antidote. So will you, sir—eh? A drop of real first-rate cognac?"

"Thank you, sir—old man—I don't mind dipping a feather and drawing it across my lips."

Jamie had been so frightened by the encounter with Cruel Coppinger that he was thoroughly upset. He was a timid, nervous child, and Judith had persuaded him to go to bed. She sat by him, holding his hand, comforting him as best she might, when he sobbed over the loss of his pup, and cheering him when he clung to her in terror at the reminiscence of the threats of the Captain to deal with him as he had with Tib. Judith was under no apprehension of his re-visiting the cave; he had been too thoroughly frightened ever to venture there again. She said nothing to impress this on him; all her efforts were directed towards allaying his alarms.

Just as she hoped that he was dropping off into unconsciousness, he suddenly opened his eyes, and said, "Ju!"

"Yes, dear."

"I've lost the chain."

"What chain, my pretty?"

"Tib's chain."

The pup had been a trouble when Jamie went with the creature through the village or through a farm-yard. He would run after and nip the throats of chickens. Tib and his master had got into trouble on this account; accordingly Judith had turned out a light steel chain, somewhat rusty, and a dog collar from among the sundries that encumbered the drawers and closets of the rectory. This she had given to her brother, and whenever the little dog was near civilization he was obliged to submit to the chain.

Judith, to console Jamie for his loss, had told him that in all probability another little dog might be procured to be his companion. Alas! the collar was on poor Tib, but she represented to him that if another dog were obtained it would be possible to buy or beg a collar for him, supposing a collar to be needful. This had satisfied Jamie, and he was about to doze off, when suddenly he woke to say that the chain was lost.

"Where did you lose the chain, Jamie?"

"I threw it down."

"Why did you do that?"

"I thought I shouldn't want it when Tib was gone."

"And where did you throw it? Perhaps it may be found again."

"I won't go and look for it—indeed I won't." He shivered and clung to his sister.

"Where was it? Perhaps I can find it."

"I dropped it at the top—on the down when I came up the steps from—from that man, when he had killed Tib."

"You did not throw it over the cliff?"

"No—I threw it down. I did not think I wanted it any more."

"I dare say it may be found. I will go and see."

"No—no! Don't, Ju. You might meet that man."

Judith smiled. She felt that she was not afraid of that man—he would not hurt her.

As soon as the boy was asleep, Judith descended the stairs, leaving his door ajar, that she might hear should he wake in a fright, and entering the little sitting-room, took up her needles and wool, and seated herself quietly by the window, where the last glimmer of twilight shone, to continue her work at a jersey she was knitting for Jamie's use in the winter.

The atmosphere was charged with tobacco smoke, almost as much as that of the adjoining workshop. There was no door between the rooms; none had been needed formerly, and Mr. Menaida did not think of supplying one now. It was questionable whether one would have been an advantage, as Jamie ran to and fro, and would be certain either to leave the door open or to slam it, should one be erected. Moreover, a door meant payment to a carpenter for timber and labour. There was no carpenter in the village, and Mr. Menaida spent no more money than he was absolutely obliged to spend, and how could he on an annuity of fifty pounds?

Judith dropped her woolwork in her lap and fell into meditation. She reviewed what had just taken place: she saw before her again Coppinger, strongly built, with his dark face, and eyes that glared into the soul to its lowest depths, illumining all, not as the sun, but as the lightning, and suffering not a thought, not a feeling to remain obscure.

A second time had Jamie done what angered him, but on this occasion he had curbed his passion and had contented himself with a threat—nay, not even that—with a caution. He had expressly told Jamie that he himself would not hurt him, but that he ran into danger from others.

She was again looking at Coppinger as he spoke; she saw the changes in his face, the alterations of expression in his eyes, in his intonation. She recalled the stern, menacing tone in which he had spoken to Jamie, and then the inflexion of voice as he referred to her. A dim surmise—a surmise she was ashamed to allow could be true—rose in her mind and thrilled her with alarm. Was it possible that he liked her—liked—she could, she would give even in thought no other term to describe that feeling which she feared might possibly have sprung up in his breast. That he liked her—after all she had done? Was that why he had come to the cottage the day after his accident? Was that what had prompted the strange note sent to her along with the keg of spirits to Uncle Zachie? Was that the meaning of the offer of the choice of all his treasures?—of the vehemence with which he had seized her hand and had kissed it? Was that the interpretation of those words of excuse in which he had declared her his queen? If this were so, then much that had been enigmatical in his conduct was explained—his interference with the valuers for dilapidations, the strange manner in which he came across her path almost whenever she went to the rectory. And this was the signification of the glow in his eyes, the quaver in his voice, when he addressed her.

Was it so?—could it be so?—that he liked her?— he—Cruel Coppinger—Cruel Coppinger—the terror of the country round—liked her, the weakest creature that could be found?

The thought of such a possibility frightened her. That the wild smuggler-captain should hate her she could have borne with better than that he should like her. That she was conscious of a sense of pleased surprise, intermixed with fear, was inevitable, for Judith was a woman, and there was something calculated to gratify feminine pride in the presumption that the most lawless and headstrong man on the Cornish coast should have meant what he said when he declared himself her subject.

These thoughts, flushing and paling her cheek, quickening and staying her pulse, so engrossed Judith that, though she heard the voices in the adjoining apartment, she paid no heed to what was said.

The wind, which had been fresh all day, was blowing stronger. It battered at the window where Judith sat, as though a hand struck and brushed over the panes.

"Hot or cold?" asked Uncle Zachie.

"Thanky', neither. Water can be got everywhere, but such brandy as this, old man—only here."

"You are good to say so. It is Coppinger's present to me."

"Coppinger!—his very good health, and may he lie in clover to-morrow night. He's had one arm bound, I've seen; perhaps he may have two before the night grows much older."

Mr. Menaida raised his brows.

"I do not understand you."

"I daresay not," said Scantlebray. "It's the duty of all right-minded men to clear the world of rascals. I will do my duty, please the pigs. Would you mind—just another drop?"

After his glass had been refilled, Mr. Scantlebray leaned back in his chair and said—

"It's a wicked world, and, between you and me and the sugar dissolving at the bottom of my glass, you won't find more rascality anywhere than in my profession, and one of the biggest rascals in it is Mr. Cargreen. He's on the side against the orphings. If you've the faculty of pity in you, pity them—first, because they've him agin' 'em, and, secondly, because they've lost me as their protector. You know whom they got in place of me? I wish them joy of him. But they won't have his wing over them long, I can tell you."

"You think not?"

"Sure of it."

"You think he'll throw it up?"

"I rather suspect he won't be at liberty to attend to it. He'll want his full attention to his own consarns."

Mr. Scantlebray tipped off his glass.

"It's going to be a dirty night," said he. "You won't mind my spending an hour or two with you, will you?"

"I shall be delighted. Have you any business in the place?"

"Business—no. A little pleasure, may be." After a pause, he said, "But, old man, I don't mind telling you what it is. You are mum, I know. It is this—the trap will shut to-night. Snap it goes, and the rats are fast. You haven't been out on the cliffs today, have you?"

"No—bless me!—no, I have not."

"The Black Prince is in the offing."

"The Black Prince?"

"Aye, and she will run her cargo ashore to-night. Now, I'm one who knows a little more than most. I'm one o' your straightfor'ard 'uns, always ready to give a neighbour a lift in my buggy, and a helping hand to the man that is down, and a frank, outspoken fellow am I to every one I meet—so that, knocking about as I do, I come to know and to hear more than do most, and I happen to have learnt into what cove the Black Prince will run her goods. I've a bone to pick with Captain Cruel, so I've let the Preventive men have the contents of my information-pottle, and they will be ready to-night for Coppinger and the whole party of them. The cutter will slip in between them and the sea, and a party will be prepared to give them the kindliest welcome by land. That is the long and short of it—and, old man, I shall dearly love to be there and see the sport. That is why I wish to be with you for an hour or two. Will you come as well?"

"Bless me!" exclaimed Mr. Menaida, "not I! You don't suppose Coppinger and his men will allow themselves to be taken easily? There'll be a fight."

"And pistols go off," said Scantlebray. "I shall not be surprised or sorry if Captain Cruel be washed up one of these next tides with a bullet through his head. Ebenezer Wyvill is one of the guards, and he has his brother's death to avenge."

"Do you really believe that Coppinger killed him?"

Mr. Scantlebray shrugged his shoulders. "It don't matter much what I think, to-night, but what the impression is that Ebenezer Wyvill carries about with him. I imagine that if Ebenezer comes across the Captain he won't speak to him by word of mouth, nor trouble himself to feel for a pair of handcuffs. So—fill my glass again, old man, and we'll drink to a cold bed and an indigestible lump—somewhere—in his head or in his gizzard—to Cruel Coppinger, and the wiping off of old scores—always a satisfaction to honest men." Scantlebray rubbed his hands. "It is a satisfaction to the conscience—to ferret out the rats sometimes."

# CHAPTER XIV
# WARNING OF DANGER

JUDITH, lost for awhile in her dreams, had been brought to a sense of what was the subject of conversation in the adjoining room by the mention of Coppinger's name more than once. She heard the desultory talk for awhile without giving it much attention, but Scantlebray's voice was of that harsh and penetrating nature that to exclude it the ears must be treated as Ulysses treated the ears of his mariners as he passed the rock of the Syrens.

Presently she became alive to the danger in which Coppinger stood. Scantlebray spoke plainly, and she understood. There could be no doubt about it. The Black Prince belonged to the Captain, and his dealings with and through that vessel were betrayed. Not only was Coppinger, as the head of a gang of smugglers, an object worth capture to the Preventive men, but the belief that he had caused the death of at least one of their number had embittered them against him to such an extent that, when the opportunity presented itself to them of capturing him red-handed engaged in his smuggling transactions, they were certain to deal with him in a way much more summary than the processes of a court of justice. The brother of the man who had been murdered was among the coastguard, and he would not willingly let slip a chance of avenging the death of Jonas Wyvill. Coppinger was not in a condition to defend himself effectively. On that day, for the first time, had he left off his bandages, and his muscles were stiff and the newly-set bones still weak.

What was to be done? Could Judith go to bed and let Coppinger run into the net prepared for his feet—go to his death?

No sooner, however, had Judith realized the danger that menaced Coppinger than she resolved on doing her utmost to avert it. She, and she alone, could deliver him from the disgrace, if not the death, that menaced him.

She stole lightly from the room and got her cloak, drew the hood over her head, and sallied forth into the night. Heavy clouds rolled over the sky, driven before a strong gale. Now and then they opened and disclosed the twilight sky, in which faintly twinkled a few stars, and at such times a dim light fell over the road, but in another moment lumbering masses of vapour were carried forward, blotting out the clear tract of sky, and at the same time blurring all objects on earth with one enveloping shadow.

Judith's heart beat furiously, and timidity came over her spirit as she left the cottage, for she was unaccustomed to be outside the house at such an hour; but the purpose she had before her eyes gave her strength and courage. It seemed to her that Providence had suddenly constituted her the guardian angel of Coppinger, and she flattered herself that, were she to be the means of delivering him from the threatened danger, she might try to exact of him a promise to discontinue so dangerous and so questionable a business. If this night she were able to give him warning in time, it would be some return made for his kindness to her, and some reparation made for the injury she had done him. When for an instant there was a rist in the clouds, and she could look up and see the pure stars, it seemed to her that they shone down on her like angels' eyes, watching, encouraging, and promising her protection. She thought of her father—of how his mind had been set against Coppinger; now, she felt convinced, he saw that his judgment had been warped, and that he would bless her for doing that which she had set her mind to accomplish. Her father had been ever ready frankly to acknowledge himself in the wrong when he had been convinced that he was mistaken, and now in the light of eternity, with eyes undarkened by prejudice, he must know that he was in error in his condemnation of Coppinger, and be glad that his daughter was doing something to save that man from an untimely and bloody death.

Not a soul did Judith meet or pass on her way. She had determined in the first case to go to Pentyre Glaze. She would see if Captain Cruel were there. She trusted he was at his house. If so, her course was simple; she would warn him and return to Mr. Menaida's cottage as quickly as her feet would bear her. The wind caught at her cloak, and she turned in alarm, fancying that it was plucked by a human hand. No one, however, was behind her.

In Pentyre lane it was dark, very dark. The rude half-walls, half-hedges stood up high, walled towards the lane, hedged with earth and planted with thorns towards the fields. The wind hissed through the bushes; there was an ash tree by a gate. One branch sawed against another, producing a weird, even shrill sound, like a cry.

The way led past a farm, and she stole along before it with the utmost fear as she heard the dog in the yard begin to bark furiously, and she believed that it was not chained up, might rush forth at her. It might fall upon her, and hold her there till the farmer came forth and found her, and inquired into the reason of her being there at night. If found and recognized, what excuse could she give? What explanation could satisfy the inquisitive?

She did not breathe freely till she had come out on the down; the dog was still barking, but, as he had not pursued her, she was satisfied that he was not at large. Her way now lay for a while over open common, and then again entered a lane between the hedges that enclosed the fields and meadows of the Glaze.

A dense darkness fell over the down, and Judith for a while was uncertain of her way, the track being undistinguishable from the short turf on either side. Suddenly she saw some flashes of light that ran along the ground and then disappeared.

"This is the road," said a voice.

Judith's heart stood still, and her blood curdled in her veins. If the cloud were to roll away—and she could see far off its silvery fringe, she would become visible. The voice was that of a man, but whether that of a smuggler or of a coastguard she could not guess. By neither did she care to be discovered. By the dim, uncertain light she stole off the path, and sank upon the ground among some masses of gorse that stood on the common. Between the prickly tufts she might lie, and in her dark cloak be mistaken for a patch of furze. She drew her feet under the skirt, that the white stockings might not betray her, and plucked the hood of her cloak closely round her face. The gorse was sharp, and the spikes entered her hands and feet, and pricked her as she turned herself about between the bushes to bring herself deeper among them.

From where she lay she could see the faintly illumined horizon, and against that horizon figures were visible, one—then another—a third—she could not count accurately, for there came several together; but she was convinced there must have been over a dozen men.

"It's a'most too rough to-night, I reckon," said one of the men.

"No it is not—the wind is not direct on shore. They'll try it."

"Coppinger and his chaps are down in the cove already," said a third. "They wouldn't go out if they wasn't expecting the boats from the Black Prince."

"You are sure they're down, Wyvill?"

"Sure and sartain. I seed 'em pass, and mighty little I liked to let 'em go by—without a pop from my pistol. But I'd my orders. No orders against the pistol going off of itself, Captain, if I have a chance presently?"

No answer was given to this; but he who had been addressed as Captain asked—

"Are the asses out?"

"Yes; a whole score, I reckon."

"Then they'll come up the mule-path. We must watch that. Lieutenant Hanson will be ready with the cutter to run out and stop their way back by water to the Prince. The Prince's men will take to the sea, and he'll settle with them: but Coppinger's men will run up the cliffs, and we must tackle them. Go on."

Several now disappeared into the darkness, moving towards the sea.

"Here, a word with you, Wyvill," said the Captain.

"Right, sir—here I be."

"Dash it!—it is so dark! Here, step back—a word in your ear."

"Right you are, sir."

They came on to the turf close to where Judith crouched.

"What is that?" said the Captain, hastily.

"What, sir?"

"I thought I trod on something like cloth. Have you a light?"

"No, sir! Horne has the dark lantern."

"I suppose it is nothing. What is all that dark stuff there?"

"I'll see, sir," said Wyvill, stooping, and groping with his hand. "By George, Sir! it's naught but fuzz."

"Very well, Wyvill—a word between us. I know that if you have the chance you intend to send a bullet into Coppinger. I don't blame you. I won't say I wouldn't do it—unofficially—but looky' here, man, if you can manage without a bullet—say a blow with the butt-end on his forehead and a roll over the cliffs—I'd prefer it. In self-defence of course we must use fire-arms. But there's some squeamish stomachs, you understand; and if it can come about accidentally, as it were—as if he'd missed his footing—I'd prefer it. Make it pleasant all round, if you can."

"Yes, sir; leave it to me."

"It oughtn't to be difficult, you know, Wyvill. I hear he's broke one arm, so is like to be insecure in his hold climbing the cliffs. Then no questions asked, and more pleasant, you know. You understand me?"

"Yes, sir; thank you, sir."

Then they went on, and were lost to sight and to hearing. For some minutes Judith did not stir. She lay, recovering her breath; she had hardly ventured to breathe whilst the two men were by her, the Captain with his foot on her skirt. Now she remained motionless, to consider what was to be done. It was of no further use her going on to Pentyre Glaze. Coppinger had left it. Wyvill, who had been planted as spy, had seen him with his carriers defile out of the lane with the asses that were to bring up the smuggled goods from the shore.

She dare not take the path by which on the preceding afternoon she had descended with Jamie to the beach, for it was guarded by the Preventive men.

There was but one way by which she could reach the shore and warn Coppinger, and that was by the chimney of the cave—a way dangerous in daylight, one, moreover, not easy to find at night. The mouth of the chimney opened upon a ledge that overhung the sea half-way down the face of the precipice, and this ledge could only be reached by a narrow track—a track apparently traced by sheep.

Judith thought that she might find her way to that part of the down from which the descent was to be made: for she had noticed that what is locally called a "new-take" wall came near it, and if she could hit this wall, she believed she could trace it up to where it approached the cliff: and the track descended somewhere thereabouts. She waited where she lay till the heavy clouds rolled by, and for a brief space the sky was comparatively clear. Then she rose, and took the direction in which she ought to go to reach the "new-take" wall. As she went over the down, she heard the sea roaring threateningly; on her left hand the glint of the lighthouse on Trevose Head gave her the direction she must pursue. But, on a down like that, with a precipice on one hand; in a light, uncertain at best, often in complete darkness, it was dangerous to advance except by thrusting the foot forward tentatively, before taking a step. The sea and the gnawing winds caused the cliffs to crumble; bits were eaten out of the surface, and in places there were fissures in the turf where a rent had formed, and where shortly a mass would fall.

It is said that the duties on customs were originally instituted in order to enable the Crown to afford protection to trade against pirates. The pirates ceased to infest the seas, but the duties were not only not taken off, but were increased, and became a branch of the public revenue. Perhaps some consciousness that the profits were not devoted to the purpose originally intended, bred in the people on the coast a feeling of resentment against the imposition of duties. There certainly existed an impression, a conviction rather, that the violation of a positive law of this nature was in no respect criminal. Adventures embarked in the illicit traffic without scruple, as they did in poaching. The profit was great, and the danger run enhanced the excitement of the pursuit, and gave a sort of heroic splendour to the achievements of the successful smuggler.

The Government, to stop a traffic that injured legitimate trade, and affected the revenue, imposed severe penalties. Smuggling was classed among the felonies, "without benefit of clergy," the punishment for which was death and confiscation of goods. The consciousness that they would be dealt with with severity did not deter bold men from engaging in the traffic, but made them desperate in self-defence when caught. Conflicts with Revenue officers were not uncommon, and lives were lost on both sides. The smugglers were not bound together by any link, and sometimes one gang was betrayed by another, so as to divert suspicion and attention from their own misdeeds, or out of jealousy, or on account of a quarrel. It was so on this occasion: the success of Coppinger, the ingenuity with which he had carried on his defiance of the law, caused envy of him, because he was a foreigner—was, at all events, not a Cornishman; this had induced a rival to give notice to the Revenue officers, through Scantlebray —a convenient go-between in a good many question able negotiations. The man who betrayed Coppinger dared not be seen entering into communication with the officers of the law. He, therefore, employed Scantlebray as the vehicle through whom, without suspicion resting on himself, his rival might be fallen upon and his proceedings brought to an end.

It was now very dark. Judith had reached and touched a wall; but in the darkness lost her bearings. The Trevose light was no longer visible, and directly she left the wall to strike outwards she became confused as to her direction, and in the darkness groped along with her feet, stretching her hands before her. Then the rain came down, lashing in her face. The wind had shifted somewhat during the evening, and it was no guidance to Judith to feel from what quarter the rain drove against her. Moreover, the cove formed a great curve in the coast-line, and was indented deeply in some places, so that to grope round the edge without light in quest of a point only seen or noticed once seemed a desperate venture. Suddenly Judith's foot caught. It was entangled, and she could not disengage it. She stooped, and put her hand on a chain. It was Jamie's steel dog-chain, one link of which had caught in a tuft of restharrow.

She had found the spot she wanted, and now waited only till the rain had rushed further inland, and a fringe of light appeared in the sky, to advance to the very edge of the cliff. She found it expedient to stoop as she proceeded, so as to discover some indications of the track. There were depressions where feet had worn the turf, and she set hers therein, and sought the next. Thus creeping and groping, she neared the edge.

And now came the moment of supreme peril, when, trusting that she had found the right path, she must go over the brink. If she were mistaken, the next step would send her down two hundred feet, to where she heard the roar, and felt the breath of the sea stream up to her from the abyss. Here she could distinguish nothing; she must trust to Providence to guide her steps. She uttered a short and earnest prayer, and then boldly descended. She could not stoop now. To stoop was to dive headlong down. She felt her way, however, with her feet, reached one firm station, then another. Her hands touched the grass and earth of the ragged margin, then with another step she was below it, and held to the rain-splashed fangs of rock.

Clinging, with her face inward, feeling with her feet, and never sure but that the next moment might see her launched into air, she stole onward, slowly, cautiously, and ever with the gnawing dread in her heart lest she should be too late. One intense point of consciousness stood out in her brain—it told her that if, whilst thus creeping down, there should come the flash and explosion of firearms, her courage would fail, her head would spin, and she would be lost.

How long she was descending she could not tell, how many steps she took was unknown to her—she had not counted—but it seemed to her an entire night that passed, with every change of position an hour was marked; then, at last, she was conscious that she stood on more level ground. She had reached the terrace.

A little further, and on her left-hand would open the mouth of the shaft, and she must descend that, in profoundest darkness. A cry! A light flashed into her eyes and dazzled her. A hand at the same moment clutched her, or she would have reeled back and gone over the cliff.

The light was held to pour over her face. Who held it and who grasped her she could not see; but she knew the moment she heard a voice exclaim—

"Judith!"

In her terror and exhaustion she could but gasp for breath for a few moments.

By degrees her firmness and resolution returned, and she exclaimed, in broken tones, panting between every few words—

"Captain Cruel!—you are betrayed—they are after you!"

He did not press her. He waited till she could speak again, lowering the lantern.

Then, without the glare in her eyes, she was able to speak more freely.

"There is a boat—a Revenue cutter—waiting in the bay—and—above—are the Preventive men—and they will kill you."

"Indeed," said he. "And you have come to warn me?"

"Yes."

"Tell me—are there any above, where you came down?"

"None; they are on the ass-path."

"Can you ascend as you came down?"

"Yes."

He extinguished his lantern, or covered it.

"I must no more show light. I must warn those below." He paused, then said—

"Dare you mount alone?"

"I came down alone."

"Then do this one thing more for me. Mount, and go to Pentyre. Tell your aunt—three lights, red, white, red. Then ten minutes, and then, red, red, white. Can you remember? Repeat after me: 'Three lights—red, white, red; then ten minutes, and next, red, red, and white.'"

Judith repeated the words.

"That is right. Lose no time. I dare not give you a light. None must now be shown. The boat from the Black Prince is not in—this lantern was her guide. Now it is out she will go back. You will remember the signals? I thank you for what you have done. There is but one woman would have done it, and that Judith."

He stepped inside the shaft to descend. When hidden, he allowed his light again to show, to assist him in his way down. Judith only waited till her eyes, that had been dazzled by the light, were recovered, and then she braced herself to resume her climb; but now it was to be up the cliff.

# CHAPTER XV
# CHAINED

TO ASCEND is easier than to go down. Judith was no longer alarmed. There was danger still, that was inevitable; but the danger was as nothing now to what it had been. It is one thing to descend in total darkness into an abyss where one knows that below are sharp rocks, and a drop of two hundred feet to a thundering, raging sea, racing up the sand, pouring over the shelves of rock, foaming where divided waves clash. When Judith had been on the beach in the afternoon the tide was out, now it was flowing, and had swept over all that tract of white sand and pebble where she had walked. She could not indeed now see the water, but she heard the thud of a billow as it smote a rock, the boil and the hiss of the waves and spray. To step downward, groping the way, with a depth and a wild throbbing sea beneath, demanded courage, and courage of no mean order; but it was other to mount, to be able to feel with the foot the ascent in the track, and to grope upwards with the hand from one point of clutch to another, to know that every step upwards was lessening the peril, and bringing nearer to the sward and to safety.

Without great anxiety, therefore, Judith turned to climb. Cruel Coppinger had allowed her to essay it unaided. Would he have done that had he thought it involved danger, or rather, serious danger? Judith was sure he would not. His confidence that she could climb to the summit unassisted made her confident. As she had descended she had felt an interior qualm and sinking at every step she took; there was no such sensation now as she mounted.

She was not much inconvenienced by the wind, for the wind was not directly on shore; but it soughed about her, and eddies caught her cloak and jerked it. It would have been better had she left her cloak above on the turf. It incommoded her in her climb; it caught in the prongs of rock.

The rain, the water running off the rock, had wet her shoes, soaked them, and every step was in moisture that oozed out of them. She was glad now to rest on her right hand. In descending the left had felt and held the rock, and it had been rubbed and cut. Probably it was bleeding.

Surely there was a little more light in the sky where the sky showed between the dense masses of vapour. Judith did not observe this, for she did not look aloft; but she could see a steely tract of sea, fretted into foam, reflecting an illumination from above, greater than the twilight could cast. Then she remembered that there had been a moon a few nights before, and thought that it was probably risen by this time.

Something chill and wet brushed her face. It startled her for a moment, and then she knew by the scent that it was a bunch of samphire growing out of the side of the crag.

Shrill in her ear came the scream of a gull that rushed by in the darkness, and she felt, or believed she felt, the fan from the wings. Again it screamed, and near the ear it pierced her brain like an awl, and then again, still nearer, unnerving her. In the darkness she fancied that this gull was about to attack her with beak and claws, and she put up her left arm as a protection to her eyes. Then there broke out a jabber of sea-birds' voices, laughing mockingly, at a little distance.

Whither had she got?

The way was no longer easy—one step before another —there was a break of continuity in the path, if path the track could be called.

Judith stood still, and put forward her foot to test the rock in front. There was no place where it could rest. Had she, bewildered by that gull, diverged from the track? It would be well to retreat a few steps. She endeavoured to do this, and found that she encountered a difficulty in finding the place where she had just planted her foot.

It was but too certain that she was off the track line. How to recover it she knew not. With the utmost difficulty she did reach a point in her rear where she could stand, clinging to the rock; but she clung now with both hands. There was no tuft of samphire to brush her face as she descended. She must have got wrong before she touched that. But where was the samphire? She cautiously felt along the surface of the crag in quest of it, but could not find it. There was, however, a little above her shoulder, a something that felt like a ledge, and which might be the track. If she had incautiously crept forward at a level without ascending rapidly enough, she was probably below the track. Could she climb to this point?—climb up the bare rock, with sheer precipice below her? And, supposing that the shelf she felt with her hand were not the track, could she descend again to the place where she had been?

Her brain spun. She lost all notion as to where she might be—perhaps she was below the path, perhaps she was above it. She could not tell. She stood with arms extended, clinging to the rock, and her heart beat in bounds against the flinty surface. The clasp of her cloak was pressing on her throat, and strangling her. The wind had caught the garment, and was playing with the folds, carrying it out and flapping it behind her over the gulf. It was irksome; it was a danger to her. She cautiously slid one hand to her neck, unhasped the mantle, and it was snatched from her shoulders and carried away. She was lighter without it, could move with greater facility; cold she was not, wet she might become, but what mattered that if she could reach the top of the cliff?

Not only on her own account was Judith alarmed. She had undertaken a commission. She had promised to bear a message to her aunt from Coppinger that concerned the safety of his men. What the signal meant she did not know, but suspected that it conveyed a message of danger.

She placed both her hands on the ledge, and felt with her knee for some point on which to rest it, to assist her in lifting herself from where she stood to the higher elevation. There was a small projection, and after a moment's hesitation she drew her foot from the shelf whereon it had rested and leaned the left knee on this hunch. Then she clung with both hands, and with them and her knee endeavoured to heave herself up about four feet, that is, to the height of her shoulders. A convulsive quiver seized on her muscles. She was sustained by a knee and her hands only. If they gave way she could not trust to recover her previous lodgment place. One desperate strain, and she was on the ledge, on both knees, and was feeling with her hands to ascertain if she had found the track. Her fingers touched thrift and passed over turf. She had not reached what she sought. She was probably further from it than before. As all her members were quivering after the effort, she seated herself on the shelf she had reached, leaned back against the wet rock, and waited till her racing pulses had recovered evenness of flow, and her muscles had overcome the first effects of their tension.

Her position was desperate. Rain and perspiration mingled dripped from her brow, ran over and blinded her eyes. Her breath came in sobs between her parted lips. Her ears were full of the booming of the surge far below, and the scarcely less noisy throb of her blood in her pulses.

When she had started on her adventurous expedition she had seen some stars that had twinkled down on her, and had appeared to encourage her. Now, not a star was visible, only, far off on the sea, a wan light that fell through a rent in the black canopy over an angry deep. Beyond that all was darkness, between her and that all was darkness.

As she recovered her self-possession, with the abatement of the tumult in her blood she was able to review her position, and calculate her chances of escape from it.

Up the track from the cave the smugglers would almost certainly escape, because that was the only way, unwatched, by which they could leave the beach without falling into the hands of the Preventive men.

If they came by the path—that path could not be far off, though in which direction it lay she could not guess. She would call, and then Coppinger or some of his men would come to her assistance.

By this means alone could she escape. There was nothing for her to do but to wait.

She bent forward and looked down. She might have been looking into a well; but a little way out she could see, or imagine she saw, the white fringes of surf stealing in. There was not sufficient light for her to be certain whether she really saw foam, or whether her fancy, excited by the thunder of the tide, made her suppose she saw it.

The shelf she occupied was narrow and inclined; if she slipped from it she could not trust to maintain herself on the lower shelf, certainly not if she slid down in a condition of unconsciousness. And now reaction after the strain was setting in, and she feared lest she might faint. In her pocket was the dog-chain that had caught her foot. She extracted that now, and groping along the wall of rock behind her, caught a stout tuft of coarse heather, wiry, well rooted; and she took the little steel chain and wound it about the branches and stem of the plant, and also about her wrist—her right wrist—so as to fasten her to the wall. That was some relief to her, to know that in the event of her dropping out of consciousness there was something to hold her up, though that was only the stem of an erica, and her whole weight would rest on its rootlets. Would they suffice to sustain her? It was doubtful; but there was nothing else on which she could depend.

Suddenly a stone whizzed past, struck the ledge, and rebounded. Then came a shower of earth and pebbles. They did not touch her, but she heard them clatter down.

Surely they had been displaced by a foot, and that a foot passing above.

Then she heard a shot—also overhead, and a cry. She looked aloft, and saw against the half-translucent vapours a black struggling figure on the edge of the cliff. She saw it but for an instant, and then was struck on the face by an open hand, and a body crashed on to the shelf at her side, rolled over the edge, and plunged into the gulf below.

She tried to cry, but her voice failed her. She felt her cheek stung by the blow she had received. A feeling as though all the rock were sinking under her came on, as though she were sliding—not shooting— but sliding down, down, and the sky went up higher, higher—and she knew no more.

## CHAPTER XVI
## ON THE SHINGLE

THE smugglers, warned by Coppinger, had crept up the path in silence, and singly, at considerable intervals between each, and on reaching the summit of the cliffs had dispersed to their own homes, using the precaution to strike inland first, over the "new-take" wall.

As the last of the party reached the top he encountered one of the coastguards, who, by the orders of his superior, was patrolling the down to watch that the smugglers did not leave the cove by any other path than the one known—that up and down which donkeys were driven. This donkey-driving to the beach was not pursued solely for the sake of contraband; the beasts brought up loads of sand, which the farmers professed they found valuable as manure on their stiff soil, and also the masses of seaweed cast on the strand after a gale, and which was considered to be possessed of rare fertilizing qualities.

No sooner did the coastguard see a man ascend the cliff, or rather come up over the edge before him, than he fired his pistol to give the signal to his fellows, whereupon the smuggler turned, seized him by the throat, and precipitated him over the edge.

Of this Coppinger knew nothing. He had led the procession, and had made his way to Pentyre Glaze by a roundabout route, so as to evade a guard set to watch for him approaching from the cliffs, should one have been so planted.

On reaching his door, his first query was whether the signals had been made.

"What signals?" asked Miss Trevisa.

"I sent a messenger here with instructions."

"No messenger has been here."

"What, no one—not—" he hesitated, and said, "not a woman?"

"Not a soul has been here—man, woman, or child— since you left."

"No one to see you?"

"No one at all, Captain."

Coppinger did not remove his hat; he stood in the doorway biting his thumb. Was it possible that Judith had shrunk from coming to his house to bear the message? Yet she had promised to do so. Had she been intercepted by the Preventive men? Had—had she reached the top of the cliff? Had she, after reaching the top, lost her way in the dark, taken a false direction, and— Coppinger did not allow the thought to find full expression in his brain. He turned, without another word, and hastened to the cottage of Mr. Menaida. He must ascertain whether she had reached home.

Uncle Zachie had not retired to bed; Scantlebray had been gone an hour; Zachie had drunk with Scantlebray, and he had drunk after the departure of that individual to indemnify himself for the loss of his company. Consequently Mr. Menaida was confused in mind and thick in talk.

"Where is Judith?" asked Coppinger, bursting in on him.

"In bed, I suppose," answered Uncle Zachie, after a while, when he comprehended the question, and had time to get over his surprise at seeing the Captain.

"Are you sure? When did she come in?"

"Come in?" said the old man, scratching his forehead with his pipe. "Come in— bless you, I don't know; some time in the afternoon. Yes, to be sure it was, some time in the afternoon."

"But she has been out to-night?"

"No—no—no," said Uncle Zachie, "it was Scantlebray."

"I say she has—she has been to—" he paused, then said—"to see her aunt."

"Aunt Dunes! bless my heart, when?"

"To-night."

"Impossible!"

"But I say she has. Come, Mr. Menaida. Go up to her room, knock at the door, and ascertain if she be back. Her aunt is alarmed—there are rough folks about."

"Why, bless me!" exclaimed Mr. Menaida; "so there are. And—well, wonders 'll never cease. How came you here? I thought the guard were after you. Scantlebray said so."

"Will you go at once and see if Judith Trevisa is home?"

Coppinger spoke with such vehemence, and looked so threateningly at the old man, that he staggered out of his chair, and, still holding his pipe, went to the stairs.

"Bless me!" said he, "whatever am I about? I've forgot a candle. Would you oblige me with lighting one? My hand shakes, and I might light my fingers by mistake."

After what seemed to Coppinger to be an intolerable length of time, Uncle Zachie stumbled down the stairs again.

"I say," said Mr. Menaida, standing on the steps, "Captain—did you ever hear about Tincombe Lane?— 'Tincombe Lane is all up-hill, Or down hill, as you take it; You tumble up and crack your crown, Or tumble down and break it.' —It's the same with these blessed stairs. Would you mind lending me a hand? By the powers, the banister is not firm! Do you know how it goes on?— 'Tincombe Lane is crooked and straight As pot-hook or as arrow. 'Tis smooth to foot, 'tis full of rut, 'Tis wide, and then 'tis narrow.' —Thank you, sir, thank you. Now take the candle. Bah! I've broke my pipe—and then comes the moral— 'Tincombe Lane is just like life From when you leave your mother, 'Tis sometimes this, 'tis sometimes that, 'Tis one thing or the other.'"

In vain had Coppinger endeavoured to interrupt the flow of words, and to extract from thick Zachie the information he needed, till the old gentleman was back in his chair.

Then Uncle Zachie observed—"Blessy'—I said so— I said so a thousand times. No—she's not there. Tell Aunt Dunes so. Will you sit down and have a drop? The night is rough, and it will do you good—take the chill out of your stomach and the damp out of your chest."

But Coppinger did not wait to decline the offer. He turned at once, left the house, and dashed the door back as he stepped out into the night. He had not gone a hundred paces along the road before he heard voices, and recognized that of Mr. Scantlebray—

"I tell you the vessel is the Black Prince, and I know he was to have unloaded her to-night."

"Anyhow he is not doing so. Not a sign of him."

"The night is too dirty."

"Wyvill—" Coppinger knew that the Captain at the head of the coastguard was speaking. "Wyvill, I heard a pistol-shot. Where is Jenkyns? If you had not been by me I should have said you had acted wide of your orders. Has any one seen Jenkyns?"

"No, sir."

"Who is that?"

Suddenly a light flashed forth, and glared upon Coppinger. The Captain in command of the coastguard uttered an oath.

"You out to-night, Mr. Coppinger? Where do you come from?"

"As you see—from Polzeath."

"Humph! From no other direction?"

"I'll trouble you to let me pass."

Coppinger thrust the Preventive man aside, and went on his way.

When he was beyond ear-shot, Scantlebray said— "I trust he did not notice me along with you. You see, the night is too dirty. Let him bless his stars, it has saved him."

"I should like to see Jenkyns," said the officer. "I am almost certain I heard a pistol-shot; but when I sent in the direction whence it came, there was no one to be seen. It's a confounded dark night."

"I hope they've not give us the slip, Captain?" said Wyvill.

"Impossible," answered the officer. "Impossible. I took every precaution. They did not go out to-night. As Mr. Scantlebray says, the night was too dirty."

Then they went on.

In the meantime Coppinger was making the best of his way to the downs. He knew his direction even in the dark—he had the "new-take" wall as a guide. What the coastguard did not suspect was that this "new-take" had been made for the very purpose of serving as a guide by which the smugglers could find their course in the blackest of winter's nights; moreover, in the fiercest storm the wall served as a shelter, under lea of which they might approach their cave. Coppinger was without a lantern. He doubted if one would avail him, in his quest: moreover, the night was lightening, as the moon rode higher.

The smuggler captain stood for a moment on the edge of the cliffs to consider what course he should adopt to find Judith. If she had reached the summit, it was possible enough that she had lost her way and had rambled inland among lanes and across fields, pixy-led. In that case it was a hopeless task to search for her; moreover, there would be no particular necessity for him to do so, as, sooner or later, she must reach a cottage or a farm, where she could learn her direction. But if she had gone too near the edge, or if, in her ascent, her foot had slipped, then he must search the shore. The tide was ebbing now, and left a margin on which he could walk. This was the course he must adopt. He did not descend by the track to the chimney, as the creeping down of the latter could be effected in absolute darkness only with extreme risk; but he bent his way over the down skirting the crescent indentation of the cove to the donkey-path, which was now, as he knew, unwatched. By that he swiftly and easily descended to the beach. Along the shore he crept carefully towards that portion which was overhung by the precipice along which the way ran from the mouth of the shaft. The night was mending, or at all events seemed better. The moon, as it mounted, cast a glimmer through the least opaque portions of the driving clouds. Coppinger looked up, and could see the ragged fringe of down torn with gullies, and thrust up into prongs, black as ink against the grey of the half-translucent vapours. And near at hand was the long dorsal ridge that concealed the entrance to the cave, sloping rapidly upwards and stretching away before him into shadow.

Coppinger mused. If one were to fall from above, would he drop between the cliff and this curtain, or would he strike and be projected over it on to the shelving sand up which stole the waves? He knew that the water eddying against friable sandstone strata that came to the surface had eaten them out with the wash, and that the hard flakes of slate and ribs of quartz stood forth, overhanging the cave. Most certainly, therefore, had Judith fallen, her body must be sought on the sea-face of the masking ridge. The smuggler stood at the very point where in the preceding afternoon Jamie and the dog had scrambled up that fin-like blade of rock and disappeared from the astonished gaze of Judith. The moon, smothered behind clouds, and yet, in a measure self-assertive, cast sufficient light down into the cove to glitter on, and transmute into steel, that sea-washed and smoothed, and still wet, ridge, sloping inland as a sea-wall. As Coppinger stood looking upwards he saw in the uncertain light something caught on the fangs of this saw-ridge, moving uneasily this way, then that, something dark, obscuring the glossed surface of the rock, as it might be a mass of gigantic sea-tangles.

"Judith!" he cried. "Is that you?" And he plunged through the pool that intervened, and scrambled up the rock.

He caught something. It was cloth. "Judith! Judith!" he almost shrieked in anxiety. That which he had laid hold of yielded, and he gathered to him a garment of some sort, and with it he slid back into the pool, and waded on to the pebbles. Then he examined his capture by the uncertain light, and by feel, and convinced himself that it was a cloak—a cloak with clasp and hood—just such as he had seen Judith wearing when he flashed his lantern over her on the platform at the mouth of the shaft.

He stood for a moment, numbed as though he had been struck on the head with a mallet, and irresolute. He had feared that Judith had fallen over the edge, but he had hoped that it was not so. This discovery seemed to confirm his worst fears.

If the cloak were there—she also would probably be there also, a broken heap. She who had thrown him down and broken him, had been thrown down herself, and broken also—thrown down and broken because she had come to rescue him from danger. Coppinger put his hand to his head. His veins were beating as though they would burst the vessels in his temples, and suffuse his face with blood. As he stood thus clasping his brow with his right hand, the clouds were swept for an instant aside, and for an instant the moon sent down a weird glare that ran like a wave along the sand, leaped impediments, scrambled up rocks, and flashed in the pools. For one moment only—but that sufficed to reveal to him a few paces ahead a black heap: there was no mistaking it. The rounded outlines were not those of a rock. It was a human body lying on the shingle half immersed in the pool at the foot of the reef!

A cry of intensest, keenest anguish burst from the heart of Coppinger. Prepared though he was for what he must see by the finding of the cloak, the sight of that motionless and wrecked body was more than he could endure with composure. In the darkness that ensued after the moon gleam he stepped forward, slowly, even timidly, to where that human wreck lay, and knelt on both knees beside it on the wet sand.

He waited. Would the moon shine out again and show him what he dreaded seeing? He would not put down a hand to touch it. One still clasped his brow, the other he could not raise so high, and he held it against his breast where it had lately been strapped. He tried to hold his breath, to hear if any sound issued from what lay before him. He strained his eyes to see if there were any, the slightest, movement in it. Yet he knew there could be none. A fall from these cliffs above must dash every spark of life out of a body that reeled down them. He turned his eyes upwards to see if the cloud would pass; but no—it seemed to be one that was all-enveloping, unwilling to grant him that glimpse which must be had, but which would cause him acutest anguish.

He could not remain kneeling there in suspense any longer. In uncertainty he was not. The horror was before him, inevitable—and must be faced.

He thrust his hand into his pocket, and drew forth tinder-box and flint. With a hand that had never trembled before, but now shaking as with an ague, he struck a light. The sparks flew about, and were long in igniting the touch-wood. But finally it was kindled, and glowed red. The wind fanned it into fitful flashes, as Coppinger, stooping, held the lurid spark over the prostrate form, and passed it up and down on the face. Then suddenly it fell from his hand, and he drew a gasp. The dead face was that of a bearded man.

A laugh—a wild, boisterous laugh—rang out into the night, and was re-echoed by the cliff, as Coppinger leaped to his feet. There was hope still. Judith had not fallen.

# CHAPTER XVII
## FOR LIFE OR DEATH

COPPINGER did not hesitate a moment now to leave the corpse on the beach where he had found it, and to hasten to the cave.

There was a third alternative to which hitherto he had given no attention. Judith, in ascending the cliff, might have strayed from the track, and be in such a position that she could neither advance nor draw back. He would, therefore, explore the path from the chimney mouth, and see if any tokens could be found of her having so done.

He again held his smouldering tinder, and by this feeble glimmer made his way up the inclined beach within the cave, passed under the arch of the rock where low, and found himself in that portion where was the boat.

Here he knew of a receptacle for sundries, such as might be useful in an emergency, and to that he made his way, and drew from it a piece of candle and a lantern. He speedily lighted the candle, set it in the lantern, and then ascended the chimney.

On reaching the platform at the orifice in the face of the rock, it occurred to him that he had forgotten to bring rope with him. He would not return for that, unless he found a need for it. Rope there was below, of many yards length. Till he knew that it was required, it seemed hardly worth his while to encumber himself with a coil that might be too long or too short for use. He did not even know that he would find Judith. It was a chance, that was all. It was more probable that she had strayed on the down, and was now back at Polzeath, and safe and warm in bed.

From the ledge in front of the shaft Coppinger proceeded with caution and leisurely, exploring every portion of the ascent with lowered lantern. There were plenty of impressions of feet wherever the soft and crumbly beds had been traversed, and where the dissolved stone had been converted into clay or mud, but these were the impressions of the smugglers escaping from their den. Step by step he mounted, till he had got about half-way up, when he noticed, what he had not previously observed, that there was a point at which the track left the ledge of stratified vertical rock that had inclined its broken edge upwards, and by a series of slips mounted to another fractured stratum, a leaf of the story-book turned up with the record of infinite ages sealed up in it. It was possible that one unacquainted with the course might grope onwards, following the ledge instead of deserting it for a direct upward climb. As Coppinger now perceived, one ignorant of the way and unprovided with a light would naturally follow the shelf. He accordingly deserted the track, and advanced along the ledge. There was a little turf in one place, in the next a tuft of armeria, then mud or clay, and there—assuredly a foot had trodden. There was a mark of a sole that was too small to have belonged to a man.

The shelf at first was tolerably broad, and could be followed without risk by one whose head was steady; but for how long would it so continue? These rough edges, these laminæ of upheaved slate were treacherous—they were sometimes completely broken down, forming gaps, in places stridable, in others discontinuous for many yards.

The footprint satisfied Coppinger that Judith had crept along this terrace, and so had missed the right course. It was impossible that she could reach the summit by this way—she must have fallen or be clinging at some point further ahead, a point from which she could not advance, and feared to retreat.

He held the lantern above his head, and peered before him, but could see nothing. The glare of the artificial light made the darkness beyond its radius the deeper and more impervious to the eye. He called, but received no answer. He called again, with as little success. He listened, but heard no other sound than the mutter of the sea, and the wail of the wind. There was nothing for him to do but to go forward; and he did that, slowly, searchingly, with the light near the ground, seeking for some further trace of Judith. He was obliged to use caution, as the ledge of rock narrowed. Here it was hard, and the foot passing over it made no impression. Then ensued a rift and a slide of shale, and here he thought he observed indications of recent dislodgment.

Now the foot-hold was reduced, he could no longer stoop to examine the soil; he must stand upright and hold to the rock with his right hand, and move with precaution lest he should be precipitated below.

Was it conceivable that she had passed there? —there in the dark? And yet—if she had not, she must have been hurled below.

Coppinger, clinging with his fingers, and thrusting one foot before the other, then drawing forward that foot, with every faculty on the alert, passed to where, for a short space, the ledge of rock expanded, and there he stooped once more with the light to explore. Beyond was a sheer fall, and the dull glare from his lantern showed him no continunance of the shelf. As he rose from his bent position, suddenly the light fell on a hand—a delicate, childish hand—hanging down. He raised the lantern, and saw her whom he sought. At this point she had climbed upwards to a higher ledge, and on that she lay, one arm raised, fastened by a chain to a tuft of heather— her head fallen against the rock, and feet and one arm over the edge of the cliff. She was unconscious, sustained by a dog-chain and a little bunch of ling.

Coppinger passed the candle over her face. It was white, and the eyes did not close before the light.

His position was vastly difficult. She hung there chained to the cliff, and he doubted whether he could sustain her weight if he attempted to carry her back whilst she was unconscious, along the way he and she had come. It was perilous for one alone to move along that strip of surface; it seemed impossible for one to effect it bearing in his arms a human burden.

Moreover, Coppinger was well aware that his left arm had not recovered its strength. He could not trust her weight on that. He dare not trust it on his right arm, for to return by the way he came the right hand would be that which was toward the void. The principal weight must be thrown inwards.

What was to be done? This, primarily: to release the insensible girl from her present position, in which the agony of the strain on her shoulder perhaps prolonged her unconsciousness.

Coppinger mounted to the shelf on which she lay, and bowing himself over her, whilst holding her, so that she should not slip over the edge, he disentangled the chain from her wrist and the stems of the heather. Then he seated himself beside her, drew her towards him, with his right arm about her, and laid her head on his shoulder.

And the chain?

That he took and deliberately passed it round her waist and his own body, fastened it, and muttered, "For life or for death!"

There, for a while, he sat. He had set the lantern beside him. His hand was on Judith's heart, and he held his breath, and waited to feel if there were pulsation there; but his own arteries were in such agitation, the throb in his finger-ends prevented with his being able to satisfy himself as to what he desired to know.

He could not remain longer in his present position. Judith might never revive. She had swooned through over-exhaustion, and nothing could restore her to life but the warmth and care she would receive in a house; he cursed his folly, his thoughtlessness, in having brought with him no flask of brandy. He dared remain no longer where he was, the ebbing powers in the feeble life might sink beyond recall.

He thrust his right arm under her, and adjusted the chain about him so as to throw some of her weight off the arm, and then cautiously slid to the step below, and, holding her, set his back to the rocky wall.

So, facing the Atlantic Ocean, facing the wild night sky, torn here and there into flakes of light, otherwise cloaked in storm-gloom, with the abyss below, an abyss of jagged rock and shingle shore, he began to make his way along the track by which he had gained that point.

He was at that part where the shelf narrowed to a foot, and his safety and hers depended largely on the power that remained to him in his left arm. With the hand of that arm he felt along and clutched every projecting point of rock, and held to it with every sinew strained and starting. He drew a long breath. Was Judith stirring on his arm?

The critical minute had come. The slightest movement, the least displacement of the balance, and both would be precipitated below.

"Judith!" said he, hoarsely, turning his head towards her ear. "Judith!"

There was no reply.

"Judith! For Heaven's sake—if you hear me— do not lift a finger. Do not move a muscle."

The same heavy weight on him without motion.

"Judith! For life—or death!"

Then suddenly from off the ocean flashed a tiny spark—far, far away.

It was a signal from the Black Prince.

He saw it, fixed his eyes steadily on it, and began to move sideways, facing the sea, his back to the rock, reaching forward with his left arm, holding Judith in the right.

"For life!"

He took one step sideways, holding with the disengaged hand to the rock. The bone of that arm was but just knit. Not only so, but that of the collar was also recently sealed up after fracture. Yet the salvation of two lives hung on these two infirm joints. The arm was stiff; the muscles had not recovered flexibility, nor the sinews their strength.

"For death!"

A second sidelong step, and the projected foot slid in greasy marl. He dug his heel into the wet and yielding soil, he stamped in it; then, throwing all his weight on the left heel, aided by the left arm, he drew himself along and planted the right beside the left.

He sucked the air in between his teeth with a hiss. The soft soil was sinking—it would break away. The light from the Black Prince seemed to rise. With a wrench he planted his left foot on rock—and drew up the right to it.

"Judith! For life!"

That star on the black sea—what did it mean? He knew. His mind was clear, and though in intense concentration of all his powers on the effort to pass this strip of perilous path, he could reason of other things, and knew why the Black Prince had exposed her light. The lantern that he had borne, and left on the shelf, had been seen by her, and she supposed it to be a signal from the terrace over the cave.

The next step was full of peril. With his left foot advanced, Coppinger felt he had reached the shale. He kicked into it, and kicked away an avalanche of loose flakes that slid over the edge. But he drove his foot deep into the slope, and rammed a dent into which he could fix the right foot when drawn after it.

"For death!"

Then he crept along upon the shale.

He could not see the star now. His sweat, rolling off his brow, had run over his eyelids and charged the lashes as with tears. In partial blindness he essayed the next step.

"For life!"

Then he breathed more freely. His foot was on the grass.

The passage of extreme danger was over. From the point now reached the ledge widened, and Coppinger was able to creep onward with less stress laid on the fractured bones. The anguish of expectation of death was lightened; and as it lightened nature began to assert herself. His teeth chattered as in an ague fit, and his breath came in sobs.

In ten minutes he had attained the summit—he was on the down above the cliffs.

"Judith," said he, and he kissed her cheeks and brow and hair. "For life—for death—mine, only mine."

# CHAPTER XVIII
## UNA

WHEN Judith opened her eyes, she found herself in a strange room, but as she looked about her she saw Aunt Dionysia with her hands behind her back looking out of the window.

"Oh, aunt! Where am I?"

Miss Trevisa turned.

"So you have come round at last, or pleased to pretend to come round. It is hard to tell whether or not dissimulation was here."

"Dissimulation, aunt?"

"There's no saying. Young folks are not what they were in my day. They have neither the straight-forwardness nor the consideration for their elders and betters."

"But—where am I?"

"At the Glaze; not where I put you, but where you have put yourself."

"I did not come here, auntie, dear."

"Don't auntie dear me, and deprive me of my natural sleep."

"Have I?"

"Have you not? Three nights have I had to sit up. And natural sleep is as necessary to me at my age as is stays. I fall abroad without one or the other. Give me my choice—whether I'd have nephews and nieces crawling about me or erysipelas, and I'd choose the latter."

"But, aunt—I'm sorry if I am a trouble to you."

"Of course you are a trouble. How can you be other? Don't burs stick? But that is neither here nor there."

"Aunt, how came I to Pentyre Glaze?"

"I didn't invite you, and I didn't bring you—you may be sure of that. Captain Coppinger found you somewhere on the down at night, when you ought to have been at home. You were insensible, or pretended to be so—it's not for me to say which."

"Oh, aunt, I don't want to be here."

"Nor do I want you here—and in my room, too. Hoity-toity! nephews and nieces are just like pigs— you want them to go one way and they run the other."

"But I should like to know where Captain Coppinger found me, and all about it. I don't remember anything."

"Then you must ask him yourself."

"I should like to get up; may I?"

"I can't say till the doctor comes. There's no telling—I might be blamed. I shall be pleased enough, when you are shifted to your own room," and she pointed to a door.

"My room, auntie?"

"I suppose so; I don't know whose else it is."

Then Miss Trevisa whisked out of the room.

Judith lay quietly in bed trying to collect her thoughts and recall something of what had happened. She could recollect fastening her wrist to the shrub by her brother's dog-chain; then, with all the vividness of a recurrence of the scene—the fall of the man, the stroke on her cheek, his roll over and plunge down the precipice. The recollection made a film come over her eyes and her heart stand still. After that she remembered nothing. She tried hard to bring to mind one single twinkle of remembrance, but in vain. It was like looking at a wall and straining the eyes to see through it.

Then she raised herself in bed to look about her. She was in her aunt's room, and in her aunt's bed. She had been brought there by Captain Coppinger. He, therefore, had rescued her from the position of peril in which she had been. So far she could understand. She would have liked to know more, but more, probably, her aunt could not tell her, even if inclined to do so.

Where was Jamie? Was he at Uncle Zachie's? Had he been anxious and unhappy about her? She hoped he had got into no trouble during the time he had been free from her supervision. Judith felt that she must go back to Mr. Menaida's and to Jamie. She could not stay at the Glaze. She could not be happy with her ever-grumbling, ill-tempered aunt. Besides, her father would not have wished her to be there.

What did Aunt Dunes mean when she pointed to a door and spoke of her room?

Judith could not judge whether she were strong till she tried her strength. She slipped her feet to the floor, stood up and stole over the floor to that door which her aunt had indicated. She timidly raised the latch, after listening at it, opened and peeped into a small apartment. To her surprise she saw the little bed she had occupied at her dear home, the rectory, her old washstand, her mirror, the old chairs, the framed pictures that had adorned her walls, the common and trifling ornaments that had been arranged on her chimney-piece. Every object with which she had been familiar at the parsonage for many years, and to which she had said good-bye, never expecting to have a right to them any more—all these were there, furnishing the room that adjoined her aunt's apartment.

She stood looking round in surprise, till she heard a step on the stair outside, and, supposing it was that of Aunt Dionysia, she ran back to bed, and dived under the clothes and pulled the sheets over her golden head.

Aunt Dunes entered the room, bringing with her a bowl of soup. Her eye at once caught the opened door into the little adjoining chamber.

"You have been out of bed!"

Judith thrust her head out of its hiding-place, and said, frankly, "Yes, auntie! I could not help myself. I went to see. How have you managed to get all my things together?"

"I? I have had nothing to do with it."

"But—who did it, auntie?"

"Captain Coppinger; he was at the sale."

"Is the sale over, aunt?"

"Yes, whilst you have been ill."

"Oh, I am so glad it is over, and I knew nothing about it."

"Oh, exactly! Not a thought of the worry you have been to me; deprived of my sleep—of my bed—of my bed," repeated Aunt Dunes, grimly. "How can you expect a bulb to flower if you take it out of the earth and stick it on a bedroom chair stirring broth? I have no patience with you young people. You are consumed with selfishness."

"But, auntie! Don't be cross. Why did Captain Coppinger buy all my dear crinkum-crankums?"

Aunt Dionysia snorted and tossed her head.

Judith suddenly flushed; she did not repeat the question, but said hastily, "Auntie, I want to go back to Mr. Menaida."

"You cannot desire it more than I do," said Miss Trevisa, sharply. "But whether he will let you go is another matter."

"Aunt Dunes, if I want to go, I will go!"

"Indeed!"

"I will go back as soon as ever I can."

"Well, that can't be to-day, for one thing."

The evening of that same day Judith was removed into the adjoining room, "her room," as Miss Trevisa designated it. "And mind you sleep soundly, and don't trouble me in the night. Natural sleep is as suitable to me as green peas to duck."

When, next morning, the girl awoke, her eyes ranged round and lighted everywhere on familiar objects. The two mezzotints of Happy and Deserted Auburn, the old and battered pieces of Dresden ware, vases with flowers encrusted round them, but with most of the petals broken off—vases too injured to be of value to a purchaser, valuable to her because full of reminiscences— the tapestry firescreen, the painted fans with butterflies on them, the mirror blotched with damp, the inlaid wafer-box and ruler, the old snuffer-tray. Her eyes filled with tears. A gathering together into one room of old trifles did not make that strange room to be home. It was the father, the dear father, who, now that he was taken away, made home an impossibility, and the whole world, however crowded with old familiar odds and ends, to be desert and strange. The sight of all her old "crinkum crankums," as she had called them, made Judith's heart smart. It was kindly meant by Coppinger to purchase all these things and collect them there; but it was a mistake of judgment. Grateful she was, not gratified.

In the little room there was an ottoman with a woolwork cover representing a cluster of dark red, pink, and white roses; and at each corner of the ottoman was a tassel, which had been a constant source of trouble to Judith, as the tassels would come off, sometimes because the cat played with them, sometimes because Jamie pulled them off in mischief, sometimes because they caught in her dress. Her father had embroidered those dreadful roses on a buff ground one winter when confined to the house by a heavy cold and cough. She valued that ottoman for his sake, and would not have suffered it to go into the sale had she possessed any place she could regard as her own where to put it. She needed no such article to remind her of the dear father—the thought of him would be for ever present to her without the assistance of ottomans to refresh her memory.

On this ottoman, when dressed, Judith seated herself, and let her hands rest in her lap. She was better; she would soon be well; and when well would take the first opportunity to depart.

The door was suddenly thrown open by her aunt, and in the doorway stood Coppinger looking at her. He raised his hand to his hat in salutation, but said nothing. She was startled, and unable to speak. In another moment the door was shut again.

That day she resolved that nothing should detain her longer than she was forced. Jamie—her own dear Jamie—came to see her, and the twins were locked in each other's arms.

"Oh, Ju! darling Ju! You are quite well, are you not? And Captain Coppinger has given me a grey donkey instead of Tib; and I'm to ride it about whenever I choose!"

"But, dear, Mr. Menaida has no stable, and no paddock."

"Oh, Ju! that's nothing. I'm coming up here, and we shall be together—the donkey and you and me and Aunt Dunes!"

"No, Jamie. Nothing of the sort. Listen to me. You remain at Mr. Menaida's. I am coming back."

"But I've already brought up my clothes."

"You take them back. Attend to me. You do not come here. I go back to Mr. Menaida's immediately."

"But, Ju! you've got all your pretty things from the parsonage here!"

"They are not mine. Mr. Coppinger bought them for himself."

"But—the donkey?"

"Leave the donkey here. Pay attention to my words. I lay a strict command on you. As you love me, Jamie, do not leave Mr. Menaida's; remain there till my return."

That night there was a good deal of noise in the house. Judith's room lay in a wing, nevertheless she heard the riot, for the house was not large, and the sounds from the hall penetrated every portion of it. She was frightened, and went into Miss Trevisa's room.

"Aunt! what is this dreadful racket about?"

"Go to sleep—you cannot have every one shut his mouth because of you."

"But what is it, auntie?"

"It is nothing but the master has folk with him, if you wish particularly to know. The whole cargo of the Black Prince has been run, and not a finger has been laid by the coastguard on a single barrel or bale. So they are celebrating their success. Go to bed and sleep. It is naught to you."

"I cannot sleep, aunt. They are singing now."

"Why should they not; have you aught against it? You are not mistress here, that I am aware of."

"But, auntie, are there many downstairs?"

"I do not know. It is no concern of mine—and certainly none of yours."

Judith was silenced for a while by her aunt's ill-humour; but she did not return to her room. Presently she asked— "Are you sure, aunt, that Jamie is gone back to Polzeath?"

Miss Trevisa kicked the stool from under her feet, in her impatience.

"Really! you drive me desperate. I did not bargain for this. Am I to tear over the country on post-horses to seek a nephew here and a niece there? I can't tell where Jamie is, and what is more, I do not care. I'll do my duty by you both. I'll do no more; and that has been forced on me, it was not sought by me. Heaven be my witness."

Judith returned to her room. The hard and sour woman would afford her no information.

In her room she threw herself on her bed, and began to think. She was in the very home and head-quarters of contrabandism. But was smuggling a sin? Surely not that, or her father would have condemned it decidely. She remembered his hesitation relative to it, in the last conversation they had together. Perhaps it was not actually a sin—she could recall no text in Scripture that denounced it—but it was a thing forbidden, and though she did not understand why it was forbidden, she considered that it could not be an altogether honourable and righteous traffic. Judith was unable to rest. It was not the noise that disturbed her so much as her uneasiness about Jamie. Had he obeyed her and gone back to Uncle Zachie? Or had he neglected her injunction, and was he in the house, was he below, along with the revellers?

She opened the door gently, and stole along the passage, to the head of the stairs, and listened. She could smell the fumes of tobacco; but to these she was familiar. The atmosphere of Mr. Menaida's cottage was redolent of the Virginian weed. The noise was, however, something to which she was utterly unaccustomed: the boisterous merriment, the shouts, and occasional oaths. Then a fiddle was played. There was disputation, a pause, then the fiddle recommenced; it played a jig; there was a clatter of feet, then a roar of laughter—and then—she was almost sure she heard the voice of her brother.

Regardless of herself, thinking only of him, without a moment's consideration, she ran down the stairs and threw open the door into the great kitchen, or hall.

It was full of men—wild, rough fellows—drinking and smoking; there were lights and a fire. The atmosphere was rank with spirits and tobacco; on a chair sat a sailor fiddling, and in the midst of the room, on a table, was Jamie dancing a jig, to the laughter and applause of the revellers.

The moment Judith appeared silence ensued—the men were surprised to see a pale and delicate girl stand before them, with a crown of gold like a halo round her ivory-white face. But Judith took no notice of any one there—her eyes were on her brother, and her hand raised to attract his attention. Judith had been in bed, but, disturbed by the uproar, had risen, and drawn on her gown; her feet, however, were bare, and her magnificent hair poured over her shoulders unbound. Her whole mind, her whole care, was for Jamie; on hersel not a thought rested; she had forgotten that she was but half clothed.

"Jamie! Jamie!" she cried. "My brother! my brother!"

The fiddler ceased, lowered his violin, and stared at her.

"Ju, let me alone! It is such fun," said the boy.

"Jamie! this instant you shall come with me. Get down off the table!"

As he hesitated, and looked round to the men who had been applauding him for support against his sister, she went to the table, and caught him by the feet.

"Jamie! in pity to me! Jamie! think—papa is but just dead."

Then tears of sorrow, shame, and entreaty filled her eyes.

"No, Ju! I'm not tied to your apron-strings," said the lad, disengaging himself.

But in an instant he was caught from the table by the strong arm of Coppinger, and thrust towards the door. "Judith, you should not have come here."

"Oh, Mr. Coppinger—and Jamie! why did you let him—"

Coppinger drew the girl from the room into the passage.

"Judith, not for the world would I have had you here," said he, in an agitated voice. "I'll kill your aunt for letting you come down."

"Mr. Coppinger, she knew nothing of my coming. Come I must—I heard Jamie's voice."

"Go," said the Captain, shaking the boy. He was ashamed of himself and angry. "Beware how you disobey your sister again."

Coppinger's face was red as fire. He turned to Judith—

"Your feet are bare. Let me carry you upstairs— carry you once more."

She shook her head. "As I came down so I can return."

"Will you forgive me?" he said, in a low tone.

"Heaven forgive you," she answered, and burst into tears. "You will break my heart, I foresee it."

# CHAPTER XIX
## A GOLDFISH

NEXT day—just in the same way as the day before— when Judith was risen and dressed, the door was thrown open, and again Coppinger was revealed, standing outside, looking at her with a strange expression, and saying no word.

But Judith started up from her chair and went to him in the passage, put forth her delicate white hand, laid it on his cuff, and said: "Mr. Coppinger, may I speak to you?"

"Where?"

"Where you like—downstairs will be best, in the hall, if no one be there."

"It is empty."

He stood aside, and allowed her to precede him.

The staircase was narrow, and it would have been dark but for a small dormer-window through which light came from a squally sky covered with driving white vapours. But such light as entered from a white and wan sun fell on her head as she descended—that head of hair was like the splendour of a beech tree touched by frost before the leaves fall.

Coppinger descended after her.

When they were both in the hall, he indicated his armchair by the hearth for her to sit in, and she obeyed. She was weak and now also nervous. She must speak to the smuggler firmly, and that required all her courage.

The room was tidy; all traces of the debauch of the preceding night had disappeared.

Coppinger stood a few paces from her. He seemed to know that what she was going to say would displease him, and he did not meet her clear eyes, but looked with a sombre frown upon the floor.

Judith put the fingers of her right hand to her heart to bid it cease beating so fast, and then rushed into what she had to say, fearing lest delay should heighten the difficulty of saying it.

"I am so—so thankful to you, sir, for what you have done for me. My aunt tells me that you found and carried me here. I had lost my way on the rocks, and but for you I would have died."

"Yes," he said, raising his eyes suddenly and looking piercingly into hers, "but for me you would have died."

"I must tell you how deeply grateful I am for this and for other kindnesses. I shall never forget that this foolish, silly little life of mine I owe to you."

Again her heart was leaping so furiously as to need the pressure of her fingers on it to check it.

"We are quits," said Coppinger, slowly. "You came—you ran a great risk to save me. But for you I might be dead. So, this rude and worthless—this evil life of mine," he held out his hands, both palms before her, and spoke with quivering voice—"I owe to you."

"Then," said Judith, "as you say, we are quits. Yet—no. If one accounts is cancelled, another remains unclosed. I threw you down and broke your bones. So there still remains a score against me."

"That I have forgiven long ago," said he. "Throw me down, break me, kill me, do with me what you will—and—I will kiss your hand."

"I do not wish to have my hand kissed," said Judith, hastily, "I let you understand that before."

He put his elbow against the mantel-shelf, and leaned his brow against his open hand, looking down at her, so she could not see his face without raising her eyes, but he could rest his on her and study her, note her distress, the timidity with which she spoke, the wince when he said a word that implied his attachment to her.

"I have not only to thank you, Captain Coppinger —but I have to say good-bye."

"What—go?"

"Yes—I shall go back to Mr. Menaida to-day."

He stamped, and his face became blood-red. "You shall not. I will it—here you stay."

"It cannot be," said Judith, after a moment's pause to let his passion subside. "You are not my guardian, though very generously you have undertaken to be valuer for me in dilapidations. I must go, I and Jamie."

He shook his head. He feared to speak, his anger choked him.

"I cannot remain here myself, and certainly I will not let Jamie be here."

"Is it because of last night's foolery you say that?"

"I am responsible for my brother. He is not very clever; he is easily led astray. There is no one to think for him, to care for him, but myself. I could never let him run the risk of such a thing happening again."

"Confound the boy!" burst forth Coppinger. "Are you going to bring him up as a milk-sop? You are wrong altogether in the way you manage him."

"I can but follow my conscience."

"And is it because of him that you go?"

"Not because of him only."

"But I have spoken to your aunt; she consents."

"But I do not," said Judith.

He stamped again, passionately.

"I am not the man who will bear to be disobeyed and my will crossed. I say— Here you shall stay."

Judith waited a moment, looking at him steadily out of her clear, glittering irridescent eyes, and said slowly, "I am not the girl to be obliged to stay where my common sense and my heart say Stay not."

He folded his arms, lowered his chin on his breast, and strode up and down the room. Then, suddenly, he stood still opposite her and asked, in a threatening tone—

"Do you not like your room? Does that not please your humour?"

"It has been most kind of you to collect all my little bits of rubbish there. I feel how good you have been, how full of thought for me; but, for all that, I cannot stay."

"Why not?"

"I have said, on one account, because of Jamie."

He bit his lips—"I hate that boy."

"Then most certainly he cannot be here. He must be with those who love him."

"Then stay."

"I cannot—I will not. I have a will as well as you. My dear papa always said that my will was strong."

"You are the only person who has ever dared to resist me."

"That may be; I am daring—because you have been kind."

"Kind to you. Yes—to you only."

"It may be so, and because kind to me, and me only, I, and I only, presume to say No when you say Yes."

He came again to the fireplace and again leaned against the mantel-shelf. He was trembling with passion.

"And what if I say that, if you go, I will turn old Dunes—I mean your aunt—out of the house?"

"You will not say it, Mr. Coppinger; you are too noble, too generous, to take a mean revenge."

"Oh! you allow there is some good in me?"

"I thankfully and cheerfully protest there is a great deal of good in you—and I would there were more."

"Come—stay here and teach me to be good—be my crutch; I will lean on you, and you shall help me along the right way."

"You are too great a weight, Mr. Coppinger," said she, smiling—but it was a frightened and a forced smile. "You would bend and break the little crutch."

He heaved a long breath. He was looking at her from under his hand and his bent brows.

"You are cruel—to deny me a chance. And what if I were to say that I am hungry, sick at heart, and faint. Would you turn your back and leave me?"

"No, assuredly not."

"I am hungry."

She looked up at him, and was frightened by the glitter in his eyes.

"I am hungry for the sight of you, for the sound of your voice."

She did not say anything to this, but sat, with her hands on her lap, musing, uncertain how to deal with this man, so strange, impulsive, and yet so submissive to her, and even appealing to her pity.

"Mr. Coppinger, I have to think of and care for Jamie, and he takes up all my thoughts and engrosses all my time."

"Jamie, again!"

"So that I cannot feed and teach another orphan."

"Put off your departure—a week. Grant me that. Then you will have time to get quite strong, and also you will be able to see whether it is not possible for you to live here. Here is your aunt—it is natural and right that you should be with her. She has been made your guardian by your father. Do you not bow to his directions."

"Mr. Coppinger, I cannot stay here."

"I am at a disadvantage," he exclaimed. "Man always is when carrying on a contest with a woman. Stay—stay here and listen to me." He put out his hand and pressed her back into the chair, for she was about to rise. "Listen to what I say. You do not know—you cannot know—how near death you and I —yes, you and I—were, chained together." His deep voice shock. "You and I were on the face of the cliff. There was but one little strip, the width of my hand"—he held out his palm before her—"and that was not secure. It was sliding away under my feet. Below was death, certain death—a wretched death. I held you. That little chain tied us two—us two together. All your life and mine hung on was my broken arm and broken collar-bone. I held you to me with my right arm and the chain. I did not think we should live. I thought that together—chained together, I holding you—so we would die—so we would be found —and my only care, my only prayer was, if so, that so we might be washed to sea and sink together, I holding you and chained to you, and you to me. I prayed that we might never be found; for I thought if rude hands were laid on us that the chain would be unloosed, my arm unlocked from about you, and that we should be carried to separate graves. I could not endure that thought. Let us go down together—bound, clasped together—into the depths of the deep sea, and there rest. But it was not to be so. I carried you over that stage of infinite danger. An angel or a devil—I cannot say which—held me up. And then I swore that never in life should you be loosed from me, as I trusted that in death we should have remained bound together. See!" He put his hand to her head and drew a look of her golden hair and wound it about his hand and arm. "You have me fast now—fast in a chain of gold—of gold infinitely precious to me—infinitely strong—and you will cast me off, who never thought to cast you off when tied to you with a chain of iron. What say you? Will you stand in safety on your cliff of pride and integrity and unloose the golden band and say, 'Go down—down. I know nothing in you to love. You are naught to me but a robber, a wrecker, a drunkard, a murderer—go down into Hell?'"

In his quivering excitement he acted the whole scene, unconscious that he was so doing, and the drops of agony stood on his brow and rolled—drip— drip—drip— from it. Man does not weep; his tears exude more bitter than those that flow from the eyes, and they distill from his pores.

Judith was awed by the intensity of passion in the man, but not changed in her purpose. His vehemence reacted on her, calming her, giving her determination to finish the scene decisively and finally.

"Mr. Coppinger," she said, looking up to him, who still held her by the hair wound about his hand and arm, "it is you who hold me in chains, not I you. And so I—your prisoner—must address a gaoler. Am I to speak in chains, or will you release me?"

He shook his head, and clenched his hand on the gold hair.

"Very well," said she, "so it must be; I, bound, plead my cause with you—at a disadvantage. This is what I must say at the risk of hurting you; and, Heaven be my witness, I would not wound one who has been so good to me—one to whom I owe my life, my power now to speak and entreat." She paused a minute to gain breath and strengthen herself for what she had to say.

"Mr. Coppinger—do you not yourself see that it is quite impossible that I should remain in this house —that I should have anything more to do with you? Consider how I have been brought up—what my thoughts have been. I have had, from earliest childhood, my dear papa's example and teachings, sinking into my heart till they have coloured my very life blood. My little world and your great one are quite different. What I love and care for is folly to you, and your pursuits and pleasures are repugnant to me. You are an eagle—a bird of prey."

"A bird of prey," repeated Coppinger.

"And you soar and fight, and dive, and rend in your own element; whereas I am a little silver trout—"

"No"—he drew up his arm wound round with her hair—"No—a goldfish."

"Well, so be it; a goldfish swimming in my own crystal element, and happy in it. You would not take me out of it to gasp and die. Trust me, Captain Coppinger, I could not—even if I would—live in your world."

She put up her hands to his arm and drew some of the hair through his fingers, and unwound it from his sleeve. He made no resistance. He watched her, in a dream. He had heard every word she had said, and he knew that she spoke the truth. They belonged to different realms of thought and sensation. He could not breathe—he would stifle—in hers, and it was possible—it was certain—that she could not endure the strong, rough quality of his.

Her delicate fingers touched his hand, and sent a spasm to his heart. She was drawing away another strand of hair, and untwisting it from about his arm, passing the wavy fire-gold from one hand to the other. And as every strand was taken off, so went light and hope from him, and despair settled down on his dark spirit.

He was thinking whether it would not have been better to have thrown himself down when he had her in his arms, and bound to him by the chain.

Then he laughed.

She looked up, and caught his wild eye. There was a timid inquiry in her look, and he answered it.

"You may unwind your hair from my arm, but it is woven round and round my heart, and you cannot loose it thence."

She drew another strand away, and released that also from his arm. There remained now but one red-gold band of hair fastening her to him. He looked entreatingly at her, and then at the hair.

"It must indeed be so," she said, and released herself wholly.

Then she stood up, a little timidly, for she could not trust him in his passion and his despair. But he did not stir; he looked at her with fixed, dreamy eyes. She left her place, and moved towards the door. She had gone forth from Mr. Menaida's without hat or other cover for her head than the cloak with its hood, and that she had lost. She must return bareheaded. She had reached the door; and there she waved him a farewell.

"Goldfish!" he cried.

She halted.

"Goldfish, come here; one—one word only."

She hesitated whether to yield. The man was dangerous. But she considered that with a few strides he might overtake her if she tried to escape. Therefore she returned towards him, but came not near enough for him to touch her.

"Hearken to me," said he. "It may be as you say. It is as you say. You have your world; I have mine. You could not live in mine, nor I in yours." But his voice thrilled, "Swear to me—swear to me now—that whilst I live not other shall hold you, as I would have held you, to his side; that no other shall take your hair and wind it round him, as I have—I could not endure that. Will you swear to me that?—and you shall go."

"Indeed I will; indeed, indeed I will."

"Beware how you break this oath. Let him beware who dares to seek you." He was silent, looking on the ground, his arms folded. So he stood for some minutes, lost in thought. Then suddenly he cried out, "Goldfish!"

He had found a single hair, long—a yard long—of the most intense red-gold, lustrous as a cloud in the west over the sunken sun. It had been left about his arm and hand.

"Goldfish!"

But she was gone.

## CHAPTER XX
## BOUGHT AND SOLD

CRUEL Coppinger remained brooding in the place where he had been standing, and as he stood there his face darkened. He was a man of imperious will and violent passions; a man unwont to curb himself; accustomed to sweep out of his path whoever or whatever stood between him and the accomplishment of his purpose; a man who never asked himself whether that purpose were good or bad. He had succumbed, in a manner strange and surprising to himself, to the influence of Judith—a sort of witchery over him that subdued his violence and awed him into gentleness and modesty. But when her presence was withdrawn the revolt of the man's lawless nature began. Who was this who had dared to oppose her will to his? a mere child of eighteen. Women were ever said to be a perverse generation, and loved to domineer over men; and man was weak to suffer it. So thinking, chafing, he had worked himself into a immersing rage when Miss Trevisa entered the hall, believing it to be empty. Seeing him, she was about to withdraw, when he shouted to her to stay.

"I beg your pardon for intruding, sir; I am in quest of my niece. Those children keep me in a whirl like a teetotum."

"Your niece is gone."

"Gone! where to?"

"Back—I suppose to that old fool Menaida. He is meet to be a companion for her and that idiot, her brother; not I—I am to be spurned from her presence."

Miss Trevisa was surprised, but she said nothing. She knew his moods.

"Stand there, Mother Dunes!" said Coppinger, in his anger and humiliation, glad to have some one on whom he could pour out the lava that boiled up in his burning breast. "Listen to me. She has told me that we belong to different worlds—she and I— and to different races, kinds of being, and that there can be no fellowship betwixt us. Where I am she will not be. Between me and you there is a great gulf fixed—see you? and I am as Dives tormented in my flame, and she stands yonder, serene, in cold and complacent blessedness, and will not cross to me with her finger dipped in cold water to cool my tongue; and as for my coming near to her"—he laughed fiercely—"that can never be."

"Did she say all that?" asked Miss Trevisa.

"She looked it; she implied it, if she did not say it in these naked words. And, what is more," shouted he, coming before Aunt Dionysia threateningly, so that she recoiled, "it is true. When she sat there in yonder chair, and I stood here by this hearthstone, and she spoke, I knew it was true; I saw it all—the great gulf unspanned by any bridge. I knew that none could ever bridge it, and there we were, apart for ever, I in my fire burning, she in Blessedness—indifferent."

"I am very sorry," said Miss Trevisa, "that Judith should so have misconducted herself. My brother brought her up in a manner, to my mind, most improper for a young girl. He made her read Rollin's 'Ancient History' and Blair's 'Chronological Tables,' and really, upon my word, I cannot say what else."

"I do not care how it was," said Coppinger. "But here stands the gulf."

"Rollin is in sixteen octavo volumes," said Aunt Dionysia; "and they are thick also."

Coppinger strode about the room, with his hands in his deep coat pockets, his head down.

"My dear brother," continued Miss Trevisa, apologetically, "made of Judith his daily companion, told her all he thought, asked her opinion, as though she were a full-grown woman, and one whose opinion was worth having, whereas he never consulted me, never cared to talk to me about anything, and the consequence is the child has grown up without that respect for her elders and betters, and that deference for the male sex which the male sex expects. I am sure when I was a girl, and of her age, I was very different, very different indeed."

"Of that I have not the smallest doubt," sneered Coppinger. "But never mind about yourself. It is of her I am speaking. She is gone, has left me, and I cannot endure it. I cannot endure it," he repeated.

"I beg your pardon," said Aunt Dionysia, "you must excuse me saying it, Captain Coppinger, but you place me in a difficult position. I am the guardian of my niece, though, goodness knows, I never desired it, and I don't know what to think. It is very flattering and kind, and I esteem it great goodness in you to speak of Judith with such warmth, but—"

"Goodness! kindness!" exclaimed Coppinger. "I am good and kind to her! She forces me to it. I can be nothing else, and she throws me at her feet and tramples on me."

"I am sure your sentiments, sir, are—are estimable; but, feeling as you seem to imply towards Judith, I hardly know what to say. Bless me! what a scourge to my shoulders these children are; nettles stinging and blistering my skin, and not allowing me a moment's peace!"

"I imply nothing," said Coppinger. "I speak out direct and plain what I mean. I love her. She has taken me, she turns me about, she gets my heart between her little hands and tortures it."

"Then, surely, Captain, you cannot ask me to let her be here. You are most kind to express yourself in this manner about the pert hussy, but, as she is my niece, and I am responsible for her, I must do my duty by her, and not expose her to be—talked about. Bless me!" gasped Aunt Dunes, "when I was her age I never would have put myself into such a position as to worry my aunt out of her seven senses, and bring her nigh to distraction."

"I will marry her, and make her mistress of my house and all I have," said Coppinger.

Miss Trevisa slightly curtsied, then said, "I am sure you are over-indulgent, but what is to become of me? I have no doubt it will be very comfortable and acceptable to Judith to hear this, but—what is to become of me? It would not be very delightful for me to be housekeeper here under my own niece, a pert, insolent, capricious hussy. You can see at once, Captain Coppinger, that I cannot consent to that."

The woman had the shrewdness to know that she could be useful to Coppinger, and the selfishness that induced her to make terms with him to secure her own future, and to show him that she could stand in his way till he yielded to them.

"I never asked to have these children thrust down my throat, like the fish-bone that strangled Lady Godiva—no, who was it? Earl Godiva; but I thank my stars I never waded through Rollin, and most certainly kept my hands off Blair. Of course, Captain Coppinger, it is right and proper of you to address yourself to me, as the guardian of my niece, before speaking to her."

"I have spoken to her, and she spurns me."

"Naturally, because you spoke to her before addressing me on the subject. My dear brother—I will do him this justice—was very emphatic on this point. But you see, sir, my consent can never be given."

"I do not ask your consent."

"Judith will never take you without it."

"Consent or no consent," said Coppinger, "that is a secondary matter. The first is, she does not like me, whereas I—I love her. I never loved a woman before. I knew not what love was. I laughed at the fools, as I took them to be, who sold themselves into the hands of women; but now, I cannot live without her. I can think of nothing but her all day. I am in a fever, and cannot sleep at night—all because she is tormenting me."

All at once, exhausted by his passion, desperate at seeing no chance of success, angry at being flouted by a child, he threw himself into the chair, and settled his chin on his breast, and folded his arms.

"Go on," said he. "Tell me what is my way out of this?"

"You cannot expect my help or my advice, Captain, so as to forward what would be most unsatisfactory to me."

"What! do you grudge her to me?"

"Not that; but, if she were here, what would become of me? Should I be turned out into the cold at my age by this red-headed hussy, to find a home for myself with strangers? Here I never would abide with her as mistress, never."

"I care naught about you."

"No, of that I am aware, to my regret, sir; but that makes it all the more necessary for me to take care for myself."

"I see," said Coppinger, "I must buy you. Is your aid worth it? Will she listen to you?"

"I can make her listen to me," said Aunt Dunes, "if it be worth my while. At my age, having roughed it, having no friends, I must think of myself and provide for the future, when I shall be too old to work."

"Name your price."

Miss Trevisa did not answer for a while; she was considering the terms she would make. To her coarse and soured mind there was nothing to scruple at in aiding Coppinger in his suit. The Trevisas were of a fine old Cornish stock, but then Judith took after her mother, the poor Scottish governess, and Aunt Dunes did not feel towards her as though she were of her own kin. The girl looked like her mother. She had no right, in Miss Trevisa's eyes, to bear the name of her father, for her father ought to have known better than stoop to marry a beggarly, outlandish governess. Not very logical reasoning, but what woman, where her feelings are engaged, does reason logically? Aunt Dunes had never loved her niece; she felt an inner repulsion such as sprang from encountering a nature superior, purer, more refined than her own, and the mortification of being forced to admit to herself that it was so. Judith, moreover, was costing her money, and Miss Trevisa parted with her hard-earned savings as reluctantly as with her heart's blood. She begrudged the girl and her brother every penny she was forced, or believed she would be forced, to expend upon them. And was she doing the girl an injury in helping her to a marriage that would assure her a home and a comfortable income?

Aunt Dionysia knew well enough that things went on in Pentyre Glaze that were not to be justified, that Coppinger's mode of life was not one calculated to make a girl of Judith's temperament happy, but—"Hoity-toity!" said Miss Trevisa to herself, "if girls marry, they must take men as they find them. Beggars must not be choosers. You must not look a gift horse in the mouth. No trout can be eaten apart from its bones, nor a rose plucked that is free from thorns." She herself had accommodated herself to the ways of the house, to the moods and manners of Coppinger; and if she could do that, so could a mongrel Trevisa. What was good enough for herself was overgood for Judith.

She had been saddled with these children, much against her wishes, and if she shifted the saddle to the shoulders of one willing to bear it, why not? She had duties to perform to her own self as well as to those thrust on her by the dead hand of that weak, that inconsiderate brother of hers, Peter Trevisa.

Would her brother have approved of her forwarding this union? That was a question that did not trouble her much. Peter did what he thought best for his daughter when he was alive, stuffing her head with Rollin and Blair, and now that he was gone, she must do the best she could for her, and here was a chance offered that she would be a fool not to snap at.

Nor did she concern herself greatly whether Judith's happiness were at stake. Hoity-toity! girls' happiness! They are bound to make themselves happy when they find themselves. The world was not made to fit them, but they to accommodate themselves to the places in which they found themselves in the world.

Miss Trevisa had for some days seen the direction matters were taking, she had seen clearly enough the infatuation—yes, infatuation she said it was—that had possessed Coppinger. What he could see in the girl passed her wits to discover. To her, Judith was an odious little minx—very like her mother. Miss Trevisa, therefore, had had time to weigh the advantages and the disadvantages that might spring to her, should Coppinger persist in his suit and succeed; and she had considered whether it would be worth her while to help or to hinder his suit.

"You put things," said Aunt Dionysia, "in a blunt and a discourteous manner, such as might offend a lady of delicacy, like myself, who am in delicacy a perfect guava jelly—but, Captain, I know your ways, as I ought to, having been an inmate of this house for many years. It is no case of buying and selling, as you insinuate, but the case is plainly this: I know the advantage it will be to my niece to be comfortably provided for. She and Jamie have between them but about a thousand pounds, a sum to starve, and not to live, upon. They have no home and no relative in the world but myself, who am incapable of giving them a home and of doing anything for them except at an excruciating sacrifice. If Judith be found, through your offer, a home, then Jamie also is provided for."

He said nothing to this, but moved his feet impatiently. She went on—"The boy must be provided for. And if Judith become your wife, not only will it be proper for you to see that he is so, but Judith will give neither you nor me our natural rest until the boy is comfortable and happy."

"Confound the boy!"

"It is all very well to say that, but he who would have anything to say to Judith must reckon to have to consider Jamie also. They are inseparable. Now, I assume that by Judith's marriage Jamie is cared for. But how about myself? Is every one to lie in clover and I in stubble? Am I to rack my brains to find a home for my nephew and niece, only that I may be thrust out myself? To find for them places at your table, that I may be deprived of a crust and a bone under it? If no one else will consider me, I must consider myself. I am the last representative of an ancient and honourable family—" She saw Coppinger move his hand, and thought he expressed dissent. She added hastily, "As to Judith and Jamie, they take after their Scotch mother. I do not reckon them as Trevisas."

"Come—tell me what you want," said Coppinger, impatiently.

"I want to be secure for my old age, that I do not spend it in the poor-house."

"What do you ask?"

"Give me an annuity of fifty pounds for my life, and Othello Cottage that is on your land."

"You ask enough."

"You will never get Judith without granting me that."

"Well—get Judith to be mine, and you shall have it."

"Will you swear to it?"

"Yes."

"And give me—I desire that—the promise in writing."

"You shall have it."

"Then I will help you."

"How?"

"Leave that to me. I am her guardian."

"But not of her heart?"

"Leave her to me. You shall win her."

"How?"

"Through Jamie."

## CHAPTER XXI
## OTHELLO COTTAGE

TO REVERT to the old life as far as possible under changed circumstances, to pass a sponge over a terrible succession of pictures, to brush out the vision of horrors from her eyes, and shake the burden of the past off her head—if for a while only—was a joy to Judith. She had been oppressed with nightmare, and now the night was over, her brain clear, and should forget its dreams.

She and Jamie were together, and were children once more; her anxiety for her brother was allayed, and she had broken finally with Cruel Coppinger. Her heart bounded with relief. Jamie was simple and docile as of old; and she rambled with him through the lanes, along the shore, upon the downs, avoiding only one tract of common and one cove.

A child's heart is elastic; eternal droopings it cannot bear. Beaten down, bruised and draggled by the storm, it springs up when the sun shines, and laughs into flower. It is no eucalyptus that ever hangs its leaves; it is a sensitive plant, wincing, closing, at a trifle, feeling acutely, but not for long.

And now Judith had got an idea into her head, that she communicated to Jamie, and her sanguine anticipations kindled his torpid mind. She had resolved to make little shell baskets and other chimney ornaments, not out of the marine shells cast up by the sea, for on that coast none came ashore whole, but out of the myriad snail-shells that strew the downs. They were of all sizes, from a pin's head to a gooseberry, and of various colours—salmon-pink, sulphur-yellow, rich brown and pure white. By judicious arrangement of sizes and of colours, with a little gum on cardboard, what wonderful erections might be made, certain to charm the money out of the pocket, and bring in a little fortune to the twins.

"And then," said Jamie, "I can build a linney, and rent a paddock, and keep my Neddy at Polzeath."

"And," said Judith, "we need be no longer a burden to auntie."

The climax of constructive genius would be exhibited in the formation of a shepherd and shepherdess, for which Judith was to paint faces and hands; but their hats, their garments, their shoes, were to be made of shells. The shepherdess was to have a basket on her arm, and in this basket were to be flowers, not made out of complete shells, but out of particles of sea-shells of rainbow colours.

What laughter, what exultation there was over the shepherd and shepherdess! How in imagination they surpassed the fascinations of Dresden china figures. And the price at which they were to be sold was settled. Nothing under a pound would be accepted, and that would be inadequate to represent the value of such a monument of skill and patience! The shepherd and shepherdess would have to be kept under glass bells, on a drawing-room mantel-shelf.

Judith's life had hitherto been passed between her thoughtful, cultured father and her thoughtless, infantile brother. In some particulars she was old for her age, but in others she was younger than her years. As the companion of her father, she had gained powers of reasoning, a calmness in judging, and a shrewdness of sense which is unusual in a girl of eighteen. But as also the associate of Jamie in his play, she had a childish delight in the simplest amusements, and a readiness to shake off all serious thought and fretting care in an instant, and to accommodate herself to the simplicity of her brother.

Thus—a child with a child—Judith and Jamie were on the common one windy, showery day, collecting shells, laughing, chattering, rejoicing over choice snail-shells, as though neither had passed through a wave of trouble, as though life lay serene before them.

Judith had no experience of the world. With her natural wit and feminine instinct she had discovered that Cruel Coppinger loved her. She had also no hesitation in deciding that he must be repulsed. Should he seek her, she must avoid him. They could not possibly unite their lives. She had told him this, and there the matter ended. He must swallow his disappointment, and think no more about her. No one could have everything he wanted. Other people had to put up with rejection, why not Coppinger? It might be salutary to him to find that he could not have his way in all things. So she argued, and then she put aside from her all thought of the Captain, and gave herself up to consideration of snail-shell boxes, baskets, and shepherds and shepherdesses.

Jamie was developing a marvellous aptitude for bird-stuffing. Mr. Menaida had told Judith repeatedly that if the boy would stick to it, he might become as skilful as himself. He would be most happy, thankful, to be able to pass over to him some of the work that accumulated, and which he could not execute. "I am not a professional; I am an amateur. I only stuff birds to amuse my leisure moments. Provokingly enough, gentlemen do not believe this. They write to me as if I were a tradesman, laying their commands upon me, and I resent it. I have a small income of my own, and am not forced to slave for my bread and 'baccy. Now, if Jamie will work with me and help me, I will cheerfully share profits with him. I must be director—that is understood."

But it was very doubtful whether poor Jamie could be taught to apply himself regularly to the work, and that under a desultory master, who could not himself remain at a task many minutes without becoming exhausted and abandoning it. Jamie could be induced to work only by being humoured. He loved praise. He must be coaxed and flattered to undertake any task that gave trouble. Fortunately, taxidermy did not require any mental effort, and it was the straining of his imperfect mental powers that irritated and exhausted the boy.

With a little cajolery he might be got to do as much as did Uncle Zachie, and if Mr. Menaida were as good as his word—and there could be little doubt that so kind, amiable, and honourable a man would be that—Jamie would really earn a good deal of money. Judith also hoped to earn more with her shell-work, and together she trusted they would be able to support themselves without further tax on Miss Trevisa.

And what a childish pleasure they found in scheming their future, what they would do with their money, where they would take a house, how furnish it! They laughed over their schemes, and their pulses fluttered at the delightful pictures they conjured up. And all their rosy paradise was to rise out of the proceeds of stuffed birds and snail-shell chimney ornaments.

"Ju! come here, Ju!" cried Jamie.

Then again, impatiently, "Ju! come here, Ju!"

"What is it, dear?"

"Here is the very house for us. Do come and see."

On the down, nestled against a wall that had once enclosed a garden, but was now ruinous, stood a cottage. It was built of wreck-timber, thatched with heather and bracken, and with stones laid on the thatching, which was bound with ropes, as protection against the wind. A quaint, small house, with little windows under the low eaves; one storey high, the window-frames painted white; the glass frosted with salt blown from the sea, so that it was impossible to look through the small panes, and discover what was within. The door had a gable over it, and the centre of the gable was occupied by a figure-head of Othello. The Moor of Venice was black and well battered by storm, so that the paint was washed and bitten off him. There was a strong brick chimney in the midst of the roof, but no smoke issued from it, nor had the house the appearance of being inhabited. There were no blinds to the windows, there were no crocks, no drying linen about the house; it had a deserted look, and yet was in good repair.

"Oh, Ju!" said Jamie, "we will live here. Will it not be fun? And I shall have a gun and shoot birds."

"Whose house can it be?" asked Judith.

"I don't know. Ju, the door is open; shall we go in?"

"No, Jamie, we have no right there."

A little gate was in the wall, and Judith looked through. There had at one time certainly been a garden there, but it had been neglected, and allowed to be over-run with weeds. Roses, escallonica, lavender had grown in untrimmed luxuriance. Marigolds rioted over the space like a weed. Pinks flourished, loving the sandy soil, but here and there the rude blue thistle had intruded and asserted its right to the sea-border land as its indigenous home.

Down came the rain, so lashing that Judith was constrained to seek shelter, and, in spite of her protest that she had no right to enter Othello Cottage, she passed the threshold.

No one was within but Jamie, who had not attended to her objection; led by curiosity, and excusing himself by the rain, he had opened the door and gone inside.

The house was unoccupied, and yet was not in a condition of neglect and decay. If no one lived there, yet certainly some one visited it, for it had not that mouldy atmosphere that pervades a house long shut up, nor were dust and sand deep on floor and table. There was furniture, though scanty. The hearth showed traces of having had a fire in it at no very distant period. There were benches. There were even tinder-box and candle on the mantel-shelf.

Jamie was in high excitement and delight. This was the ogre's cottage to which Jack had climbed up the bean-stalk. He was sure to find somewhere the hen that laid golden eggs, and the harp that played of itself.

Judith seated herself on one of the benches and sorted her shells, leaving Jamie to amuse himself. As the house was uninhabited, it did not seem to her that any gross impropriety existed in allowing him to run in and out and peep round the rooms, and into the corners.

"Judith," he exclaimed, coming to her from an adjoining room, "there is a bed in here, and there are crooks in the wall!"

"What are the crooks for, dear?"

"For climbing, I think."

Then he ran back, and she saw no more of him for a while, but heard him scrambling.

She rose and went to the door into the adjoining apartment to see that he was after no mischief. She found that this apartment was intended for sleeping in. There was a bedstead with a mattress on it, but no clothes. Jamie had found some crooks in the wall, and was scrambling up these, with hands and feet, towards the ceiling, where she perceived an opening, apparently into the attic.

"Oh Jamie! what are you doing there?"

"Ju, I want to see whether there is anything between the roof and the ceiling. There may be the harp there, or the hen that lays golden eggs."

"The shower is nearly over; I shall not wait for you."

She seated herself on the bed and watched him. He thrust open a sliding board, and crawled through into the attic. He would soon tire of exploring among the rafters, and would return dirty, and have to be cleared of cobwebs and dust. But it amused the boy. He was ever restless, and she would find it difficult to keep him occupied sitting by her below till the rain ceased, so she allowed him to scramble and search as he pleased. Very few minutes had passed before Judith heard a short cough in the main room, and she at once rose and stepped back into it to apologize for her intrusion. To her great surprise she found her aunt there, at the little window, measuring it.

"A couple of yards will do—double width," said Miss Trevisa.

"Auntie!" exclaimed judith. "Who ever would have thought of seeing you here?"

Miss Trevisa turned sharply round, and her lips tightened.

"And who would have thought of seeing you here," she answered, curtly.

"Auntie, the rain came on; I ran in here so as not to be wet through. To whom does this house belong?"

"To the master—to whom else? Captain Coppinger."

"Are you measuring the window for blinds for him?"

"I am measuring for blinds, but not for him."

"But—who lives here?"

"No one as yet."

"Is any one coming to live here?"

"Yes—I am."

"Oh auntie! and are we to come here with you?"

Miss Trevisa snorted, and stiffened her back.

"Are you out of your senses, like Jamie, to ask such a question? What is the accommodation here? Two little bedrooms, one large kitchen, and a lean-to for scullery—that is all—a fine roomy mansion for three people indeed!"

"But, auntie, are you leaving the Glaze?"

"Yes, I am. Have you any objection to that?"

"No, aunt, only I am surprised. And Captain Cruel lets you have this dear little cottage."

"As to its being dear, I don't know, I am to have it; and that is how you have found it open to poke and pry into. I came up to look round and about me, and then found I had not brought my measuring tape with me, so I returned home for that, and you found the door open and thrust yourself in."

"I am very sorry if I have given you annoyance."

"Oh, it's no annoyance to me. The place is not mine yet."

"But when do you come here, Aunt Dunes?"

"When?" Miss Trevisa looked at her niece with a peculiar expression in her hard face that Judith noticed, but could not interpret. "That," said Miss Trevisa, "I do not know yet."

"I suppose you will do up that dear little garden," said Judith.

Miss Trevisa did not vouchsafe an answer; she grunted, and resumed her measuring.

"Has this cottage been vacant for long, auntie?"

"Yes."

"But, auntie, some one comes here. It is not quite deserted."

Miss Trevisa said to herself, "Four times two and one breadth torn in half to allow for folds will do it. Four times two is eight, and one breadth more is ten."

Just then Jamie appeared, shyly peeping through the door. He had heard his aunt's voice, and was afraid to show himself. Her eye, however, observed him, and in a peremptory tone she ordered him to come forward.

But Jamie would not obey her willingly, and he deemed it best for him to make a dash through the kitchen to the open front door.

"That boy!" growled Miss Trevisa, "I'll be bound he has been at mischief."

"Auntie, I think the rain has ceased, I will say good-bye."

Then Judith left the cottage.

"Ju," said Jamie, when he was with his sister beyond earshot of the aunt, "such fun—I have something to tell you."

"What is it, Jamie?"

"I won't tell you till we get home."

"Oh, Jamie, not till we get back to Polzeath?"

"Well, not till we get half-way home—to the white gate. Then I will tell you."

# CHAPTER XXII
## JAMIE'S RIDE

"Now, Jamie! the white gate."

"The white gate!—what about that?" He had forgotten his promise.

"You have a secret to tell me."

Then the boy began to laugh and to tap his pockets.

"What do you think Ju! look what I have found. Do you know what is in the loft of the cottage we were in? There are piles of tobacco, all up hidden away in the dark under the rafters. I have got my pockets stuffed as full as they will hold. It is for Uncle Zachie. Won't he be pleased?"

"Oh Jamie! you should not have done that."

"Why not? Don't scold, Ju!"

"It is stealing."

"No, it is not. No one lives there."

"Nevertheless it belongs to some one, by whatever means it was got, and for whatever purpose stowed away there. You had no right to touch it."

"Then why do you take snail-shells?"

"They belong to no one, no one values them. It is other with this tobacco. Give it up. Take it back again."

"What—to Aunt Dunes? I daren't, she's so cross."

"Well, give it to me, and I will take it to her. She is now at the cottage, and the tobacco can be replaced."

"Oh, Ju, I should like to see her scramble up the wall!"

"I do not think she will do that; but she will contrive somehow to have the tobacco restored. It is not yours, and I believe it belongs to Captain Cruel. If it be not given back now he may hear of it, and be very angry."

"He would beat me," said the boy, hastily emptying his pockets. "I'd rather have Aunt Dunes'jaw than Captain Cruel's stick." He gave the tobacco to his sister, but he was not in a good humour. He did not see the necessity for restoring it. But Jamie never disobeyed his sister, when they were alone, and she was determined with him. Before others he tried to display his independence, by feeble defiances never long maintained, and ending in a reconciliation with tears and kisses, and promises of submission without demur for the future. With all, even the most docile children, there occur epochs when they try their wings, strut and ruffle their plumes, and crow very loud—epochs of petulance or boisterous out-break of self-assertion in the face of their guides and teachers. If the latter be firm, the trouble passes away to be renewed at a future period till manhood or womanhood is reached, and then guide and teacher who is wise falls back, lays down control, and lets the pupils have their own way. But if at the first attempts at mastery, those in authority, through indifference or feebleness or folly, give way, then the fate of the children is sealed, they are spoiled for ever.

Jamie had his rebellious fits, and they were distressing to Judith, but she never allowed herself to be conquered. She evaded provoking them whenever possible; and as much as possible led him by his affection. He had a very tender heart, was devotedly attached to his sister, and appeals to his better nature were usually successful, not always immediately, but in the long run.

Her association with Jamie had been of benefit to Judith; it had strengthened her character. She had been forced from earliest childhood to be strong where he was weak, to rule because he was incapable of ruling himself. This had nurtured in her a decision of mind, a coolness of judgment, and an inflexibility of purpose unusual in a girl of her years.

Judith walked to Othello Cottage, carrying the tobacco in her skirt, held up by both hands; and Jamie sauntered back to Polzeath, carrying his sister's basket of shells, stopping at intervals to add to the collection, then ensconsing himself in a nook of the hedge to watch a finch, a goldhammer, or a blackbird, then stopped to observe and follow a beetle of gorgeous metallic hues that was running across the path.

Presently he emerged into the highway, the parish road; there was no main road in those parts maintained by toll-gates, and then observed a gig approach in which sat two men, one long and narrow-faced, the other tall, but stout and round-faced. He recognized the former at once as Mr. Scantlebray, the appraiser. Mr. Scantlebray, who was driving, nudged his companion, and with the butt-end of the whip pointed to the boy.

"Heigh! hi-up! Gaffer!" called Mr. Scantlebray, flapping his arms against his sides, much as does a cock with his wings. "Come along; I have something of urgent importance to say to you—something so good that it will make you squeak; something so delicious that it will make your mouth water."

This was addressed to Jamie, as the white mare leisurely trotted up to where the boy stood. Then Scantlebray drew up, with his elbows at right angles to his trunk.

"Here's my brother thirsting, ravening to make your acquaintance—and by George! you are in luck's way, young hopeful, to make his. Obadiah! this here infant is an orphing. Orphing! this is Obadiah Scantlebray, whom I call Scanty because he is fat. Jump up, will y', into the gig."

Jamie looked vacantly about him. He had an idea that he ought to wait for Judith or go directly home. But she had not forbidden him to have a ride, and a ride was what he dearly loved.

"Are you coming?" asked Scantlebray; "or do you need a more ceremonious introduction to Mr. Obadiah, eh?"

"I've got a basket of shells," said Jamie. "They belong to Ju."

"Well, put Ju's basket in—the shells won't hurt—and then in with you. There's a nice little portmantle in front, on which you can sit and look us in the face, and if you don't tumble off with laughing, it will be because I strap you in. My brother is the very comicalest fellow in Cornwall. It's a wonder I haven't died of laughter. I should have, but our paths diverged; he took up the medical line, and I the valuation and all that, so my life was saved. Are you comfortable there?"

"Yes, sir," said Jamie, seating himself where advised.

"Now for the strap round ye," said Scantlebray. "Don't be alarmed; it's to hold you together, lest you split your sides with merriment, and to hold you in, lest you tumble overboard convulsed with laughter. That brother of mine is the killingest man in Great Britain. Look at his face. Bless me! in church I should explode when I saw him, but that I am engrossed in my devotions. On with you, Juno!"

That to the grey mare, and a whip applied to make the grey mare trot along, which she did, with her head down lost in thought, or as if smelling the road, to make sure that she was on the right track.

" 'Tisn't what he says," remarked Mr. Scantlebray, seeing a questioning expression on Jamie's innocent face, "it's the looks of him. And when he speaks— well, it's the way he says it more than what he says. I was at a Charity Trust dinner, and Obadiah said to the waiter, 'Cutlets, please!' The fellow dropped the dish, and I stuffed my napkin into my mouth, ran out, and went into a fit. Now, Scanty, show the young gentleman how to make a rabbit."

Then Mr. Scantlebray tickled up the mare with the lash of his whip, cast some objurgations at a horse-fly that was hovering and then darting at Juno.

Mr. Obadiah drew forth a white but very crumpled kerchief from his pocket, and proceeded to fold it on his lap.

"Just look at him," said the agent, "doing it in spite of the motion of the gig. It's wonderful. But his face is the butchery. I can't look at it for fear of letting go the reins."

The roads were unfrequented; not a person was passed as the party jogged along. Mr. Scantlebray hissed to the mare between his front teeth, which were wide apart; then, turning his eye sideways, observed what his brother was about.

"That's his carcase," said he, in reference to the immature rabbit.

Then a man was sighted coming along the road, humming a tune. It was Mr. Menaida.

"How are you? Compliments to the young lady orphing, and say we're jolly—all three," shouted Scantlebray, urging his mare to a faster pace, and keeping her up to it till they had turned a corner, and Menaida was no more in sight.

"Just look at his face, as he's a-folding of that there pockyhandkercher," said the appraiser. "It's exploding work."

Jamie looked into the stolid features of Mr. Obadiah, and laughed—laughed heartily, laughed till the tears. ran down his cheeks. Not that he saw aught humorous there, but that he was told it was there, he ought to see it, and would be a fool if he were not convulsed by it.

Precisely the same thing happens with us. We look at and go into raptures over a picture, because it is by a Royal Academician who has been knighted on account of his brilliant successes. We are charmed at a cantata, stifling our yawns, because we are told by the art critics who are paid to puff it that we are fools, and have no ears if we do not feel charmed by it. We rush to read a new novel, and find it vastly clever, because an eminent statesman has said on a postcard it has pleased him.

We laugh when told to laugh, condemn when told to condemn, and would stand on our heads if informed that it was bad for us to walk on our feet.

"There!" said Mr. Scantlebray, the valuer. "Them's ears."

"Crrrh!" went Mr. Obadiah, and the handkerchief, converted into a white bunny, shot from his hand up his left sleeve.

"I can't drive, 'pon my honour; I'm too ill. You have done for me to-day," said Scantlebray the elder, the valuer. "Now, young hopeful, what say you? Will you make a rabbit also? I'll give you a shilling if you will."

Thereupon Jamie took the kerchief and spread it out and began to fold it. Whenever he went wrong Mr. Obadiah made signs, either by elevation of his brows and a little shake of his head, or by pointing, and his elder brother caught him at it and protested. Obadiah was the drollest fellow, he was incorrigible, as full of mischief as an egg is full of meat. There was no trusting him for a minute when the eye was off him.

"Come, Scanty! I'll put you on your honour. Look the other way." But a moment after—"Ah, for shame! there you are at it again. Young hopeful, you see what a vicious brother I have; perfectly untrustworthy, but such a comical dog. Full of tricks up to the ears. You should see him make shadows on the wall. He can represent a pig eating out of a trough. You see the ears flap, the jaws move, the eye twinkle in appreciation of the barley-meal. It is to the life, and all done by the two hands—by one, I may say, for the other serves as trough. What! Done the rabbit? First rate! Splendid! Here is the shilling. But, honour bright, you don't deserve it; that naughty Scanty helped you."

"Please," said Jamie, timidly, "may I get out now and go home?"

"Go home! What for?"

"I want to show Ju my shilling."

"By ginger! that is too rich. Not a bit of it. Do you know Mistress Polgrean's sweetie shop?"

"But that's at Wadebridge."

"At Wadebridge; and why not? You will spend your shilling there. But look at my brother. It is distressing; his eyes are alight at the thoughts of the tartlets, and the sticks of peppermint sugar, and the almond rock. Are you partial to almond rock, orphing?"

Jamie's mind was at once engaged.

"Which is it to be? Gingerbreads or tartlets, almond rock or barley-sugar?"

"I think I'll have the peppermint," said Jamie.

"Then peppermint it shall be. And you will give me a little bit, and Scanty a bit, and take a little bit home to Ju, eh?"

"Yes, sir."

"He'll take a little bit home to Ju, Obadiah, old man."

The funny brother nodded.

"And the basket of shells?" asked the elder.

"Yes, she is making little boxes with them to sell," said Jamie.

"I suppose I may have the privilege of buying some," said Mr. Scantlebray senior. "Oh, look at that brother of mine! How he is screwing his nose about! I say, old man, are you ill? Upon my life, I believe he is laughing."

Presently Jamie got restless.

"Please, Mr. Scantlebray, may I get out? Ju will be frightened at my being away so long."

"Poor Ju!" said Scantlebray the elder. "But no —don't you worry your mind about that. We passed Uncle Zachie, and he will tell her where you are, in good hands, or rather, nipped between most reliable knees—my brother's and mine. Sit still. I can't stop Juno; we're going down-hill now, and if I stopped Juno she would fall. You must wait—wait till we get to Mrs. Polgrean's." Then, after chuckling to himself, Scantlebray senior said, "Obadiah, old man, I wonder what Missie Ju is thinking? I wonder what she will say, eh?" Again he chuckled. "No place in your establishment for that party, eh?"

The outskirts of Wadebridge were reached.

"Now may I get out?" said Jamie.

"Bless my heart! Not yet. Wait for Mrs. Polgrean's."

But presently Mrs. Polgrean's shop-window was passed.

"Oh, stop! stop!" cried Jamie. "We have gone by the sweetie shop."

"Of course we have," answered Scantlebray, senior. "I daren't trust that brother of mine in there; he has such a terrible sweet tooth. Besides, I want you to see the pig eating out of the trough. It will kill you. If it don't, I'll give you another shilling."

Presently he drew up at the door of a stiff, square built house, with a rambling wing thrown out on one side. It was stuccoed and painted drab—drab walls, drab windows, and drab door.

"Now, then, young man," said Scantlebray, cheerily, "I'll unbuckle the strap and let you out. You come in with me. This is my brother's mansion, roomy, pleasant, and comprehensive. You shall have a dish of tea."

"And then I may go home?"

"And then—we shall see; shan't we, Obadiah, old man?"

They entered the hall, and the door was shut and fastened behind them; then into a somewhat dreary room, with red flock paper on the walls, no pictures, leather-covered old mahogany chairs, and a book or two on the table—one of these a Bible.

Jamie looked wonderingly about him, a little disposed to cry. He was a long way from Polzeath, and Judith would be waiting for him and anxious, and the place into which he was ushered was not cheery, not inviting.

"Now then," said Mr. Scantlebray, "young hopeful, give me my shilling."

"Please, I'm going to buy some peppermint and burnt almonds for Ju and me as I go back."

"Oh, indeed! But suppose you do not have the chance?"

Jamie looked vacantly in his face, then into that of the stolid brother, who was not preparing to show him the pig feeding out of a trough, nor was he calling for tea.

"Come," said Scantlebray the elder; "suppose I take charge of that shilling till you have the chance of spending it, young man."

"Please, I'll spend it now."

"Not a bit. You won't have the chance. Do you know where you are?"

Jamie looked round in distress. He was becoming frightened at the altered tone of the valuer.

"My dear," said Mr. Scantlebray, "you're now an honourable inmate of my brother's Establishment for Idiots, which you don't leave till cured of imbecility. That shilling, if you please?"

## CHAPTER XXIII
## ALL IS FOR THE BEST IN THE BEST OF WORLDS

JUDITH returned to the cottage of Mr. Menaida, troubled in mind, for Aunt Dunes had been greatly incensed at the taking of the tobacco by Jamie, and not correspondingly gratified by the return of it so promptly by Judith. Miss Trevisa was a woman who magnified and resented any wrong done, but minimized and passed over as unworthy of notice whatever was generous, and every attempt made to repay an evil. Such attempts not only met with no favour from her, but were perverted in her crabbed mind into fresh affronts or injuries. That the theft of Jamie would not have been discovered, had not Judith spoken of it, and brought back what had been taken, was made of no account by Aunt Dionysia; she attacked Judith with sharp reproach for allowing the boy to be mischievous, for indulging him and suffering him to run into danger through his inquisitiveness and thoughtlessness. "For," said Aunt Dionysia, "had the master or any of his men found out what Jamie had done, there is no telling how he might have been served." Then she had muttered, "If you will not take precautions, other folk must, and the boy must be put where he can be properly looked after and kept from interfering with the affairs of others."

On reaching Mr. Menaida's cottage, Judith called her brother, but as she did not receive an answer, she went in quest of him, and was met by the servant, Jump. "If you please, miss," said Jump, "there's been two gen'lemen here, as said they was come from Mrs. Trevisa, and said they was to pack and take off Master Jamie's clothes. And please, miss, I didn't know what to do—they was gen'lemen, and the master —he was out, and you was out, miss—and Master Jamie, he wasn't to home n'other."

"Taken Jamie's clothes!" repeated Judith, in amazement.

"Yes, miss, they brought a portmantle a-purpose; and they'd a gig at the door; and they spoke uncommon pleasant, leastwise one o' them did."

"And where is Jamie? Has he not come home?"

"No, miss."

At that moment Mr. Menaida came in.

"What is it, Judith? Jamie? Where Jamie is?—why, having a ride, seated between the two Scantlebrays, in their gig. That is where he is."

"Oh, Mr. Menaida, but they have taken his clothes!"

"Whose clothes?"

"Jamie's."

"I do not understand."

"The two gentlemen came to this house when you and I were out, and told Jump that they were empowered by my aunt to pack up and carry off all Jamie's clothing, which they put into a portmanteau they had brought with them."

"And then picked up Jamie. He was sitting on the portmanteau," said Uncle Zachie; then his face became grave. "They said that they acted under authority from Mrs. Trevisa?"

"So Jump says."

"It can surely not be that he has been moved to the asylum."

"Asylum, Mr. Menaida?"

"The idiot asylum."

Judith uttered a cry, and staggered back against the wall.

"Jamie! my brother Jamie!"

"Mr. Obadiah Scantlebray has such a place at Wadebridge."

"But Jamie is not an idiot."

"Your aunt authorized them—" mused Uncle Zachie. "Humph! you should see her about it. That is the first step, and ascertain whether she has done it, or whether they are acting with a high hand for themselves. I'll look at my law-books—if the latter it would be actionable."

Judith did not hesitate for a moment. She hastened to Pentyre. That her aunt had left Othello Cottage she was pretty sure, as she was preparing to leave it when Judith returned with the tobacco. Accordingly she took the road to Pentyre at once. Tears of shame and pain welled up in her eyes at the thought of her darling brother being beguiled away to be locked up among the imbecile in a private establishment for the insane. Then her heart was contracted with anger and resentment at the scurvy trick played on her and him. She did not know that the Scantlebrays had been favoured by pure accident. She conceived that men base enough to carry off her brother would watch and wait for the opportunity when to do it unobserved and unopposed. She hardly walked. She ran till her breath failed her, and the rapid throbbing of her heart would no longer allow her to run. Her dread of approaching the Glaze after the declaration made by Captain Cruel was overwhelmed in her immediate desire to know something about Jamie, in her anguish of fear for him. On Coppinger she did not cast a thought—her mind was so fully engrossed in her brother.

She saw nothing of the Captain. She entered the house, and proceeded at once to her aunt's apartment. She found Miss Trevisa there, seated near the window, engaged on some chintz that she thought would do for the window at Othello Cottage, when she took possession of it. She had measured the piece, found that it was suitable, and was turning down a hem and tacking it. It was a pretty chintz, covered with sprigs of nondescript pink and blue flowers.

Judith burst in on her, breathless, her brow covered with dew, her bosom heaving, her face white with distress, and tears standing on her eyelashes. She threw herself on her knees before Miss Trevisa, half crying out and half sobbing—

"Oh, aunt! they have taken him!"

"Who have taken whom?" asked the elderly lady, coldly.

She raised her eyes and cast a look full of malevolence at Judith. She never had, did not, never would feel towards that girl as a niece. She hated her for her mother's sake, and now she felt an unreasonable bitterness against her, because she had fascinated Coppinger—perhaps, also, because in a dim fashion she was aware that she herself was acting towards the child in an unworthy, unmerciful manner, and we all hate those whom we wrong.

"Auntie! tell me it is not so. Mr. Scantlebray and his brother have carried my darling Jamie away."

"Well, and what of that?"

"But—will they let me have him back?"

Miss Trevisa pulled at the chintz. "I will trouble you not to crumple this," she said.

"Aunt! dear aunt! you did not tell Mr. Scantlebray to take Jamie away from me?"

The old lady did not answer, she proceeded to release the material at which she was engaged from under the knees of Judith. The girl, in her vehemence, put her hands to her aunt's arms, between the elbows and shoulders, and held and pressed them back, and with imploring eyes looked into her hard face.

"Oh, auntie! you never sent Jamie to an asylum?"

"I must beg you to let go my arms," said Miss Trevisa. "This conduct strikes me as most indecorous towards one of my age and relationship."

She avoided Judith's eye, her brow wrinkled, and her lips contracted. The gall in her heart rose and overflowed.

"I am not ashamed of what I have done."

"Auntie!" with a cry of pain. Then Judith let go the old lady's arms, and clasped her hands over her eyes.

"Really," said Miss Trevisa, with asperity, "you are a most exasperating person. I shall do with the boy what I see fit. You know very well that he is a thief."

"He never took anything before to-day—never—and you had settled this before you knew about the tobacco!" burst from Judith, in anger and with floods of tears.

"I knew that he has always been troublesome and mischievous, and he must be placed where he can be properly managed by those accustomed to such cases."

"There is nothing the matter with Jamie."

"You have humoured and spoiled him. If he is such a plague to all who know him, it is because he has been treated injudiciously. He is now with men who are experienced, and able to deal with the like of Jamie."

"Aunt, he must not be there. I promised my papa to be ever with him, and to look after him."

"Then it is a pity your father did not set this down in writing. Please to remember that I, and not you, am constituted his guardian, by the terms of the will."

"Oh, aunt! aunt! let him come back to me!"

Miss Trevisa shook her head.

"Then let me go to him!"

"Hoity-toity! here's airs and nonsense. Really, Judith, you are almost imbecile enough to qualify for the asylum. But I cannot afford the cost of you both. Jamie's cost in that establishment will be £70 in the year, and how much do you suppose that you possess?"

Judith remained kneeling upright, with her hands clasped, looking earnestly through her tears at her aunt.

"You have in all, between you, but £45 or £50. When the dilapidations are paid, and the expenses of the funeral, and the will-proving, and all that, I do not suppose you will be found to have a thousand pounds between you, and that put out to interest will not bring you more than I have said; so I shall have to make up the deficiency. That is not pleasing to me, you may well suppose. But I had rather pay £25 out of my poor income, than have the name of the family disgraced by Jamie."

"Jamie will never, never disgrace the name. He is too good. And—it is wicked, it is cruel to put him where you have. He is not an idiot."

"I am perhaps a better judge than you; so also is Mr. Obadiah Scantlebray, who has devoted his life to the care and study of the imbecile. Your brother has weak intellects."

"He is not clever, that is all. With application—"

"He cannot apply his mind. He has no mind that can be got to be applied."

"Aunt, he's no idiot. He must not be kept in that place."

"You had best go back to Polzeath. I have decided on what I considered right. I have done my duty."

"It cannot be just. I will see what Mr. Menaida says. He must be released; if you will not let him out, I will."

Miss Trevisa looked up at her quickly between her half-closed lids; a bitter, cruel smile quivered about her lips. "If any one can deliver him, it will be you."

Judith did not understand her meaning, and Aunt Dionysia did not care at that time to further enlighten her thereon. Finding her aunt inflexible, the unhappy girl left pentyre Glaze and hurried back to Polzeath, where she implored Mr. Menaida to accompany her to Wadebridge. Go there she would—she must—that same evening. If he would not attend her, she would go alone. She could not rest, she could not remain in the house, till she had been to the place where Jamie was, and seen whether she could not release him thence by her entreaties, her urgency.

Mr. Menaida shook his head. But he was a kind-hearted old man, and was distressed at the misery of the girl, and would not hear of her making the expedition alone, as she could not well return before dark. So he assumed his rough and shabby beaver hat, put on his best cravat, and sallied forth with Judith upon her journey to Wadebridge, one that he assured her must be fruitless, and had better be postponed till the morrow.

"I cannot! I cannot!" she cried. "I cannot sleep, thinking of my darling brother in that dreadful place, with such people about him—he crying, frightened, driven mad by the strangeness of it all, and being away from me. I must go. If I cannot save him and bring him back with me, I can see him and console him, and bid him wait in patience and hope."

Mr. Menaida, with a soft heart and a weak will, was hung about with scraps of old-world polish, scraps only. In him nothing was complete—here and there a bare place of rustic uncouthness, there patches of velvet courtesy of the Queen Anne age; so, also, was he made up of fine culture, of classic learning alternating with boorish ignorance—here high principle, there none at all—a picture worked to a miniature in points, and in others rudely roughed in and neglected. Now he was moved as he had not been moved for years by the manifest unhappiness of the girl, and he was willing to do his utmost to assist her, but that utmost consisted in little more than accompanying her to Wadebridge and ringing at the house-bell of Mr. Obadiah Scantlebray's establishment. When it came to the interview that ensued with the proprietor of the establishment and gaoler of Jamie, he failed altogether. Judith and Uncle Zachie were shown into the dreary parlour, without ornaments, and presently to them entered Mr. Obadiah.

"Oh, sir! is he here?—have you got Jamie here?"

Mr. Scantlebray nodded his head, then went to the door and knocked with his fists against the wall. A servant maid appeared. "Send missus," said he, and returned to the parlour.

Again Judith entreated to be told if her brother were there with all the vehemence and fervour of her tattered heart.

Mr. Obadiah listened with stolid face and vacant eyes that turned from her to Mr. Menaida, and then back to her again. Presently an idea occurred to him, and his face brightened. He went to a sideboard, opened a long drawer, brought out a large book, thrust it before Judith, and said, "Pictures." Then, as she took no notice of the book, he opened it.

"Oh, please, sir," pleaded Judith, "I don't want that. I want to know about Jamie. I want to see him."

Then in at the door came a lady in black silk, with small curls about her brow. She was stout, but not florid.

"What!" said she, "my dear, are you the young lady whose brother is here? Don't you fret yourself. He is as comfortable as a chick in a feathered nest. Don't you worry your little self about him now. Now your good days have begun. He will not be a trouble and anxiety to you any more. He is well cared for. I dare be sworn he has given you many an hour of anxiety. Now, O be joyful! that is over, and you can dance and play with a light heart. I have lifted the load off you, I and Mr. Scantlebray. Here he will be very comfortable and perfectly happy. I spare no pains to make my pets snug, and Scantlebray is inexhaustible in his ability to amuse them. He has a way with these innocents that is quite marvellous. Wait a while—give him and me a trial, and see what the result is. You may believe me as one of long and tried experience. It never does for amateurs—for relations—to undertake these cases; they don't know when to be firm, or when to yield. We do—it is our profession. We have studied the half-witted."

"But my brother is not half-witted."

"So you say, and so it becomes you to say. Never admit that there is imbecility or insanity in the family. You are quite right, my dear; you look forward to being married some day, and you know very well it might stand in the way of an engagement, were it supposed that you had idiocy in the family blood. It is quite right. I understand all that sort of thing. We call it nervous debility, and insanity we term nervous excitement. Scantlebray, my poppet, isn't it so?"

Mr. Obadiah nodded.

"You leave all care to us; thrust it upon our shoulders. They will bear it; and never doubt that your brother will be cared for in body and in soul. In body—always something nice and light for supper, tapioca, rice-pudding, batter; to-night, rolly-poly. After that, prayers. We don't feed high, but we feed suitably. If you like to pay a little extra, we will feed higher. Now, my dear, you take all as for the best, and rely on it everything is right."

"But Jamie ought not to be locked up."

"My dear, he is at school under the wisest and most experienced of teachers. You have mismanaged him. Now he will be treated professionally; and Mr. Scantlebray superintends not the studies only, but the amusements of the pupils. He has such a fund of humour in him." Obadiah at once produced his pocket-handkerchief and began to fold it. "No, dear, no, ducky, no rabbit now! You fond thing, you! always thinking of giving entertainment to some one. No, nor the parson preaching either." He was rolling his hands together and thrusting up his thumb as the representative of a sacred orator in his pulpit. "No, ducky darling! another time. My husband is quite a godsend to the nervously prostrate. He can amuse them by the hour; he never wearies of it; he is never so happy as when he is entertaining them. You cannot doubt that your brother will be content in the house of such a man. Take my word for it, there is nothing like believing that all is for the best as it is. Our pupils will soon be going to bed. Rolly-poly and prayers, and then to bed—that is the order."

"Oh, let me see Jamie now."

"No, my dear. It would be injudicious. He is settling in; he is becoming reconciled, and it would disturb him, and undo what has already been done. Don't you say so, poppet?"

The poppet nodded his head.

"You see, this great authority agrees with me. Now, this evening Jamie and the others shall have an extra treat. They shall have the pig eating out of the trough. There—what more can you desire? As soon as lights are brought in, then rolly-poly, prayers, and the pig and the trough. Another time you shall see him. Not to-night. It is inadvisable. Take my word for it, your brother is as happy as a boy can be. He has found plenty of companions of the same condition as himself."

"But he is not an idiot."

"My dear, we know all about that; very nice and sweet for you to say so—isn't it, duckie?"

The duckie agreed it was so.

"There is the bell. My dear, another time. You will promise to come and see me again? I have had such a delightful talk with you. Good-night, good-night. 'All is for the best in the best of worlds.' Put that maxim under your head and sleep upon it."

## CHAPTER XXIV
## A NIGHT EXCURSION

SOME people are ever satisfied with what is certain to give themselves least trouble, especially if that something concerns other persons.

Mr. Menaida was won over by the volubility of Mrs. Scantlebray and the placidity of Mr. Scantlebray to the conviction that Jamie was in the very best place he could possibly be in. A lady who called Judith "my dear" and her husband "duckie" must have a kindly heart, and a gentleman like Mr. Obadiah, so full of resources, could not fail to divert and gratify the minds of those under his charge, and banish care and sorrow. And as Mr. Menaida perceived that it would be a difficult matter to liberate Jamie from the establishment where he was, and as it was an easy matter to conclude that the establishment was admirably adapted to Jamie, he was content that Aunt Dionysia had chosen the wisest course in putting him there, and that it would be to the general advantage to cherish this opinion. For, in the first place, it would pacify Judith, and then, by pacifying her, would give himself none of that inconvenience, that running to and fro between Polzeath and Wadebridge, that consultation of law-books, that correspondence, that getting of toes and fingers into hot water, likely to result from the impatience, the unflagging eagerness of Judith to liberate her brother.

Accordingly Uncle Zachie used his best endeavours to assure Judith that Jamie certainly was happy, had never been so happy in his life before, and that, under the treatment of so kind and experienced a man as Mr. Obadiah Scantlebray, there was reason to believe that in a short time Jamie would issue from under his tuition a light so brilliant as to outshine the beacon on Trevose Head.

Judith was unconvinced. Love is jealous and timorous. She feared lest all should not be as was represented. There was an indefinable something in Mrs. Scantlebray that roused her suspicion. She could not endure that others should step into the place of responsibility towards Jamie she had occupied so long, and which she had so solemnly assured her father she would never abandon. Supposing that Scantlebray and his wife were amiable and considerate persons, might they not so influence the fickle Jamie as to displace her from his affections and insinuate themselves in her room?

But it was not this mainly that troubled her. She was tormented with the thought of the lonely, nervous child in the strange house, among strange people, in desolation of heart and deadly fear.

Whenever he had become excited during the day he was sleepless at night, and had to be soothed and coaxed into slumber. On such occasions she had been wont, with the infinite, inexhaustible patience of true love, to sit by his bed, pacifying his alarms, allaying his agitation, singing to him, stroking his hair, holding his hand, till his eyes closed. And how often, just as he seemed about to drop asleep, had he become again suddenly awake, through some terror, or some imagined discomfort? then all the soothing process had to be gone through again, and it had always been gone through without a murmur or an impatient word.

Now Jamie was alone—or perhaps worse than alone —in a dormitory of idiots, whose strange ways filled him with terror, and his dull mind would be working to discover how he came to be there, how it was that his Ju was not with him. Who would lull his fears, who sing to him old familiar strains? Would any other hand rest on the hot brow and hold it down on the pillow?

Judith looked up to heaven, to the stars already glimmering there. She was not hearkening to the talk of Uncle Zachie: she was thinking her own thoughts. She was indeed walking back to Polzeath; but her mind was nailed to that dull drab house in the suburbs of Wadebridge with the brass plate on the door, inscribed, "Mr.

Scantlebray, Surgeon." As her eyes were raised to the stars, she thought of her father. He was above, looking down on her, and it seemed to her that in the flicker of the stars she saw the trouble in her father's face at the knowledge that his children were parted, and his poor little half-bright boy was fallen among those who had no love for him, might have no patience with his waywardness, would not make allowance for his infirmities.

She sobbed, and would not be comforted by Mr. Menaida's assurances. Tired, foot-weary, but more tired and weary in heart and mind, she reached the cottage. She could not sleep; she was restless. She sought Jamie's room, and seated herself on the chair by his little bed, and sobbed far on into the night. Her head ached, as did her burning and blistered feet; and as she sat she dozed off, then awoke with a start, so distinctly did she seem to hear Jamie's voice—his familiar tone when in distress—crying, "Ju! Come to me, Ju!" So vividly did the voice sound to her that she could not for a moment or two shake off the conviction that she had in reality heard him. She thought that he must have called her. He must be unhappy. What were those people doing to him? Were they tormenting the poor little frightened creature? Were they putting him into a dark room by himself, and was he nearly mad with terror? Were they beating him, because he cried out in the night and disturbed the house?

She imagined him sitting up on a hard bed, shivering with fear, looking round him in the dark, and screaming for her—and she could not help him.

"Oh, Jamie!" she cried, and threw herself on her knees and put her hands over her eyes to shut out the horrible sight, over her ears to close them to the piercing cry. "They will drive him mad! Oh, papa! my papa! what will you say to me? Oh, my Jamie! what can I do for you?"

She was half mad herself, mad with fancies, conjured up by the fever of distress into which she had worked herself. What could she do? She could not breathe in that room. She could not breathe in the house. She could not remain so far from Jamie—and he crying for her. His voice rang still in her ears. It sounded in her heart, it drew her irresistibly away. If she could but be outside that drab establishment in the still night, to listen, and hear if all were quiet within, or whether Jamie were calling, shrieking for her. He would cry himself into fits. He would become really deranged, unless he were pacified. Oh! those people! —she imagined they were up, not knowing what to do with the boy, unable to soothe him, and were now wishing that she were there, wishing they had not sent her away.

Judith was in that condition which is one of half craze through brooding on her fears, through intense sympathy with the unhappy boy so ruthlessly spirited away, through fever of the blood, caused by long-protracted nervous strain, through over-weariness of mind and body. Jamie's distress, his need for her became an idea that laid hold of her, that could not be dispelled, that tortured her into recklessness. She could not lie on her bed, she could not rest her head for one moment. She ran to the window, panting, and smoked the glass with her burning breath, so that she could not see through it.

The night was still, the sky clear, and there were stars in it. Who would be abroad at that time? What danger would ensue to her if she went out and ran back to Wadebridge? If any foot were to be heard on the road, she could hide. She had gone out at night in storm to save Cruel Coppinger—should she not go out in still starlight to aid her own twin-brother, if he needed her? Providence had shielded her before—it would shield her now.

The house was quiet. Mr. Menaida had long ago gone to bed, and was asleep. His snores were usually audible at night through the cottage. Jump was asleep, sound in sleep as any hard-worked sewing-wench. Judith had not undressed, had not taken off her shoes; she had wandered, consumed by restlessness, between her own room and that of her brother.

It was impossible for her to remain there. She felt that she would die of imaginings of evil unless she were near Jamie, unless there were naught but a wall between him and her.

Judith descended the stairs and once again went forth alone into the night, not now to set her face seaward, but landward; before she had gone with a defined aim in view, to warn Coppinger of his danger, now she was moved by a vague suspicion of evil.

The night was calm, but there was summer lightning on the horizon, attended by no thunder, a constant flicker, sometimes a flare, as though some bonfire were kindled beyond the margin of the world, that was being stirred and added to. The air was close.

Judith had no one to look to in the world to help her and Jamie—not her aunt, her sole relative, it was she who had sent her brother to this place of restraint; not Mr. Menaida, he had not the moral courage and energy of purpose to succour her in her effort to release Jamie; not Captain Coppinger—him she dare not ask, lest he should expect too much in return. The hand of misfortune was heavy on the girl; if anything was to be done to relieve the pressure, she must do it herself.

As she was going hastily along the lane she suddenly halted. She heard some one a little way before her. There was no gate near by which she could escape. The lane was narrow, and the hedges low, so as not to afford sufficient shadow to conceal her. By the red summer flashes she saw a man reeling towards her round the corner. His hat was on one side of his head, and he lurched first to one side of the lane, then to the other.

"There went three trav'lers over the moor—  Ri-tiddle-riddle-rol, huph! said he. Three trav'lers over the moor so green, The one sang high, the third sang low,  Ri-tiddle-riddle-rol, huph! said he, And the second he trolled between."

Then he stood still.

"Huph! huph!" he shouted. "Some one else go on, I'm done for—'Ri-tiddle-de.'"

He saw Judith by the starlight and by the flicker of the lightning, and put his head on one side and capered towards her with arms extended, chirping—"'Ri-tiddle-riddle-rol, huph! said he.'"

Judith started on one side, and the drunken man pursued her, but in so doing, stumbled, and fell sprawling on the ground. He scrambled to his feet again, and began to swear at her and send after her a volley of foul and profane words. Had he contented himself with this it would have been bad enough, but he also picked up a stone and threw it. Judith felt a blow on her head, and the lightning flashes seemed to be on all sides of her, and then great black clouds to be rising like smoke out of the earth about her. She staggered into the hedge, and sank on her knees.

But fear lest the tipsy ruffian should pursue her nerved her to make an effort to escape. She quickly rose and ran along the lane, turned the corner, and ran on till her feet would no longer bear her, and her breath failed. Then, looking back, and seeing that she was not followed, she seated herself, breathless, and feeling sick, in the hedge, where a glow-worm was shining, with a calm, steady light, very different from the flicker of the stars above.

As she there sat, she was conscious of something warm on her neck, and putting her hand up, felt that it was moist. She held her fingers to the faint glow of the worm in the grass; there was a dark stain on her hand, and she was sure that it was blood.

She felt her head swim, and knew that in another moment she would lose consciousness, unless she made an effort to resist. Hastily she bound a white handkerchief about her head where wounded by the stone, to stay the flow, and walked resolutely forward.

There was now a shadow stealing up the sky to the south, and obscuring the stars, a shadow behind which danced and wavered the electrical light, but Judith heard no thunder, she had not the leisure to listen for it; all her anxiety was to reach Wadebridge. But the air, the oppressively sultry air, was charged with sound, the mutter and growl of the Atlantic. The ocean, never at rest, ever gives forth a voice, but the volume of its tone varies. Now it was loud and threatening, loud and threatening as it had been on that afternoon when Judith sat with her father in the rectory garden, tossing guelder-roses. Then, the air had been still, but burdened with the menace of the sea. So was it now at midnight; the ocean felt the influence of the distant storm that was playing far away to the south.

Judith could not run now. Her feet were too sore, her strength had given way. Resolute though her will might be, it could not inspire with masculine strength the fragile little body, recently recovered from sickness. But it carried her into the suburbs of Wadebridge, and in the starlight she reached the house of Mr. Obadiah Scantlebray, and stood before it, looking up at it despairingly. It was not drab in colour now, it was lampblack against a sky that flashed in the russet-light. The kerchief she had tied about her head had become loose. Still looking at the ugly, gloomy house, she put up her arms and rebound it, knotting the ends more tightly, using care not to cover her ears, as she was intent to hear the least sound that issued from the asylum. But for some time she could hear nothing save the rush of her blood in her ears, foaming, hissing, like the tide entering a bay over reefs. With this was mingled the mutter of the Atlantic, beyond the hills—and now—yes, certainly now— the rumble of remote thunder.

Judith had stood on the opposite side of the street looking up at Scantlebray's establishment; she saw no light anywhere. Now she drew near and crept along the walls. There was a long wing, with its back to the street, without a window in the wall, and she thought it probable that the inmates of the asylum were accommodated therein, a dormitory upstairs, play or school-rooms below. There Jamie must be. The only windows to this wing opened into the garden; and consequently Judith stole along the garden wall, turned the angle, down a little lane, and stood listening. The wall was high, and the summit encrusted with broken glass. She could see the glass prongs by the flicker of the lightning. She could not possibly see over the wall; the lane was too narrow for her to go back far, and the wall on the further side too high to climb. Not a sound from within reached her ears.

In the still night she stood holding her breath.

Then a scream startled her. It was the cry of a gull flying inland.

If a gull's cry could be heard, then surely that of her brother, were he awake and unhappy, and wanting her.

She went further down the wall, and came on a small garden gate in it, fastened, locked from within. It had a stone step. On that she sank, and laid her head in her hands.

## CHAPTER XXV
## FOUND

STRANGE mystery of human sympathy! inexplicable, yet very real. Irrational, yet very potent. The young mother has accepted an invitation to a garden-party. She knows that she never looked better than at present, with a shade of delicacy about her. She has got a new bonnet that is particularly becoming, and which she desires to wear in public. She has been secluded from society for several months, and she longs to meet her friends again. She knows that she is interesting, and believes herself to be more interesting than she really is. So she goes. She is talking, laughing, a little flushed with pleasure, when suddenly she becomes grave, the hand that holds the plate of raspberries and cream trembles. All her pleasure is gone. She knows that baby is crying. Her eye wanders in quest of her husband, she runs to him, touches his arm, says—

"Do order the carriage; baby is crying."

It is all fiddle-de-dee. Baby has the best of nurses, the snuggest, daintiest little cot; has a fresh-opened tin of condensed Swiss milk. Reason tells her that; but no! and nurse cannot do anything to pacify the child, baby is crying, nurse is in despair.

In like manner now did Judith argue with herself, without being able to convince her heart. Her reason spoke and said to her—

No sound of cries comes from the asylum. There is no light in any window. Every inmate is asleep, Jamie among them. He does not need you. He is travelling in dreamland. The Scantlebrays have been kind to him. The lady is a good, motherly body; the gentleman's whole soul is devoted to finding amusement and entertainment for the afflicted creatures under his care. He has played tricks before Jamie, made shadow-pictures on the wall, told funny stories, made jacks-in-the-box with his hands, and Jamie has laughed till he was tired, and his heavy eyes closed with a laugh not fully laughed out on his lips. The Scantlebrays are paid £70 for taking care of Jamie, and £70 in Judith's estimation was a very princely sum. For £70 per annum Mr. Scantlebray would corruscate into his richest fun, and Mrs. Scantlebray's heart overflow with warmest maternal affection.

But it was in vain that Judith thus reasoned, her heart would not be convinced. An indescribable unrest was in her, and would not be laid. She knew by instinct that Jamie wanted her, was crying for her, was stretching out his hands in the dark for her.

As she sat on the step not only did reason speak, but judgment also. She could do nothing there. She had acted a foolish part in coming all that way in the dark, and without a chance of effecting any deliverance to Jamie now she had reached her destination. She had committed an egregious error in going such a distance from home, from any one who might serve as protector to her in the event of danger, and there were other dangers she might encounter than having stones thrown at her by drunken men. If the watch were to find her there, what explanation of her presence could she give? Would they take her away and lock her up for the rest of the night? They could not leave her there. Large, warm drops, like tears from angels' eyes, fell out of heaven upon her folded hands, and on her bowed neck.

She began to feel chilled after having been heated by her walk, so she rose, and found that she had become stiff. She must move about, however sore and weary her feet might be.

She had explored the lane as far as was needful. She could not see from it into the house, the garden, and playground. Was it possible that there was a lane on the further side of the house which would give her the desired opportunity?

Judith resolved to return by the way she had come, down the lane into the main street, then to walk along the front of the house, and explore the other side. As she was descending the lane she noticed about twenty paces from the door, on the further side, a dense mass of Portugal laurel that hung over the opposite wall, casting a shadow of inky blackness into the lane. This she considered might serve her as shelter when the threatening storm broke and the rain poured down. She walked through this shadow, and would have entered the street, but that she perceived certain dark objects passing noiselessly along it. By the flashes of lightning she could distinguish men with laden asses, and one she saw turn to enter the lane where she was. She drew back hastily into the blot cast by the bush that swung its luxuriance over the wall, and drew as closely back to the wall as was possible. Thus she could not be seen, for the reflection of the lightning would not fall on her; every glare made the shadow seem the deeper. Though concealed herself, and wholly invisible, she was able to distinguish a man with an ass passing by, and then halting at the door in the wall that surrounded Mr. Obediah's tenement. There the man knocked, and uttered a peculiar whistle. As there ensued no immediate answer he knocked and whistled again, whereupon the door was opened, and a word or two was passed.

"How many do you want, sir?"

"Four."

"Any to help to carry the half-ankers?"

"No."

"Well, no odds. I'll carry one and you the t'other. We'll make two journeys, that's all. I can't leave Neddy for long, but I'll go with you to your house door."

Probably the person addressed nodded a reply in the darkness, he made no audible answer.

"Which is it, Mr. Obadiah. Rum or brandy?"

"Brandy."

"Right you are, then. These are brandy. You won't take three brandies and one rum?"

"Yes."

"All right, sir; lead the way. It's deuced dark."

Judith knew what this signified. Some of the householders of Wadebridge were taking in their supplies of spirits from the smugglers. Owing to the inconvenience of it being unlawful to deal with these men for such goods, they had to receive their purchases at night, and with much secrecy. There were watchmen at Wadebridge, but on such nights they judiciously patrolled another quarter of the town than that which received its supplies. The watchmen were municipal officials, and were not connected with the excise, had no particular regard for the Inland Revenue, anyhow, owed no duties to the officers of the coast-guard. Their superior was the mayor, and the mayor was fond of buying his spirits at the cheapest market.

Both men disappeared. The door was left open behind them. The opportunity Judith had desired had come. Dare she seize it? For a moment she questioned her heart, then she resolutely stepped out of the shadow of the Portugal laurel, brushed past the patient ass, entered the grounds of Mr. Scantlebray's establishment through the open garden door, and drew behind a syringa bush to consider what further step she should take. In another moment both men were back.

"You are sure you don't mind one rum?"

"No."

"Right you are, then; I'll have it for you direct. The other kegs are at t'other end of the lane. You come with me, and we'll have 'em down in a jiffy."

Judith heard both men pass out of the door. She looked towards the house. There was a light low down in a door opening into the garden or yard where she was.

Not a moment was to be lost. As soon as the last kegs were brought in the house door would be locked, and though she had entered the garden she would be unable to penetrate to the interior of the asylum. Without hesitation, strong in her earnest purpose to help Jamie to the utmost of her power, and grasping at every chance that offered, she hastened, cautiously indeed, but swiftly, to the door whence the light proceeded. The light was but a feeble one, and cast but a fluttering ray upon the gravel. Judith was careful to walk where it could not fall on her dress.

The whole garden front of the house was not before her. She was in a sort of gravelled yard, with some bushes against the walls. The main block of the house lay to her right, and the view of it was intercepted by a wall. Clearly the garden space was divided, one portion for the house, and another, that into which she had entered, for the wing. That long wing rose before her, with its windows all dark above, and the lower, or ground floor, also dark. Only from the door issued the light, and she saw that a guttering tallow candle was set there on the floor.

Hastily she drew back. She heard feet on the gravel. The men were returning. Mr. Obadiah Scantlebray and the smuggler, each laden with a small cask of spirits.

"Right you are," said the man, as he set his keg down in the passage; "that's yours—and I could drink your health, sir."

"You wouldn't—prefer—?"

Mr. Scantlebray made contortions with his hands between the candle and the wall, and threw a shadow on the surface of plaster.

"No thanky, sir. I'd prefer a shilling."

Mr. Scantlebray fumbled in his pocket, grunted—

"Umph! purse upstairs." Felt again. "No." Groped inside the breast of his waistcoat. "Another time—not forget."

The man muttered something not complimentary, and turned to go through the yard.

"Must lock door," said Mr. Obadiah, and went after him.

Now was Judith's last chance. She took it at once; the moment the backs of the two men were turned she darted into the passage and stood back against the door out of the flare of the candle.

The passage was a sort of hall, with slated floor, the walls plastered, and whitewashed at one time, but the wash and plaster had been picked off to about five feet from the floor wherever not strongly adhesive, giving a diseased and sore look to the wall. The slates of the floor were broken and dirty.

Judith looked along the hall for a place to which she could retreat on the return of the proprietor of the establishment. She had entered that portion of the building tenanted by the unhappy patients. The meanness of the passage, the picked walls, the situation on one side of the comfortable residence, showed her this. A door there was on the right hand, ajar, that led into the private dwelling-house, but into that Judith did not care to enter. One further down on the left probably gave access to some apartment devoted to the "pupils," as Mrs. Scantlebray called the patients.

There was, however, another door that was open, and from it descended a flight of brick steps to what Judith conjectured to be the cellars. At the bottom a second candle, in a tin candlestick, was guttering and flickering in the draught that blew in at the yard door, and descended to this underground story. It was obvious to the girl that Mr. Scantlebray was about to carry or roll the kegs he had just acquired down the brick steps to his cellar. For that purpose he had set a candle there. It would not, therefore, do for her in her attempt to avoid him to descend to this lower region. She must pass the door that gave access to the cellars, a door usually locked, as she judged, for a large iron key stood in the lock, and enter the room the door of which opened further down the passage.

She was drawing her skirts together so as to slip past the candle on the passage floor for this purpose, when her heart stood still as though she had received a blow on it. She heard, proceeding from somewhere beneath, down those steps, a moan, then a feeble cry of, "Ju! where are you? Ju! Ju! Ju!"

She all but cried out herself. A gasp of pain and horror did escape her, and then, without a thought of how she could conceal herself, how avoid Scantlebray, she ran down the steps to the cellars.

On reaching the bottom she found that there were four doors, two of which had square holes cut in them, but with iron bars before these openings. The door of one of the others, one on the left, was open, and she could see casks and bottles. It was a wine and spirit cellar, and the smell of wine issued from it.

She stood panting, frightened, fearing what she might discover, doubting whether she had heard her brother's voice, or whether she was a prey to fancy.

Then again she heard a cry and a moan. It issued from the nearest cell on her right hand.

"Jamie! my Jamie!" she cried.

"Ju! Ju!"

The door was hasped, with a crook let into a staple, so that it might, if necessary, be padlocked. But now it was simply shut, and a wooden peg was thrust through the eye of the crook.

She caught up the candle, and with trembling hand endeavoured to unfasten the door; but so agitated was she, so blinded with horror, that she could not do so till she had put down the candle again. Then she forced the peg from its place and raised the crook. She stooped and took up the candle once more, and then, with a short breath and a contraction of the breast, threw open the door, stepped in, and held up the light.

The candle flame irradiated what was but a cellar compartment, vaulted with brick, once whitewashed, now dirty with cobwebs and accumulated dust and damp-stains. It had a stone shelf on one side, on which lay a broken plate and some scraps of food. Against the further wall was a low truckle bed with a mattress on it and some rags of blanket. Huddled on this lay Jamie, his eyes dilated with terror, and yet red with weeping; all his clothes had been removed, except his shirt; his long red-gold hair had lost its gloss and beauty, it was wet with sweat and knotted; the boy's face was ghastly in the flickering light.

Judith dropped the candle on the floor, and rushed with outstretched arms, and a cry, piercing, but beaten back on her by the walls and vault of the cell, and caught the frightened boy to her heart.

"Jamie; oh, my Jamie!—my Jamie!"

She swayed herself crying on the bed, holding him to her, with no thought, her whole being absorbed in a spasm of intensest, most harrowing pain.

The tallow candle was on the slate floor, fallen, melting, spluttering, flaring. And in the door, holding the brandy keg upon his shoulder, stood, with open eyes and open mouth, Mr. Obadiah Scantlebray.

# CHAPTER XXVI
## ESCAPED

MR. OBADIAH stood open-mouthed, staring at the twins clasped in each other's arms, unable at first to understand what he saw. Then a suspicion entered his dull brain, he uttered a growl, put down the keg, his heavy brows contracted, he shut his mouth, drawing in the lips so that they disappeared, and he clenched his hands.

"Wait—I'll beat you!" he said.

The upset candle was on the floor, now half molten into a pond of tallow, burning with a lambent blue flicker, trembling on extinction, then shooting up in a yellow flare.

In that uncertain, changeful, upward light the face of the man looked threatening, remorseless, so that Judith, in a paroxysm of fear for her brother and herself, dropped on her knee, and caught at the tin candlestick as the only weapon of defence accessible. It was hot, and burnt her fingers, but she did not let go; and as she stood up, the dissolved candle fell from it among some straw that littered the pavement. This at once kindled and blazed up into golden flame.

For a moment the cell was full of light. Mr. Obadiah immediately saw the danger. His casks of brandy were hard by, the fume of alcohol was in the air; if the fire spread and caught his stores, a volume of flame would sweep up the cellar stairs and set his house on fire. He hastily sprang in, and danced about the cell, stamping furiously at the ignited wisps. Judith, who saw him rush forward, thought he was about to strike her or Jamie, and raised the tin candlestick in self-defence; but when she saw him engaged in trampling out the fire, tearing at the bed to drag away the blankets with which to smother the embers, she drew Jamie aside beyond his reach, sidled, with him clinging to her, along the wall, and, by a sudden spring, reached the passage, slammed the door, fastened the hasp, and had the gaoler secured in his own gaol.

For a moment Mr. Scantlebray was unaware that he was a prisoner, so busily engaged was he in trampling out the fire, but the moment he did realize the fact he flung himself with all his force against the door.

"Let me out!"

Judith looked round her. There was now no light in the cellar but the feeble glimmer that descended the stairs from the candle above. The flame of that was now burning steadily, for the door opening into the yard had been shut, and the draught was excluded.

In dragging Jamie along with her Judith had drawn forth a scanty blanket that was about his shoulders; she wrapped it round the boy.

"Let me out!" roared Scantlebray. "Don't understand. Fun—rolicking fun!"

Judith paid no attention to his bellow. She was concerned only to escape with Jamie. She was well aware that her only chance was by retaining Mr. Obadiah where he was.

"Let me out!" again shouted the prisoner, and he threw himself furiously against the door. But though it jarred on its hinges and made the hasp leap, he could not break it down. Nevertheless, so big and strong was the man, that it was by no means improbable that his repeated efforts might start a staple, or snap a hinge band, and he and the door might come together crashing down into the passage between the cells.

Judith drew Jamie up the steps, and, on reaching the top, shut the cellar door. Below, Mr. Scantlebray roared, swore, shouted, and beat against the door; but now his voice and the sound of his blows were muffled, and would almost certainly be inaudible in the dwelling-house.

No wonder that Judith had not heard the cries of her brother. It had never occurred to her that the hapless victims of the keeper of the asylum might be chastised, imprisoned, variously maltreated in regions underground, whence no sounds of distress might reach the street, and apprise the passers-by that all was not laughter within.

Standing in the passage or hall above, Judith said—

"Oh, Jamie! where are your clothes?"

The boy looked into her face with a vacant and distressed expression. He could not answer, he did not even understand her question, so stupefied was he by his terrors and the treatment he had undergone.

Judith took the candle from the floor and searched the hall. Nothing was there save Mr. Scantlebray's coat, which he had removed and cast across one of the kegs when he prepared to convey them down to his cellar. Should she take that? She shook her head at the thought. She would not have it said that she had taken anything out of the house, except only—as that was an extreme necessity—the blanket wrapped about Jamie. She looked into the room that opened beyond the cellar door. It was a great bare apartment, containing nothing save a table and some forms.

"Jamie," she said, "we must get away from this place as we are. There is no help for it. Do you not know where your clothes were put?"

He shook his head. He clung to her with both arms, as though afraid if he held by but one that she would slip away and vanish; he was as one drowning, clinging to the only support that sustained him from sinking.

"Come, Jamie; it cannot be otherwise!" she set down the candle, opened the door into the yard, and issued forth into the night, along with the boy. The clouds had broken, and poured down their deluge of warm thunder-rain. In the dark Judith was unable to find her direction at once, she reached the boundary wall where was the door.

Jamie uttered a cry of pain.

"What is it, dear?"

"The stones cut my feet."

She felt along the wall with one hand till she touched the jamb, then pressed against the door itself. It was shut. She groped for the lock. No key was in it. She could as little escape from that enclosure as she could enter into it from without. The door was very solid, and the lock big and secure. What was to be done? Judith considered for a moment, standing in the pouring rain, through which the lightning flashed obscurely, illuminating nothing. It seemed to her that there was but one course open to her—to return and obtain the key from Mr. Obadiah Scantlebray. But it would be no easy matter to induce him to surrender it.

"Jamie, will you remain at the door? Here under the wall is some shelter. I must go back."

But the boy was frightened at the prospect of being deserted.

"Then, Jamie, will you come back with me to the house?"

No, he would not do that.

"I must go for the key, dearest," she said, coaxingly. "I cannot open the door so that we can escape unless I have the key. Will you do something for Ju? Sit here on the step, where you are somewhat screened from the rain, and sing to me something—one of our old songs—'A jolly goshawk, and his wings were grey'? Sing that, that I may hear your voice and find my way back to you. Oh—and here, Jamie, your feet are just the size of mine, and so you shall pull on my shoes. Then you will be able to run alongside of me and not hurt your soles."

With a little persuasion she induced him to do as she asked. She took off her own shoes and gave them to him, then went across the yard to where was the house. She discovered the door by a little streak of light below it and above the well-trampled and deeply worn threshold stone. She opened the door, took up the candle, and again descended the steps to the cellar floor. On reaching the bottom she held up the light, and saw that the door was still sound; at the square, barred opening was the red face of Mr. Scantlebray.

"Let me out!" he roared.

"Give me the key of the garden door."

"Will you let me out if I do?"

"No; but this I promise: as soon as I have escaped from your premises I will knock and ring at your front door till I have roused the house, and then you will be found and released. By that time we shall have got well away."

"I will not give you the key."

"Then here you remain," said Judith, and began to re-ascend the steps. It had occurred to her, suddenly, that very possibly the key she desired might be in the pocket of the coat Mr. Scantlebray had cast off before descending to the cellar. She would hold no further communication with him till she had ascertained this. He yelled after her—

"Let me out, and you shall have the key."

But she paid no attention to his promise. On reaching the top of the stairs she again shut the door, and took up his coat. She searched the pockets. No key was in them. She must go to him once more.

He began to shout as he saw the flicker of the candle approach, "Here is the key; take it, and do as you said."

His hand, a great coarse hand, was thrust through the opening in the door, and in it was the key she required.

"Very well," said she, "I will do as I undertook."

She put her hand, the right hand, up to receive the key; in her left was the candlestick. Suddenly he let go the key, that clinked down on the floor outside, and made a clutch at her hand and caught her by the wrist. She grasped the bar in the little window, or he would have drawn her hand in, dragged her by the arm up against the door and broken her bones. He now held her wrist, and with his strong hand strove to wrench her fingers from their clutch.

"Unhasp the door!" he howled at her.

She did not answer otherwise than with a cry of pain, as he worked with his hand at her wrist, and verily it seemed as though the fragile bones must snap under his grasp.

"Unhasp the door!" he roared again.

With his great fingers and thick nails he began to thrust at and ploughed her knuckles. He had her by the wrist with one hand, and he was striving to loosen her hold of the bar with the other.

"Unhasp the door!" he yelled a third time, "or I'll break every bone in your fingers!" and he brought his fist down on the side of the door to show how he would pound them by a blow. If he did not do this at once it was because he dreaded by too heavy a blow to strike the bar, and wound himself whilst crushing her hand.

She could not hold the iron stancheon for more than another instant, and when her strength failed, then he would drag her arm in, as a lion in its cage, when it has laid hold of the incautious visitor, tears him to itself through the bars.

Then she brought the candle flame up against his hand that grasped her wrist, and it played round it. He uttered a scream of pain and let go for one moment; but that moment sufficed. She was free. The key was on the floor, she stooped to pick it up, but her fingers were as though paralysed, she was forced to take it with the left hand, and leave the candle on the floor. Then, holding the key, she ran up the steps, ran out into the yard, and heard her brother waiting. "Ju, I want you! Where are you, Ju?" Guided by his cries she reached the door. The key she put into the lock, and with a little effort turned it. The door opened. She and Jamie were free.

The door shut behind them. They were in the dark lane under a pouring rain. But Judith thought nothing of the darkness, nothing of the rain. She threw her arms round her brother, put her wet cheek against his, and burst into tears.

"My Jamie! Oh, my Jamie!"

But the deliverance of her brother was not complete, she must bring him back to Polzeath. She could allow herself but a moment for the relief of her heart, and then she caught him to her side, and pushed on with him along the lane till they entered the street. Here she stood for a moment in uncertainty. Was she bound to fulfil her engagement to Mr. Obadiah? She had obtained the key, but he had behaved to her with treachery. He had not intended the key to be other than a bait to draw her within his clutch, that he might torture her into opening the door of his cell. Nevertheless, she had the key, and Judith was too honourable to take advantage of him. With Jamie still clinging to her, she went up the pair of steps to the front door, rang the night bell, and knocked long and loud. Then, all at once, her strength that had lasted gave way, and she sank on the doorstep, without indeed losing consciousness, but losing in one instant all power of doing or thinking, or striving any more for Jamie or for herself.

## CHAPTER XXVII
## AT HER FEET

A WINDOW overhead was thrown open, and a voice, that Judith recognized as that of Mrs. Obadiah Scantlebray, called: "Who is there? What is wanted?"

The girl could not answer. The power to speak was gone from her. It was as though all her faculties, exerted to the full, had at once given way. She could not rise from the step on which she had sunk: the will to make the effort was gone. Her head had fallen against the jamb of the door, and the knot of the kerchief was between her head and the wood, and it hurt her; but even the will to lift her hands and shift the bandage one inch aside was not present.

The mill-wheel revolves briskly, throwing the foaming water out of its buckets with a lively rattle, then its movement slackens, it strains, the buckets fill and over-spill, but the wheel seems to be reduced to stationariness. That stress-point is but for a moment, then the weight of the water overbalances the strain, and whirr! round plunges the wheel, and the bright, foaming water is whisked about, and the buckets disgorge their contents.

It is the same with the wheel of human life. It has its periods of rapid and glad revolution, and also its moments of supreme tension, when it is all but overstrung, when its movement is hardly perceptible. The strain put on Judith's faculties had been excessive, and now those faculties failed her, failed her absolutely. The prostration might not last long—it might last for ever. It is so sometimes when there has been overexertion: thought stops, will ceases to act, sensation dies into numbness, the heart beats slow—slower—then perhaps stops finally.

It was not quite come to that with Judith. She knew that she had rushed into danger again, the very danger from which she had just escaped; she knew it, but she was incapable of acting on the knowledge.

"Who is below?" was again called from an upper window.

Judith, with open eyes, heard that the rain was still falling heavily, heard the shoot of water from the roof plash down into the runnel of the street, felt the heavy drops come down on her from the architrave over the door, and she saw something in the road-way—shadows stealing along, the same as she had seen before, but passing in a reversed direction. These were again men and beasts, but their feet and hoofs were no longer inaudible: they trod in the puddles and splashed and squelched the water and mud about at each step. The smugglers had delivered the supplies agreed on at the houses of those who dealt with them, and were now returning, the asses no longer laden.

And Judith heard the door behind her unbarred and unchained and unlocked. Then it was opened, and a ray of light was cast into the street, turning the falling rain-drops into drops of liquid gold, and revealing, ghostly, a passing ass and its driver.

"Who is there? Is any one there?"

Then the blaze of light was turned on Judith, and her eyes shut with a spasm of pain.

In the doorway stood Mrs. Scantlebray, half garmented, that is to say, with a gown on, the folds of which fell in very straight lines from her waist to her feet, and with a night-cap on her head, and her curls in papers. She held a lamp in her hand, and this was now directed upon the girl lying, or half sitting, in the doorway, her bandaged head leaning against the jamb, one hand in her lap, the fingers open, the other fallen at her side, hanging down the steps, the fingers in the running current of the gutter, in which also was one shoeless foot.

"Why—goodness! Mercy on us!" exclaimed Mrs. Scantlebray, inconsiderately thrusting the lamp into the girl's face and contracting eyes. "It can never be—yet—surely it is—"

"Judith!" exclaimed a deep voice, the sound of which sent a sudden flutter through the girl's nerves and pulses. "Judith!" and from out the darkness and falling rain plunged a man in full mantle wrapped about him and overhanging broad-brimmed hat. Without a word of excuse he snatched the light from Mrs. Scantlebray and raised it above Judith's head.

"Merciful powers!" he cried, "what is the meaning of this? What has happened? There is blood here— blood! Judith—speak! For Heaven's sake, speak!"

The light fell on his face, his glittering eyes, and she slightly turned her head and looked at him. She opened her mouth to speak, but could form no words; but the appeal in those dim eyes went to his heart. He thrust the lamp roughly back into Mrs. Scantlebray's hand, knelt on the steps, passed one arm under the girl, the other about her waist, lifted and carried her without a word inside the house. There was a leather covered ottoman in the hall, and he laid her on that, hastily throwing off his cloak, folding it, and placing it as a pillow beneath her head.

Then, on one knee at her side, he drew a flask from his breast pocket, and poured some drops of spirit down her throat. The strength of the brandy made her catch her breath, and brought a flash of red to her cheek. It had served its purpose, helped the wheel of life to turn beyond the stress-point at which it threatened to stay wholly. She moved her head, and looked eagerly about her for Jamie. He was not there. She drew a long breath, a sigh of relief.

"Are you better?" he asked, stooping over her: and she could read the intensity of his anxiety in his face. She tried to smile a reply, but the muscles of her lips were too stiff for more than a flutter.

"Run!" ordered Captain Coppinger, standing up. "You, woman! Are you a fool? Where is your husband? He is a doctor; fetch him. The girl might die."

"He—Captain, he is engaged, I believe, taking in his stores."

"Fetch him! Leave the lamp here."

Mrs. Scantlebray groped about for a candle, and having found one proceeded to light it.

"I'm really shocked to appear before you, Captain, in this state of undress."

"Fetch your husband!" said Coppinger, impatiently.

Then she withdrew.

The draught of spirits had acted on Judith, and had revived her. Her breath came more evenly, her heart beat regularly, and the blood began to circulate again. As her bodily powers returned, her mind began to work once more, and again, anxiously, she looked about her.

"What is it you want?" asked Captain Cruel.

"Where is Jamie?"

He muttered a low oath. Always Jamie. She could think of no one but that silly boy.

Then suddenly she realized her position—in Scantlebray's house, and the wife was on the way to the cellars, would find him, release him; and though she knew that Coppinger would not suffer Obadiah to injure her, she feared, in her present weakness, a violent scene. She sat up, dropped her feet on the floor, and stretched both her hands to the smuggler.

"Oh, take me—take me from this place!"

"No, Judith," he answered; "you must have the doctor to see you—after that—"

"No! No! take me before he comes. He will kill me!"

Coppinger laughed. He would like to see the man who would dare to lay a finger on Judith whilst he stood by.

Now they heard a noise from the wing of the house occupied by the patients, and that communicated with the dwelling by a door which Mrs. Scantlebray had left ajar. There were exclamations, oaths, a loud, angry voice, and the shrill tones of the woman mingled with the bass notes of her husband. The colour that had risen to the girl's cheeks left them, she put her hands on Coppinger's breast, and looking him entreatingly in the eyes, said—

"I pray you! I pray you!"

He snatched her up in his arms, drew her close to him, went to the door, cast it open with his foot, and bore her out into the rain. There stood his mare, Black Bess, with a lad holding him.

"Judith, can you ride?"

He lifted her into the saddle.

"Boy," said he, "lead on gently. I will stay her lest she fall."

Then they moved away, and saw through the sheet of falling rain the lighted door, and Scantlebray in it, in his shirt-sleeves, shaking his fists, and his wife behind him endeavouring to draw him back by the buckle and strap of his waistcoat.

"Oh, where is Jamie? I wonder where Jamie is?" said Judith, looking round her in the dark; but she could see no signs of her brother.

There were straggling houses for half a mile; a little gap of garden, or paddock; then a cottage; then a cluster of trees and an ale-house; then hedges, and no more houses. A cooler wind was blowing, dispelling the close, warm atmosphere, and the rain fell less heavily. There was a faint light among the clouds, like a watering of satin. It showed that the storm was passing away. The lightning flashes were, moreover, at longer intervals, fainter, and the thunder rumbled distantly. With the fresher air, some strength and life came back to Judith. The wheel, though on the turn, was not yet revolving rapidly.

Coppinger walked by the horse; he had his arm up, holding Judith, for he feared lest, in her weakness, she might fall; and, indeed, by her weight upon his hand, he was aware that her power to sustain herself unassisted was not come. He looked up at her; he could hardly fail to do so, standing, striding so close to her, her wet garments brushing his face; but he could not see her, or he saw her indistinctly. He had thrust her little foot into the leather of his stirrup, as the strap was too long for her to use the steel, and he did not tarry to shorten it.

Coppinger was much puzzled to learn how Judith had come at such an hour to the door of Mr. Obadiah Scantlebray, shoeless, and with wounded head; but he asked no questions. He was aware that she was not in condition to answer them. He held her up with his right hand in the saddle, and with his left he hold her foot in the leather. Were she to fall, she might drag by the foot, and he must be on his guard against that. Pacing in the darkness, holding her, his heart beat, and his thoughts tossed and boiled within him. This girl—so feeble, so childish—he was coming across incessantly, thrown in her way, to help her, and he was bound to her by ties invisible, impalpable, and yet of such strength that he could not break through them and free himself.

He was a man of indomitable will, of iron strength, staying up this girl, who had flickered out of unconsciousness, and might slide back into it again at any moment, and yet he felt—he knew—that he was powerless before her—that if she said to him, "Lie down, that I may trample on you," he would throw himself in the foul road without a word, to be trodden under by those shoeless feet. There was but one command she could lay on him that he would not perform, and that was, "Let me go by myself! Never come near me!" That he could not obey. The rugged moon revolves about the earth. Would the moon fly away into space were the terrestrial orb to bid it cease to be a satellite? And if it did, whither would it go? Into far-off space, into outer darkness and deathly cold, to split and shiver into fragments in the inconceivable frost in the abyss of blackness. And Judith threw a sort of light and heat over this fierce, undisciplined man that trembled in his veins and bathed his heart, and was to him a spring of beauty, a summer of light. Could he leave her? To leave her would be to be lost to everything that was beginning to transform his existence. The thought came over him now as he walked along in silence—that she might bid him let go, and he felt that he could not obey. He must hold her; he must hold her not from him on the saddle, not as merely staying her up, but to himself, to his heart, as his own, his own for ever.

Suddenly, an exclamation from Judith—"Jamie! Jamie!" Something was visible in the darkness, something whitish, in the hedge. In another moment it came bounding up.

"Ju! oh, Ju! I ran away."

"You did well," she said. "Now I am happy. You are saved."

Coppinger looked impatiently round, and saw by the feeble light that the boy had come close to him, and that he was wrapped in a blanket.

"He has nothing on him," said Judith; "oh, poor Jamie!"

She had revived; she was almost herself again. She held herself more firmly in the saddle, and did not lean so heavily on Coppinger's hand.

Coppinger was vexed at the appearance of the boy Jamie. He would fain had paced along in silence by the side of Judith. If she could not speak, it mattered not so long as he held her. Now that this fool should spring out of the darkness and join company with him and her, and at once awake her interest and loosen her tongue, irritated him. But, as she was able to speak, he would address her, and not allow her to talk over his head with Jamie.

"How have you been hurt?" he asked. "Why have you tied that bandage about your head?"

"I have been cut by a stone."

"How came that?"

"A drunken man threw it at me."

"What was his name?"

"I do not know."

"That is well for him." Then, after a short pause, he asked further, "And your unshod feet?"

"Oh! I gave my shoes to Jamie."

Coppinger turned sharply round on the boy. "Take off those shoes instantly, and give them back to your sister."

"No—indeed, no!" said Judith; "he is running, and will cut his poor feet—and I, through your kindness, am riding."

Coppinger did not insist. He asked, "But how comes this boy to be without clothes?"

"Because I rescued him, as he was, from the asylum."

"You? Is that why you are out at night?"

"Yes; I knew he had been taken by the two Mr. Scantlebrays to Wadebridge, and I could not rest. I felt sure he was miserable, and was crying for me."

"So—in the night you went to him?"

"Yes."

"But how did you get him his freedom?"

"I found him locked in the black hole, in the cellar."

"And did Scantlebray look on passively whilst you released him?"

"Oh, no; I let Jamie out, and locked Mr. Scantlebray in, in his place."

"You—Scantlebray in the black hole?"

"Yes."

Then Coppinger laughed, laughed long and boisterously. His hand that held Judith's foot and the stirrup-leather shook with his laughter.

"By Heaven! you are wonderful—very wonderful. Any one who opposes you is ill-treated, knocked down and broken, or locked in a black hole in the dead of night."

Judith, in spite of her exhaustion, was obliged to smile.

"You see, I must do what I can for Jamie."

"Always—Jamie."

"Yes, Captain Coppinger, always Jamie. He is helpless and must be thought for. I am mother, nurse, sister to him."

"His Providence," sneered Coppinger.

"The means under Providence of preserving him," said Judith.

"And me—would you do aught for me?"

"Did I not go down the cliffs for you?" asked the girl.

"Heaven forgive me that I forgot that for one moment," he answered, with vehemence. "Happy—happy—happiest of any in this vile world is the man for whom you think, and scheme, and care, and dare—as you do for Jamie."

"There is none such," said Judith.

"No—I know that," he answered, gloomily, and strode forward with his head down.

Ten minutes had elapsed in silence, and Polzeath was approached. Then suddenly Coppinger let go his hold of Judith, caught the rein of Black Bess, and arrested her. Standing beside Judith, he said in a peevish, low tone, "I touched your hand, and said I was subject to a queen." He bent, took her foot, and kissed it. "You repulsed me as subject; you are my mistress—accept me as your slave."

## CHAPTER XXVIII
## AN EXAMINATION

SOME days had elapsed. Judith had not suffered from her second night expedition as she had from the first; but the intellectual abilities of Jamie had deteriorated. The fright he had undergone had shaken his nerves, and had made him more restless, timid, and helpless than heretofore, exacting more of Judith's attention, and more trying her endurance. But she trusted that these ill effects would pass away in time. From his rambling talk she had been able to gather some particulars which to a degree modified her opinion relative to the behaviour of Mr. Obadiah Scantlebray. It appeared from the boy's own account that he had been very troublesome. After he had been taken into the wing of the establishment that was occupied by the imbecile, his alarm and bewilderment had grown. He had begun to cry and to clamour for his release, or for the presence of his sister. As night came on, paroxysms of impotent rage had alternated with fits of whining. The appearance of his companions in confinement, some of them complete idiots, with half-human gestures and faces, had enhanced his terrors. He would eat no supper, and when put to bed in the common dormitory had thrown off his clothes, torn his sheets, and refused to lie down—had sat up and screamed at the top of his voice. Nothing that could be done, no representations, would pacify him. He prevented his fellow inmates of the asylum from sleeping, and he made it not at all improbable that his cries would be overheard by passers-by in the street, or those occupying neighbouring houses, and thus give rise to unpleasant surmises, and perhaps inquiry. Finally, Scantlebray had removed the boy to the place of punishment—the black hole—a compartment of the cellars, there to keep him till his lungs were exhausted, or his reason had gained the upper hand. And Judith supposed, with some justice, that Scantlebray had done this only, or chiefly, because he himself would be up and about the cellars, engaged in housing his supplies of brandy, and that he had no intention of locking the unhappy boy up for the entire night in solitude in the cellars. He had not left him in complete darkness, for a candle had been placed on the ground outside the black-hole door.

As Judith saw the matter now, it seemed to her that though Scantlebray had acted with harshness and lack of judgment, there was some palliation for his conduct. That Jamie could be most exasperating, that she knew full well by experience. When he went into one of his fits of temper and crying, it took many hours and much patience to pacify him. She had now and again spent long time and exhausted her efforts in striving to bring him to a subdued frame of mind on occasions when the most irrational and trifling matters had angered him. Nothing answered with him then, save infinite forbearance and exuberant love. On this occasion there was good excuse for Jamie's fit: he had been frightened, and frightened out of his few wits. As Judith said to herself, had she been treated in the same manner—spirited off, without preparation, to a strange house, confined among afflicted beings, deprived of every familiar companion—she would have been filled with terror, and reasonably so. She would not have exhibited it, however, in the same manner as Jamie.

Scantlebray had not acted with gentleness; but he had not, on the other hand, exhibited wanton cruelty. That he was a man of coarse nature, likely on provocation to break through the superficial veneer of amiability, she concluded from her own experience, and she did not doubt that those of the unfortunate inmates of the asylum who overtaxed his forbearance met with very rough handling. But that he took a malignant pleasure in harassing and torturing them, that she did not believe.

On the day following the escape from the asylum, Judith sent Mr. Menaida to Wadebridge with the blanket that had been carried off round the shoulders of her brother, and with a request to have Jamie's clothes surrendered. Uncle Zachie returned with the garments, that were not refused him; and Judith and her brother settled down into the routine of employment and amusement as before. The lad assisted Mr. Menaida with his bird skins, talking a little more childishly than before, and sticking less assiduously to his task; and Judith did her needlework, and occasionally played on the piano the pieces of music at which Uncle Zachie had hammered ineffectually for many years, and she played them to the old man's satisfaction.

At last the girl ventured to induce Jamie to recommence his lessons. He resisted at first, and when she did, on a rainy day, persuade him to set to his school tasks, she was careful not to hold him to them for more than a few minutes, and to select those lessons which made him least impatient.

There was a Goldsmith's Geography, illustrated with copper-plates of Indians attacking Captain Cook, the Geysers, Esquimaux fishery, &c., that always amused the boy. Accordingly more geography was done during these first days of resumption of work than history, arithmetic, or reading. Latin had not yet been attempted, as that was Jamie's particular aversion. However, the Eton Latin Grammar was produced, and placed on the table, to familiarise his mind with the idea that it had to be tackled some day.

Judith had one morning spread the table with lesson-books, with slate and writing-copies, when she was surprised at the entry of four gentlemen, two of whom she recognized immediately as the brothers Scantlebray. The other two she did not know. One was thin-faced, with red hair, a high forehead extending to the crown, with the hair drawn over it and well pomatumed to keep it in place and conceal the baldness; the other a short man, in knee-breeches and top-boots, with a red face, and with breath that perfumed the whole room with spirits. Mr. Scantlebray senior came up with both hands extended.

"This is splendid! How are you? Never more charmed in my life—and ready to impart knowledge as the sun diffuses light. Obadiah, old man, look at your pupil; better already for having passed through your hands. I can see it at a glance; there's a brightness, a je ne sais quoi about him that was not there before. Old man, I congratulate you. You have a gift—shake hands."

The gentlemen seated themselves without invitation. Surprise and alarm made Judith forget her usual courtesy. She feared lest the sight of his gaoler might excite Jamie. But it was not so. Whether in his confused mind he did not associate Mr. Obadiah with his troubles on that night of distress, or whether his attention was distracted by the sight of so many, was doubtful, but Jamie did not seem to be disconcerted—rather, on the contrary, glad of some excuse for escape from lessons.

"We are come," said the red-headed man, "at Mrs. Trevisa's desire—but really, Mr. Scantlebray, for shame of you. Where are your manners? Introduce me."

"Mr. Vokes," said Scantlebray, "and the accomplished and charming Miss Judith Trevisa, orphing."

"And now, dear young lady," said the red-headed man. "Now, positively, it is my turn. My friend, Mr. Jukes. Jukes, man! Miss Judith Trevisa."

Then Mr. Vokes coughed into his thin, white hand, and said, "We are come, naturally—and I am sure you wish what Mrs. Trevisa wishes—to just look at your brother, and give an opinion on his health."

"Oh, he is quite well," said Judith.

"Ah! you think so, naturally; but we would decide for ourselves, dearest young lady, though not for the world would we willingly differ from you. But, you know, these are questions on which varieties of opinion are allowable, and yet do not disturb the most heartfelt friendship. It is so, is it not, Jukes?"

The rubicund man in knee-breeches nodded.

"Shall I begin, Jukes? Why, my fine little man! what an array of books! What scholarship! And at your age, too—astounding! What age did you say you were?" This to Jamie in an insinuating tone. Jamie stared, looked appealingly to Judith, and said nothing.

"We are the same age; we are twins," said Judith.

"Ah! it is not the right thing to appear anxious to know a lady's age. We will put it another way, eh, Jukes?"

The red-faced man leaned his hands on his stick, his chin on his hands, and winked, as in that position he could not nod.

"Now, my fine little man, when is your birthday? when you have your cake— raisin cake, eh?"

Jamie looked questioningly at his sister.

"Ah! come, not the day of the month, but the month, eh?"

Jamie could not answer.

"Come now," said the red-headed, long man, stretching his legs before him, legs vested in white trousers, strapped down tight. "Come now, my splendid specimen of humanity, in which quarter of the year? between sickle and scythe, eh?" He waited, and, receiving no answer, pulled out a pocket-book and made a note, after having first wetted the end of his pencil. "Don't know when he was born! What do you say to that, Jukes? Will you take your turn?"

The man with an inflamed face, now gradually becoming purple, as he leaned forward on his stick, said, "Humph! a Latin Grammar, Propria quæ maribus —I remember it, but it was a long time ago I learnt it. Now, whipper-snapper! how do you go on? Propria qua maribus—go on." He waited. Jamie looked at him in astonishment. "Come! Tribu—" Again he waited. "Come. Tribuuntur mascula dicas— go on." Again a pause. Then with an impatient growl, "Ut sunt Divorum, Mars, Bacchus, Apollo. This will never do. Go on with the scaramouch, Vokes. I'll make my annotation."

"He's too hard on my little chap, ain't he?" asked the thin man in ducks. "We won't be done. We are not old enough."

"He is but eighteen," said Judith.

"He is but eighteen," repeated the red-headed man. "Of course he has not got so far as that, but musæ, musæ—"

Jamie turned sulky.

"Not musa, musa—and eighteen years! Jukes, this is serious, Jukes, eh, Jukes?"

"Now look here, you fellows," said Scantlebray, senior, "you are too exacting. It's holiday time, ain't it, orphing? We won't be put upon, not we. We'll sport and frolic and be joyful. Look here, Scanty, old man, take the slate and draw a pictur' to my describing. Now then, Jamie, look at him and hearken to me. He's the funniest old man that ever was, and he'll surprise you. Are you ready, Scanty?"

Mr. Obadiah drew the slate before him, and signed with the pencil to Jamie to observe him. The boy was quite ready to see him draw.

"There was once upon a time," began Mr. Scantlebray senior, "a man that lived in a round tower. Look at him draw it. There you are; that is the tower. Go on. And in the tower was a round winder. Do you see the winder, orphing? This man every morning put his hand out of the winder to ascertain which way the wind blew. He put it out thus, and drew it in thus. No! don't look at me; look at the slate, and there you'll see it all. Now this man had a large pond, preserved full of fish." Scratch, scratch went the pencil on the slate. "Them's the fish," said Scantlebray, senior. "Now below the situation of that pond, in two huts, lived a pair of thieves. You see them poky things my brother has drawn? Them's the 'uts. When night set in, these wicked thieves came walking up to the pond—see my brother drawing their respective courses—and, on reaching the pond, they opened the sluice, and whish! whish! out poured the water." Scratch, scratch, squeak, squeak, went the pencil on the slate. "There now! the naughty robbers went after fish and got a goose. Look! a goo-oose."

"Where's the goose?" asked Jamie.

"Where? Before your eyes—under your nose. That brilliant brother of mine has drawn one. Hold the slate up, Scanty?"

"That's not a goose," said Jamie.

"Not a goose! You don't know what geese are."

"Yes I do," retorted the boy, resentfully. "I know the wild goose and the tame one—which do you call that?"

"Oh, wild goose, of course."

"It's not one. A goose hasn't a tail like that, nor such legs," said Jamie, contemptuously.

Mr. Scantlebray senior looked at Messrs. Vokes and Jukes and shook his head.

"A bad case. Don't know a goose when he sees it—and he is eighteen."

Both Vokes and Jukes made an entry in their pocket-books.

"Now, Jukes," said Vokes, "will you take a turn, or shall I?"

"Oh, you, Vokes," answered Jukes; "I haven't recovered Propria quæ maribus yet."

"Very well, my interesting young friend. Suppose now we change the subject and try arithmetic."

"I don't want any arithmetic," said Jamie, sulkily.

"No, come now, we won't call it by that name. Suppose some one were to give you a shilling."

Jamie looked up, interested.

"And suppose he were to say, 'There, go and buy sweeties with this shilling.' Tartlets at three for twopence, and barley-sugar at three farthings a stick, and—"

"I want my shilling back," said Jamie, looking straight into the face of Mr. Scantlebray senior.

"And that there were burnt almonds at twopence an ounce—"

"I want my shilling," exclaimed the boy, angrily.

"Your shilling, puff! puff!" said the red-headed man. "This is ideal. An ideal shilling and ideal jam tarts, almond-rock, burnt almonds, or what you like."

"Give me back my shilling? I won it fair," persisted Jamie.

Then Judith, distressed, interfered. "Jamie, dear, what do you mean? You have no shilling owing you."

"I have! I have!" screamed the boy. "I won it fair of that man there, because I made a rabbit, and he took it from me again."

"Hallucinations," said Jukes.

"Quite so," said Vokes.

"Give me my shilling? It is a cheat!" cried Jamie, now suddenly roused into one of his fits of passion.

Judith caught him by the arm, and endeavoured to pacify him.

"Let go, Ju! I will have my shilling. That man took it away. He is a cheat, a thief! Give me my shilling?"

"I am afraid he is excitable," said Vokes.

"Like all irrational beings," answered Jukes. "I'll make a note: 'Rising out of hallucination.'"

"I will have my shilling," persisted Jamie. "Give me my shilling, or I'll throw the ink at you!"

He caught up the ink-pot, and, before Judith had time to interfere, had flung it across the table, intending to hit Mr. Scantlebray senior; but the pot missed him; the black fluid was, however, scattered over Mr. Vokes' white trousers.

"Bless my life!" exclaimed this gentleman, springing to his feet, pulling out his handkerchief to wipe away the ink, and only smearing it the more over his "ducks," and discolouring as well his handkerchief. "Bless my life, Jukes! a dangerous lunatic. Note at once. Clearly comes within the Act—clearly."

In a few minutes all had left, and Judith was endeavouring to pacify her irritated brother. His fingers were blackened, and finally she persuaded him to go upstairs and wash his hands clear of the ink. Then she ran into the adjoining room to Mr. Menaida.

"Oh! dear Mr. Menaida," she said, "what does this mean? Why have they been here?"

Uncle Zachie looked grave and discomposed.

"My dear," said he, "those were doctors, and they have been here, sent by your aunt, to examine into the condition of Jamie's intellects, and to report on what they have observed. There was little going beyond the law, perhaps, at first. That is why they took it so easily when you carried Jamie off. They knew you were with an old lawyer; they knew that you or I could sue for a writ of habeas corpus."

"But do you really think that Aunt Dionysia is going to have Jamie sent back to that man at Wadebridge?"

"I am certain of it. That is why they came here to-day."

"Can I not prevent it?"

"I do not think so. If you go to law—"

"But, if they once get him, they will make an idiot or a madman of him."

"Then you must see your aunt, and persuade her not to send him there."

## CHAPTER XXIX
## ON A PEACOCK'S FEATHER

AS MR. MENAIDA spoke, Miss Dionysia Trevisa entered, stiff, hard, and when her eyes fell on Judith they contracted with an expression of antipathy. In the eyes alone was this observable, for her face was immovable.

"Auntie!" exclaimed Judith, drawing her into the sitting-room, and pressing her to take the armchair. "Oh, auntie! I have so longed to see you. There have been some dreadful men here—doctors, I think—and they have been teazing Jamie till they had worked him into one of his temper fits."

"I sent them here, and for good reasons; Jamie is to go back to Wadebridge."

"No—indeed no, auntie; do not say that. You would not say it if you knew all."

"I know quite enough—more than is pleasing to me. I have heard of your outrageous and unbecoming conduct. Hoity-toity! To think that a Trevisa—but there, you are one only in name—should go out at night about the streets and lanes like a common thing. Bless me! you might have knocked me down with a touch when I was told of it."

"I did nothing outrageous and unbecoming, aunt. You may be sure of that. I am quite aware that I am a Trevisa, and a gentlewoman, and something higher than that, aunt—a Christian. My father never let me forget that."

"Your conduct was—well, I will give it no expletive."

"Aunt, I did what was right. I was sure that Jamie was unhappy and wanted me. I cannot tell you how I knew it, but I was certain of it, and I had no peace till I went; and as I found the garden door open I went in, and, when I went in, I found Jamie locked up in the cellar, and I freed him. Had you found him there you would have done the same."

"I have heard all about it. I want no repetition of a very scandalous story. Against my will I am burdened with an intolerable obligation to look after an idiot nephew, and a niece that is a self-willed and perverse miss."

"Jamie is no idiot," answered Judith, firmly.

"Jamie is what those pronounce him to be who by their age, their profession, and their experience are calculated to judge, better than an ignorant girl not out of her teens."

"Auntie, I believe you have been misinformed. Listen to me, and I will tell you what happened. As for those men—"

"Those men were doctors. Perhaps they were misinformed when they went through the College of Surgeons, were misinstructed by all the medical books they have read, were misdirected by all the study of the mental and bodily maladies of men they have made, in their professional course."

"I wish, dear Aunt Dionysia, you would take Jamie to be with you a few weeks, talk to him, play with him, go walks with him, and you will never say that he is an idiot. He needs careful management, and also a little application—"

"Enough on that theme," interrupted Miss Trevisa; "I have not come here to be drawn into an argument, or to listen to your ideas on the condition of that unhappy, troublesome, that provoking boy. I wish to Heaven I had no the responsibility for him, that has been thrust on me: but as I have to exercise it, and there is no one to relieve me of it, I must do my best, though it is a great expense to me. Seventy pounds is not seventy shillings, nor is it seventy pence."

"Aunt, he is not to go back to the asylum! He must not go."

"Hoity-toity! must not, indeed! You, a minx of eighteen, to dictate to me! Must not, indeed! You seem to think that you, and not I, are Jamie's guardian."

"Papa entrusted him to me with his last words."

"I know nothing about last words. In his will I am constituted his guardian and yours, and as such I shall act as my convenience—conscience, I mean—dictates."

"But, aunt, Jamie is not to go back to Wadebridge. Aunt! I entreat you! I know what that place is. I have been inside it, you have not. I have seen the horrible black hole. You have not. And just think of Jamie on the very first night being locked up there."

"He richly deserved it, I will be bound."

"Oh, aunt! How could he? How could he?"

"Of that Mr. Obadiah Scantlebray was the best judge. Why he had to be punished you do not know."

"Indeed, I do. He cried because the place was strange, and he was among strange faces. Aunt, if you were whipped off to Timbuctoo, and suddenly found yourself among savages, and in a rush apron, as the squaw of a black chief, or whatever they call them in Timbuctooland, would not you scream?"

"Judith," said Miss Trevisa, bridling up. "You forget yourself."

"No, aunt. I am only pleading for Jamie; trying to make you feel for him when he was locked up in an asylum. How would you like it, aunt, if you were snatched away to Bartholomew Fair, and suddenly found yourself among tight-rope dancers, and Jack Puddings?"

"Judith! I insist on you holding your tongue. I object to be associated, even in fancy, with such creatures."

"Well—but Jamie was associated, not in fancy, but in horrible reality, with idiots."

"Jamie goes to Scantlebray's Asylum to-day."

"Auntie!"

"He is already in the hands of the Brothers Scantlebray."

Oh, auntie—no—no!"

"It is no pleasure to me to have to find the money, you may well believe. Seventy pounds is not, as I said, seventy pence, it is not seventy farthings. But duty is duty, and however painful and unpleasant and costly, it must be performed."

Then from the adjoining room, "the shop," came Mr. Menaida.

"I beg pardon for an interruption and for interference," said he. "I happen to have overheard what has passed, as I was engaged in the next room, and I believe that I can make a proposal which will perhaps be acceptable to you, Mrs. Trevisa, and grateful to Miss Judith."

"I am ready to listen to you," said Aunt Dionysia, haughtily.

"It is this," said Uncle Zachie. "I understand that pecuniary matters concerning Jamie are a little irksome. Now, the boy, if he puts his mind to it, can be useful to me. He has a remarkable aptitude for taxidermy. I have more orders on my hands than I can attend to. I am a gentleman, not a tradesman, and I object to be oppressed—flattened out—with the orders piled on top of me. But if the boy will help, he can earn sufficient to pay for his living here, with me."

"Oh, Mr. Menaida! dear Mr. Menaida! thank you so much!" exclaimed Judith.

"Perhaps you will allow me to speak," said Miss Trevisa, with asperity. "I am guardian, and not you: whatever you may think from certain vague expressions dropped casually from my poor brother's lips, and to which you have attached an importance he never gave to them—"

"Aunt, I assure you, my dear papa—"

"That question is closed. We will not reopen it. I am a Trevisa; I can't for a moment imagine where you got those ideas. Not from your father's family, I am sure. Tight-rope dancers and Timbuctoo indeed!" Then she turned to Mr. Menaida, and said, in her hard, constrained voice, as though she were exercising great moral control to prevent herself from snapping at him with her teeth: "Your proposal is kind and well intentioned, but I cannot accept it."

"Oh, aunt! why not?"

"That you shall hear. I must beg you not to interrupt me. You are so familiar with the manners of Timbuctoo and of Bartelmy Fair, that you forget those pertaining to England and to polished society." Then, turning to Mr. Menaida, she said, "I thank you for your well-intentioned proposal, which, however, it is not possible for me to close with. I must consider the boy's ulterior advantage, not the immediate relief to my sorely-tasked purse. I have thought proper to place James with a person, a gentleman of experience, and highly qualified to deal with those mentally afflicted. However much I may value you, Mr. Menaida, you must excuse me for saying that firmness is not a quality you have cultivated with assiduity. Judith, my niece, has almost ruined the boy by humouring him. You cannot stiffen a jelly by setting it in the sun, or in a chair before the fire, and that is what my niece has been doing. The boy must be isinglassed into solidity by those who know how to treat him. Mr. Obadiah Scantlebray is the man—"

"To manufacture idiots, madam, out of simple innocents; it is worth his while at seventy pounds a year," said Uncle Zachie, petulantly.

Miss Trevisa looked at him sternly, and said—

"Sir! I suppose you know best. But it strikes me that such a statement relative to Mr. Obadiah Scantlebray is actionable; but you know best, being a solicitor."

Mr. Menaida winced, and drew back.

Judith leaned against the mantel-shelf, trembling with anxiety, and some anger. She thought that her aunt was acting in a heartless manner towards Jamie; that there was no good reason for refusing the generous offer of Uncle Zachie. In her agitation, unable to keep her fingers at rest, the girl played with the little chimney ornaments. She must occupy her nervous, twitching hands about something; tears of distress and mortification were swelling in her heart, and a fire was burning in two flames in her cheeks. What could she do to save Jamie? What would become of the boy at the asylum? It seemed to her that he would be driven out of his few wits by terror and ill-treatment, with distress at leaving her, and at losing his liberty to ramble about the cliffs where he liked. In a vase on the chimney-piece was a bunch of peacocks' feathers, and in her agitation, not thinking what she was about, desirous only of having something to pick at and play with in her hands, to disguise the trembling of the fingers, she took out one of the plumes, and trifled with it, waving it, and letting the light undulate over its wondrous surface of gold and green and blue.

"As long as I have responsibility for the urchin—" said Miss Dionysia.

"Urchin!" muttered Judith.

"As long as I have the charge I shall do my duty according to my lights, though they may not be those of a rush-aproned squaw in Timbuctoo, nor of a Jack Pudding balancing a feather on his nose." There was here a spiteful glance at Judith. "When my niece has a home of her own, is settled into a position of security and comfort, then I wash my hands of the responsibility; she may do what she likes then—bring her brother to live with her, if she chooses and her husband consents—that will be naught to me."

"And in the meantime," said Judith, holding the peacock's feather very still before her—"In the meantime Jamie's mind is withered and stunted—his whole life is to be spoiled. Now—now alone can he be given a turn aright and towards growth."

"That entirely depends on you," said Miss Trevisa, coldly. "You know best what opportunities have offered—"

"Aunt, what do you mean?"

"Wait," said Uncle Zachie, rubbing his hands. "My boy Oliver is coming home. He has written; his situation is a good one now."

Miss Trevisa turned on him with a face of marble.

"I entirely fail to see what your son Oliver has to do with the matter, more than the man in the moon. May I trouble you, as you so deeply interest yourself in our concerns, to step outside to Messrs. Scantlebray and that boy, and ask them to bring him in here. I have told them what the circumstances are, and they are prepared."

Mr. Menaida left the room, not altogether unwilling to escape.

"Now," said Aunt Dionysia, "I am relieved to find that for a minute we are by ourselves, not subjected to the prying and eavesdropping of the impertinent and the meddlesome. Mr. Menaida is a man who in his life never did good to himself or to any one else, though a man with the best intentions under the sun. Now Judith, I am a plain woman—that is to say, not plain, but straightforward—and I like to have everything above board. The case stands thus: I, in my capacity as guardian of that boy, am resolved to consign him immediately to the asylum, and to retain him there as long as my authority lasts, though it will cost me a pretty sum. You do not desire that he should go there. Well and good. There is but one way, but that is effectual, by means of which you can free Jamie from restraint. Let me tell you he is now in the hands of Mr. Obadiah, and gagged that he may not arouse the neighbourhood with his screams." Miss Trevisa fixed her hard eyes on Judith. "As soon as you take the responsibility off me, and on to yourself, you do with the boy what you like."

"I will relieve you at once."

"You are not in a condition to do so. As soon as I am satisfied that your future is secure, that you will have a house to call your own, and a certainty of subsistence for you both, then I will lay down my charge."

"And you mean—"

"I mean that you must first accept Captain Coppinger, who has been good enough to find you not intolerable. He is—in this one particular—unreasonable; however, he is what he is, in this matter. He makes you the offer, gives you the chance. Take it, and you provide Jamie and yourself with a home; the boy gets his freedom, and you can manage or mismanage him as you list. Refuse the chance, and Jamie is lodged in Mr. Scantlebray's establishment within an hour."

"I cannot decide this on the spur of the moment."

"Very well. You can let Jamie go, provisionally, to the asylum, and stay there till you have made up your mind."

"No—no—no—aunt! Never! never!"

"As you will." Miss Trevisa shrugged her shoulders, and cast a glance at her niece like a dagger-stab.

"Auntie, I am but a child."

"That may be. But there are times when even children must decide momentous questions. A boy, as a child, decides on his profession; a girl, may be, on her marriage."

"Oh, dear auntie! Do leave Jamie here for, say, a fortnight, and in a fortnight from to-day you shall have my answer."

"No," answered Miss Trevisa; "I also must decide on my future, for your decision affects not Jamie only, but me also."

Judith had listened in great self-restraint, holding the feather before her. She held it between thumb and forefinger of both hands, not concerning herself about it, and yet with her eyes watching the undulations from the end of the quill to the deep blue eye set in a halo of gold at the further end, and the feather undulated with every rise and fall of her bosom.

"Surely, auntie, you cannot wish me to marry Cruel Coppinger?"

"I have no wishes one way or the other. Please yourself."

"But, auntie—"

"You profess to be ready to do all you can for Jamie, and yet hesitate about relieving me of an irksome charge, and Jamie of what you consider barbarous treatment."

"You cannot be serious—I to marry Captain Cruel!"

"It is a serious offer."

"But papa! what would he say?"

"I never was in a position to tell his thoughts and guess what his words would be."

"But—auntie, he is such a bad man."

"You know a great deal more about him than do I, of course."

"But—he is a smuggler, I do know that."

"Well—and what of that. There is no crime in that."

"It is not an honest profession. They say, too, that he is a wrecker."

"They say! Who say? What do you know?"

"Nothing; but I am not likely to trust my future to a man of whom such tales are told, auntie. Would you, supposing that you were—"

"I will have none of your suppositions. I never did wear a rush apron, nor act as Juck Pudding."

"I cannot—Captain Cruel of all men."

"Is he so hateful to you?"

"Hateful—no; but I cannot like him. He has been kind; but somehow I can't think of him as—as— as a man of our class and thoughts and ways, as one worthy of my own, own papa. No—it is impossible; I am still a child."

She took the end of the peacock's feather; the splendid eye lustrous with metallic beauty, and bowed the plume, without breaking it, and, unconscious of what she was doing, stroked her lips with it. What a fragile, fine quill that was on which hung so much beauty! and how worthless the feather would be when that quill was broken! And so with her—her fine, elastic, strong spirit, that when bowed sprang to its uprightness the moment the pressure was withdrawn: that strong spirit on which all her charm, her beauty, hung.

"Captain Coppinger has, surely, never asked you to put this alternative to me?"

"No—I do it myself. As you are a child you are unfit to take the charge of your brother. When you are engaged to be married you are a woman; I shift my load on you then."

"And you wish it?"

"I repeat I have no wishes in the matter."

"Give me time to consider."

"No; it must be decided now—that is to say, if you do not wish Jamie to be taken away. Don't fancy I want to persuade you; but I want to be satisfied about my own future. I shall not remain in Pentyre with you. As you enter by the front door, I leave by the back."

"Where will you go?"

"That is my affair."

Then in at the door came the two Scantlebrays, having Jamie between them, gagged, and with his hands bound behind his back. The boy had run out directly his examination was over, and had been secured almost without resistance, so taken by surprise was he, and reduced to a condition of helplessness.

Judith leaned against the mantel-shelf, with every tinge of colour gone out of her cheeks. Jamie's frightened eyes met hers, and he made a slight struggle to speak, and to escape to her.

"You have a close conveyance ready for your patient?" asked Aunt Dionysia of the brothers.

"Oh, yes, a very snug little box on wheels. Scanty and I will sit with our young man, to prevent his feeling dull, you know."

"You understand, gentlemen, what I told you, that in the decision whether the boy is to go with you or not, I am not the only one to be considered? If I have my will, go he shall, as I am convinced that your establishment is the very place for him; but my niece, Miss Judith, has at her option the chance of taking the responsibility for the boy off my shoulders, and if she chooses to do that, why then I fear she will continue to spoil him, as she has done heretofore."

"It has cost us time and money," said Scantlebray senior.

"And you shall be paid, whichever way is decided," said Miss Trevisa. "Everything now rests with my niece."

Judith seemed as one petrified. One hand was on her bosom, staying her heart, the other held the peacock's feather before her, horizontally. Every particle of colour had deserted, not her face only, but her hands as well. Her eyes were sunken, her lips contracted and livid. She was motionless as a marble statue; she hardly seemed to breathe. She perfectly understood what her aunt had laid before her, and her bodily sensations were dead, whilst a conflict of ideas raged in her brain. She was the arbiter of Jamie's fate. She did not disguise from herself that if consigned to the keeper of the asylum, though only for a week or two, he would not leave his charge the same as he entered. And what would it avail her or him to postpone the decision for a week or for a fortnight?

The brothers Scantlebray knew nothing of the question agitating her, but they saw that the determination which she was resolving to arrive at was one that cost her all her powers. Mr. Obadiah's heavy mind did not exert itself to probe the secret, but the more eager intellect of his elder brother was alert, and wondering what might be the matter that so affected the girl, and made it difficult for her to pronounce her decision. The hard eyes of Miss Trevisa were fixed on her. Judith's answer would decide her future; on it depended Othello Cottage, and an annuity of fifty pounds. Jamie looked through a veil of tears at his sister, and never for a moment turned his eyes from her from the moment of his entry into the room. Instinctively the boy felt that his freedom and happiness depended on her.

One or the other must be sacrificed, that Judith saw. Jamie was dull of mind, but there were possibilities of development in it. And, even if he remained where he was, he was happy, happy and really harmless, if a little mischievous; an offer had been made which was likely to lead him on into industrious ways, and to teach him application. He loved his liberty, loved it as does the gull. In an asylum he would pine, his mind become more enfeebled, and he would die. But then—what a price must be paid to save him? Oh, if she could have put the question to her father! But she had none to appeal to for advice. If she gave to Jamie liberty and happiness, it was at the certain sacrifice of her own. But there was no evading the decision, one or the other must be sacrificed.

She stretched forth the peacock's feather, laid the great indigo blue eye on the bands that held Jamie, on his gagged lips, and said, "Let him go."

"You agree," exclaimed Miss Trevisa.

Judith doubled the peacock's feather and broke it.

# CHAPTER XXX
## THROUGH THE TAMARISKS

FOR some days after Judith had given her consent, and had released Jamie from the hands of the Scantlebrays, she remained silent and white. Uncle Zachie missed the music to which he had become used, and complained. She then seated herself at the piano, but was distraught, played badly, and the old bird-stuffer went away, grumbling, to his shop.

Jamie was happy, delighted not to be afflicted with lessons, and forgot past troubles in present pleasures. That the recovery of his liberty had been bought at a heavy price, he did not know, and would not have appreciated it had he been told the sacrifice Judith had been ready to make for his sake.

In the garden behind the cottage was an arbour composed of half a boat set up, that is to say, an old boat sawn in half, and erected, so that it served as a shelter to a seat, which was fixed into the earth on posts. From one side of this boat a trellice had been drawn, and covered with escallonia, and a seat placed here as well, so that in this rude arbour it was possible for more than one person to find accommodation. Here Judith and Jamie often sat; the back of the boat was set against the prevailing wind from the sea, and on this coast the air is usually soft at the same time that it is bracing, enjoyable wherever a little shelter is provided against its violence. For violent it can be, and can buffet severely, yet its blows are those of a pillow.

Here Judith was sitting one afternoon alone, lost in a dream, when Uncle Zachie came into the garden with his pipe in his mouth, to stretch his legs, after a few minutes' work at stuffing a cormorant.

In her lap lay a stocking Judith was knitting for her brother, but she had made few stitches, and yet had been an hour in the summer-house. The garden of Mr. Menaida was hedged off from a neighbour's grounds by a low wall of stone and clay and sand, in and out of which grew rankly strong tamarisks, now in their full pale pink blossom. The eyes of Judith had been on these tamarisks waving like plumes in the sea air, when she was startled from her reverie by the voice of Uncle Zachie.

"Why, Miss Judith! What is the matter with you? Dull, eh? Ah, wait a bit, when Oliver comes home we shall have mirth. He is full of merriment. A bright boy and a good son; altogether a fellow to be proud of, though I say it. He will return at the fall."

"I am glad to hear it, Mr. Menaida. You have not seen him for many years?"

"Not for ten."

"It will be a veritable feast to you. Does he remain long in England?"

"I cannot say. If his employers find work for him at home, then at home he will tarry; but if they consider themselves best served by him at Oporto, then to Portugal must he return."

"Will you honour me by taking a seat near me—under the trellis?" asked Judith. "It will, indeed, be a pleasure to me to have a talk with you; and I do need it very sore. My heart is so full, that I feel I must spill some of it before a friend."

"Then, indeed, I will hold out both hands to catch the sweetness."

"Nay—it is bitter, not sweet, bitter as gall, and briny as the ocean."

"Not possible, a little salt gives savour."

She shook her head, took up the stocking, did a couple of stitches, and put it down again. The sea-breeze that tossed the pink branches of tamarisk waved stray tresses of her red-gold hair, but somehow the brilliancy, the burnish, seemed gone from it. Her eyes were sunken, and there was a greenish tinge about the ivory white surrounding her mouth.

"I cannot work, dear Mr. Menaida; I am so sorry that I should have played badly that sonata last night; I know it fretted you, but I could not help myself, my mind is so selfishly directed, that I cannot attend to anything even of Beethoven's in music, nor to stocking knitting even for Jamie."

"And what are the bitter, briny thoughts?"

Judith did not answer at once, she looked down into her lap, and Mr. Menaida, whose pipe was choked, went to the tamarisks and plucked a little piece, stripped off the flower, and proceeded to clear the tube with it.

Presently, whilst Uncle Zachie's eyes were engaged on the pipe, Judith looked up, and said hastily, "I am very young, Mr. Menaida."

"A fault in process of rectification every day," said he, blowing through the stem of his pipe. "I think it is clear now."

"I mean—young to be married."

"To be married—zounds!" He turned his eyes on her in surprise, holding the tamarisk spill in one hand, and the pipe in the other, poised in the air.

"You have not understood that I got Jamie off the other day only by taking full charge of him upon myself, and relieving my aunt."

"But, good gracious, you are not going to marry your brother."

"My aunt would not transfer the guardianship to me unless I were qualified to undertake and exercise it properly, according to her ideas, and that could be only by my becoming engaged to be married to a man of substance."

"Goodness help me! what a startlement! And who is the happy man to be? Not Scantlebray, senior, I trust, whose wife is dying?"

"No—Captain Coppinger."

"Cruel Coppinger!" Uncle Zachie put down his pipe so suddenly on the bench by him that he broke it. "Cruel Coppinger! Never!"

She said nothing to this, but rose and walked, with her head down, along under the bank, and put her hands among the waving pink branches of tamarisk bloom, sweeping the heads with her own delicate hand as she passed. Then she came back to the boat-arbour and reseated herself.

"Dear me! Bless my heart! I could not have credited it," gasped Mr. Menaida; "and I had such different plans in my head—but there, no more about them."

"I had to make my election whether to take him and qualify to become Jamie's guardian, or refrain, and then he would have been snatched away and imprisoned in that odious place again."

"But my dear Miss Judith—" The old man was so agitated that he did not know what he was about; he put the stick of tamarisk into his mouth in place of his pipe, and took it out to speak, put down his hand, picked up the bowl of his pipe, and tapped the end of the tamarisk spill with that. "Mercy save me! What a world we do live in! And I had been building for you a castle—not in Spain, but in a contiguous country. Who'd have thought it? And Cruel Coppinger too! Upon my soul, I don't want to say I am sorry for it, and I can't find in my heart to say I'm glad."

"I do not expect that you will be glad—not if you have any love for me."

The old man turned round; his eyes were watering and his face twitching.

"I have. Heaven knows I have, Ju—I mean Miss Judith!"

"Mr. Menaida," said the girl, "you have been so kind, so considerate, that I should like to call you what every one else does when speaking of you to one another—not to your face—Uncle Zachie."

He put out his hand—it was shaking—and caught hers. He put the ends of the fingers to his lips, but he kept his face averted, and the water that had formed in his eyes ran down his cheeks. He did not venture to speak. He had lost command over his voice.

"You see, uncle, I have no one of whom to ask counsel. I have only aunt, and she—somehow I feel that I cannot go to her and get from her the advice best suited to me. Now papa is dead I am entirely alone, and I have to decide on matters most affecting my own life and that of Jamie. I do so crave for a friend who could give me an opinion, but I have no one if you refuse."

He pressed her hand.

"Not that now I can go back from my word. I have passed that to Aunt Dionysia, and draw back I may not; but somehow, as I sit and think and think, and try to screw myself up to the resolution that must be reached of giving up my hand and my whole life into the power of—of that man, I cannot attain to it. I feel like one who is condemned to cast himself down a precipice and shrinks from it, cannot make up his mind to spring, but draws back after every run made to the edge. Tell me—uncle—tell me truly, what do you think about Captain Coppinger? What do you know about him? Is he a very wicked man?"

"You ask me what I think, and also what I know," said Mr. Menaida, releasing her hand. "I know nothing, but I have my thoughts."

"Then tell me what you think."

"As I have said, I know nothing. I do not know whence he comes. Some say he is a Dane, some that he is a Frenchman. I cannot tell, I know nothing, but I think his intonation is Irish, and I have heard that there is a family of that name in Ireland. But this is all guess-work. One thing I do know—he speaks French like a native. Then, as to his character. I believe him to be a man of ungovernable temper, who, when his blood is roused, will stick at nothing. I think him a man of very few scruples. But he has done liberal things; he is open-handed—that all say. A hard liver, and with a rough tongue, and yet with some of the polish of a gentleman; a man with the passions of a devil, but not without in him some sparks of divine light. That is what I think him to be. And, if you ask me further, whether I think him a man calculated to make you happy, I say decidedly that he is not."

Barely ever before in his life had Mr. Menaida spoken with such decision.

"He has been kind to me," said Judith, "very kind."

"Because he is in love with you."

"And gentle—"

"Have you ever done aught to anger him?"

"Yes; I threw him down and broke his arm and collar-bone."

"And won his heart by so doing."

"Uncle Zachie, he is a smuggler."

"Yes; there is no doubt about that."

"Do you suppose, if I were to entreat him, that he would abandon smuggling? I have already had it in my heart to ask him this, but I could not bring the request over my lips."

"I have no doubt if you asked him to throw up his smuggling that he would promise to do so. Whether he would keep his promise is another matter. Many a girl has made her lover swear to give up gambling, and on that understanding has married him, but I reckon none have been able to keep their husbands to the engagement. Gambling, smuggling, and poaching, my dear, are in the blood. A man brings the love of adventure, the love of running a risk, into the world with him. If I had been made by my wife to swear when I married never to touch a musical instrument, I might, out of love for her, have sworn, but I could not have kept my oath. And you, if you vowed to keep your fingers from needle and thread, and you saw your gown in rags, or your husband's linen frayed, would find an irresistible itch in the fingers' ends to mend and hem, and you would do it in spite of your vow. So with a gambler, a poacher, and a smuggler—the instinct, the passion is in them, and is irresistible. Don't impose any promise on Captain Cruel; it will not tie him."

"They tell me he is a wrecker."

"What do you mean by a wrecker? We are all wreckers, after a storm, when a merchantman has gone to pieces on the rocks, and the shore is strewn with prizes. I have taken what I could, and I see no harm in it. When the sea throws treasures here and there, it is a sin not to take them up and use them, and be thankful."

"I do not mean that. I mean that he has been the means of luring ships to their destruction."

"Of that I know nothing. Stories circulate whenever there is a wreck not in foul weather or with a wind on shore. But who can say whether they be true or false?"

"And what about that man Wyvill? Did he kill him?"

"There, also, I can say nothing, because I know nothing. All that can be said about the matter is that the Preventive man Wyvill was found at sea, or washed ashore without his head. A shark may have done it, and sharks have been found off our coast. I cannot tell. There is not a shadow of evidence that could justify an indictment. All that can be stated that makes against Coppinger is that the one is a smuggler, the other was a Preventive man, and that the latter was found dead, and with his head off, an unusual circumstance, but not sufficient to show that he had been decapitated by any man, nor that the man who decapitated him was Coppinger."

Then Mr. Menaida started up. "And—you sell yourself to this man for Jamie?"

"Yes, uncle, to make a man of Jamie."

"On the chance, Judith, on the very doubtful chance, of making a man of Jamie you rush on the certainty of making a ruin of yourself. That man—that Coppinger to be trusted with you! A fair little vessel, richly laden, with silken said and cedar sides, comes skimming over the sea, and—Heaven forgive me if I judge wrongly—but I think he is a wrecker, enticing, constraining you on to the reefs where you will break up, and all your treasures will—not fall to him—but sink; and all that will remain of you will be a battered and broken hull and a draggled, discoloured sail. I cannot—I cannot endure the thought."

"Yet it must be endured, faced and endured by me," said Judith. "You are a cruel comforter, Uncle Zachie. I called you to encourage me, and you cast me down, to lighten my load, and you heap more on."

"I can do no other," gasped Mr. Mendaida. Then he sprang back, with open mouth, aghast. He saw Cruel Coppinger on the other side of the hedge; he had put his hands to the tamarisk bushes, and had thrust them apart, and was looking through.

"Goldfish!" called Captain Coppinger—"Goldfish, come!"

Judith knew the voice, and looked in the direction whence it came, and saw the large hands of Coppinger holding back the boughs of tamarisk, his dark face in the gap. She rose at once, and stepped towards him.

"You are ill," he said, fixing his sombre eyes on her.

"I am not ill in body. I have had much to harass my mind."

"Yes, that Wadebridge business."

"Much that has sprung out of it."

"Shall I come to you, or will you to me?—through the tamarisks?"

"As you will, Captain Coppinger."

"Come, then—up on to the hedge and jump. I will catch you in my arms. I have held you there ere this."

"Yes, you have taken me up; now must I throw—"

She did not finish the sentence; she meant must she voluntarily throw herself into his arms. She caught hold of the bushes, and raised herself to the top of the hedge.

"By Heaven!" said he, "the tamarisk flowers have more colour in them than your face."

She stood on the summit of the bank, the tamarisks rising to her knees, waving in the wind about her. Must she resign herself to that man of whom she knew so little, whom she feared so greatly? There was no help for it. She must. He held out his arms. She sprang, and he caught her.

"I have you now," he said, with a laugh of triumph. "You have come to me, and I will never give you up."

## CHAPTER XXXI
## AMONG THE SAND-HEAPS

COPPINGER held her in his arms, shook her hair out so that it streamed over his arm; and thus he looked into her upturned face.

"Indeed you are light—lighter than when I bare you in my arms before; and you are thin and white, and the eyes, how red! You have been crying. What! the spirit, strong as a steel spring, is so subdued that it gives way to weeping!"

Judith's eyes were closed against the strong light from the sky above, and against the sight of his face bent over hers, and the fire-glint of his eyes, dark as a thundercloud, and as full charged with lightnings. And now there was a flashing of fire from them, of love, and pride, and admiration. The strong man trembled beneath his burden in the vehemence of his emotion, with the boiling and foaming of his heart within him, as he held the frail child in his arms, and knew that in a short space she was to be his own, his own wholly. It was for the moment to him as though all earth and sea and heaven were dissolved into nebulous chaos, and the only life, the only pulses, in the universe were in him and the little creature he held to his breast. He looked into her face, down on her as Vesuvius must have looked down on lovely, marble-white Pompeii, with its gilded roofs and incense-scented temples, and restrained itself so long as it could restrain its molten heart, before it poured forth its fires and consumed the pearly city lying in its arms.

He looked at her closed eyelids, with the long golden lashes resting on the dark sunken dip beneath, at the delicate mouth drawn as with pain, at the white temples in which slowly throbbed the blue veins, at the profusion of red-gold hair streaming over his arm and almost touching the ground.

She knew that his eyes—on fire—were on her, and she dared not meet them, for there would be a shrinking from him, no responsive leap of flame from hers.

"Shall I carry you about like this?" he asked. "I could, and I would, to the world's end, and leap with you thence into the unfathomed abyss."

Her head, leaning back on his arm, with the gold rain from it falling, exposed her long and delicate throat of exquisite purity of tint and beauty of modelling, and on it lay a little tuft of pink tamarisk blossom, brushed off in her leap into his arms, and then caught in the light edging of her gown at the neck.

"And you came to me of your own will!" he said.

Then Judith slightly turned her head to avoid his eyes, and said, "I have come—it was unavoidable. Let me down that we may speak together."

He obeyed with reluctance. Then, standing before him, she bound up and fastened her hair.

"Look!" said he, and threw open his collar. A ribbon was tied about his throat. "Do you see this?" He loosed the band and held it to her. One delicate line of gold ran along the silk, fastened to it by threads at intervals. "Your one hair—the one left with me when you first heard me speak my heart's wish, and you disdained me and went your way. You left me that one hair, and that one hair I have kept wound round my neck ever since, and it has seemed to me that I might still hope so long as I retained that hair. And see—I have caught my goldfish, my saucy goldfish that at first swam away from my hook."

Judith said, calmly, "Let us walk together somewhere—to S. Enodoc, to my father's grave, and then, over that sand-heap, we will settle what must be settled."

"I will go with you where you will. You are my queen—I your subject; it is my place to obey."

"The subject has sometimes risen and destroyed the queen. It has been so in France."

"Yes, when the subject has been too hardly treated, too downtrodden, not allowed to look on and adore the queen."

"And," said Judith, further, "let us walk in silence. Allow me the little space between here and my father's grave to collect my thoughts. Bear with me for that short distance."

"As you will. I am your slave, as I have told you, and you, my mistress, have but to command."

"Yes, but the slave sometimes becomes the master, and then is all the more tyrannous because of his former servitude."

So they walked together, yet apart, from Polzeath, to S. Enodoc, neither speaking, and it might have been a mourner's walk at a funeral. She held her head down, and did not raise her eyes from the ground, but he continued to gaze on her with a glow of triumph and exultation in his face.

They reached at length the deserted church, sunken in the sands; it had a hole broken in the wall under the eaves on the south, rudely barricaded, through which the sacred building might be entered for such functions as a marriage, or the first part of the funeral office, that must be performed in a church.

The roof was of pale grey slate, small, much broken, folding over the rafters, like the skin on the ribs of an old horse past work. The churchyard was covered with blown sand, gravestones were in process of being buried, like those whom they commemorated. Some stood a little above the sand, with a fat cherub's head peering above the surface, others stood high on the land side, but were banked up by sand towards the sea. Here the churchyard surface was smooth, there it was tossed into undulations, according as the sand had been swept over portions tenanted by the poor who were uncommemorated with headstones, or over those where lay the well-to-do with their titles and virtues registered above them.

There was as yet no monument erected over the grave of the Reverend Peter Trevisa, sometime rector of S. Enodoc. The mound had been turfed over and bound down with withies. The loving hands of his daughter had planted above where he lay some of the old favourite flowers from the long walk at the rectory, but they had not as yet taken to the soil; the sand ill-agreed with them, and the season of the year when their translation had taken place dissatisfied them; they looked forlorn, drooping, and doubted whether they would make the struggle to live.

Below the church lay the mouth of the Camel, blue between sand-hills, with the Doom Bar, a long and treacherous bank of shifting sands, in the midst.

On reaching the churchyard Judith signed to Captain Coppinger to seat himself on a flat tombstone on the south side of her father's grave, and she herself leaned against the headstone that marked her mother's tomb.

"I think we should come to a thorough understanding," she said, with composure, "that you may not expect of me what I cannot give, and may know the reason why I give you anything. You call me goldfish. Why?"

"Because of your golden hair."

"No, that was not what sprung the idea in your brain; it was something I said to you—that you and I stood to each other in the relation of bird of prey to fish, belonging to distinct modes of life and manner of thinking, and that we could never to be one another in any other relation than that, the falcon and his prey, the flame and its fuel, the wrecker and the wrecked."

Coppinger started up and became red as blood.

"These are strange words," he said.

"It is the same that I said before."

"Then why have you given yourself to me?"

"I have resigned myself to you as I cannot help myself, any more than can the fish that is pounced on by the sea bird, or the fuel that is enveloped by the flame, or the ship that is boarded by the wreckers."

She looked up at him steadily; he was quivering with excitement, anger, and disappointment.

"It is quite right that you should know what to expect, and make no more demands on me than I am capable of answering. You cannot ask of me that I should become like you, and I do not entertain the foolish thought that you could be brought to be like me—to see through my eyes, feel with my heart. My dead father lies between us now, and he will ever be between us—he a man of pure life, noble aspirations, a man of books, of high principle, fearing God and loving men. What he was, that he tried to make me. Imperfectly, faultily, I follow him, but, though unable to be like him, I strive after what he showed me should be my ideal."

"You are a child. You will be a woman, and new thoughts will come to you."

"Will they be good and honourable and contented thoughts? Shall I find these in your house?"

Coppinger did not reply; his brows were drawn together, and his face became dark.

"Why, then, have you promised to come to me?"

"Because of Jamie."

He uttered an oath, and with his hands clenched the upper stone of the tomb.

"I have promised my aunt that I will accept you if you will suffer my poor brother to live where I live, and permit me to be his protector. He is helpless, and must have some one to think and watch for him. My aunt would have sent him to Mr. Obadiah Scantlebray's asylum, and that would have been fatal to him. To save him from that I said that I would be yours, on the condition that my home should be him home. I have passed my word to my aunt, and I will not go from it, but that does not mean that I have changed my belief that we are unfitted for each other, because we belong to different orders of being."

"This is cold comfort."

"It is cold as ice, but it is all that I have to give to you. I wish to put everything plainly before you now, that there may be no misapprehension later, and you may be asking of me what I cannot give, and be angry at not receiving what I never promised to surrender."

"So! I am only accepted for the sake of that boy James."

"It is painful for me to say what I do—as painful as it must be for you to hear it, but I cannot help myself. I wish to put all coldly and hardly before you before an irrevocable step is taken, such as might make us both wretched. I take you for Jamie's sake. Were his happiness, his well-being, not in the scale, I would not take you. I would remain free."

"That is plain enough," exclaimed Coppinger, setting his teeth, and he broke off a piece of the tombstone on which he was half sitting.

"You will ask of me love, honour, and obedience. I will do my best to love you—like you I do now, for you have been kind and good to me, and I can never forget what you have done for me. But it is a long leap from liking to loving. Still I will try my best, and if I fail it will not be for lack of effort. Honour is another matter. That lies in your own power to give. If you behave as a good and worthy man to your follows, and justly towards me, of course I shall honour you. I must honour what is deserving of honour, and where I honour there I may come to love. I cannot love where I do not honour, so perhaps I may say that my heart is in your hands, and that if those hands are clean and righteous in their dealings, it may become yours come time. As to obedience—that you shall command. That I will render to you frankly and fully in all things lawful."

"You offer me an orange from which all the juice has been squeezed, a nut without a kernel."

"I offer you all I have to offer. Is it worth your while having this?"

"Yes!" said he, angrily, starting up; "I will have what I can, and wring the rest out of you when once you are mine."

"You never will wring anything out of me. I give what I may, but nothing will I yield to force."

He looked at her sullenly and said, "A child in years, with an old head and a stony heart."

"I have always lived with my father, and so have come to think like one that is old," said Judith. "And now, alone in the world, I must think with ripened wits."

"I do not want that precocious, wise soul, if that be the kernel. I will have the shell—the glorious shell. Keep your wisdom and righteousness and piety for yourself. I do not value them a rush; but your love I will have."

"I have told you there is but one way by which that may be won. But, indeed, Captain Coppinger, you have made a great mistake in thinking of me. I am not suited to you to make you happy and content, any more than you are suited to me. Look out for some girl more fit to be your mate."

"Of what sort? Come, tell me!" said Coppinger, scornfully.

"A fine, well-built girl, dark-haired, dark-eyed, with cheeks as apricots, lively in mood, with nimble tongue, good-natured, not bookish, not caring for brush or piano; one who can take a rough word and return it; who will not wince at an oath, and shrink away at coarse words flung about where she is. All these things you know very well must be encountered by your wife in your house. Did you ever read 'Hamlet,' Captain Coppinger?"

He made no answer; he was plucking at the slab-cover of the tomb, and grinding his heels into the sand.

"In 'Hamlet' we read of a king poisoned by his queen, who dipped the juice of cursed hebenon into his ears, and it curdled all his blood. It is the same with the sort of language that is found in your house when your seamen are there. I cannot endure it, it curdles my heart. Choose a girl who is indifferent."

"You shall not be subjected to it," said Coppinger; "and, as to the girl you have sketched, I care not for her. Such as you describe are to be found thick as whortleberries on a moor. Do you not know that man seeks in marriage not his counterpart but his contrast? It is because you are in all things different from me that I love you."

"Then, will naught that I have said make you desist?"

"Naught."

"I have told you that I take you only so as to be able to make a home for Jamie."

"Yes."

"And that I do not love you, and hardly think I ever can."

"Yes."

"And still—you will have me?"

"Yes."

"And that by taking me you wreck my life, spoil my happiness."

He raised his head, then dropped it again, and said— "Yes."

She remained silent, also looking on the ground. Presently she raised her head and said—

"I gave you a chance, and you have cast it from you. I am sorry."

"A chance? What chance?"

"The chance of taking a first step up the ladder in my esteem."

"I do not understand you."

"Therefore I am sorry."

"What is your meaning?"

"Captain Coppinger," said Judith, firmly, looking straight into his dark face and flickering eyes, "I am very, very sorry. When I told you that I accepted your offer only because I could not help myself, because I was a poor, feeble orphan, with a great responsibility laid on me, the charge of my unfortunate brother—that I only accepted you for his sake; when I told you that I did not love you; that our characters, our feelings, were so different, that it would be misery to me to become your wife, that it would be the ruin of my life —then, had you been a man of generous soul, you would have said: 'I will not force myself upon you, but I will do one thing for you, assist you in protecting Jamie from the evil that menaces him.' Had you said that, I would have honoured you, and, as I said just now, where I honour there I may love. But you could not think such a thought, no such generous feeling stirred you. You hold me to my bond."

"I hold you to your bond!" exclaimed Coppinger, in livid rage; "I hold you, indeed. Even though you can neither love nor honour me, you shall be mine. You likened me to a bird of prey that must have its prey or die; to a fire, and that must have its fuel; to a wrecker, and he must have his wreck. I care not. I will have you as mine whether you love me or not."

"So be it, then," said Judith, sadly. "You had your opportunity, and have put it from you. We understand each other. The slave is master—and a tyrant."

# CHAPTER XXXII
## A DANGEROUS GIFT

"I du love a proper muddle cruel bad, I du," said Jump; and had what she loved, for the preparations for Judith's marriage threw Mr. Menaida's twin cottage into a "proper muddle." There were the cakes to be baked, and for a while the interior of the house was pervaded by that most delicious aroma of baking bread, superior to Frangipanni, Jockey Club, and Wood Violet. Then came the dusting, and after that the shaking and beating of rugs, and sofa and chairs. Then it was discovered that the ceiling and walls would be the better for white and colour-wash. This entailed the turning out of everything previously dusted and tidied and arranged. Neither Mr. Menaida nor Jump had any other idea of getting things into order than that of throwing all into a muddle in the hopes that out of chaos creation and order might spring.

A dressmaker had been engaged, and material purchased for the fabrication of a trousseau. This naturally interested Jump vastly, and Jump paid repeated visits to the dressmaker whilst engaged on her work. On one such occasion she neglected the kitchen, and allowed some jam to become burnt. On another she so interested the needlewoman, and diverted her attention from her work whilst cutting out, that the latter cut out two right arms to the wedding-gown. This involved a difficulty, as it was not practicable either to turn the one sleeve, and convert it into a left arm, nor to remove Judith's left arm and attach it to the right side of her body, and so accommodate her to the gown. The mercer at Camelford was communicated with, from whom the material had been procured, but he was out of it. He, however, was in daily expectation of a consignment of more of the same stuff. A fortnight later he was able to supply the material, sufficient for a left sleeve, but unfortunately of a different colour. The gown had to be laid aside till some one could be found of Judith's size and figure, with two right arms, and also who wanted a wedding-dress, and, also, would be disposed to take this particular one at half the cost of the material, or else to let the gown stand over till after the lapse of a century or thereabouts, when the fashion would prevail for ladies to wear sleeves of a different substance and colour from their bodies and skirts.

"'Taint a sort o' a courtin' as I'd give a thankee for," said Jump. "There was Camelford Goose Fair, and whether he axed her to go wi' him and pick a goose I can't tell, but I know her never went. Then a' Sundays they don't walk one another out. And he don't come arter her to the back garden, and she go to him, and no whisperings and kissings. I've listened a score o' times a hoping and a wishing to see and hear the likes, and never once, as I'm a Christian and a female. There were my sister Jane, when she was going to be married, her got that hot and blazin' red that I thought it were scarlatina, but it was naught but excitement. But the young mistress—bless 'ee! her gets whiter and colder every day, and I'd say, if such a thing were possible, that her'd rather her never was a going to be married, but you see that ain't in natur'— leastways wi' us females. I tell 'ee I never seed him once put his arm round her waist. If this be courtin' among gentlefolks, all I say is, preserve and deliver me from being a lady."

It was as Jump in her vulgar way put it. Judith alone in the house appeared to take no interest in the preparations. It was only after a struggle with her aunt that she had yielded to have the wedding in November. She had wished it postponed till the spring, but Cruel Coppinger and Aunt Dionysia were each for their several ends desirous to have it in the late autumn. Coppinger had the impatience of a lover, and Miss Trevisa the desire to be free from a menial position, and lodged in her own house before winter set in. She had amused herself over Othello Cottage ever since that Judith had yielded her consent, and her niece saw little of her accordingly.

It suited Coppinger's interest to have a tenant for the solitary cottage, and that a tenant who would excite no suspicion, as the house was employed as a store for various run goods, and it was understood between him and Miss Trevisa that he was still to employ the garret for the purposes that suited him.

Had Othello Cottage remained long unoccupied, it was almost certain to attract the attention of the Preventive men, awake their suspicions, and be subjected to a visit. Its position was convenient, it was on the cliff of that cove where was the cave in which the smugglers' boats were concealed.

Coppinger visited Polzeath, and saw Judith whenever he came to Mr. Menaida's house, but his wooing met with no response. She endured his attentions, shrinking from the slightest approach to familiarity, and though studiously courteous, was never affectionate. It would have taken a heavy charge of self-conceit to have made the Captain blind to the fact that she did not love him, that, in truth, she viewed her approaching marriage with repugnance. Coppinger was a proud, but not a conceited, man, and her coldness and aversion roused his anger, for it galled his pride. Had he been a man of noble impulse, he would have released her, as she had plainly told him, but he was too selfish, too bent on carrying out his own will to think of abandoning his suit.

Her lack of reciprocation did not abate his passion; it aggravated it. It enlisted his self-esteem in the cause, and he would not give her up, because he had set his mind upon obtaining her, and to confess his defeat would have been a humiliation insufferable to his haughty spirit. But it was not merely that he would not, it was also that he could not. Coppinger was a man who had all his life long done what he willed, till his will had become in him the mainspring of his existence, and drove him to execute his purposes in disregard of reason, safety, justice. What he willed he must do. He could not brook opposition. He would eat out his own furious heart in impotent rage, if his will encountered impossibility of execution. And he was of a sanguine temperament. Hitherto every opposition had been overthrown before him, therefore he could not conceive that the heart of a young girl, a mere child, could stand out against him permanently. For a while it might resist, but ultimately it must yield, and then the surrender would be absolute, unconditional.

Every time he came to see her, he came with hopes, almost with confidence, that the icy barrier would dissolve, but when he was in her presence, the chill from it struck him, numbed his heart, silenced his tongue, deadened his thoughts. Yet no sooner was he gone from the house, than his pulses leaped, his brain whirled, and he was consumed with mortified pride and disappointed love. He could not be rough, passionate, and imperious with her. A something he could not understand, certainly not define, streamed from her that kept him at a distance and quelled his insolence. It was to him at moments as if he hated her; but this hate was but the splutter of frustrated love. He recalled the words she had spoken to him, the terms she had employed in speaking of the relation in which they stood to each other, the only relation to her conceivable in which they could stand to each other, and each such word was a spark of fire, a drop of flaming phosphorus on his heart, torturing it with pain, and unquenchable. A word once spoken can never be recalled, and these words had been thrown red hot at him, had sunk in and continued to consume where they had fallen. He was but a rapacious bird and she the prey, he the fire and she the fuel, he the wrecker and she the wreck. There could be no reciprocity between them; the bird in the talons of the hawk, rent by his beak, could do no other than shiver and shriek, and struggle to be free. The fuel could but expect to be consumed to ashes in the flame; and the wrecked must submit to the wrecker. He brooded over these similes, he chafed under the conviction that there was truth in them, he fought against the idea that a return of his love was impossible—and then his passion raged and roared up in a fury that was no other than hatred of the woman who could not be his in heart. Then, in another moment, he cooled down, and trusted that what he dreaded would not be. He saw before him the child, white as a lily, with hair as the anthers of the lily—so small, so fragile, so weak; and he laughed to think that one such, with no experience of life, one who had never tasted love, could prove insensible to his devouring passion. The white asbestos in the flame glows, and never loses its delicacy and its whiteness.

And Judith was, as Jump observed, becoming paler and more silent as her marriage drew on. The repugnance with which she had viewed it instead of abating, intensified with every day. She woke in the night with a start of horror, and a cold sweat poured from her. She clasped her hands over her eyes, and buried her face in her pillow and trembled, so that the bed rattled. She lost all appetite. Her throat was contracted when she touched food. She found it impossible to turn her mind to the preparations that were being made for her wedding; she suffered her aunt to order for her what she liked; she was indifferent when told of the blunder made by the dressmaker in her wedding-gown. She could not speak at meals. When Mr. Menaida began to talk, she seemed to listen, but her mind was elsewhere. She resumed lessons with Jamie, but was too abstracted to be able to teach effectually. A restlessness took hold of her, and impelled her to be out of doors and alone. Any society was painful to her. She could endure only to be alone; and when alone, she did nothing save pluck at her dress, or rub her fingers one over the other—the tricks and convulsive movements of one on the verge of death.

But she did not yield to her aversion without an effort to accustom herself to the inevitable. She rehearsed to herself the good traits she had observed in Coppinger, his kindness, his forbearance towards herself. She took cognizance of his efforts to win her regard, to afford her pleasure; his avoidance of everything that he thought might displease her. And when she knew he was coming to visit her, she strove with herself and formed the resolution to break down her coldness, and to show him some of that semblance of affection which he might justly expect. But it was in vain. No sooner did she hear his step, or the first words he uttered—no sooner did she see him, than she turned to stone, and the power to even feign an affection she did not possess, left her. And when Coppinger had departed, there was stamped red hot on her brain the conviction that she could not possibly endure life with him.

She prayed long and often, sometimes by her father's grave, always in bed when lying wakeful, tossing from side to side in anguish of mind, often, very often when on the cliffs looking out to sea, to the dark, leaden, sullen sea, that had lost all the laughter and colour of summer. But prayer afforded her no consolation. The thought of marriage to such a man, whom she could not respect, whose whole nature was inferior to her own, was a thought of horror. She could have nerved herself to death by the most excruciating of torments, but for this—not all the grace of heaven could fortify her.

To be his mate, to be capable of loving him, she must descend to his level, and that she neither could nor would do. His prey, his fuel, his wreck—that she must became, but she could be nothing else—nothing else. As the day of her marriage approached, her nervous trepidation become so acute that she could hardly endure the least noise. A strange footfall startled her and threw her into a paroxysm of trembling. The sudden opening of a door made her heart stand still.

When her father had died, poignant though her sorrow had been, she had enjoyed the full powers of her mind. She had thought about the necessary preparations for the funeral, she had given orders to the servants, she had talked over the dear father to Jamie, she had wept his loss till her eyes were red. Not so now: she could not turn her thoughts from the all-absorbing terror; she could not endure an allusion to it from any one, least of all to speak of it to her brother. And the power to weep was taken from her. Her eyes were dry—they burnt, but were unfilled by tears.

When her father was dead she could look forward, think of him in Paradise, and hope to rejoin him after having trustily executed the charge imposed on her by him. But now she could not look ahead. A shadow of horror lay before her, an impenetrable curtain. Her father was covering his face, was sunk in grief in his celestial abode; he could not help her. She could not go to him with the same open brow and childish smile as before. She must creep to his feet, and lay her head there, sullied by association with one against whom he had warned her, one whom he had regarded as the man that had marred his sacred utility, one who stood far below the stage of virtue and culture that belonged to his family, and on which he had firmly planted his child. What was in her heart Judith could pour out before none; certainly not before Aunt Dionysia, devoid of a particle of sympathy with her niece. Nor could she speak her trouble to Uncle Zachie, a man void of resources, kind, able for a minute or two to sympathize, but never to go deeply into any trouble, and understand more of a wound than the fester on the surface. Besides, of what avail to communicate the anguish of her heart to any one, when nothing could be done to alter the circumstances. She could not now draw back. Indeed it never occurred to her to be possible to go back from her undertaking. To save Jamie from an idiot asylum she had passed her word to give her hand at the altar to Cruel Coppinger, and her word was sacred. Aunt Dionysia trusted her word. Coppinger held to it. Knowing that she gave it on compulsion and reluctantly, yet he showed his perfect confidence in its security.

"My dear Judith," said Mr. Menaida, "I am so sorry about losing you, and what is more, losing Jamie, for. I know very well that when he is at the Glaze, he will find plenty to amuse him without coming to see me, or, anyhow, coming to work with me."

"I hope not, dear uncle."

"Yes, I lose a promising pupil." Then, turning to the boy, he said: "Jamie, I hope you will not give up stuffing birds, or—if you have not the patience to do that, that you will secure the skins and prepare them for me."

"Yes, I will," said Jamie.

"Yes, yes, my dear boy," said Menaida; "but don't you fancy I am going to trust you with arsenic for preparing the skins. I shall give that to your sister, and she will keep the supply, eh?—will you not Judith?"

"Yes, I will take charge of it."

"And let him have it as needed, never more than is needed."

"Why not?" asked Jamie.

"Because it is a dangerous thing to have lying about." Menaida ran into the workshop, and came back with a small tin box of the poison. "Look here! here is a little bone spoon. Don't get the powder over your fingers. Why—a spoonful would make a man very ill, and two would kill him. So, Judith, I trust this to you. When Jamie has a skin to prepare, he will go to you, and you will let him have only so much as he requires."

"Yes uncle."

She took the little tin of arsenic and put it into her work-box, under the tray that contained reels and needles.

## CHAPTER XXXIII
## HALF A MARRIAGE

ONE REQUEST Judith had made, relative to her marriage, and one only, after she had given way about the time when it was to take place, and this request concerned the place. She desired to be married, not in the parish church of S. Minver, but in that of S. Enodoc, in the yard of which lay her father and mother, and in which her father had occasionally ministered.

It was true that no great display could be made in a building half filled with sand, but neither Judith nor Coppinger, nor Aunt Dionysia desired display, and Jump, the sole person who wished that the wedding should be in full gala, was not consulted in the matter.

November scowled over sea and land, perverting the former into lead, and blighting the latter to a dingy brown.

The wedding day was sad. Mist enveloped the coast, wreathed the cliffs, drifted like smoke over the glebe, and lay upon the ocean dense and motionless, like a mass of cotton wool. Not a smile of sun, not a glimmer of sky, not a trace of outline in the haze over head. The air was full of minute particles of moisture, flying aimlessly, lost to all sense of gravity, in every direction. The mist had a fringe but no seams, and looked as if it were as unrendable as felt. It trailed over the soil, here lifting a ragged flock or tag of fog a few feet above the earth, there dropping it again, and smearing water over all it touched.

Vapour condensed on every twig and leaf, but only leisurely, and slowly dripped from the ends of thorns and of leaves, but the weight of the water on some of the frosted and sickly foliage brought the leaves down with it. Every stone in every wall was lined with trickles of water like snail crawls. The vapour penetrated within doors, and made all articles damp, of whatever sort they were. Fires were reluctant to kindle, chimneys smoked. The grates and irons broke out into eruptions of rust, mildew appeared on walls, leaks in roofs. The slate floors became dark and moist. Forks and spoons adhered to the hands of those who touched them, and on the keys of Mr. Menaida's piano drops formed.

What smoke did escape from a chimney trailed down the roof. Decomposed leaves exhaled the scent of decay. From every stackyard came a musty odour of wet straw and hay. Stableyards emitted their most fetid exudation, that oozed through the gates and stained the roads. The cabbages in the kailyards, touched by frost, announced that they were in decomposition, and the turnips that they were in rampant degeneration and rottenness. The very seaweed, washed ashore, impregnated the mist with the flavour of decay.

The new rector, the Reverend Desiderius Mules, had been in residence at S. Enodoc for three months. He had received but a hundred and twenty-seven pounds four and ninepence farthing for dilapidations, and was angry, declared himself cheated, and vowed he would never employ the agent Cargreen any more. And a hundred and twenty-seven pounds four and ninepence farthing went a very little way towards repairing and altering the rectory to make it habitable to the liking of the Reverend Desiderius. The Reverend Peter Trevisa and his predecessors had been West Country men, and as such loved the sun, and chose to have the best rooms of the house with a southern aspect. But the Reverend Desiderius Mules had been reared in Barbadoes, and hated the sun, and elected to have the best rooms of the house to look north. This entailed great alterations. The kitchen had to be converted into a parlour, and the parlour into a kitchen, the dining-room into a scullery, the scullery into a study, and the library enlarged to serve as a dining-room. All the downstair windows had to be altered. Mr. Desiderius Mules liked to have French windows opening to the ground.

In the same manner great transformations were made in the garden. Where Mr. Peter Trevisa had built up and planted a hedge, there Mr. Desiderius Mules opened a gate, and where the late rector had laid down a drive there the new rector made garden beds. In the same manner shrubberies were converted into lawns and lawns into shrubberies. The pump was now of no service outside the drawing-room window, it had to be removed to the other side of the house, and to serve the pump with water a new well had to be dug, and the old well that had furnished limpid and wholesome water was filled up. The site of the conservatory was considered the proper one for the new well, and this entailed the destruction of the conservatory, removal was intended, with a new aspect, to the north, as a frigidarium; but when touched it fell to pieces, and in so doing furnished Mr. Desiderius Mules with much comment on the imposition to which he had been subjected, for he had taken this conservatory at a valuation, and that valuation had been for three pounds seven and fourpence half-penny, whereas the real value of the conservatory was, so he declared, three pounds seven and fourpence without the half-penny at the end or the three pounds.

When the Reverend Desiderius Mules heard that Captain Coppinger and Judith Trevisa were to be married in his church, "By Jove," said he, "they shall pay me double fees, as extra parochial. I shall get that out of them at all events. I have been choused sufficiently."

A post-chaise from Wadebridge conveyed Judith, Miss Trevisa, Uncle Zachie, and Jamie from Polzeath.

The bride was restless. At one moment she leaned back, then forward, her eyes turned resolutely through the window at the fog. Her hands plucked at her veil, or at her gloves, she spoke not a word throughout the drive; Aunt Dionysia was also silent. Opposite her sat Mr. Menaida in blue coat with brass buttons, white waistcoat outside a coloured one, and white trousers tightly strapped. Though inclined to talk, he was unable to resist the depressing influence of his vis-à-vis, Miss Trevisa, who sat scowling at him, with her thin lips closed. Jamie was excited, but as no one answered him when he spoke, he also lapsed into silence.

When the churchyard gate of S. Enodoc was reached, Mr. Menaida jumped out of the chaise with a sigh of relief, and muttered to himself that had he known what to expect he would have brought his pocket-flask with him, and have had a nip of cognac on the way.

A goodly number of sightseers had assembled from Polzeath and S. Enodoc, and stood in the churchyard magnified by the mist to gigantic size. Over the graves of drowned sailors were planted the figureheads of wrecked vessels, and these in the mist might have been taken as the dead risen and mingling with the living to view this dreary marriage.

The bride herself looked ghostlike, or as a waft of the fog but little condensed, blown through the graveyard towards the gap in the church wall, and blown through that also to the altar within.

That gap was usually blocked with planks from a wreck, supported by beams; when the church was to be put in requisition, then the beams were knocked away, whereupon down clattered the boards and they were tossed aside. It had been so done on this occasion, and the fragments were heaped untidily about among the graves under the church wall. The clerk-sexton had, indeed, considered that morning, with his hands in his pockets, whether it would be worth his while, assisted by the five bell-ringers, to take this accumulation of wreckage and pile it together out of sight, but he had thought that, owing to the fog, a veil would be drawn over the disorder, and he might be saved this extra trouble.

Within the sacred building, over his boots in sand, stamped and fumed, and paced and growled, the Reverend Desiderius Mules, in surplice, hood, and stole, very ill at ease and out of humour because the wedding party arrived unpunctually, and he feared he might catch cold from the wind and fog that drifted in through the hole in the wall serving as door.

The sand within was level with the sills of the windows, it cut the tables of Commandments in half, had blotted away the majority of inhibitions against marriage within blood relationship and marriage kinship. The altar rails were below the surface. The altar table had been fished up, and set against the east wall, not on this day for the marriage, but at some previous occasion. Then the sexton had placed two pieces of slate under the feet on one side, and not having found handy any other pieces, had thought that perhaps it did not matter. Consequently the two legs on one side had sunk in the sand, and the altar table formed an incline.

A vast number of bats occupied the church, and by day hung like little moleskin purses from the roof. Complaints had been made of the disagreeableness of having these creatures suspended immediately over the head of the officient, accordingly the sexton had knocked away such as dangled immediately above the altar and step—or place where the step was, beneath the sand; but he did not think it necessary to disturb those in other parts of the church. If they inconvenienced others it was the penalty of curiosity, coming to see a wedding there. Towards the west end of the church some wooden pew tops stood above the sand, and stuck into a gimlet hole in the top rail o one was a piece of holly, dry and brown as a chip. It had been put there as a Christmas decoration the last year that the church was used for divine worship at the feast of Noel; when that was only the oldest men could remember. The sexton had looked at it several times, with his hands in his pockets, and considered whether it were worth while pulling his hands out and removing the withered fragment, and carrying it outside the church, but had arrived at the conclusion that it injured no one, and might therefore just as well remain.

There were fragments of stained glass in the windows, in the upper lights of the perpendicular windows saints and angels in white and gold, on ruby and blue grounds. In one window a fragment of a Christ on the cross. But all were much obscured by cobwebs. These cobwebs, after having entangled many flies, caught and retained many particles of sand, became impervious to light, and obscured the figures in the painted glass. The sexton had looked at these cobwebs occasionally, and mused whether it would be worth his while to sweep them down, but as he knew that the church was rarely used for divine offices, and never for regular divine worship, he deemed that there was no crying necessity for their destruction. Life was short, and time might be better employed—to wit: in talking to a neighbour, in smoking a pipe, in drinking a pint of ale, in larruping his wife, in reading the paper. Consequently the cobwebs remained.

Had Mr. Desiderius Mules been possessed of antiquarian tastes, he might have occupied the time he was kept waiting in studying the bosses of carved oak that adorned the waggon-roof of the church, which were in some cases quaint, in the majority beautiful, and no two the same. And he might have puzzled out the meaning of three rabbits with only three ears between them, forming a triangle, or three heads united in one neck, a king and queen, a bishop and a monk, or of a sow suckling a dozen little pigs. But Mr. Desiderius Mules had no artistic or archæological faculty developed in him. His one object on the present occasion was to keep draught and damp from the crown of his head, where the hair was so scanty as hardly to exist at all. He did not like to assume his hat in the consecrated building, so he stamped about in the sand, holding a red banana handkerchief on the top of his head, and grumbling at the time he was kept waiting, at the Cornish climate, at the way in which he had been "choused" in the matter of dilapidations for the chancel of the church, at the unintelligible dialect of the people, and at a good many other causes of irritation, notably at a bat which had not reverenced his bald pate when he ventured beyond the range of the sexton's sweeping.

Presently the clerk, who was outside, thrust in his head through the gap in the wall, and in a stagewhisper announced, "They's a-coming."

The Reverend Mules growled, "There ought to be a right to charge extra when the parson is kept waiting; sixpence a minute, not a penny less. But we are choused in this confounded corner of the world in every way. Hah! there is a mildew spot on my stole—all come of this villainous damp."

In the tower stood five men, ready to pull the ropes and sound a merry peal when the service was over, and earn a guinea. They had a firkin of ale in a corner, with which to moisten their clay between each round. Now that they heard that the wedding party had arrived they spat on their hands and heaved their legs out of the sand.

Through the aperture in the wall entered the bridal party, a cloud of fog blowing in with them and enveloping them. They stepped laboriously through the fine sand, at this place less firm than elsewhere, having been dug into daily by the late rector in his futile efforts to clear the church.

Mr. Mules cast a suspicious look at the rafters above him to see that no profane bat was there, and opened his book.

Mr. Menaida was to act as father to the bride, and there was no other bridesmaid than Miss Trevisa. As they waded towards the altar Judith's strength failed, and she stood still. Then Uncle Zachie put his arm round her, and half carried her over the sand towards the place where she must stand to give herself away. She turned her head and thanked him with her eyes, she could not speak. So deathly was her whiteness, so deficient in life did she seem, that Miss Trevisa looked at her with some anxiety, and a little doubt whether she would be able to go through the service.

When Judith reached her place her eyes rested on the sand. She did not look to her left side, she could hear no steps, for the sand muffled all sound of feet, but she knew by the cold shudder that thrilled through her that Captain Coppinger was at her side.

"Dearly beloved, we are gathered together here—now, then, order if you please, and quiet; we are twenty-five minutes after time," said Mr. Desiderius Mules.

The first few words, seven in all, were addressed to the wedding party, the rest to a number of men and women and children who were stumbling and plunging into the church through the improvised door, thrusting each other forward, with a "Get along," and "Out of the road," all eager to secure a good sight of the ceremony, and none able to hurry to a suitable place because of the sand that impeded every step.

"Now, then, I can't stay here all day!"

Mr. Mules sniffed, and applied the banana to his nose, as an indication that he was chilled, and that his rheum would be on the heads of the congregation were he made ill by this delay.

"Dearly beloved, we are gathered," he began again, and he was now able to proceed. "Curll," said he, in loud and emphatic tones, "wilt thou have this woman to thy wedded wife, to live together after God's ordinance in the holy estate of matrimony? Wilt thou love her, comfort her, honour, and keep her in sickness and in health; and, forsaking all other, keep thee only unto her so long as ye both shall live?"

The response of Coppinger went through the heart of Judith like a knife. Then the rector addressed her. For answer she looked up at him and moved her lips. He took her hand and placed it in that of Coppinger. It was cold as ice, and quivering like an aspen leaf. As Captain Coppinger held it it seemed to drag and become heavy in his hand, whilst he pronounced the words after the rector, making oath to take Judith as his own. Then the same words were recited to her, for her to repeat in order after the priest. She began, she moved her lips, looked him pleadingly in the face, her head swam, the fog filled the whole church and settled between her and the rector. She felt nothing save the grip of Coppinger's hand, and sank unconscious to the ground.

"Go forward," said Cruel.

Mr. Menaida and Aunt Dionysia caught Judith and held her up. She could neither speak nor stir. Her lips were unclosed; she seemed to be gasping for breath like one drowning.

"Go on," persisted Cruel; and holding her left hand he thrust the ring on her fourth finger, repeating the words of the formula.

"I cannot proceed," said the Reverend Desiderius.

"Then you will have to come again to-morrow."

"She is unconscious," objected the rector.

"It is momentary only," said Aunt Dionysia; "be quick and finish."

Mr. Mules hesitated a moment. He had no wish to return in like weather on another day; no wish again to be kept waiting five and twenty minutes. He rushed at the remainder of the office and concluded it a hand gallop.

"Now," said he, "the registers are at the rectory. Come there."

Coppinger looked at Judith.

"Not to-day. It is not possible. She is ill—faint. To-morrow. Neither she nor I, nor the witnesses, will run away. We will come to you to-morrow."

Uncle Zachie offered to assist Judith from the church.

"No," said Cruel, peremptorily, "she is mine now."

With assistance she was able to walk. She seemed to recover for a moment in the air outside, but again lapsed into faintness on being placed in the chaise.

"To Pentyre Glaze," ordered Coppinger; "our home."

# CHAPTER XXXIV
## A BREAKFAST

"She has been over exerted and over excited," said Miss Trevisa. "Leave her to recover; in a few days she will be herself again. Remember, her father died of heart complaint, and though Judith resembles her mother rather than a Trevisa, she may have inherited from my brother just that one thing she had better have let him carry to his grave with him."

So Judith was given the little room that adjoined her aunt's, and Miss Trevisa postponed for a week her migration to Othello Cottage.

Aunt Dionysia was uneasy about her niece; perhaps her conscience did suffer from some qualms when she saw how Judith shrank from the union she had driven her into for her own selfish convenience. She treated her in the wisest manner now she had brought her to the Glaze, for she placed her in her old room next her own, and left her there to herself. Judith could hear her aunt walking about and muttering in the adjoining chamber, and was content to be alone to recover her composure and strength.

Uncle Zachie and Jump were, however, in sore distress. They had made the twin cottage ready, had prepared a wedding breakfast, engaged a helping hand or two, and no one had come to partake. Nor was Mr. Desiderius Mules in a cheerful mood. He had been invited to the breakfast, and was hungry and cold. He had to wait whilst Mr. Menaida ran up to Pentyre to know whether any one was going to honour his board. Whilst he was away the rector stamped about the parlour, growling that he believed he was about to be "choused out of his breakfast. There was really no knowing what these people in this out-of-the-world corner might do." Then he pulled off his boots and shook the sand out, rang for Jump, and asked at what hour precisely the breakfast was to be eaten, and whether it was put on table to be looked at only.

From Pentyre Glaze Mr. Menaida was not greatly successful in obtaining guests. He found some wild-looking men there in converse with Coppinger, men whom he knew by rumour to belong to a class that had no ostensible profession and means of living.

Mr. Menaida had ordered in clotted cream, which would not keep sweet many days. It ought to be eaten at once. He inquired whether Coppinger, the bride, Miss Trevisa, any one was coming to his house to consume the clotted cream. As Jamie was drifting about purposeless, and he alone seemed disposed to accompany Uncle Zachie, the old gentleman carried him off.

"I s'pose I can't on the spur of the moment go in and ask our S. Minver parson?" asked Menaida, dubiously, of the S. Enodoc parson. "You see, I dare say he's hurt not to have had the coupling of 'em himself."

"Most certainly not," said Mr. Mules; "an appetite is likely to go into faintness unless attended to at once. I know that the coats of my stomach are honeycombed with gastric juice. Shall I say grace? Another half-hour of delay will finish me."

Consequently but three persons sat down to a plentiful meal, but some goose, cold, had hardly been served, when in came Mr. Scantlebray, the agent, with a cheery salutation of—

"Hulloa, Menaida, old man! What, eating and drinking? I'll handle a knife and fork with you—unasked. Beg pardon, Mr. Mules. I'm a rough man, and an old acquaintance of our good friend here; hope I see you in the enjoyment of robust health, sir! Ah! Menaida, old man! I didn't expect such a thing as this. Now I begin to see daylight, and understand why I was turned out of the valuership, and why my brother lost this promising young pupil. Ah, ha! my man, you have been deprived of fun, such fun, roaring fun, by not being with my brother Scanty. Well, sir" —to Mr. Mules—"what was the figure of the valuation? You had a queer man on your side. I pity you. A man I wouldn't trust myself. I name no names. Now tell me, what did you get?"

"A hundred and twenty-seven pounds four and nine-pence farthing. Monstrous—a chouse!"

"As you say, monstrous. Why, that chancel! Show me the builder who will contract to do that alone at a hundred and twenty-seven pounds? And the repairs of the rectory, are they to be reckoned at four and nine-pence farthing? It is a swindle! I'd appeal. I'd refuse. You made a mistake, sir, let me tell you, in falling into certain hands. Yes, I'll have some goose, thank you."

Mr. Scantlebray ate heartily, so did the Reverend Desiderius, who had the honeycomb cells of his stomach coats to fill. Both, moreover, did justice to Mr. Menaida's wine, they did not spare it; why should they? Those for whom the board was spread had not troubled to come to it, and they must make amends for their neglect.

"Horrible weather!" said the rector. "I suppose this detestable sort of stuff of which the atmosphere is composed is the prevailing abomination one has to inhale throughout three-quarters of the year. One cannot see three yards before one."

"It's bad for some and good for others," answered Scantlebray. "There'll be wrecks, certainly, after this, especially if we get, as we are pretty sure to get, a wind on shore."

"Wrecks!" exclaimed the rector. "And pray who pays the fees for drowned men I may be expected to bury?"

"The parish," answered Uncle Zachie.

"Oh, half-a-crown a head," said Mr. Mules, contemptuously.

"There are other things to be had out of a wreck besides burial fees," said Scantlebray. "But you must be down early before the coastguard are there. Have you donkies?"

"Donkies! What for?"

"I have one—a grey beauty," exclaimed Jamie. "Captain Coppinger gave her to me."

"Well, young man, then you pick up what you can, when you have the chance, and lade her with your findings. You'll pick up something better than corpses, and make something more than burial half-crowns."

"But why do you suppose there will be wrecks?" inquired the rector of S. Enodoc. "There is no storm."

"No storm, certainly; but there is fog, and in the fog vessels coming up the Channel to Bristol get lost as to their bearings, get near our cliffs without knowing it, and then—if a wind from the west springs up and blows rough—they are done for; they can't escape to the open. That's it, old man. I beg your reverence's pardon, I mean sir. When I said that such weather was bad for some and good for others, you can understand me now—bad for the wrecked, good for the wreckers."

"But, surely, you have no wreckers here?"

Mr. Scantlebray laughed. "Go and tell the bridegroom that you think so. I'll let you into the knowledge of one thing"—he winked over his glass;—"there's a fine merchantman on her way to Bristol."

"How do you know?"

"Know! Because she was sighted off S. Ives, and the tidings has run up the coast like fire among heather. I don't doubt it that the tidings has reached Hartland by this; and, with a thick fog like to-day, there are a thousand hearts beating with expectation. Who can say? She may be laden with gold dust from Africa, or with tin from Barca, or with port from Oporto."

"My boy Oliver is coming home," said Mr. Menaida.

"Then let's hope he is not in this vessel, for, old man, she stands a bad chance in such weather as this. There is Porth-quin, and there is Hayle Bay ready to receive her, or Doom Bar, on which she may run, all handy for our people. Are you anything of a sportsman, sir?"

"A little; but I don't fancy there is much in this precious country—no cover."

"What is fox-hunting when you come to consider, or going after a snipe or a partridge? A fox!—it's naught, the brush stinks; and a snipe is but a mouthful. My dear sir, if you come to live among us, you must seek your sport not on the land, but at sea. You'll find the sport worth something when you get a haul of a barrel of first-rate sherry, or a load of silver ingots. Why, that's how Penwarden bought his farm. He got the money after a storm—drew it on the shore out of the pocket of a dead man. Do you know why the bells of S. Enodoc are so sweet? Because, so folks say, melted into them are ingots of Peruvian silver, from a ship wrecked on Doom Bar."

"I should like to get some silver or gold," said Jamie.

"I daresay you would; and so perhaps you may if you look out for it. Go to your good friend, Captain Coppinger, and tell him what you want. He has made his pickings before now, on shore and off wrecks, and has not given up the practice."

"But," said Mr. Mules, "do you mean to tell me that you Cornish people in this benighted corner of the world live like sharks, upon whatever is cast over-board."

"No, I do not," answered Scantlebray. "We have too much energy and intelligence for that. We don't always wait till it is cast overboard; we go aboard and take what we want."

"What, steal!"

"I don't call that stealing, supposing as how Providence and a south-west wind throws a ship into our laps, when we put in our fingers and pick out the articles we want. What are Porth-quin and Hayle Bay but our laps, in which lie the wrecks heaven sends us? And Doom Bar, what is that but a counter, on which the good things are spread, and those first there get the first share?"

"And pray," said Mr. Desiderius Mules, "have the owners of the vessels, the passengers, the captains, no objections to make?"

"They are not there—don't wait for our people. If they do—so much the worse for them." Then Scantlebray laughed. "There's a good story told of the Zenobia, lost four years ago. There was a lady on board. When she knew the vessel was on Doom Bar she put on all her jewellery, to escape with it; but some of our people got to the wreck before she went off it, and one lobe of her ears was torn off."

"Torn off!"

"Yes, in pulling the earrings off her."

"But who pulled the earrings off her?"

"Our people."

"Gracious heavens! Were they not brought to justice?"

"Who did it? No one knew. What became of the jewellery? No one knew. All that was known was that Lady Knighton—that was her name—lost her diamonds and the lobe of her right ear as well."

"And it was never recovered?"

"What! the lobe of her ear?"

"No, the jewellery."

"Never."

"Upon my word, I have got among a parcel of scoundrels! It was high time that I should come and reform them. I'll set to work at once. I'll have S. Enodoc dug out and restored; and I'll soon put an end to this sort of thing."

"You think so?"

"You don't know me. I'll have a bazaar. I'll have a ball in the Assembly rooms at Wadebridge. The church shall be excavated. I'm not going in there again with the bats, and to have my boots filled with sand, I can tell you. Everything shall be renovated and put to rights. I'll see to it at once. I'll have a pigeon-shooting for the sake of my chancel—I dare say I shall raise twenty pounds by that alone—and a raffle for the font, and an Aunt Sally for the pulpit. But the ball will be the main thing. I'll send and get the county people to patronize. I'll do it, and you barbarians in this benighted corner of the world shall see there is a man of energy among you."

"You'd best try your hand on a wreck. You'll get more off that."

"And I'll have a bran pie for an altar table."

"You won't get the parishioners to do anything for the restoration of the church. They don't want to have it restored."

"The Decalogue is rotten. I run my umbrella through the Ten Commandments this morning. I'll have a gipsy-camp and fortune-telling to furnish me with new Commandments."

"I've heard tell," said Scantlebray, "that at Poughill, near Stratton, is a four-post bed of pure gold, come off a wreck in Bude Bay."

"When I was up in the north," said the rector of S. Enodoc, "we had a savage who bit off the heads of rats, snap, and ate them raw, and charged sixpence entrance; but that was for the missionaries. I should hardly advocate that for the restoration of a church; besides, where is the savage to be got? We made twenty-seven pounds by that man; but expenses were heavy, and swallowed up twenty-five; we sent two pounds to the missionaries."

Mr. Menaida stood up and went to the window.

"I believe the wind has shifted to the north, and we shall have a lightening of the fog after sunset."

"Shall we not have a wreck? I hope there'll be one," said Jamie.

"What is the law about wreckage, Menaida, old man?" asked Scantlebray, also coming to the window.

"The law is plain enough: no one has a right to goods come to land; he who finds may claim salvage—naught else; and any person taking goods cast ashore, which are not legal wreck, may be punished."

"And," said Scantlebray, "what if certain persons give occasion to a ship being wrecked, and then plundering the wreck?"

"There the law is also plain: the invading and robbing of a vessel, either in distress or when wrecked, and the putting forth of false lights, in order to bring a vessel into danger, are capital felonies."

Scantlebray went to the table, took up a napkin, twisted it, and then flung it round his neck, and hung his head on one side.

"What—this, Menaida, old man?"

Uncle Zachie nodded.

"Come here, Jim, my boy. A word with you outside." Scantlebray led Jamie into the road. "There's been a shilling owing you for some time. We had roaring fun about it once. Here it is. Now listen to me. Go to Pentyre. You want to find gold dust on the shore, don't you?"

"Yes."

"Or bars of silver."

"Yes."

"Well, beg Captain Coppinger, if he is going to have a Jack o' Lantern to-night, to let you be the Jack. Do you understand? And mind—not a word about me. Then—gold dust and bars of silver and purses of shillings. Mind you ask to be Jack o' Lantern. It is fun!—such fun!—roaring fun."

## CHAPTER XXXV
## JACK O' LANTERN

EVENING closed in. Judith had been left entirely to herself. She sat in the window, looking out into the mist, and watching the failing of the light. Sometimes she opened the casement, and allowed the vapour to blow in like cold steam, then became chilled, shivered, and closed it again. The wind was rising, and piped about the house, whistled at her window. Judith, sitting there, tried with her hand to find the orifice through which the blast drove, and then amused herself with playing with her finger-tops on the opening, and regulating the whistle so as to form a tune. She frequently heard Coppinger's voice in conversation, sometimes in the hall, sometimes in the courtyard, but could not catch what was spoken. She listened with childish curiosity to the voice that was now that of her lord and husband, and endeavoured to riddle out of it some answer to her questions as to what sort of a master he would prove. She could not comprehend him. She had heard stories told of him that made her deem him the worst of men: remorseless and regardless of others, yet towards her he had proved gentle and considerate. What, for instance, could be more delicate and thoughtful that his behaviour to her at this very time? Feeling that she had married him with reluctance, he kept away from her, and suffered her to recover her composure without affording her additional struggle. A reaction after the strain on her nerves set in; the step she had dreaded had been taken, and she was the wife of the man she feared and did not love. The suspense of expectation was exchanged for the calmer grief of retrospect.

The fog all day had been white as wool, and she had noticed how parcels of vapour had been caught and entangled in the thorn bushes, as the fog swept by, very much as sheep left flocks of their fleeces in the bushes when they broke out of a field. Now that the day set, the vapour lost its whiteness and became ash-grey, but it was not so dense as it had been, or rather it was compacted in places into thick masses, with clear tracts between. The sea was not visible, nor the cliffs, but she could distinguish outbuilding, tufts of furze, and hedges. The wind blew much stronger, and she could hear the boom of the waves against the rocks, like the throbbing of the unseen heart of the world. It was louder than it had been. The sound did not come upon the wind, for the fog, that muffled all objects from sight, muffled also all sounds to the ear, but the boom came from the vibration of the land. The sea, flung against the coast-line, shook the rocks, and they quivered for a far distance inland, making every wall and tree quiver also; and the sound of the sea was heard, not through the ears, but through the soles of the feet.

Miss Trevisa came in.

"Shall I light you a pair of candles, Judith?"

"I thank you, hardly yet."

"And will you not eat?"

"Yes, presently, when supper is served."

"You will come downstairs?"

"Yes."

"I am glad to hear that."

"'Aunt, I thought you were going to Othello Cottage the day I came here?"

"Captain Coppinger will not suffer me to leave at once, till you have settled down to your duties as mistress of the house."

"Oh, auntie, I shall never be able to manage this large establishment!"

"Why not? You managed that at the rectory."

"Yes, but it was entirely different."

"How so?"

"My dear papa's requirements were so simple, and so few, and there were no men about except poor Balhachet, and he was a dear, good old humbug. Here, I don't know how many men there are, and who belong to the house, and who do not. They are in one day and out the next; and then Captain Coppinger is not like my own darling papa."

"No, indeed he is not. Shall I light the candles? I have something to show you."

"As you will, aunt."

Miss Trevisa went into her room and fetched a light, and kindled the two candles that stood on Judith's dressing-table.

"Oh, aunt! not three candles."

"Why not? We shall need light."

"But three candles together bring ill-luck; and we have had enough already."

"Pshaw! Don't be a fool. I want light, for I have something to show you."

She opened a small box and drew forth a brooch and earrings, that flashed in the rays of the candles.

"Look, child, they are yours! Captain Coppinger has given them to you. They are diamonds. See—a butterfly for the breast, and two little butterflies for the ears."

"Oh, auntie, not for me! I do not want them."

"This is ungracious. I dare say they cost many hundreds of pounds. They are diamonds."

Judith took the brooch and earrings in her hand; they sparkled. The diamonds were far from being brilliants, they were of good size and purest water.

"I really do not wish to have them. Persuade Captain Coppinger to return them to the jeweller; it is far too costly a gift for me, far, far. I should be happier without them." Then suddenly—"I do not know that they have been bought. Oh, Aunt Dunes, tell me truly. Have they been bought? I think jewellers always send out their goods in leather cases, and there is none such for these. And see, this earring, the gold is bent, as if pulled out of shape. I am sure they have not been bought. Take them back again, I pray you."

"You little fool!" said Miss Trevisa, angrily. "I will do nothing of the kind. If you refuse them, then take them back yourself. Captain Coppinger performs a generous and kind act that costs him much money, and you throw his gift in his face; you insult him. Insult him yourself with your suspicions and refusals—you have already behaved to him outrageously. I will do nothing for you that you ask. Your father put on me a task that is hateful, and I wish I were clear of it."

Then she bounced out of the room, leaving her candle burning along with the other two.

A moment later she came back hastily and closed Judith's shutters.

"Oh, leave them open," pleaded Judith. "I shall like to see how the right goes—if the fog clears away."

"No, I will not," answered Miss Trevisa, roughly. "And mind you, these shutters remain shut, or your candles go out. Your window commands the sea, and the light of your window must not show."

"Why not?"

"Because should the fog lift, it would be seen by vessels."

"Why should they not see it?"

"You are a fool. Obey, and ask no questions."

Miss Trevisa put up the bar, and then retired with the candle, leaving Judith to her own thoughts, with the diamonds on the table before her.

Her thoughts were reproachful of herself. She was ungracious, and perhaps unjust also. Her husband had sent her a present of rare value, and she was disposed to reject it, and charge him with not having come by the diamonds honestly. They were not new from a jeweller; but what of that? Could he afford to buy her a set at the price of some hundreds of pounds? And because he had not obtained them from a jeweller, did it follow that he had taken them unlawfully? He might have picked them up on the shore, or have bought them from a man who had. He might have obtained them at a sale in the neighbourhood. They might be family jewels, that had belonged to his mother, and he was showing her the highest honour a man could show a woman in asking her to wear the ornaments that had belonged to his mother.

He had exhibited to her a store-room full of beautiful things, but these might be legitimately his, brought from foreign countries by his ship the Black Prince. It was possible that they were not contraband articles.

Judith opened her door and went downstairs. In the hall she found Coppinger with two or three men, but the moment he saw her he started up, came to meet her, and drew her aside into a parlour, then went back into the hall and fetched candles. A fire was burning in this room, ready for her, should she condescend to use it.

"I hope I have not interrupted you," she said, timidly.

"An agreeable interruption. At any time you have only to show yourself and I will at once come to you, and never ask to be dismissed."

She knew that this was no empty compliment, that he meant it from the depth of his heart, and was sorry that she could not respond to an affection so deep and so sincere.

"You have been very good to me, more good than I deserve," she said, standing by the fire, with lowered eyes. "I must thank you now for a splendid and beautiful present, and I really do not know how to find words in which fittingly to acknowledge it."

"You cannot thank and gratify me better than by wearing what I have given you."

"But when? Surely not on an ordinary evening?"

"No, certainly. The rector has been up this afternoon and desired to see you; he is hot on a scheme for a public ball to be given at Wadebridge for the restoration of his church, and he has asked that you will be a patroness."

"I—oh—I! after my father's death?"

"That was in the late spring, and now it is the early winter; besides, now you are a married lady—and was not the digging out and restoring of the church your father's strong desire?"

"Yes; but he would never have had a ball for such a purpose."

"The money must be raised somehow, so I promised for you. You could not well refuse; he was impatient to be off to Wadebridge and secure the assembly rooms."

"But, Captain Coppinger—"

"Captain Coppinger?"

Judith coloured.

"I beg your pardon, I forgot. And now I do not recollect what I was going to say. It matters nothing. If you wish me to go, I will go. If you wish me to wear the diamond butterflies, I will wear them."

"I thank you." He held out his hands to her.

She drew back slightly and folded her palms, as though praying.

"I will do much to please you, but do not press me too greatly. I am strange in this house, strange in my new situation; give me time to breathe and look round and recover my confidence. Besides, we are only half married so far."

"How so?"

"I have not signed the register."

"No; but that shall be done to-morrow."

"Yes, to-morrow; but that gives me breathing time. You will be patient and forbearing with me?"

She put forward her hands folded, and he put his outside them and pressed them. The flicker of the fire lent a little colour to her cheeks, and surrounded her head with an aureole of spun gold.

"Judith, I will do anything you ask. I love you with all my soul, past speaking. I am your slave. But do not hold me too long in chains, do not tread me too ruthlessly under foot."

"Give me time," she pleaded.

"I will give you a little time," he answered.

Then she withdrew her hands from between his, and sped upstairs, leaving him looking into the fire, with troubled face.

When she returned to her room the candles were still burning, and the diamonds lay on the dressing-table where she had left them. She took the brooch and earrings to return them to their box, and then noticed for the first time that they were wrapped in paper, not in cotton wool. She tapped at her aunt's door, and, entering, asked if she had any cotton wool that she could spare her.

"No, I have not. What do you want it for?"

"For the jewelry. It cannot have come from a shop, as it was wrapped in paper only."

"It will take no hurt. Wrap it in paper again."

"I had rather not, auntie. Besides, I have some cotton wool in my workbox."

"Then use it."

"But my workbox has not been brought here. It is at Mr. Menaida's."

"You can fetch it to-morrow."

"But I am lost without my needles and thread. Besides, I do not like to leave my workbox about. I will go for it. The walk will do me good."

"Nonsense, it is falling dark."

"I will get Uncle Zachie to walk back with me. I must have my workbox. Besides, the fresh air will do me good, and the fog has lifted."

"As you will, then."

So Judith put on her cloak and drew a hood over her head, and went back to Polzeath. She knew the way perfectly: there was no danger; night had not closed in. It would be a pleasure to her to see the old bird-stuffer's face again; and she wanted to find Jamie. She had not seen him, nor heard his voice, and she supposed he must be at Polzeath.

On her arrival at the double cottage the old fellow was delighted to see her, and to see that she had recovered from the distress and faintness of the morning sufficiently to be able to walk back to his house from her new home. Her first question was after Jamie. Uncle Zachie told her that Jamie had breakfasted at his table, but he had gone away in the afternoon and he had seen no more of him. The fire was lighted, and Uncle Zachie insisted on Judith's sitting by it with him and talking over the events of the day, and on telling him that she was content with her position, reconciled to the change of her state.

She sat longer with him than she had intended, listening to his disconnected chatter, and then nothing would suffice him but she must go to the piano and play through his favourite pieces.

"Remember, Judith, it is the last time I shall have you here to give me this pleasure."

She could not refuse him his request, especially as he was to walk back to Pentyre with her. Thus time passed, and it was with alarm and self-reproach that she started up on hearing the clock strike the half-past, and learned it was half-past nine, and not half-past eight, as she supposed.

As she now insisted on departing, Mr. Menaida put on his hat.

"Shall we take a light?" he asked, and then said—"No, we had better not. On such a night as this a moving light is dangerous."

"How can it be dangerous?" asked Judith.

"Not to us, my dear child; but to a ship at sea. A stationary light might serve as a warning, but a moving light misleads. The captain of a vessel, if he has lost his bearings—as is like enough in the fog—as soon as the mist rises, would see a light gliding along, and think it was that of a vessel at sea, and so make in the direction of the light, in the belief that there was open water, and so run directly on his destruction."

"Oh, no, no, uncle, we will not take a light."

Mr. Menaida and Judith went out together, she with her workbox under her arm, he with his stick, and her hand resting on his arm. The night was dark, very dark; but the way led for the most part over down, and there was just sufficient light in the sky for the road to be distinguishable. It would be in the lane, between the walls, and where overhung by thorns, that the darkness would be most profound.

The wind was blowing strongly, and the sound of the breakers came on it now, for the cloud had lifted off land and sea, though still hanging low. Very dense overhead it could not be, or no light would have pierced the vaporous canopy.

Uncle Zachie and Judith walked on talking together, and she felt cheered by his presence, when all at once she stopped, pressed his arm, and said—

"Oh, do look, uncle! What is that light?"

In the direction of the cliffs a light was distinctly visible, now rising, now falling, observing an unevenly undulating motion.

"Oh, uncle, it is dreadful! Some foolish person is on the downs going home with a lantern, and it may lead to a dreadful error, and to a wreck."

"I hope to heaven it is only what you say."

"What do you mean?"

"That it is not done wilfully."

"Wilfully?"

"Yes, with purpose to mislead. Look. The movement of the light is exactly that of a ship on a rolling sea."

"Uncle, let us go there at once, and stop it."

"I don't know, my dear; if it be done by some unprincipled ruffian, he would not be stopped by us."

"It must be stopped. And oh! think! you told me that your Oliver is coming home. Think of him."

"We will go."

Mr. Menaida was drawn along by Judith in her eagerness. They left the road to Pentyre, and struck out over the downs, keeping their eyes on the light. The distance was deceptive. It seemed to have been much nearer than they found it actually to be.

"Look! it is coming back," exclaimed Judith.

"Yes; that is done wilfully. That is to give the appearance of a vessel tacking up channel. Stay behind, Judith; I will go on."

"No; I will go with you. You would not find me again in the darkness if we parted."

"The light is coming this way. Stand still; it will come directly on us."

They drew up. Judith clung to Uncle Zachie's side, her heart beating with excitement, indignation, and anger.

"The lantern is fastened to an ass's head," said Uncle Zachie. "Do you see how, as the creature moves his head, the light is swayed, and that, with the rise and fall in the land, makes it look as though the rise and fall were on the sea. I have my stick. Stand behind me, Judith."

But a voice was heard that made her gasp and clasp the arm of Uncle Zachie the tighter.

Neither spoke.

The light approached. They could distinguish the lantern, though they could not see what bore it; only—next moment something caught the light—the ear of a donkey thrust forward.

Again a voice, that of some one urging on the ass.

Judith let go Menaida's arm, sprang forward with a cry—

"Jamie! Jamie! What are you doing?"

In a moment she had wrenched the lantern from the head of the ass, and the creature, startled, dashed away and disappeared in the darkness. Judith put the light under her cloak.

"Oh, Jamie! Jamie! why have you done this? Who ever set you to this wicked task?"

"I am Jack o' Lantern," answered the boy. "Ju, now my Neddy is gone."

"Jamie, who sent you out to do this? Answer me!"

"Captain Coppinger."

Judith walked on in silence. Neither she nor Uncle Zachie spoke; only Jamie whimpered and muttered. Suddenly they were surrounded, and a harsh voice exclaimed—

"In the King's name! We have you now—showing false lights."

Judith hastily slung the lantern from beneath her cloak, and saw that there were several men about her, and that the speaker was Mr. Scantlebray. The latter was surprised when he recognized her.

"What!" he said. "I did not expect this—pretty quickly into your apprenticeship. What brings you here? And you, too, Menaida, old man?"

"Nothing simpler," answered Uncle Zachie. "I am accompanying Mrs. Coppinger back to the Glaze."

"What, married in the morning, and roving the downs at night?"

"I have been to Polzeath after my workbox. Here it is," said Judith.

"Oh, you are out of your road to Pentyre—I suppose you know that?" sneered Scantlebray.

"Naturally," replied Mr. Menaida. "It is dark enough for any one to stray. Why! you don't suspect me, do you, of showing false lights and endeavouring to wreck vessels? That would be too good a joke—and the offence, as I told you—capital."

Scantlebray uttered an oath, and turned to the men and said—

"Captain Cruel is too deep for us this time. I thought he had sent the boy out with the ass; instead, he has sent his wife—a wife of a few hours—and never told her the mischief she was to do with the lantern. Hark!"

From the sea—the boom of a gun.

All stood still as rooted to the spot.

Then again—the boom of a gun.

"There is a wreck!" exclaimed Scantlebray. "I thought so—and you, Mistress Orphing, you're guilty."

He turned to the men. "We can make nothing of this affair with the lantern. Let us catch the sea-wolves falling on their prey."

# CHAPTER XXXVI
# THE SEA-WOLVES

On the Doom Bar!

That very merchantman was wrecked, over which so many Cornish mouths had watered, aye, and Devonian mouths also, from the moment she had been sighted at S. Ives.

She had been entangled in the fog, not knowing where she was, all her bearings lost. The wind had risen, and, when the day darkened into night, the mist had lifted in cruel kindness to show a false glimmer that was at once taken as the light of a ship beating up the Channel. The head of the merchantman was put about, a half-reefed topsail spread, and she ran on her destruction. With a crash she was on the bar. The great bowlers that roll without a break from Labrador rushed on behind, beat her, hammered her further and further into the sand, surged up at each stroke, swept the decks with mingled foam and water and spray. The mainmast went down with a snap. Bent with the sail, at the jerk, as the vessel ran aground, it broke and came down, top-mast, rigging, and sail, in an enveloping, draggled mass. From that moment the captain's voice was no more heard. Had he been struck by the fallen mast and stunned or beaten overboard? or did he lie on deck enveloped and smothered in wet sail, or had he been caught and strangled by the cordage? None knew; none inquired. A wild panic seized crew and passengers alike. The chief mate had the presence of mind to order the discharge of signals of distress, but the order was imperfectly carried out. A flash, illumining for a second the glittering froth and heaving sea, then a boom. A lapse of a minute, another flash and another boom— almost drowned by the roar of the sea and the screams of women and oaths of sailors—and then panic laid hold of the gunner also, and he deserted his post. The word had gone round, none knew from whom, that the vessel had been lured to her destruction by wreckers, and that in a few minutes she would be boarded by these wolves of the sea. The captain, who should have kept order, had disappeared; the mate was disregarded; there was a general sauve-qui-peut. A few women were on board; at the shock they had come on deck, some with children, and the latter were wailing and shrieking with terror. The women implored that they might be saved. Men passengers ran about asking what was to be done, and were beaten aside and cursed by the frantic sailors. A Portuguese nun was ill with sea-sickness, and sank on the deck like a log, crying to S. Joseph between her paroxysms. One man alone seemed to maintain his self-possession, a young man, and he did his utmost to soothe the excited women and abate their terrors. He raised the prostrate nun, and insisted on her laying hold of a rope, lest she should be carried overboard in the swash of the water. He entreated the mate to exert his authority and bring the sailors to a sense of their duty, to save the women, instead of escaping in the boat, regardful of themselves only.

Suddenly a steady star, red in colour, glared out of the darkness, and between it and the wreck heaved and tossed a welter of waves and foam.

"There is land!" shouted the mate.

"And that shines just where that light was that led us here," retorted a sailor.

The vessel heeled to one side, and shipped water fore and aft over either rail, with a hiss and hum. She plunged, staggered, and sank deeper into the sand.

A boat had been lowered, and three men were in it, and called to the women to be sharp and join them. But this was no easy matter, for the boat at one moment leaped up on the comb of a black wave, and then sank in its yawning trough; now was close to the side of the ship, and then separated from it by a rift of water. The frightened women were let down by ropes, but in their bewilderment missed their opportunity when the boat was under them, and some fell into the water and had to be dragged out; others refused to leave the wreck and risk a leap into the littl boat.

Nothing would induce the sick nun to venture overboard. She could not understand English. The young passenger addressed her in Portuguese, and, finally, losing all patience, and finding that precious time was wasted in arguing with a poor creature who, in her present condition, was incapable of reasoning, he ordered a sailor to help him, caught her up in his arms, and proceeded to swing himself over, that he might carry her into the boat.

But at that moment dark figures occupied the deck, and a man arrested him with his hand, whilst in a loud and authoritative voice he called—

"No one leaves the vessel without my orders. Number Five, down into the boat and secure that. Number Seven, go with him. Now, one by one, and before each leaves, give over your purses and valuables that you are trying to save. No harm shall be done you; only make no resistance."

The ship was in the hands of the wreckers.

The men in the boat would have cast off at once, but the two men sent into it, Numbers Five and Seven, prevented them. The presence of the wreckers produced order where there had before been confusion. The man who had laid his hand on the Portuguese nun, and had given orders, was obeyed not only by his own men, but by the crew of the merchant vessel, and by the passengers, from whom all thoughts of resistance, if they ever rose, vanished at once. All alike, cowed and docile, obeyed without a murmur, and began to produce from their pockets whatever they had secured and had hoped to carry ashore with them.

"Nudding! me nudding!" gasped the nun.

"Let her pass down," ordered the man who acted as captain. "Now the next— you—" He turned on the young passenger who had assisted the nun.

"You scoundrel!" shouted the young man, "you shall not have a penny of mine."

"We shall see," answered the wrecker, and levelled a pistol at his head. "What answer do you make to this?"

The young man struck up the pistol, and it was discharged into the air. Then he sprang on the man acting as captain, struck him in the chest, and grappled with him.

In a moment a furious contest was engaged in between the two men on the wet, sloping deck, sloping, for the cargo had shifted.

"Hah!" shouted the wrecker, "a Cornishman!"

"Yes, a Cornishman," answered the youth.

The wrecker knew whence he came by his method of wrestling, a trick peculiar to the county.

If there had been light, crew, invaders, passengers would have gathered in a circle and watched the contest, but in the dark, lashed by foam, in the roar of the waves and the pipe of the wind, only one or two that were near were aware of the conflict. Some of the crew were below. They had got at the spirits and were drinking. One drunken sailor rushed forth swearing and blaspheming and striking about him. He was knocked down by a wrecker, and a wave that heaved over the deck lifted him and swept him over the bulwarks.

The wrestle between the two men in the dark taxed the full nerves and the skill of each. The young passenger was strong and nimble, but he had found his match in the wrecker. The latter was skilful and of great muscular power. First one went down on the knee, then the other, but each was up again in a moment. A blinding whip of foam and water slashed between them, stinging their eyes, swashing into their mouths, forcing them momentarily to relax their hold of each other, but next moment they had leaped at one another again. Now they held each other, breast to breast, and sought with their arms bowed like the legs of grasshoppers to strangle or break each other's neck. Then, like a clap of thunder, a huge billow beat against the stern and rolled in a liquid heap over the deck, enveloping the wrestlers, and lifted them from their feet and cast them writhing, pounding each other, prostrate upon the deck.

There were screams and gasps from the women as they escaped from the water; the nun shrieked to S. Joseph—she had lost her hold and fell overboard, but was caught and placed in the boat.

"Now another!" was the shout.

"Hand me your money," demanded one of the wreckers. "Madam, have no fear. We do not hurt women. I will help you into the boat."

"I have nothing; nothing but this. What shall I do if you take my money?"

"I am sorry. You must either remain and drown when the ship breaks up, or give me the purse."

She gave up the purse, and was safely lodged below.

"Who are you?" gasped the captain of the wreckers, in a moment of relaxation from the desperate struggle.

"An honest man—and you a villain," retorted the young passenger, and the contest was recommenced.

"Let go," said the wrecker, as he and the young passenger regained their feet, still clasping each other, "and you shall be allowed to depart, and carry your money with you."

"I ask no man's leave to carry what is my own," answered the youth. He put his hand to his waist and unbuckled a belt; to this belt was attached a pouch well weighted with metal. "This is all I have in the world, and with it I will beat your brains out." He whirled the belt and money-bag round his head, and brought it down with a crash upon his adversary, who staggered back. The young man struck at him again, but, in the dark, missed him, and, with the violence of the blow and weight of the purse, was carried forward, and fell on the slippery, inclined planks.

"Now I have you!" shouted the other; he flung himself on the prostrate man, and planted his knee on his back. But, assisted by the inclination of the deck, the young man slipped from beneath his antagonist, and, half rising, caught him and dashed him against the rail.

The wrecker was staggered for a moment, and had the passenger seized the occasion he might have finished the conflict; but his purse had slipped from his hand, and he groped for the belt till he found one end at his feet; and now he twisted the belt round and about his right arm, and weighted his fist with the pouch.

The captain recovered the blow, and threw himself on his adversary, grasped his arms between the shoulder and elbow, and bore him back against the bulwark, drove him against it, and cast himself upon him.

"I've spared your life so far. Now I'll spare you no more," said he, and the young man felt that one of his arms was released. He could not tell at the time, he never could decide afterwards how he knew it, whether he saw, or whether he guessed it, but he was certain that his enemy was groping at his side for a knife. Then the hand of the wrecker closed on his throat, and the young man's head was driven back over the rail, almost dislocating the neck. It was then as though he saw into the mind of the man who had cast himself against him, and who was strangling him. He knew that he could not find the required knife; but he saw nothing, only a fire and blood before his eyes that looked up into the black heavens, and he felt naught save agony at the nape of his neck where his spine was turned back on the bulwarks.

"Number Eight! any of you! an axe!" roared the wrecker. "By heaven! you shall be as Wyvill, and float headless on the waves."

"Coppinger!" cried the young man, by a desperate effort liberating his head. He threw his arms round the wrecker. A dash and a boil of froth, and both went overboard, fighting as they fell into the surf.

"In the King's name!" shouted a harsh voice. "Surround—secure them all. Now we have them, and they shall not escape."

The wreck was boarded by, and in the hands of, the coastguard.

## CHAPTER XXXVII
## BRUISED NOT BROKEN

"Come with me, uncle," said Judith.

"My dear, I will follow you like a dog, anywhere."

"I want to go to the rectory."

"To the rectory! At this time of night?"

"At once."

When the down was left, then there was no longer necessity for hiding the lantern, as they were within lanes, and the light would not be seen at sea.

The distance to the parsonage was not great, and the little party were soon there, but were somewhat puzzled how to find the door, owing to the radical transformation of the approaches effected by the new rector.

Mr. Desiderius Mules was not in bed. He was in his study, without his collar and necktie, smoking, and composing a sermon. It is not only lucus which is derived from non lucendo. A study in many a house is equally misnamed. In that of Mr. Mules' house it had some claim perhaps to its title, for in it once a week Mr. Desiderius cudgelled his brains how to impart form to an incoate mass of notes; but it hardly deserved its name as a place where the brain was exercised in absorption of information. The present study was the old pantry. The old study had been occupied by a man of reading and of thought. Perhaps it was not unsuitable that the pantry should become Mr. Mules' study, that where the maid had emptied her slop-water after cleaning forks and plates, should be the place for the making of the theological slop-water that was to be poured forth on the Sunday. But, what a word has been here employed—theological —another lucus a non lucendo, for there was nothing of theology proper in the stuff compounded by Mr. Mules. We shall best be able to judge by observing him engaged on his sermon for Sunday.

In his mouth was a pipe, on the table a jar of birds'-eye. Item: a tumbler of weak brandy and water to moisten his lips with occasionally. It was weak. Mr. Mules never took a drop more than was good for him. Before him were arranged, in a circle, his materials for composition. On his extreme left was what he termed his Treacle-pot. That was a volume of unctuous piety. Then came his Dish of Flummery. That was a volume of ornate discourses by a crack lady's preacher. Next his Spice-box. That was a little store of anecdotes, illustrations, and pungent sayings. Pearson on the Creed, Bishop Andrews, no work of solid divinity was to be found either on his table or on his shelves. A Commentary was outspread, and a Concordance.

The Reverend Desiderius Mules sipped his brandy and water, took a long whiff at his pipe, and then wrote his text. Then he turned to his Commentary, and extracted from it junks of moralization upon his text and on other texts which his Concordance told him more or less had to do with his head text. Then he peppered his paper well over with quotations, those in six lines preferred to those in three, and those in one only despised as unprofitable.

"Now," said the manufacturer of the sermon, "I must have a little treacle. I suppose those bumpkins will like it, but not much; I hate it myself. It is ridiculous! And I can dish up a trifle of flummery in here and there conveniently, and—let me see—I'll work up to a story near the tail somehow. But what heading shall I give my discourse? 'Pon my word, I don't know what its subject is. We'll call it 'General Piety.' That will do admirably—yes, 'General Piety.' Come in! Who's there?"

A servant entered, and said that there were Mr. Menaida and the lady that had been married that morning at the door wanting to speak with him. Should she show them into the study?

Mr. Mules looked at his brandy and water, then at his array of material for composition, and then at his neckerchief on the floor, and said, "No—into the drawing-room." The maid was told to light candles for them. He would put on his collar and be with them shortly. So the sermon had to be laid aside.

Presently Mr. Desiderius Mules entered his drawing-room, where Judith, Uncle Zachie, and Jamie were awaiting him.

"A late visit, but always welcome," said the rector. "Sorry I kept you waiting, but I was en déshabille. What can I do for you now, eh?"

Judith was composed; she had formed her resolution. She said, "You married me this morning when I was unconscious. I answered but one of your questions. Will you get your Prayer Book, and I will make my responses to all those questions you put to me when I was in a dead faint."

"Oh, not necessary. Sign the register, and it is all right. Silence gives consent you know."

"I wish it otherwise, particularly, and then you can judge for yourself whether silence gave consent."

Mr. Desiderius Mules ran back into his study, pulled a whiff at his pipe to prevent the fire from going out, moistened his untempered clay with brandy and water, and came back again with a book of Common Prayer.

"Here we are," said he. " 'Wilt thou have this man,' and so on—you answered to that, I believe. Then comes, 'I, Judith, take thee, Curll, to my wedded husband'—you were indistinct over that, I believe."

"I remember nothing about it. Now I will give you my intention distinctly. I will not take Curll Coppinger to my wedded husband, and thereto I will never give my troth—so help me, God."

"Goodness gracious!" exclaimed the rector. "You put me in a queer position. I married you, and you can't undo what is done. You have the ring on your finger."

"No—here it is. I return it."

"I refuse to take it. I have nothing whatever to do with the ring. Captain Coppinger put it on your hand."

"When I was unconscious."

"But am I to be choused out of my fee, as out of other things?"

"You shall have your fee. Do not concern yourself about that. I refuse to consider myself married. I refuse to sign the register. No man shall force me to it, and if it comes to law, here are witnesses—you yourself are a witness—that I was unconscious when you married me."

"I shall get into trouble. This is a very unpleasant state of affairs."

"It is more unpleasant for me than for you," said Judith.

"It is a most awkward complication. Never heard of such a case before. Don't you think that after a good night's rest and a good supper—and let me advise a stiff glass of something warm—taken medicinally, you understand—that you will come round to a better mind."

"To another mind I shall not come round. I suppose I am half married—never by my will shall that half be made into a whole."

"And what do you want me to do?" asked Mr. Mules, thoroughly put out of his self-possession by this extraordinary scene.

"Nothing," answered Judith, "save to bear testimony that I utterly and entirely refuse to complete the marriage which was half done, by answering with assent to those questions which I failed to answer in church because I fainted, and to wear the ring which was fixed on me when I was insensible, and to sign the register now that I am in full possession of my wits. We will detain you no longer."

Judith left along with Jamie and Mr. Menaida, and Mr. Mules returned to his sermon. He pulled at his pipe till the almost expired fire was rekindled into glow, and he mixed himself a little more brandy and water. Then, with his pipe in the corner of his mouth, he looked at his discourse. It did not quite please him; it was undigested.

"Dear me!" said Mr. Desiderius; "my mind is all of a whirl, and I can do nothing to this now. It must go as it is—yet, stay, I'll change the title. 'General Piety' is rather pointless. I'll call it 'Practical Piety.' "

Judith returned to Pentyre Glaze. She was satisfied with what she had done; anger and indignation were in her heart. The man to whom she had given her hand had enlisted her poor brother in the wicked work of luring unfortunate sailors to their destruction. She could hardly conceive of anything more diabolical than this form of wrecking; her Jamie was involved in the crime of drawing men to their death. A ship had been wrecked—she knew that by the minute guns—and if lives were lost from it, the guilt in a measure rested on the head of Jamie. But for her intervention, he would have been taken in the act of showing lights to mislead mariners, and would certainly have been brought before magistrates and most probably have been imprisoned. The thought that her brother, the son of such a father, should have escaped this disgrace through an accident only, and that he had been subjected to the risk by Coppinger, filled her veins with liquid fire. Thenceforth there could be nothing between her and Captain Cruel, save, on her part, antipathy, resentment and contempt. His passion for her must cool or chafe itself away. She would never yield to him a hair's breadth.

Judith threw herself on her bed, in her clothes. She could not sleep. Wrath against Coppinger seethed in her young heart. Concerned she was for the wrecked, but concern for them was overlapped by fiery indignation against the wrecker. There was also in her breast self-reproach. She had not accepted as final her father's judgment on the man. She had allowed Coppinger's admiration of herself to move her from a position of uncompromising hostility, and to awake in her suspicions that her dear, dear father might have been mistaken, and that the man he condemned might not be so guilty as he supposed.

As she lay tossing on her bed, turning from side to side, her face now flaming, then white, she heard a noise in the house. She sat up on her bed and listened. There was now no light in the room, and she would not go into that of her aunt to borrow one: Miss Trevisa might be asleep, and would be vexed to be disturbed. Moreover, resentment against her aunt for having forced her into the marriage was strong in the girl's heart, and she had no wish to enter into any communications with her.

So she sat on her bed listening. There was certainly disturbance below. What was the meaning of it?

Presently she heard her aunt's voice downstairs. She was, therefore, not asleep in her room.

Thereupon Judith descended the stairs to the hall. There she found Captain Coppinger being carried to his bedroom by two men, whilst Miss Trevisa held a light. He was streaming with water that made pools on the floor.

"What is the matter? Is he hurt? Is he hurt seriously?" she asked, her woman's sympathy at once aroused by the sight of suffering.

"He has had a bad fall," replied her aunt. "He went to a wreck that has been cast on Doom Bar, to help to save the unfortunate, and save what they value equally with their lives—their goods, and he was washed overboard, fell into the sea, and was dashed against the boat. Yes, he is injured. No bones broken this time. This time he had to do with the sea and with men. But he is badly bruised. Go on," she said to those who were conveying Coppinger. "He is in pain; do you not see this as you stand there? Lay him on his bed and remove his clothes. He is drenched to the skin. I will brew him a posset."

"May I help you, aunt?"

"I can do it myself."

Judith remained with Miss Trevisa. She said nothing to her till the posset was ready. Then she offered to carry it to her husband.

"As you will: here it is," said Aunt Dionysia.

Thereupon Judith took the draught, and went with it to Captain Coppinger's room. He was in his bed. No one was with him, but a candle burned on the table.

"You have come to me, Judith?" he said, with glad surprise.

"Yes—I have brought you the posset. Drink it out to the last drop."

She handed it to him; and he took the hot caudle.

"I need not finish the bowl?" he asked.

"Yes—to the last drop."

He complied, and then suddenly withdrew the vessel from his lips. "What is this at the bottom—a ring?"

He extracted a plain gold ring from the bowl.

"What is the meaning of this? It is a wedding-ring."

"Yes—mine."

"It is early to lose it."

"I threw it in."

"You—Judith—why?"

"I return it to you."

He raised himself on one elbow and looked at her fixedly, with threatening eyes.

"What is the meaning of this?"

"That ring was put on my finger when I was unconscious. Wait till I accept it freely."

"But, Judith, the wedding is over."

"Only a half wedding."

"Well, well, it shall soon be a whole one. We will have the register signed to-morrow."

Judith shook her head.

"You are acting strangely to-night," said he.

"Answer me," said Judith. "Did you not send out Jamie with a light to mislead the sailors, and draw them on to Doom Bar?"

"Jamie again!" exclaimed Coppinger, impatiently.

"Yes, I have to consider for Jamie. Answer me, did you not send him—"

He burst in angrily. "If you will. Yes, he took the light to the shore. I knew there was a wreck. When a ship is in distress she must have a light."

"You are not speaking the truth. Answer me—did you go on board the wrecked vessel to save those who were cast away?"

"They would not have been saved without me. They had lost their heads—every one."

"Captain Coppinger," said Judith, "I have lost all trust in you. I return you the ring which I will never wear. I have been to see the rector and have told him that I refuse you, and that I will never sign the register."

"I will force the ring on to your finger," said Coppinger.

"You are a man, stronger than I, but I can defend myself, as you know to your cost. Half married we are, and so must remain, and never, never shall we be more than that."

Then she left the room, and Coppinger dashed the posset cup to the ground, but held the ring and turned it in his fingers, and the light flickered on it, a red-gold ring like that red-gold hair that was about his throat.

# CHAPTER XXXVIII
## A CHANGE OF WIND

AFTER many years of separation, father and son were together once more. Early in the morning after the wreck on Doom Bar, Oliver Menaida appeared at his father's cottage, bruised and wet through, but in health and with his purse in hand.

When he had gone overboard with the wrecker, the tide was falling and he had been left on the sands of the Bar, where he had spent a cold and miserable night, with only the satisfaction to warm him that his life and his money were his. He was not floating, like Wyvill, a headless trunk, nor was he without his pouch that contained his gold and valuable papers.

Mr. Menaida was roused from sleep very early to admit Oliver. The young man had recognized where he was, as soon as sufficient light was in the sky, and he had been carried across the estuary of the Camel by one of the boats that was engaged in clearing the wreck, under the direction of the captain of the coastguard. Three men only had been arrested on the wrecked vessel, three of those who had boarded her for plunder; all the rest had effected their escape, and it was questionable whether these three could be brought to justice, as they protested they had come from shore as salvors. They had heard the signals of distress and had put off to do what they could for those who were in jeopardy. No law forbad men coming to the assistance of the wrecked. It could not be proved that they had laid their hands on, and kept for their own use, any of the goods of the passengers or any of the cargo of the vessel. It was true that from some of the women their purses had been exacted, but the men taken professed their innocence of having done this, and the man who had made the demand—there was but one— had disappeared. Unhappily he had not been secured.

It was a question also whether proceedings could be taken relative to the exhibition of lights that had misguided the merchantman. The coastguard had come on Mr. Menaida and Judith on the downs with a light, but he was conducting her to her new home, and there could be entertained against them no suspicion of having acted with evil intent.

"Do you know, father," said Oliver, after he was rested, had slept and fed, "I am pretty sure that the scoundrel who attacked me was Captain Coppinger. I cannot swear. It is many years now since I heard his voice, and when I did hear it in former years, it was but occasionally. What made me suspect at the time that I was struggling with Captain Cruel was that he had my head back over the gunwale, and called for an axe, swearing that he would treat me like Wyvill. That story was new when I left home, and folk said that Coppinger had killed the man."

Mr. Menaida fidgeted.

"That was the man who was at the head of the entire gang. He it was who issued the orders which the rest obeyed; and he, moreover, was the man who required the passengers to deliver up their purses and valuables before he allowed them to enter the boat."

"Between ourselves," said Uncle Zachie, rubbing his chin and screwing up his mouth—"between you and me and the poker, I have no doubt about it, and I could bring his neck into the halter if I chose."

"Then why do you not do so, father? The ruffian would not have scrupled to hack off my head, had an axe been handy, or had I waited till he had got hold of one."

Mr. Menaida shook his head.

"There are a deal of things that belong to all things," he said. "I was on the down with my little pet and idol, Judith, and we had the lantern, and it was that lantern that proved fatal to your vessel."

"What, father! we owe our wreck to you?"

"No—and yet it must be suffered to be so supposed, I must allow many hard words to be rapped out against me, my want of consideration, my scatterbrainedness. I admit that I am not a Solomon, but I should not be such an ass—such a criminal—as on a night like the last to walk over the downs above the cliffs with a lantern. Nevertheless, I cannot clear myself."

"Why not?"

"Because of Judith."

"I do not understand."

"I was escorting her home—to her husband's—"

"Is she married"

"'Pon my word I can't say—half-and-half."

"I do not understand you."

"I will explain later," said Mr. Menaida. "It's a perplexing question; and, though I was brought up at the law, upon my word I can't say how the law would stand in the matter."

"But how about the false lights?"

"I am coming to that. When the Preventive men came on us, led by Scantlebray—and why he was with them, and what concern it was of his, I don't know— when the guard found us, it is true Judith had the lantern, but it was under her cloak."

"We, however, saw the light for some time."

"Yes—but neither she nor I showed it. We had not brought a light with us. We knew that it would be wrong to do so; but we came on some one driving an ass with the lantern affixed to the head of the brute."

"Then say so."

"I cannot. That person was Judith's brother."

"But he is an idiot."

"He was sent out with the light."

"Well, then, that person who sent him will be punished, and the silly boy will come off scot free."

"I cannot. He who sent the boy was Judith's husband."

"Judith's husband! Who is that?"

"Captain Coppinger."

"Well, what of that? The man is a double-dyed villain. He ought to be brought to justice. Consider the crimes of which he has been guilty. Consider what he has done this past night. I cannot see, father, that merely because you esteem a young person, who may be very estimable, we should let a consummate scoundrel go free, solely because he is her husband. He has brought a fine ship to wreck, he has produced much wretchedness and alarm. Indeed, he has been the occasion of some lives being lost, for one or two of the sailors, thinking we were going to Davy Jones' locker, got drunk and were carried overboard. Then, consider, he robbed some of the unhappy, frightened women as they were escaping. Bless me!"—Oliver sprang up and paced the room—"it makes my blood seethe. The fellow deserves no consideration. Give him up to justice. Let him be hung or transported."

Mr. Menaida passed his hand through his hair, and lit his pipe.

"'Pon my word," said he, "there's a good deal to be said on your side—and yet—"

"There is everything to be said on my side," urged Oliver, with vehemence. "The man is engaged in his nefarious traffic. Winter is setting in. He will wreck other vessels as well, and if you spare him now, then the guilt of causing the destruction of other vessels, and the loss of more lives will rest in a measure on you."

"And yet," pleaded Menaida senior, "I don't know. I don't like—you see—"

"You are moved by a little sentiment for Miss Judith Trevisa, or—I beg her pardon—Mrs. Cruel Coppinger. But it is a mistake, father. If you had had this sentimental regard for her, and value for her, you should not have suffered her to marry such a scoundrel past redemption."

"I could not help it. I told her that the man was bad—that is to say, I believed he was a smuggler, and that he was generally credited with being a wrecker as well. But there were other influences, other forces, at work. I could not help it."

"The sooner we can rid her of this villain the better," persisted Oliver. "I cannot share your scruples, father."

Then the door opened and Judith entered.

Oliver stood up. He had re-seated himself on the opposite side of the fire to his father, after the ebullition of wrath that had made him pace the room.

He saw before him a delicate, girlish figure—a child in size and in innocence of face, but with a woman's force of character in the brow, clear eyes, and set mouth. She was very white, her golden hair was spread out about her face, blown by the wind—it was a veritable halo, such as is worn by an angel of da Fiesole or the Venus of Botticelli. Her long, slender, white throat was bare, she had short sleeves to the elbows, and bare arms. Her stockings were white, under her dark blue gown.

Oliver Menaida had spent a good many years in Portugal, and had seen flat faces, sallow complexions, and dark hair—women without delicacy of tone, and grace of figure; and on his return to England the first woman he saw was Judith. This little, pale, red-gold-headed creature was wonderful to him with her iridescent eyes full of a soul that made them sparkle and change colour with every change of emotion in the heart and of thought in the busy brain.

Oliver was a fine man, tall, with a bright and honest face, fair hair, and blue eyes. He started back from his seat, and looked attentively at this child-bride who entered his father's cottage. He knew at once who she was, from the descriptions he had received of her from his father, in letters from home.

He did not understand how she had become the wife of Cruel Coppinger. He had not heard the story from his father, still less could he comprehend the enigmatical words of his father relative to her half-and-half marriage. As now he looked on this little figure, that breathed an atmosphere of perfect purity, of white innocence, and yet not mixed with that weakness which so often characterizes innocence; on the contrary, blended with a strength and force beyond her years. Oliver's heart rose with a bound, and smote against his ribs. He was overcome with a qualm of infinite pity for this poor little fragile being, whose life was linked with that of one so ruthless as Coppinger. Looking at that anxious face, at those lustrous eyes, set in lids that were reddened with weeping, he knew that the iron had entered into her soul, that she had suffered, and was suffering then; nay, more, that the life opening before her would be one of almost unrelieved contrariety and sorrow.

At once he understood his father's hesitation when he urged him not to increase the load of shame and trouble that lay on her. He could not withdraw his eyes from Judith. She was to him a vision so wonderful, so strange, so thrilling, so full of appeal to his admiration and to his chivalry.

"Here, Ju! Here is my Oliver of whom I have told you so much," said Menaida, running up to Judith. "Oliver, boy, she has read your letters, and I believe they gave her almost as great pleasure as they did to me. She was always interested in you—I mean, ever since she came into my house—and we have talked together about you; and upon my word, it really seemed as if you were to her as a brother."

A faint smile came on Judith's face; she held out her hand and said—

"Yes; I have come to love your dear father, who has been to me so kind, and to Jamie also; he has been full of thought—I mean kindness. What has interested him has interested me. I call him uncle, so I will call you cousin. May it be so?"

He touched her hand, he did not dare to grasp the frail, slender white hand. But as he touched it, there boiled up in his heart a rage against Coppinger, that he—this man steeped in iniquity—should have obtained possession of a pearl set in ruddy gold—a pearl that he was, so thought Oliver, incapable of appreciating.

"How came you here?" asked Judith. "Your father has been expecting you some time, but not so soon."

"I am come off the wreck."

She started back and looked fixedly on him.

"What—you were wrecked?—in that ship, last night?"

"Yes. After the fog lifted we were quite lost as to where we were, and ran aground."

"What led you astray?"

"Our own bewilderment and ignorance as to where we were."

"And you got ashore?"

"Yes. I was put across by the Preventive men. I spent half the night on Doom Bar.

"Were any lives lost?"

"Only those lost their lives who threw them away. Some tipsy sailors, who got at the spirits and drank themselves drunk."

"And—did any others—I mean did any wreckers come to your ship?"

"Salvors? Yes; salvors came to save what could be saved. That is always so."

Judith drew a long breath of relief; but she could not forget Jamie and the ass.

"You were not led astray by false lights?"

"Any lights we might have seen were sure to lead us astray, as we did not in the least know where we were."

"Thank you," said Judith. Then she turned to Uncle Zachie. "I have a favour to ask of you."

"Anything you ask I will do."

"It is to let Jamie live here. He is more likely to be well employed, less likely to get in wrong courses, than at the Glaze. Alas! I cannot be with him always and everywhere, and I cannot trust him there. Here he has his occupation; he can help you with the birds. There he has nothing, and the men he meets are not such as I desire that he should associate with. Besides —you know, uncle, what occurred last night, and why I am anxious to get him away."

"Yes," answered the old man; "I'll do my best. He shall be welcome here."

"Moreover, Captain Coppinger dislikes him. He might in a fit of anger maltreat him; I cannot say that he would, but he makes no concealment of his dislike."

"Send Jamie here."

"And then I can come every day and see him, how he is getting on, and can encourage him with his work, and give him his lessons as usual."

"It will always be a delight to me to have you here."

"And to me—to come." She might have said, "to be away from Pentyre," but she refrained from saying that.

With a faint smile—a smile that was but the twinkle of a tear—she held out her hand to say farewell.

Uncle Zachie clasped it, and then, suddenly, she bent and kissed his hand.

"You must not do that," said he, hastily.

She looked piteously into his eyes, and said in a whisper that he alone could hear, "I am so lonely."

When she was gone the old man returned to the ingle nook and resumed his pipe. He did not speak, but every now and then he put one finger furtively to his cheek, wiped off something, and drew very vigorous whiffs of tobacco.

Nor was Oliver inclined to speak; he gazed dreamily into the fire, with contracted brows, and hands that were clenched.

A quarter of an hour thus passed. Then Oliver looked up at his father, and said—

"There is worse wrecking than that of ships. Can nothing be done for this poor little craft, drifting in fog —aimless, and going on to the rocks?"

Uncle Zachie again wiped his cheek, and in his thoughtlessness wiped it with the bowl of his pipe and burnt himself. He shook his head.

"Now tell me what you meant when you said she was but half married," said Oliver.

Then his father related to him the circumstances of Judith's forced engagement, and of the incomplete marriage of the day before.

"By my soul!" exclaimed Oliver, "he must—he shall not treat her as he did our vessel."

"Oh, Oliver! If I had had my way—I had designed her for you."

"For me!"

Oliver bent his head and looked hard into the fire, where strange forms of light were dancing—dancing and disappearing.

Then Mr. Menaida said, between his whiffs: "Surely a change of wind, Oliver. A little while ago, and she was not to be considered: justice above all, and Judith sacrificed, if need be. Now it is Judith above all.'

"Yes," musingly, "above all."

## CHAPTER XXXIX
## A FIRST LIE

AS A FAITHFUL, as a loving wife almost, did Judith attend to Coppinger for the day or two before he was himself again. He had been bruised, that was all. The waves had driven him against the boat, and he had been struck by an oar; but the very fact that he was driven against the boat had proved his salvation, for he was drawn on board, and his own men carried him swiftly to the bank, and, finding him unable to walk, conveyed him home.

On reaching home a worse blow than that of the oar had struck him, and struck him on the heart, and it was dealt him by his wife. She bade him put away from him for ever the expectation, the hope, of her becoming his in more than name.

Pain and disappointment made him irritable. He broke out into angry complaint, and Judith had much to endure. She did not answer him. She had told him her purpose, and she would neither be bullied nor cajoled to alter it.

Judith had much time to herself; she wandered through the rooms of Pentyre during the day without encountering any one, and then strolled on the cliffs; wherever she went she carried her trouble with her, gnawing at her heart. There was no deliverance for her, and she did not turn her mind in that direction. She would remain what she was—Coppinger's half-wife, a wife without a wedding ring, united to him by a most dubiously legal ceremony. She bore his name, she was content to do that; she must bear with his love turned to fury by disappointment. She would do that till it died away before her firm and unchangeable opposition.

"What will be said," growled Coppinger, "when it is seen that you wear no ring?"

"I will wear my mother's, and turn the stone within," answered Judith, "then it will be like our marriage, a semblance, nothing more."

She did appear next day with a ring. When the hand was closed it looked like a plain gold wedding-hoop. When she opened and turned her hand, it was apparent that within was a small brilliant. A modest ring, a very inexpensive one, that her father had given to her mother as a guard. Modest and inexpensive because his purse could afford no better; not because he would not have given her the best diamonds available, had he possessed the means to purchase them.

This ring had been removed from the dead finger of her mother, and Mr. Peter Trevisa had preserved it as a present for the daughter.

Almost every day Judith went to Polzeath to give lessons to Jamie, and to see how the boy was going on. Jamie was happy with Mr. Menaida, he liked a little desultory work, and Oliver was kind to him, took him walks, and talked to him of scenes in Portugal.

Very often, indeed, did Judith, when she arrived, find Oliver at his father's. He would sometimes sit through the lesson, often attend her back to the gate of Pentyre. His conduct towards her was deferential, tinged with pity. She could see in his eyes, read in his manner of address, that he knew her story, and grieved for her, and would do anything he could to release her from her place of torment, if he knew how. But he never spoke to her of Coppinger, never of her marriage, and the peculiar features that attended it. She often ventured on the topic of the wreck, and he saw that she was probing him to discover the truth concerning it, but he on no occasion allowed himself to say anything that could give her reason to believe her husband was the cause of the ship being lost, nor did he tell her of his own desperate conflict with the wrecker captain on board the vessel.

He was a pleasant companion, cheerful and entertaining. Having been abroad, though not having travelled widely, he could tell much about Portugal, and something about Spain. Judith's eager mind was greedy after information, and it diverted her thoughts from painful topics to hear and talk about orange and lemon groves, the vineyards, the flower-gardens, the manners and customs of the people of Portugal, to see sketches of interesting places, and of the costumes of the peasantry. What drew her to Oliver especially was, however, his consideration for Jamie, to whom he was always kind, and whom he was disposed to amuse.

The wreck of the merchantman on Doom Bar had caused a great commotion among the inhabitants of Cornwall. All the gentry, clergy, and the farmers and yeomen not immediately on the coast, felt that wrecking was not only a monstrous act of inhumanity, but was a scandal to the county, and ought to be peremptorily suppressed, and those guilty of it brought to justice. It was currently reported that the merchantman from Oporto was wilfully wrecked, and that an attempt had been made to rob and plunder the passengers and the vessel. But the evidence in support of this view was of little force. The only persons who had been found with a light on the cliffs were Mr. Menaida, whom every one respected for his integrity, and Judith, the daughter of the late rector of S. Enodoc, the most strenuous and uncompromising denouncer of wrecking. No one, however malicious, could believe either to be guilty of more than imprudence.

The evidence as to the attempt of wreckers to invade the ship, and plunder it and the passengers also, broke down. One lady alone could swear that her purse had been forcibly taken from her. The Portuguese nun could hardly understand English, and though she asserted that she had been asked for money, she could not say that anything had been taken from her. It was quite possible that she had misunderstood an order given her to descend into the boat. The night had been dark, the lady who had been robbed could not swear to the identity of the man who had taken her purse, she could not even say that it was one of those who had come to the vessel, and was not one of the crew. The crew had behaved notoriously badly, some had been drunk, and it was possible that one of these fellows, flushed with spirits, had demanded and taken her money.

There were two or three S. Enodoc men arrested because found on the ship at the time, but they persisted in the declaration that, hearing signals of distress, they had kindled a light and set it in the tower window of the church as a guide to the shipwrecked, and had gone to the vessel aground on Doom Bar, with the intention of offering every assistance in their power to the castaways. They asserted that they had found the deck in confusion, the seamen drunk and lost to discipline, the passengers helpless and frightened, and that it was only owing to them that some sort of order was brought about, or attempted. The arrival of the coastguard interfered with their efforts to be useful.

The magistrates were constrained to dismiss the case, although possessed with the moral conviction that the matter was not as the accused represented. The only person who could have given evidence that might have consigned them to prison was Oliver, and he was not called upon to give witness.

But, although the case had broken down completely, an uneasy and angry feeling prevailed. People were not convinced that the wreck was accidental, and they believed that but for the arrival of the guard, the passengers would have been robbed and the ship looted. It was true enough that a light had been exhibited from S. Enodoc tower, but that served as a guide to those who rushed upon the wreck, and was every whit as much to their advantage as to that of the shipwrecked men. For, suppose that the crew and passengers had got off in their boats, they would have made, naturally, for the light, and who could say but that a gang of ruffians was not waiting on the shore to plunder them as they landed?

The general feeling in the county was one of vexation that more prompt action had not been taken, or that the action taken had not been more successful. No man showed this feeling more fully than Mr. Scantlebray, who hunted with the coastguard for his own ends, and who had felt sanguine that in this case Coppinger would be caught.

That Coppinger was at the bottom of the attempt, which had been partly successful, few doubted, and yet there was not a shadow of proof against him. But that, according to common opinion, only showed how deep was his craft.

The state of Judith's mind was also one of unrest. She had a conviction seated in her heart that all was not right, and yet she had no sound cause for charging her husband with being a deliberate wrecker. Jamie had gone out with his ass and the lantern, that was true, but was Jamie's account of the affair to be relied on? When questioned he became confused. He never could be trusted to recall twenty-four hours after an event the particulars exactly as they occured; any suggestive queries drew him aside, and without an intent to deceive he would tell what was a lie, simply because he could not distinguish between realities and fleeting impressions. She knew that if she asked him whether Coppinger had fastened the lantern to the head of his donkey, and had bidden him drive the creature slowly up and down the inequalities of the surface of the cliffs, he would assent, and say it was so; but, then, if she were to say to him, "Now, Jamie, did not Captain Coppinger tell you on no account to show the light till you reached the shore at S. Enodoc's, and then to fix it steadily," that his face would for a moment assume a vacant, then a distressed expression, and that he would finally say he believed it really was so. No reliance was to be placed on anything he said, except at the moment, and not always then. He was liable to misunderstand directions, and by a stupid perversity to act exactly contrary to the instructions given him.

Judith heard nothing of the surmises that floated in the neighbourhood, but she knew enough to be uneasy. She had been somewhat reassured by Oliver Menaida; she could see no reason why he should withhold the truth from her. Was it, then, possible after all that Captain Coppinger had gone to the rescue of the wrecked people, that he had sent the light not to mislead, but to direct them aright?

It was Judith's fate—so it seemed—to be never certain whether to think the worst of Coppinger, or to hold that he had been misjudged by her. He had been badly hurt in his attempt to rescue the crew and passengers—according to Aunt Dionysia's account. If she were to believe this story then he was deserving of respect.

Judith began to recover some of her cheerfulness, some of her freshness of looks. This was due to the abatement of her fears. Coppinger had angrily, sullenly, accepted the relation which she had assured him must subsist between them, and which could never be altered.

Aunt Dionysia was peevish and morose indeed. She had been disappointed in her hope of getting into Othello Cottage before Christmas; but she had apparently received a caution from Coppinger not to exhibit ill-will towards his wife by word or token, and she restrained herself, though with manifest effort. That sufficed Judith. She no longer looked for, cared for love from her aunt. It satisfied her if Miss Trevisa left her unmolested.

Moreover, Judith enjoyed the walk to Polzeath every day, and, somehow, the lessons to Jamie gave her an interest that she had never found in them before. Oliver was so helpful. When Jamie was stubborn, he persuaded him with a joke or a promise to laugh and put aside his ill-humour, and attack the task once more. The little gossiping talk after the lesson with Oliver, or with Oliver and his father, was a delight to her. She looked forward to it from day to day, naturally, reasonably, for at the Glaze she had no one with whom to converse, no one with the same general interests as herself, the same knowledge of books, and pleasure in the acquisition of information.

On mountain sides there are floral zones. The rhododendron and the gentian luxuriate at a certain level, above is the zone of the blue hippatica, the soldanella, and white crocus, below is the belt of mealy primula and lilac clematis. So is it in the world of minds—they have their levels, and can only live on those levels. Transplant them to a higher or to a lower zone and they suffer, and die.

Judith found no one at Pentyre with whom she could associate with pleasure. It was only when she was at Polzeath with Uncle Zachie and Oliver that she could talk freely and feel in her element.

One day Oliver said to her, "Judith,"—for, on the understanding that they were cousins, they called each other by their Christian names—"Judith, are you going to the ball at Wadebridge after Christmas?"

"Ball, Oliver, what ball?"

"That which Mr. Mules is giving for the restoration of his church."

"I do not know. I—yes, I have heard of it; but I had clean forgotten all about it. I had rather not."

"But you must, and promise me three dances at least."

"I do not know what to say. Captain Coppinger"— she never spoke of her husband by his Christian name, never thought of him as other than Captain Coppinger. Did she think of Oliver as Mr. Menaida, junior?— "Captain Coppinger has not said anything to be about it of late. I do not wish to go. My dear father's death—-"

"But the dance is after Christmas. And, you know, it is for a sacred purpose. Think, every whirl you take puts a new stone on the foundations, and every setting to your partner in quadrilles adds a pane of glass to the battered windows."

"I do not know," again said Judith, and became grave. Her heart fluttered. She would like to be at the ball, and dance three dances with Oliver, but would Captain Coppinger suffer her? Would he expect to dance with her all the evening? If that were so, she would not like to go. "I really do not know," again she said, clasped her hands on her knees, and sighed.

"Why that sigh, Judith?"

She looked up, dropped her eyes in confusion, and said faintly, "I do not know." And that was her first lie.

# CHAPTER XL
## THE DIAMOND BUTTERFLY

POOR little fool! Shrewd in maintaining her conflict with Cruel Coppinger—always on the defensive, ever on guard, she was sliding unconsciously, without the smallest suspicion of danger, into a state that must eventually make her position more desperate and intolerable. In her inexperience she had never supposed that her own heart could be a traitor within the city walls. She took pleasure in the society of Oliver, and thought no wrong in so doing. She liked him, and would have reproached herself had she not done so.

Her relations with Coppinger remained strained. He was a good deal from home, indeed he went a cruise in his vessel, the Black Prince, and was absent for a month. He hoped that in his absence she might come to a better mind. They met when he was at home at meals, at other times not at all; he went his way, she went hers. Whether the agitation of men's minds relative to the loss of the merchantman, and the rumours concerning the manner of its loss, had made Captain Cruel think it were well for him to absent himself for a while till they had blown away, or whether he thought that his business required his attention elsewhere, or that by being away from home his wife might be the readier to welcome him, and come out of her vantage castle, and lay down her arms, cannot be said for certain; probably all these motives combined to induce him to leave Pentyre for five or six weeks. Whilst he was away Judith was lighter in heart.

He returned shortly before Christmas, and was glad to see her more like her old self, with cheeks rounder, less livid, eyes less sunken, less like those of a hunted beast, and with a step that had resumed its elasticity. But he did not find her more disposed to receive him with affection as a husband. He thought that probably some change in the monotony of life at Pentyre might be of advantage, and he somewhat eagerly entered into the scheme for the ball at Wadebridge. She had been kept to books and to the society of her father too much in days gone by, and had become whimsical and prudish. She must learn some of the enjoyments of life, and then she would cling to the man who opened to her a new sphere of happiness.

"Judith," said he, "we will certainly go to this ball. It will be a pleasant one. As it is for a charitable purpose, all the neighbourhood will be there. Squire Humphrey Prideaux of Prideaux Place, the Matthews of Roscarrock, the Molesworths of Pencarrow, and every one worth knowing in the country round for twelve miles. But you will be the queen of the ball."

Judith at first thought of appearing at the dance in her simplest evening dress; she was shy and did not desire to attract attention. Her own position was anomalous, because that of Coppinger was anomalous. He passed as a gentleman in a part of the country not very exacting that the highest culture should prevail in the upper region of society. He had means, and he owned a small estate. But no one knew whence he came, or what was the real source whence he derived his income. Suspicion attached to him as engaged in both smuggling and wrecking, neither of which were regarded as professions consonant with gentility. The result of this uncertainty relative to Coppinger was that he was not received into the best society. The gentlemen knew him and greeted him in the hunting-field, and would dine with him at his house. The ladies, of course, had never been invited, because he was an unmarried man. The gentlemen probably had dealings with him about which they said nothing to their wives. It is certain that the Bodmin wine merchant grumbled that the great houses of the North of Cornwall did not patronise him as they ought, and that no wine merchant was ever able to pick up a subsistence at Wadebridge. Yet the country gentry were by no means given to temperance; and their cellars were being continually refilled.

It was not their interest to be on bad terms with Coppinger, one must conjecture, for they went somewhat out of their way to be civil to him.

Coppinger knew this, and thought that now he was married an opportunity had come in this charity ball, for the introduction of Judith to society, and that to the best society, and he trusted to her merits and beauty, and to his own influence with the gentlemen, to obtain for her admission to the houses of the neighbourhood. As the daughter of the Rev. Peter Trevisa, who had been universally respected, not only as a gentleman and a scholar, but also as the representative of an ancient Cornish family of untold antiquity, she had a perfect right to be received into the highest society of Cornwall, but her father had been a reserved and poor man. He did not himself care for associating with fox-hunting and sporting squires, nor would he accept invitations when he was unable to return them. Consequently Judith had gone about very little when at S. Enodoc Rectory. Moreover, she had been but a child, and was known only by name to those who lived in the neighbourhood, she was personally acquainted with none of the county people.

Captain Cruel had small doubt but that, the ice once broken, Judith would make friends, and would be warmly received. The neighbourhood was scantily peppered over with county family seats, and the families found the winters tedious, and were glad of any accession to their acquaintance, and of another house opened to them for entertainment.

If Judith were received well, and found distraction from her morbid and fantastic thoughts, then she would be grateful to him—so thought Coppinger— grateful for having brought her into a more cheerful and bright condition of life than that in which she had been reared. Following thereon, her aversion from him, or shyness towards him, would give way.

And Judith—what were her thoughts? Her mind was a little fluttered, she had to consider what to wear. At first she would go simply clad, then her aunt insisted that, as a bride, she must appear in suitable gown—that in which she had been married, not that with the two sleeves for one side, which had been laid by. Then the question of the jewellery arose. Judith did not wish to wear it, but yielded to her aunt's advice. Miss Trevisa represented to her that, having the diamonds, she ought to wear them, and that not to wear them would hurt and offend Captain Coppinger, who had given them to her. This she was reluctant to do. However, she consented to oblige and humour him in such a small matter.

The night arrived, and Judith was dressed for the ball. Never before had Coppinger seen her in evening costume, and his face beamed with pride as he looked on her in her white silk dress, with ornaments of white satiny bugles in sprigs edging throat and sleeve, and forming a rich belt about the waist. She wore the diamond butterfly in her bosom, and the two earrings to match. A little colour was in her delicately pure cheeks, brought there by excitement. She had never been at a ball before, and with an innocent, childish simplicity she wondered what Oliver Menaida would think of her in her ball dress.

Judith and Coppinger arrived somewhat late, and most of those who had taken tickets were already there. Sir William and Lady Molesworth were there, and the half-brother of Sir William, John Molesworth, rector of S. Breock, and his wife, the daughter of Sir John S. Aubyn. With the baronet and his lady had come a friend, staying with them at Pencarrow, and Lady Knighton, wife of an Indian judge. The Matthews were there; the Tremaynes came all the way from Heligan, as owning property in S. Enodoc, and so in duty bound to support the charity; the Prideaux were there from Place; and many, if not all, of the gentry of various degrees who resided within twelve to fifteen miles of Wadebridge were also there.

The room was not one of any interest, it was long, had a good floor, which is the main thing considered by dancers, a gallery at one end for the instrumentalists, and a draught which circulated round the walls, and cut the throats of the old ladies who acted as wallfruit. There was, however, a room to which they could adjourn to play cards. And many of the dowagers and old maids had brought with them little silver-linked purses in which was as much money as they had made up their minds to lose that evening.

The Dowager Lady Molesworth in a red turban was talking to Lady Knighton, a lady who had been pretty, but whose complexion had been spoiled by Indian suns. and to her Sir William was offering a cup of tea.

"You see," said Lady Knighton, "how tremulous my hand is. I have been like this for some years— indeed ever since I was in this neighbourhood before."

"I did not know you had honoured us with a visit on a previous occasion," said Sir William.

"It was very different from the present, I can assure you," answered the lady. "Now it is voluntarily—then it was much the contrary. Now I have come among very dear and kind friends, then—I fell among thieves."

"Indeed!"

"It was on my return from India," said Lady Knighton. "Look at my hand!" She held forth her arm, and showed how it shook as with palsy. "This hand was firm then. I even played several games of spellikins on board ship on the voyage home, and, Sir William, I won invariably, so steady was my hold of the crook, so evenly did I raise each of the little sticks. But ever since then I have had this nervous tremor that makes me dread holding anything."

"But how came it about?" asked the baronet.

"I will tell you, but—who is that just entered the room?" she pointed with trembling finger.

Judith had come in along with Captain Coppinger, and stood near the door, the light of the wax candles twinkling in her bugles, glancing in flashes from her radiant hair. She was looking about her, and her bosom heaved. She sought Oliver, and he was near at hand. A flush of pleasure sprang into her cheeks as she caught his eye, and held out her hand.

"I demand my dance!" said he.

"No, not the first, Oliver," she answered.

Coppinger's brows knit.

"Who is this?" he asked.

"Oh! do you not know? Mr. Menaida's son, Mr. Oliver."

The two men's eyes met, their irises contracted.

"I think we have met before," said Oliver.

"That is possible," answered Captain Cruel, contemptuously, looking in another direction.

"When we met, I knew you without your knowing me," pursued the young man in a voice that shook with anger. He had recognized the tone of the voice that had spoken on the wreck.

"Of that I, neither, have any doubt as to its possibility. I do not recollect every Jack I encounter."

A moment after an idea struck him, and he turned his head sharply, fixed his eyes on young Menaida, and said, "Where did we meet?"

" 'Encounter' was your word."

"Very well—encounter?"

"On Doom Bar."

Coppinger's colour changed. A sinister flicker came into his sombre eyes.

"Then," said he slowly, in low vibrating tones, "we shall meet again."

"Certainly, we shall meet again, and conclude our —I use your term—encounter."

Judith did not hear the conversation. She had been pounced upon by Mr. Desiderius Mules.

"Now—positively I must walk through a quadrille with you," said the rector. "This is all my affair; it all springs from me, I arranged everything. I beat up patrons and patronesses. I stirred up the neighbourhood. It all turns as a wheel about me as the axle. Come along, the band is beginning to play. You shall positively walk through a quadrille with me."

Mr. Mules was not the man to be put on one side, not one to accept a refusal; he carried off the bride to the head of the room, and set her in one square.

"Look at the decorations," said Mr. Mules, "I designed them. I hope you will like the supper. I drew up the menu. I chose the wines, and I know they are good. The candles I got at wholesale price— because for a charity. What beautiful diamonds you are wearing. They are not paste, I suppose?"

"I believe not."

"Yet good old paste is just as irridescent as real diamonds. Where did you get them? Are they family jewels? I have heard that the Trevisas were great people at one time. Well, so were the Mules. We are really De Moels. We came in with the Conqueror. That is why I have such a remarkable Christian name, Desiderius is the French Désiré—and a Norman Christian name. Look at the wreaths of laurel and holly. How do you like them?"

"The decorations are charming."

"I am so pleased that you have come," pursued Mr. Mules. "It is your first appearance in public as Mrs. Captain Coppinger. I have been horribly uncomfortable about—you remember what. I have been afraid I had put my foot into it, and might get into hot water. But now you have come here, it is all right; it shows me that you are coming round to a sensible view, and that to-morrow you will be at the Rectory and sign the register. If inconvenient, I will run up with it under my arm to the Glaze. At what time am I likely to catch you both in? The witnesses, Miss Trevisa and Mr. Menaida, one can always get at. Perhaps you will speak to your aunt and see that she is on the spot, and I'll take the old fellow on my way home."

"Mr. Mules, we will not talk of that now."

"Come! you must see, and be introduced to, Lady Molesworth."

In the meanwhile Lady Knighton was telling her story to a party round her.

"I was returning with my two children from India; it is now some years ago. It is so sad, in the case of Indians, either the parents must part from their children, or the mother must take her children to England and be parted from her husband. I brought my little ones back to be with my husband's sister, who kindly undertook to see to them. We encountered a terrible gale as we approached this coast; do you recollect the loss of the Andromeda?"

"Perfectly," answered Sir William Molesworth; "were you in that?"

"'Yes, to my cost. One of my darlings so suffered from the exposure that she died. But, really, I do not think it was the wreck of the vessel which was worst. It was not that, or not that alone, which brought this nervous tremor on me."

"I remember that case," said Sir William. "It was a very bad one, and disgraceful to our county. We have recently had an ugly story of a wreck on Doom Bar, with suspicion of evil practices; but nothing could be proved, nothing brought home to any one. In the case of the Andromeda there was something of the same sort."

"Yes, indeed, there were evil practices. I was robbed."

"You! surely, Lady Knighton, it was not of you that the story was told?"

"If you mean the story of the diamonds, it was," answered the Indian lady. "We had to leave the wreck, and carry all our portable valuables with us. I had a set of jewellery of Indian work given me by Sir James—well, he was only plain Mr.

Knighton then. It was rather quaint in design: there was a brooch representing a butterfly, and two emeralds formed the—-"

"Excuse me one moment, Lady Knighton," said Sir William. "Here comes the new rector of S. Enodoc with the bride to introduce her to my wife. I am ashamed to say we have not made her acquaintance before."

"Bride! what—his bride?"

"Oh, no! the bride of a certain Captain Coppinger, who lives near here."

"She is pretty, very pretty; but how delicate!"

Suddenly Lady Knighton sprang to her feet, with an exclamation so shrill and startling that the dancers ceased, and the conductor of the band, thinking an accident had occurred, with his baton stopped the music. All attention was drawn to Lady Knighton, who, erect, trembling from head to foot, stood pointing with shaking finger to Judith.

"See! see! my jewels, that were torn from me! Look!" She lifted the hair, worn low over her cheeks, and displayed one ear; the lobe was torn away.

No one stirred in the ball-room; no one spoke. The fiddler stood with bow suspended over the strings, the flutist with fingers on all stops. Every eye was fixed on Judith. It was still in that room as though a ghost had passed through in winding-sheet. In this hush, Lady Knighton approached Judith, pointing still with trembling hand.

"I demand whence comes that brooch? where—from whom did you get those earrings? They are mine; given me in India by my husband. They are Indian work, and not to be mistaken. They were plucked from me one awful night of wreck by a monster in human form who came to our vessel, as we sought to leave it, and robbed us of our treasures. Answer me— who gave you those jewels?"

Judith was speechless. The lights in the room died to feeble stars. The floor rolled like a sea under her feet; the ceiling was coming down on her.

She heard whispers, murmurs—a humming as of a swarm of bees approaching ready to settle on her and sting her. She looked round her. Every one had withdrawn from her. Mr. Desiderius Mules had released her arm, and stood back. She tried to speak, but could not. Should she make the confession which would incriminate her husband?

Then she heard a deep man's voice, heard a step on the floor. In a moment an arm was round her, sustaining her, as she tottered.

"I gave her the jewels. I, Curll Coppinger, of Pentyre. If you ask where I got it, I will tell you. I bought them of Willy Mann, the pedlar. I will give you any further information you require to-morrow. Make room; my wife is frightened."

Then, holding her, looking haughtily, threateningly, from side to side, Coppinger helped Judith along—the whole length of the ball-room—between rows of astonished, open-eyed, mute dancers. Near the door was a knot of gentlemen. They sprang apart, and Coppinger conveyed Judith through the door, out of the light. down the stair, into the open air.

# CHAPTER XLI
## A DEADLOCK

THE INCIDENT of the jewellery of Lady Knighton occasioned much talk. On the evening of the ball it occupied the whole conversation, as the sole topic on which tongues could run and brains work. I say tongues run and brains work, and not brains work and tongues run, for the former is the natural order in chatter. It was a subject that was thrashed by a hundred tongues of the dancers. Then it was turned over and re-thrashed. Then it was winnowed. The chaff of the tale was blown into the kitchens and servants'-halls, it drifted into taprooms, where the coachmen and grooms congregated and drank; and there it was re-thrashed and re-winnowed.

On the day following the ball the jewels were returned to Lady Knighton, with a courteous letter from Captain Coppinger, to say that he had obtained them through the well-known Willy Mann, a pedlar who did commissions for the neighbourhood, who travelled from Exeter along the south coast of Devon and Cornwall, and returned along the north coast of both counties.

Every one had made use of this fellow to do commissions, and trustworthy he had always proved. That was not a time when there was a parcels post, and few could afford the time and the money to run at every requirement to the great cities, where were important shops, when they required what could not be obtained in small country towns. He had been employed to match silks, to choose carpets, to bring medicines, to select jewellery, to convey love letters.

But Willy Mann had, unfortunately, died a month ago, having fallen off a waggon and broken his neck.

Consequently it was not possible to follow up any further the traces of the diamond butterflies. Willy Mann, as was well known, had been a vehicle of conveying sundry valuables from ladies who had lost money at cards, and wanted to recoup by parting with bracelets and brooches. That he may have received stolen goods and valuables obtained from wrecks was also probable.

So, after all the thrashing and winnowing, folks were no wiser than before, and no nearer the solution of the mystery. Some thought that Coppinger was guilty, others thought not, and others maintained a neutral position. Some again thought one thing one day and the opposite the next; and some always agreed with the last speaker's views; whereas others again always took a contrary opinion to those who discussed the matter with them.

Moreover, the matter went through a course much like a fever. It blazed out, was furious, then died away; languor ensued, and it gave symptoms of disappearing.

The general mistrust against Coppinger was deepened, certainly, and the men who had wine and spirits and tobacco through him resolved to have wine and spirits and tobacco from him, but nothing more. They would deal with him as a trader, and not acknowledge him as their social fellow. The ladies pitied Judith, they professed their respect for her; but as beds are made so must they be lain on, and as is cooked so must be eaten. She had married a man whom all mistrusted, and must suffer accordingly; one who is associated with an infected patient is certain to be shunned as much as the patient. Such is the way of the world, and we cannot alter it, as the making of that way has not been entrusted to us.

On the day following the ball, Judith did not appear at Polzeath, nor again on the day after that.

Oliver became restless. The cheerful humour, the merry mood that his father had professed were his, had deserted him. He could not endure the thought that one so innocent, so childlike as Judith, should have her fortunes linked to those of a man of whom he knew the worst. He could not, indeed, swear to his identity with the man on the wreck who had attempted to rob the passengers, and who had fought with him. He had no doubt whatever in his own mind that his adversary and assailant had been Coppinger; but he was led to this identification by nothing more tangible than the allusion made to Wyvill's death, and a certain tone of voice which he believed he recognized. The evidence was insufficient to convict him, of that Oliver was well aware. He was confident, moreover, that Coppinger was the man who had taken the jewels from Lady Knighton; but here again he was wholly unsupported by any sound basis of fact on which his conviction could maintain itself.

Towards Coppinger he felt an implacable anger, and a keen desire for revenge. He would like to punish him for that assault on the wreck, but chiefly for the wrongs done to Judith. She had no champion, no protector. His father, as he acknowledged to himself, was a broken reed for one to lean on, a man of good intentions, but of a confused mind, of weakness of purpose, and lack of energy. The situation of Judith were a pitiful one, and if she were to be rescued from it, he must rescue her. But when he came to consider the way and means, he found himself beset with difficulties. She was married after a fashion. It was very questionable whether the marriage were legal, but nevertheless it was known through the county that a marriage had taken place, Judith had gone to Coppinger's house, and had appeared at the ball as his wife. If he established before the world that the marriage was invalid, what would she do? How would the world regard her? Was it possible for him to bring Coppinger to justice? Oliver went about instituting inquiries. He endeavoured to trace to their source, the rumours that circulated relative to Coppinger but always without finding anything on which he could lay hold. It was made plain to him that Captain Cruel was but the head of a great association of men, all involved in illegal practices; men engaged in smuggling, and ready to make their profit out of a wreck when a wreck fell in their way. They hung together like bees. Touch one, and the whole hive swarmed out. They screened one another, were ready to give testimony before magistrates that would exculpate whoever of the gang was accused. They evaded every attempt of the coastguard to catch them; they laughed at the constables and magistrates. Information was passed from one to another with incredible rapidity; they had their spies and their agents along the coast. The magistrates and country gentry, though strongly reprobating wrecking, and bitterly opposed to poaching, were of broad and generous views regarding smuggling, and the Preventive officer complained that he did not receive that support from the squirearchy which he expected and had a right to demand.

There were caves along the whole coast from Land's End to Hartland, and there were, unquestionably, stores of smuggled goods in a vast number of places, centres whence they were distributed. When a vessel engaged in the contraband trade appeared off the coast, and the guard were on the alert in one place, she ran a few miles up or down, signalled to shore, and landed her cargo before the coastguard knew where she was. They were being constantly deceived by false information, and led away in one direction whilst the contraband goods were being conveyed ashore in an opposite quarter.

Oliver learned much concerning this during the ensuing few days. He made acquaintance with the officer in command of the nearest station, and resolved to keep a close watch on Coppinger, and to do his utmost to effect his arrest. When Captain Cruel was got out of the way, then something could be done for Judith. An opportunity came in Oliver's way of learning tidings of importance, and that when he least expected it. As already said, he was wont to go about on the cliffs with Jamie, and after Judith ceased to appear at Mr. Menaida's cottage, in his unrest he took Jamie much with him, out of consideration for Judith, who, as he was well aware, would be content to have her brother with him, and kept thereby out of mischief.

On one of these occasions he found the boy lag behind, become uneasy, and at last refuse to go further. He inquired the reason, and Jamie, in evident alarm, replied that he dare not—he had been forbidden.

"By whom?"

"He said he would throw me over, as he did my doggie, if I came here again."

"Who did?"

"Captain Coppinger."

"But why?"

Jamie was frightened, and looked round.

"I mustn't say," he answered, in a whisper.

"Must not say what, Jamie?"

"I was to let no one know about it."

"About what?"

"I am afraid to say. He would throw me over. I found it out and showed it to Ju. I have never been down there since."

"Captain Coppinger found you somewhere, and forbade your ever going to that place again?"

"Yes," in a faltering voice.

"And threatened to fling you over the cliffs if you did?"

"Yes," again timidly.

Oliver said quietly, "Now run home and leave me here."

"I daren't go by myself. I did not mean to come here."

"Very well. No one has seen you. Let me see, this wall marks the spot. I will go back with you."

Oliver was unusually silent as he walked to Polzeath with Jamie. He was unwilling further to press the boy. He would probably confuse him by throwing him into a paroxysm of alarm. He had gained sufficient information for his purpose from the few words let drop. "I have never been down there since," Jamie had said. There was, then, something that Coppinger desired should not be generally known concealed between the point on the cliff where the "new-take" wall ended and the beach immediately beneath.

He took Jamie to his father, and got the old man to give him some setting up of birds to amuse and occupy him, and then returned to the cliff. It did not take him long to discover the entrance to the cave beneath, behind the curtain of slate reef, and as he penetrated this to the furthest point, he was placed in possession of one of the secrets of Coppinger and his band.

He did not tarry there, but returned home another way, musing over what he had learned, and considering what advantage he was to take of it. A very little thought satisfied him that his wisest course was to say nothing about what he had learnt, and to await the turns of fortune, and the incautiousness of the smugglers.

From this time, moreover, he discontinued his visits to the coastguard station, which was on the further side of the estuary of the Camel, and which could not well be crossed without attracting attention. There was no trusting any one, Oliver felt—the boatman who put him across was very possibly in league with the smugglers, and was a spy on those who were in communication with the officers of the Revenue.

Another reason for his cessation of visits was that, on his return to his father's house, after having explored the cave and the track in the face of the cliff leading to it, he heard that Jamie had been taken away by Coppinger. The Captain had been there during his absence, and had told Mr. Menaida that Judith was distressed at being separated from her brother, and that, as there were reasons which made him desire that she should forego her walks to Polzeath, he, Captain Coppinger, deemed it advisable to bring Jamie back to Pentyre.

Oliver asked himself, when he heard this, with some unease, whether this was due to his having been observed with the boy on the downs near the place from which access to the cave was had. Also, whether the boy would be frightened at the appearance of Captain Cruel so soon after he had approached the forbidden spot, and, in his fear, reveal that he had been there with Oliver and had partially betrayed the secret.

There was another question he was also constrained to ask himself, and it was one that made the colour flash into his cheek. What was the particular reason why Captain Coppinger objected to the visits of his wife to Polzeath at that time? Was he jealous? He recalled the flame in his eyes at the ball, when Judith turned to him, held out her hand, and called him by his Christian name.

From this time all communication with Pentyre Glaze was cut off; tidings relative to Judith and Jamie were not to be had. Judith was not seen, Aunt Dionysia rarely, and from her nothing was to be learned. It would hardly comport with discretion for inquiries to be made by Oliver of the servants of the Glaze; but his father, moved by Oliver and by his own anxiety, did venture to go to the house and ask after Judith. He was coldly received by Miss Trevisa, who took the opportunity to insult him by asking if he had come to have his bill settled, there being a small account in his favour for Jamie. She paid him, and sent the old fellow fuming, stamping, even swearing, home, and as ignorant of the condition of Judith as when he went. He had not seen Judith, nor had he met Captain Coppinger. He had caught a glimpse of Jamie in the yard with his donkey, but the moment the boy saw him he dived into the stable, and did not emerge from it till Uncle Zachie was gone.

Then Mr. Menaida, still urged by his son and by his own feelings, incapable of action unless goaded by these double spurs, went to the rectory to ask Mr. Mules if he had seen Judith, and whether anything had been done about the signatures in the register.

Mr. Desiderius was communicative. He had been to Pentyre about the matter. He was, as he said, "in a stew over it" himself. It was most awkward; he had filled in as much as he could of the register, and all that lacked were the signatures—he might say all but that of the bride and of Mr. Menaida, for there had been a scene. Mrs. Coppinger had come down, and, in the presence of the Captain and her aunt, he had expostulated with her, had pointed out to her the awkward position in which it placed himself, the scruple he felt at retaining the fee when the work was only half done; how, that by appearing at the ball, she had shown to the whole neighbourhood that she was the wife of Captain Coppinger, and that, having done this, she might as well append her name to the entry in the register. Then Captain Coppinger and Miss Trevisa had made the requisite entries, but Judith had again calmly, but resolutely, refused.

Mr. Mules admitted there had been a scene. Mr. Coppinger became angry, and used somewhat violent words. But nothing that he himself could say, no representations made by her aunt, no urgency on the part of her husband could move the resolution of Judith, "which was a bit of arrant tomfoolery," said Mr. Desiderius, "and I told her so. Even that—the knowledge that she went down a peg in my estimation —even that did not move her."

"And how was she?" asked Mr. Menaida.

"Obstinate," answered the rector—"obstinate as a m—, I mean as a donkey. That is the position of affairs. We are at a deadlock."

## CHAPTER XLII
## TWO LETTERS

OLIVER MENAIDA was summoned to Bristol by the heads of the firm which he served, and he was there detained for ten days.

Whilst he was away, Uncle Zachie felt his solitude greatly. Had he had even Jamie with him he might have been content, but to be left completely alone was a trial to him, especially since he had become accustomed to having the young Trevisa in his house. He missed his music. Judith's playing had been to him an inexpressibly great delight. The old man for many years had gone on strumming and fumbling at music by great masters, incapable of executing it, and unwilling to hear it performed by incompetent instrumentalists. At length Judith had seated herself at his piano, and had brought into life all that wondrous world of melody and harmony which he had guessed at, believed in, yearned for, but never reached. And now that he was left without her to play to him, he felt like one deprived of a necessary of life.

But his unrest did not spring solely from a selfish motive. He was not at ease in his mind about her. Why did he not see her any more? Why was she confined to Pentyre? Was she ill? Was she restrained there against her will from visiting her old friends? Mr. Menaida was very unhappy because of Judith. He knew that she was resolved never to acknowledge Coppinger as her real husband; she did not love him, she shrank from him. And knowing what he did—the story of the invasion of the wreck, the fight with Oliver—he felt that there was no brutality, no crime which Coppinger was not capable of committing, and he trembled for the happiness of the poor little creature who was in his hands. Weak and irresolute though Mr. Menaida was, he was peppery and impulsive when irritated, and his temper had been roused by the manner of his reception at the Glaze, when he went there to inquire after Judith.

Whilst engaged on his birds, his hand shook, so that he could not shape them aright. When he smoked his pipe, he pulled it from between his lips every moment to growl out some remark. When he sipped his grog, he could not enjoy it. He had a tender heart, and he had become warmly attached to Judith. He firmly believed in the identification of the ruffian with whom Oliver had fought on the deck, and it was horrible to think that the poor child was at his mercy; and that she had no one to counsel and to help her.

At length he could endure the suspense no longer. One evening, after he had drunk a good many glasses of rum and water, he jumped up, put on his hat, and went off to Pentyre, determined to insist on seeing Judith.

As he approached the house he saw that the hall windows were lighted up. He knew which was Judith's room, from what she had told him of its position. There was a light in that window also. Uncle Zachie, flushed with anger against Coppinger, and with the spirits he had drunk, anxious about Judith, and resenting the way in which he had been treated, went boldly up to the front door and knocked. A maid answered his knock, and he asked to see Mrs. Coppinger. The woman hesitated, and bade him be seated in the porch. She would go and see.

Presently Miss Trevisa came, and shut the door behind her, as she emerged into the porch.

"I should like to see Mrs. Coppinger," said the old man.

"I am sorry—you cannot," answered Miss Trevisa.

"But why not?"

"This is not a fit hour at which to call."

"May I see her if I come at any other hour?"

"I cannot say."

"Why may I not see her?"

"She is unwell."

"If she is unwell, then I am very certain she would be glad to see Uncle Zachie."

"Of that I am no judge, but you cannot be admitted now."

"Name the day, the hour, when I may."

"That I am not at liberty to do."

"What ails her?—where is Jamie?"

"Jamie is here—in good hands."

"And Judith?"

"She is in good hands."

"In good hands!" exclaimed Mr. Menaida, "I should like to see the good, clean hands worn by any one in this house, except my dear, innocent little Judith. I must and will see her. I must know from her own lips how she is. I must see that she is happy—or at least not maltreated."

"Your words are insult to me, her aunt, and to Captain Coppinger, her husband," said Miss Trevisa, haughtily.

"Let me have a word with Captain Coppinger."

"He is not at home."

"Not at home!—I hear a great deal of noise. There must be a number of guests in the hall. Who is entertaining them, you or Judith?"

"That is no concern of yours, Mr. Menaida."

"I do not believe that Captain Coppinger is not at home. I insist on seeing him."

"Were you to see him—you would regret it afterwards. He is not a person to receive impertinences and pass them over. You have already behaved in a most indecent manner, in encouraging my niece to visit your house, and sit, and talk, and walk with, and call by his Christian name that young fellow your son."

"Oliver!" Mr. Menaida was staggered. It had never occurred to his fuddled, yet simple mind, that the intimacy that had sprung up between the young people was capable of misinterpretation. The sense that he had laid himself open to this charge made him very angry, not with himself, but with Coppinger and with Miss Trevisa.

"I'll tell you what," said the old man. "If you will not let me in, I suppose you will not object to my writing a line to Judith."

"I have received orders to allow of no communication of any kind whatsoever between my niece and you or your house."

"You have received orders—from Coppinger?" the old man flamed with anger. "Wait a bit! There is no command issued that you are not to take a message from me to your master?"

He put his hand into his pocket, pulled out a notebook, and tore out of it a page. Then, by the light from the hall window, he scribbled on it a few lines in pencil.

"Sir!—You are a scoundrel. You bully your wife. You rob, and attempt to murder those who are shipwrecked.

"Zachary Menaida."

"There," said the old man, "that will draw him, and I shall see him, and have it out with him."

He had wafers in his pocket-book. He wetted and sealed the note. Then he considered that he had not said enough, so he opened the page again, and added— "I shall tell all the world what I know about you." Then he fastened the note again and directed it. But as it suddenly occurred to him that Captain Coppinger might refuse to open the letter, he added on the outside— "The contents I know by heart; and shall proclaim them on the house-tops." He thrust the note into Miss Trevisa's hand, turned his back on the house, and walked home snorting and muttering. On reaching Polzeath, however, he had cooled, and thought that possibly he had done a very foolish thing, and that most certainly he had in no way helped himself to what he desired, to see Judith again. Moreover, with a qualm, he became aware that Oliver, on his return from Bristol, would in all probability greatly disapprove of this fiery outburst of temper. To what would it lead? Could he fight Captain Coppinger? If it came to that, he was ready. With all his faults Mr. Menaida was no coward.

On entering his house, he found Oliver there, just arrived from Camelford. He at once told him what he had done. Oliver did not reproach him; he merely said, "A declaration of war, father!—and a declaration before we are quite prepared."

"Well—I suppose so. I could not help myself. I was so incensed."

"The thing we have to consider," said Oliver, "is what Judith wishes, and how it is to be carried out. Some communication must be opened with her. If she desires to leave the house of that fellow, we must get her away. If, however, she elects to remain, our hands are tied: we can do nothing."

"It is very unfortunate that Jamie is no longer here; we could have sent her a letter through him."

"He has been removed to prevent anything of the sort taking place."

Then Oliver started up. "I will go and reconnoitre myself."

"No," said the father. "Leave all to me. You must on no account meddle in this matter?"

"Why not?"

"Because"—the old man coughed. "Do you not understand?—you are a young man."

Oliver coloured, and said no more. He had not great confidence in his father's being able to do anything effectual for Judith. The step he had recently taken was injudicious and dangerous, and could further the end in view in no way.

He said no more to old Mr. Menaida, but he resolved to act himself in spite of the remonstrance made, and the objection raised by his father. No sooner was the elder man gone to bed, than he sallied forth and took the direction of Pentyre. It was a moonlight night. Clouds indeed rolled over the sky and for a while obscured the moon, but a moment after it flared forth again. A little snow had fallen and frosted the ground, making everything unburied by the white flakes to seem inky black. A cold wind whistled mournfully over the country. Oliver walked on, not feeling the cold, so glowing were his thoughts, and came within sight of the Glaze. His father had informed him that there were guests in the hall; but when he approached the house he could see no lights from the windows. Indeed the whole house was dark, as though every one in it were asleep, or it were an uninhabited ruin. That most of the windows had shutters he was aware, and that these might be shut so as to exclude the chance of any ray issuing he also knew. He could not therefore conclude that all the household had retired for the night. The moon was near its full. It hung high aloft in an almost cloudless sky. The air was comparatively still—still it never is on that coast, nor is it ever unthrilled by sound. Now, above the throb of the ocean, could be heard the shrill clatter and cry of the gulls. They were not asleep; they were about, fishing or quarrelling in the silver light.

Oliver rather wondered at the house being so hushed —wondered that the guests were all dismissed. He knew in which wing of the mansion was Judith's room, and also which was Judith's window. The pure white light shone on the face of the house and glittered in the window panes.

As Oliver looked, thinking and wondering, he saw the casement opened, and Judith appeared at it, leaned with her elbow on the sill, and rested her face in her hand, looking up at the moon. The light air just lifted her fine hair. Oliver noticed how delicately pale and fragile she seemed—white as a gull, fragile as porcelain. He would not disturb her for a moment or two; he stood watching, with an oppression on his heart, and with a film forming over his eyes. Could nothing be done for the little creature? She was moped up in her room. She was imprisoned in this house, and she was wasting, dying in confinement.

And now he stole noiselessly nearer. There was an old cattle-shed adjoining the house, that had lost its roof. Coppinger concerned himself little about agriculture, and the shed that had once housed cows had been suffered to fall to ruin, the slates had been blown off, then the rain had wetted and rotted the rafters, and finally the decayed rafters had fallen with their remaining load of slates, leaving the walls alone standing.

Up one of the sides of this ruinous shed Oliver climbed, and then mounted to the gable, whence he could speak to Judith. But she must have heard him, and been alarmed, for she hastily closed the casement. Oliver, however, did not abandon his purpose. He broke off particles of mortar from the gable of the cow-house, and threw them cautiously against the window. No notice was taken of the first or the second particle that clickered against a pane; but at the third a shadow appeared at the window, as though Judith had come to the casement to look out. Oliver was convinced that he could be seen, as he was on the very summit of the gable, and he raised his hands and arms to ensure attention. Suddenly the shadow was withdrawn. Then hastily he drew forth a scrap of paper, on which he had written a few words before he left his father's house, in the hopes of obtaining a chance of passing it to Judith, through Jamie, or by bribing a servant. This he now wrapped round a bit of stone and fastened it with a thread. Next moment the casement was opened and the shadow reappeared.

"Back!" whispered Oliver, sufficiently loud to be heard, and he dexterously threw the stone and the letter through the open window.

Next moment the casement was shut, and the curtains were drawn.

He waited for full a quarter of an hour, but no answer was returned.

# CHAPTER XLIII
## THE SECOND TIME

NO SOONER had Oliver thrown the stone with note tied round it into Judith's room through the window, than he descended from a position which he esteemed too conspicuous should any one happen to be about in the night near the house. He ensconced himself beneath the cowshed wall in the shadow where concealed, but was ready, should the casement open, to step forth and show himself.

He had not been there many minutes before he heard steps and voices, one of which he immediately recognized as that of Cruel Coppinger. Oliver had not been sufficiently long in the neighbourhood to know the men in it by their voices, but, looking round the corner of the wall, he saw two figures against the horizon, one with hands in his pockets, and, by the general slouch, he thought that he recognized the sexton of St. Enodoc.

"The Black Prince will be in before long," said Coppinger. "I mean next week or fortnight, and I must have the goods shored here this time. She will stand off Porth-leze, and mind you get information conveyed to the captain of the coastguard that she will run her cargo there. Remember that. We must have a clear coast here. The stores are empty, and must be refilled."

"Yes, your honour."

"You have furnished him with the key to the signals?"

"Yes, Cap'n."

"And from Porth-leze there are to be signals to the Black Prince to come on here, but so that they may be read the other way—you understand?"

"Yes, Cap'n."

"And what do they give you every time you carry them a bit of information?"

"A shilling."

"A munificent Government payment! And what did they give you for the false code of signals?"

"Half a crown."

"Then here is half a guinea—and a crown for every lie you impose on them."

Then Coppinger and the sexton went further. As soon as Oliver thought he could escape unobserved, he withdrew and returned to Polzeath. Next day he had a talk with his father.

"I have had opinions, in Bristol," said he, "relative to the position of Judith."

"From whom?"

"From lawyers."

"Well—and what did they say?"

"One said one thing, and one another. I stated the case of her marriage, its incompletion, the unsigned register, and one opinion was that nevertheless she was Mrs. Coppinger. But another opinion was that, in consequence of the incompleteness of the marriage, it was none—she was Miss Trevisa. Father, before I went to the barristers and obtained their opinions, I was as wise as I am now, for I knew then what I know now, that she is either Mrs. Coppinger, or else that she is Miss Trevisa."

"I could have told you as much."

"It seems to me—but I may be uncharitable," said Oliver, grimly, "that the opinion given was this way or that way, according as I showed myself interested for the legality or against the legality of the marriage. Both of those to whom I applied regarded the case as interesting and deserving of being thrashed out in court of law, and gave their opinions so as to induce me to embark in a suit. You understand what I mean, father? When I seemed urgent that the marriage should be pronounced none at all, then the verdict of the consulting barrister was that it was no marriage at all, and very good reasons he was able to produce to show that. But when I let it be supposed that my object was to get this marriage established against certain parties keenly interested in disputing it, I got an opinion that it was a good and legal marriage, and very good reasons were produced to sustain this conclusion."

"I could have told you as much, and this has cost you money."

"Yes, naturally."

"And left you without any satisfaction."

"Yes."

"No satisfaction is to be got out of law—that is why I took to stuffing birds."

"What is that noise at the door?" asked Oliver.

"There is some one trying to come in, and fumbling at the hasp," said his father.

Oliver went to the door and opened it—to find Jamie there, trembling, white, and apparently about to faint. He could not speak, but he held out a note to Oliver.

"What is the matter with you? " asked the young man.

The boy, however, did not answer, but ran to Mr. Menaida and crouched behind him.

"He has been frightened," said the old man. "Leave him alone. He will come round presently, and I will give him a drop of spirits to rouse him up. What letter is that?"

Oliver looked at the little note given him. It had been sealed, but torn open afterwards. It was addressed to him, and across the address was written in bold, coarse letters, with a pencil, "Seen and passed.—C. C." Oliver opened the letter and read as follows:—

"I pray you leave me. Do not trouble yourself about me. Nothing can now be done for me. My great concern is for Jamie. But I entreat you to be very cautious about yourself where you go. You are in danger. Your life is threatened, and you do not know it. I must not explain myself, but I warn you. Go out of the country—that would be best. Go back to Portugal. I shall not be at ease in my mind till I know that you are gone, and gone unhurt. My dear love to Mr. Menaida.—Judith."

The hand that had written this letter had shaken; the letters were hastily and imperfectly formed. Was this the hand of Judith who had taught Jamie calligraphy, had written out his copies as neatly and beautifully as copper-plate?

Judith had sent him this answer by her brother, and Jamie had been stopped, forced to deliver up the missive, which Coppinger had opened and read. Oliver did not for a moment doubt whence the danger sprang with which he was menaced. Coppinger had suffered the warning to be conveyed to him with contemptuous indifference; it was as though he had scored across the letter, "Be forewarned, take what precautions you will, you shall not escape me."

The first challenge had come from old Menaida, but Coppinger passed over that as undeserving of attention; but he proclaimed his readiness to cross swords with the young man. And Oliver could not deny that he had given occasion for this. Without counting the cost, without considering the risk, nay, further, without weighing the right and wrong in the matter, Oliver had allowed himself to slip into terms of some familiarity with Judith, harmless enough, were she unmarried, but hardly calculated to be so regarded by a husband. They had come to consider each other as cousins, or they had pretended so to consider each other, so as to justify a half-affectionate, half-intimate association; and, before he was aware of it, Oliver had lost his heart. He could not, and he would not, regard Judith as the wife of Coppinger, because he knew that she absolutely refused to be so regarded by him, by herself, by his father, though by appearing at the ball with Coppinger, by living in his house, she allowed the world to so consider her. Was she his wife? He could not suppose it when she had refused to conclude the marriage ceremony, when there was no documentary evidence for the marriage. Let the question be mooted in a court of law. What could the witnesses say—but that she had fainted, and that all the latter portion of the ceremony had been performed over her when unconscious, and that on her recovery of her faculties she had resolutely persisted in resistance to the affixing of her signature to the register.

With respect to Judith's feelings towards himself, Oliver was ignorant. She had taken pleasure in his society because he had made himself agreeable to her, and his company was a relief to her after the solitude of Pentyre and the association there with persons with whom she was wholly out of sympathy?

His quarrel with Coppinger had shifted ground. At first he had resolved, should occasion offer, to conclude with him the contest begun on the wreck, and to chastise him for his conduct on that night. Now he thought little of that cause of resentment; he desired to punish him for having been the occasion of so much misery to Judith. He could not now drive from his head the scene of the girl's wan face at the window looking up at the moon.

Oliver would shrink from doing anything dishonourable, but it did not seem to him that there could be aught wrong and unbecoming a gentleman in endeavouring to snatch this hapless child from the claws of the wild beast that had struck it down.

"No, father!" said he, hastily, as the old fellow was pouring out a pretty strong dose of his great specific and about to administer it to Jamie—"no, father. It is not that the boy wants; and remember how strongly Judith objects to his being given spirits."

"Dear! dear!" exclaimed Uncle Zachie, "to—be— sure she does, and she made me promise not to give him any. But this is an exceptional case."

"Let him come to me; I will soothe him. The child is frightened; or, stay—get him to help you with that kittiwake. Jamie! father can't get the bird to look natural. His head does not seem to me to be right. Did you ever see a kittiwake turn his neck in that fashion? I wish you would put your fingers to the throat and bend it about, and set the wadding where it ought to be. Father and I can't agree about it."

"It is wrong," said Jamie. "Look—this is the way—"

His mind was diverted. Always volatile, always ready to be turned from one thing to another, Oliver had succeeded in interesting him, and had made him forget for a moment the terrors that had shaken him.

After Jamie had been in the house for half an hour, Oliver advised him to return to the Glaze. He would give him no message, verbal or written. But the thought of having to return renewed the poor child's fears, and Oliver could hardly allay them by promising to accompany him part of the way.

Oliver was careful not to speak to him on the subject of his alarm, but he gathered from his disjointed talk that Judith had given him the note, and impressed on him that it was to be delivered as secretly as possible, that Coppinger had intercepted him, and, suspecting something, had threatened, frightened him into divulging the truth. Then Captain Cruel had read the letter, scored over it some words in pencil, given it back to him, and ordered him to fulfil his commission—to deliver the note.

"Look you here, Jamie," was Mr. Menaida's parting injunction to the lad as he left the house, "there's no reason for you to be idle when at Pentyre. You can make friends with some of the men, and get birds shot. I don't advise your having a gun, you are not careful enough. But, if they shoot birds, you may amuse your leisure in skinning them, and I gave Judith arsenic for you. She keeps it in her workbox, and will let you have sufficient for your purpose, as you need it. I would not give it to you, as it might be dangerous in your hands as a gun. It is a deadly poison, and with carelessness you might kill a man. But go to Judith, when you have a skin ready to dress, and she will see that you have sufficient for the dressing. There, good-bye—and bring me some skins shortly."

Oliver accompanied the boy as far as the gate that led into the lane between the walls enclosing the fields of the Pentyre estate. Jamie pressed him to come further, but this the young man would not do. He bade the poor lad farewell, bid him divert himself, as his father had advised, with bird-stuffing, and remained at the gate watching him depart. The boy's face and feebleness touched and stirred the heart of Oliver. The face reminded him so strongly of his twin-sister, but it was the shadow, the pale shadow, of Judith only, without the intelligence, the character, and the force. And the helplessness of the child, his desolation, his condition of nervous alarm, roused the young man's pity. He was startled by a shot that struck his grey hat simultaneously with the report. In a moment he sprang over the hedge in the direction whence the smoke rose, and came upon Cruel Coppinger with a gun.

"Oh, you!" said the latter, with a sneer. "I thought I was shooting a rabbit."

"This is the second time," said Oliver.

"The first," was Coppinger's correction.

"Not so—the second time you have levelled at me. The first was on the wreck when I struck up your hand."

Coppinger shrugged his shoulders.

"It is immaterial. The third time is lucky, folks say."

The two men looked at each other with hostility.

"Your father has insulted me," said Coppinger. "Are you ready to take up his cause? I will not fight an old fool."

"I am ready to take up his cause, mine also, and that of—"

Oliver checked himself.

"And that of whom?" asked Coppinger, white with rage, and in a quivering voice.

"The cause of my father and mine own will suffice," said Oliver.

"And when shall we meet?" asked Captain Cruel, leaning on his gun, and glaring at his young antagonist over it.

"When and where suits me," answered Oliver, coldly.

"And when and where may that be?"

"When and where!—when and where I can come suddenly on you as you came on me upon the wreck. With such as you one does not observe the ordinary rules."

"Very well," shouted Coppinger. "When and where suits you, and when and where suits me—that is, whenever we meet again, we meet finally."

Then each turned and strode away.

# CHAPTER XLIV
# THE WHIP FALLS

FOR many days Judith had been as a prisoner in the house, in her room. Some one had spoken to Coppinger, and had roused his suspicions, excited his jealousy. He had forbidden her visits to Polzeath; and to prevent communication between her and the Menaida's, father and son, he had removed Jamie to Pentyre Glaze.

Angry and jealous he was. Time had passed, and still he had not advanced a step, rather he had lost ground. Judith's hopes that he was not what he had been represented were dashed. However plausible might be his story to account for the jewels, she did not believe it.

Why was Judith not submissive? Coppinger could now only conclude that she had formed an attachment for Oliver Menaida—for that young man whom she singled out, greeted with a smile, and called by his Christian name. He had heard of how she had made daily visits to the house of the father, how Oliver had been seen attending her home, and his heart foamed with rage and jealousy.

She had no desire to go anywhere now that she was forbidden to go to Polzeath, and when she knew that she was watched. She would not descend to the hall and mix with the company often assembled there, and though she occasionally went there when Coppinger was alone, took her knitting and sat by the fire, and attempted to make conversation about ordinary matters, yet his temper, his outbursts of rancour, his impatience of every other topic save their relations to each other, and his hatred of the Menaidas, made it intolerable for her to be with him alone, and she desisted from seeking the hall. This incensed him, and he occasionally went upstairs, sought her out, and insisted on her coming down. She would obey, but some outbreak would speedily drive her from his presence again.

Their relations were more strained than ever. His love for her had lost the complexion of love, and had assumed that of jealousy. His tenderness and gentleness towards her had been fed by hope, and when hope died they vanished. Even that reverence for her innocence, and the respect for her character that he had shown, were dissipated by the stormy gusts of jealousy.

Miss Trevisa was no more a help and stay to the poor girl than she had been previously. She was soured and embittered, for her ambition to be out of the house and in Othello Cottage had been frustrated. Coppinger would not let her go till he and his wife had come to more friendly terms.

On Judith's chimney-piece were two bunches of lavender, old bunches from the rectory garden of the preceding year. They had become so dry that the seeds fell out, and they no longer exhaled scent unless pressed.

Judith stood at her chimney-piece pressing her fingers on the dropped seeds, and picking them up by this means to throw them into the small fire that smouldered in the grate. At first she went on listlessly picking up a seed and casting it into the fire, actuated by her innate love of order, without much thought—rather without any thought—for her mind was engaged over the letter of Oliver, and his visit the previous night outside. But after a while, whilst thus gathering the grains of lavender, she came to associate them with her trouble, and as she thought—Is there any escape for me, any happiness in store? —she picked up a seed and cast it into the fire; then she asked: Is there any other escape for me than to die—to die and be with dear papa again; now not in S. Enodoc rectory garden, but in the Garden of Paradise? and again she picked up and cast away a grain. Then, as she touched her finger-tip with her tongue and applied it to another lavender seed, she said: Or must this go on—this nightmare of wretchedness, of persecution, of weariness to death without dying—for years? and she cast away the seed shudderingly. Or—and again, now without touching her finger with her tongue, as though the last thought had contaminated it—or will he finally break and subdue me, destroy me and Jamie, soul and body? Shivering at the thought, she hardly dare to touch a seed, but forced herself to do so, raised one and hastily shook it from her.

Thus she continued ringing the change, never formulating any scheme of happiness for herself—certainly in her white, guileless mind, not in any way associating Oliver with happiness, save as one who might by some means effect her discharge from this bondage, but he was not linked, not woven up with any thought of the future.

The wind clickered at the casement. She had a window towards the sea, another opposite, towards the land. Her's was a transparent chamber, and her mind had been transparent. Only now, timidly, doubtfully, not knowing herself why, did she draw a blind down over her soul, as though there were something there that she would not have all the world see, and yet which was in itself innocent.

Then a new fear woke up in her lest she should go mad. Day after day, night after night, was spent in the same revolution of distressing thought, in the same bringing up and reconsidering of old difficulties, questions concerning Coppinger, questions concerning Jamie, questions concerning her own power of endurance and resistance. Was it possible that this could go on without driving her mad?

"One thing I see," murmured she; "all steps are broken away from under me on the stair, and one thing alone remains for me to cling to—one only thing—my understanding. That"—she put her hands to her head, "that is all I have left. My name is gone from me, my friends I am separated from. My brother may not be with me. My happiness is all gone. My health may break down, but to a clear understanding I must hold, if that fails me I am lost—lost indeed."

"Lost indeed!" exclaimed Coppinger, entering abruptly.

He had caught her last words. He came in, in white rage, blinded and forgetful in his passion, and with his hat on. There was a day when he entered the rectory with his head covered, and Judith, without a word, by the mere force of her character shining out of her clear eyes, had made him retreat and uncover. It was not so now. She was careless whether he wore the hat or not when he entered her room.

"So!" said he, in a voice that foamed out of his mouth, "letters pass between you! Letters. I have read that you sent. I stayed your messenger."

"Well," answered Judith, with such composure as she could muster. She had already passed through several stormy scenes with him, and knew that her only security lay in self-restraint. "There was naught in it that you might not read. What did I say?—that my condition was fixed—that none could alter it. That is true. That my great care and sorrow of heart are for Jamie. That is true. That Oliver Menaida has been threatened. That also is true. I have heard you speak words against him of no good."

"I will make good my words."

"I wrote—and hoped to save him from a danger, and you from a crime."

Coppinger laughed.

"I have sent on the letter. Let him take what precautions he will. I will chastise him. No man ever crossed me yet but was brought to bite the dust."

"He has not harmed you, Captain Coppinger."

"He—! Can I endure that you should call him by his Christian name, whilst I am but Captain Coppinger? that you should seek him out, laugh and talk and flirt with him—"

"Captain Coppinger!"

"Yes," raged he, "always Captain Coppinger, or Captain Cruel, and he is dear Oliver! sweet Oliver!"

He well-nigh suffocated in his fury.

Judith drew herself up and folded her arms. She had in one hand a sprig of lavender, from which she had been shaking the over-ripe grains. She turned deadly white.

"Give me up his letter. Yours was an answer."

"I will give it to you," answered Judith, and she went to her workbox, raised the lid, then the little tray containing reels, and from beneath it extracted a crumpled scrap of paper. She handed it calmly, haughtily, to Coppinger, then folded her arms again, one hand still holding the bunch of lavender.

The letter was short. Coppinger's hand shook with passion so that he could hardly hold it with sufficient steadiness to read it. It ran as follows:—

"I must know your wishes, dear Judith. Do you intend to remain in that den of wreckers and cut-throats? or do you desire that your friends should bestir themselves to obtain your release? Tell us, in one word, what to do, or rather what are your wishes, and we will do what we can."

"Well," said Coppinger, looking up. "And your answer is to the point—you wish to stay."

"I did not answer thus. I said, 'Leave me.' "

"And never intended that he should leave you," raged Coppinger. He came close up to her with his eyes glittering, his nostrils distended and snorting, and his hands clenched.

Judith loosened her arms, and with her right hand swept a space before her with the bunch of lavender. He should not approach her within arm's lenght; the lavender marked the limit beyond which he might not draw near.

"Now, hear me!" said Coppinger. "I have been too indulgent. I have humoured you as a spoiled child. Because you willed this or that I have submitted. But the time for humouring is over. I can endure this suspense no longer. Either you are my wife or you are not. I will suffer no trifling over this any longer. You have, as it were, put your lips to mine, and then sharply drawn them away, and now offer them to another."

"Silence!" exclaimed Judith. "You insult me."

"You insult and outrage me!" said Coppinger, "when you run from your home to chatter with and walk with this Oliver, and never deign to speak to me. When he is your dear Oliver, and I am only Captain Coppinger; when you have smiles for him you have black looks for me. Is not that insulting, galling, stinging, maddening?"

Judith was silent. Her throat swelled. There was some truth in what he said; but, in the sight of heaven, she was guiltless of ever having thought of wrong, of having supposed for a moment that what she had allowed herself had not been harmless.

"You are silent," said Coppinger. "Now hearken! With this moment I turn over the page of humouring your fancies and yielding to your follies. I have never pressed you to sign that register; I have trusted to your good sense and good feeling. You cannot go back. Even if you desire it you cannot undo what has been done. Mine you are, mine you shall be—mine wholly and always. Do you hear?"

"Yes."

"And agree?"

"No."

He was silent a moment, with clenched teeth and hands, looking at her with eyes that smote her as though they were bullets.

"Very well," said he. "Your answer is 'No.' " "My answer is No. So held me, God."

"Very well," said he, between his teeth. "Then we open a new chapter."

"What chapter is that?"

"It is that of compulsion. That of solicitation is closed."

"You cannot, whilst I have my senses. What!" She saw that he had a great riding-whip in his hand. "What—the old story again? You will strike me?"

"No, not you. I will lash you into submission— through Jamie."

She uttered a cry, dropped the lavender, that became scattered before her, and held up her hands in mute entreaty.

"I owe him chastisement. I have owed it him for many a day—and to day above all—as a go-between."

Judith could not speak. She remained as one frozen —in one attitude, in one spot, speechless. She could not stir, she could not utter a word of entreaty, as Coppinger left the room.

In another moment a loud and shrill cry reached her ears from the court, into which one of her windows looked. She knew the cry. It was that of her twin-brother, and it thrilled through her heart, quivered in every nerve of her whole frame.

She could hear what followed; but she could not stir. She was rooted by her feet to the floor; but she writhed there. It was as though every blow dealt the boy outside fell on her: she bent, she quivered; her lips parted, but cry she could not, the sweat rolled off her brow, she beat with her hands in the air. Now she thrilled up, with uplifted arms, on tip-toe, then sank—it was like a flame flickering in a socket before it expires: it dances, it curls, it shoots up in a tongue, it sinks into a bead of light, it rolls on one side, it sways to the other, it leaps from the wick high into the air, and drops again. It was so with Judith—every stroke dealt, every scream of the tortured boy, every toss of his suffering frame, was repeated in her room, by her, in supreme, unspeaking anguish, too intense for sound to issue from her contracted throat.

Then all was still, and Judith had sunk to her knees on the scattered lavender, extending her arms, clasping her hands, spreading them again, again beating her palms together in a vague, unconscious way, as if in breathing she could not gain breath enough without this expansion and stretching forth of her arms.

But, all at once, before her stood Coppinger, the whip in his hands.

"Well, what now is your answer?"

She breathed fast for some moments, labouring for expression. Then she reared herself up and tried to speak, but could not. Before her, thrashed out on the floor, were the lavender seeds. They lay thick in one place in a film over the boards. She put her finger among them and drew—NO.

# CHAPTER XLV
## GONE FROM ITS PLACE

THERE are persons—they are not many—on whom Luck smiles and showers gold. Not a steady, daily, down-pour of money, but, whenever a little cloud darkens their sky, that same little cloud, which to others would be mere gloom, opens and discharges on them a sprinkling of gold pieces.

It is not always the case that those who have rich relatives come in for good things from them. In many cases there are such on whom Luck turns her back; but to those of whom we speak the rain of gold, and the snow of scrip and bonds, comes unexpectedly, but inevitably. Just as Pilatus catches every cloud that drifts over Switzerland, so do they by some fatality catch something out of every trouble, that tends materially to solace their feelings, lacerated by that trouble. But not so only. These little showers fall to them from relatives they have taken no trouble to keep on good terms with, from acquaintances whom they have cut, admirers whose good opinion they have not concerned themselves to cultivate, friends with whom they have quarrelled.

Gideon's fleece, on one occasion, gathered to itself all the dew that fell, and left the grass of the field around quite dry. So do these fortunate persons concentrate on themselves, fortuitously it seems, the dew of richness that descends and might have, ought to have, dropped elsewhere, at all events, ought to have been more evenly and impartially distributed. Gideon's fleece, on another occasion, was dry, when all the glebe was dripping. So is it with certain unfortunates—Luck never favours them. What they have expected and counted on they do not get, it is diverted, it drops round about them on every side, only on them it never falls.

Now, Miss Trevisa cannot be said to have belonged to either of these classes. To the latter she had pertained, till suddenly, from a quarter quite unregarded, there came down on her a very satisfactory little splash. Of relatives that were rich she had none, because she had no relatives at all. Of bosom friends she had none, for her bosom was of that unyielding nature, that no one would like to be taken to it. But, before the marriage of her brother, and before he became rector of S. Enodoc, when he was but a poor curate, she had been companion to a spinster lady, Miss Ceely, near S. Austell. Now, the companion is supposed to be a person without an opinion of her own, always standing in a cringing position to receive the opinion of her mistress, then to turn it over and give it forth as her own. She is, if she be a proper companion, a mere echo of the sentiments of her employer. Moreover, she is expected to be amiable, never to resent a rude word, never to take umbrage at neglect, always to be ready to dance attendance on her mistress, and with enthusiasm of devotion, real or simulated, to carry out her most absurd wishes, unreasoningly.

But Miss Trevisa had been, as a companion, all that a companion ought not to be. She had argued with Miss Ceely, invariably had crossed her opinions, had grumbled at her when she asked that anything might be done, raised difficulties, piled up objections, blocked the way to whatever Miss Ceely particularly set her heart on having executed. The two ladies were always quarrelling, always calling each other names, and it was a marvel to the relatives of Miss Ceely that she and her companion hung together for longer than a month. Nevertheless they did. Miss Trevisa left the old lady when Mr. Peter Trevisa became rector of S. Enodoc, and then Miss Ceely obtained in her place quite an ideal companion, a very mirror—she had but to look on her face, smile, and a smile was repeated, weep, and tears came in the mirror. The new companion grovelled at her feet, licked the dust off her shoes, fawned on her hand, ran herself off her legs to serve her, grew grey under the misery of enduring Miss Ceely's jibes and sneers and insults, finally sacrificed her health in nursing her. When Miss Ceely's will was opened it was found that she had left nothing, not a farthing, to this obsequious attendant, but had bequeathed fifteen hundred pounds, free of legacy duty, and all her furniture and her house to Miss Trevisa, with whom she had not kept up correspondence for twenty-three years. It really seemed as if leathery, rusty Aunt Dionysia, from being a dry Gideon's fleece, were about to be turned into a wet, wringable fleece. No one was more astounded than herself.

It was now necessary that Miss Trevisa should go to S. Austell, and see after what had come to her thus unsolicited and unexpectedly. All need for her to remain at Pentyre was at an end.

Before she departed—not finally, but to see about the furniture that was now hers, and to make up her mind whether to keep or to sell it—she called Judith to her.

That day, the events of which were given in last chapter, had produced a profound impression on Jamie. He had become gloomy, timid, and silent. His old idle chatter ceased. He clung to his sister, and accompanied her wherever she went; he could not endure to be with Coppinger; when he heard his voice, caught a glimpse of him, he ran away and hid. Jamie had been humoured as a child, never beaten, scolded, put in a corner, sent to bed, cut off his pudding; but the rod had now been applied to his back, and his first experience of corporal punishment was the cruel and vindictive hiding administered, not for any fault he had committed, but because he had done his sister's bidding. He was filled with hatred of Coppinger, mingled with fear, and when alone with Judith would break out into exclamations of entreaty that she would run away with him, and of detestation of the man who held them there, as it were, prisoners.

"Ju," said he, "I wish he were dead. I hate him! Why doesn't God kill him and set us free?"

At another time he said, "Ju, dear, you do not love him? I wish I were a big, strong man like Oliver, and I would do what Captain Cruel did."

"What do you mean?"

"Captain Cruel shot at Oliver."

This was the first tidings Judith had heard of the attempt on Oliver's life.

"He is a mean coward," said Jamie. "He hid behind a hedge and shot at him. But he did not hurt him."

"God preserved him," said Judith.

"Why does not God preserve us? Why did God let that beast—"

"Hush, Jamie!"

"I will not—that wretch beat me? Why did He not send lightning and strike him dead?"

"I cannot tell you, darling. We must wait and trust."

"I am tired of waiting and trusting. If I had a gun I would not shoot birds, I would go behind a hedge and shoot Captain Coppinger. There would be nothing wrong in that, Ju?"

"Yes, there would. It would be a sin."

"Not after he did that to Oliver."

"I would never, never love you if you did that."

"You would always love me, whatever I did," said Jamie.

He spoke the truth; Judith knew it. Her eyes filled she drew the boy to her, passionately, and kissed his golden head.

Then came Aunt Dionysia, and summoned her into her own room. Jamie followed.

"Judith," began Aunt Dunes, in her usual hard tones, and with the same frozen face, "I wish you particularly to understand. Look here! you have caused me annoyance enough whilst I have been here. Now I shall have a house of my own at S. Austell, and if I choose to live in it I can. If I do not, I can let it, and live at Othello Cottage. I have not made up my mind what to do. Fifteen hundred pounds is a dirty little sum, and not half as much as ought to have been left me for all I had to bear from that old woman. I am glad for one thing that she has left me something, though not much. I should have despaired of her salvation had she not. However, her heart was touched at the last, though not touched enough. Now, what I want you to understand is this—it entirely depends on your conduct, whether, after my death, this sum of fifteen hundred pounds, and a beggarly sum of about five hundred I have of my own, comes to you or not. As long as this nonsense goes on between you and Captain Coppinger—you pretending you are not married, when you are—there is no security for me that you and Jamie may not come tumbling in upon me, and become a burden to me. Captain Coppinger will not endure this fooling much longer. He can take advantage of your mistake. He can say: 'I am not married. Where is the evidence? Produce proof of the marriage having been solemnized.' And then he may send you out of his house upon the downs in the cold. What would you be then, eh? All the world holds you to be Mrs. Coppinger. A nice state of affairs if it wakes up one morning to hear that Mrs. Coppinger has been kicked out of the Glaze, that she never was the wife! What will the world say, eh? What sort of name will the world give you, when you have lived here as his wife?"

"That I have not."

"Lived here, gone to balls as his wife when you were not. What will the world call you, eh?"

Judith was silent, holding both her hands open against her bosom, Jamie beside her looking up in her face, not understanding what his aunt was saying.

"Very well—or rather, very ill," continued Miss Trevisa. "And then you and this boy here will come to me to take you in; come and saddle yourselves on me, and eat up my little fund. That is what will be the end of it, if you remain in your folly. Go at once to the rector, and put your name where it should have been two months ago, and your position is secure. He cannot drive you away, disgusted at your stubbornness, and you will relieve me of a constant source of uneasiness. It is not that only, but I must care for the good name of Trevisa, which you happen to bear, that that name may not be trailed in the dust. The common sense of the matter is precisely what you cannot see. If you are not Coppinger's wife, you should not be here. If you are Coppinger's wife, then your name should be in the register. Now, here you have come. You have appeared in public with him. You have but one course open to you, and that is to secure your position, and your name and honour. You cannot undo what is done, but you can complete what is done insufficiently. The choice between alternatives is no longer before you. If you had purposed to withdraw from marriage, break off the engagement, then you should not have come on to Pentyre and remained here. As, however, you did this, there is absolutely nothing else to be done but to sign the register. Do you hear me?"

"Yes."

"And you will obey?"

"No."

"Pig-headed fool!" said Miss Trevisa; "not one penny will I leave you, that I swear, if you remain obstinate."

"Do not let us say anything more about that, aunt. Now you are going away, is there anything connected with the house you wish me to attend to. That I will do, readily."

"Yes, there are several things," growled Miss Trevisa. "And, first of all, are you disposed to do anything, any common little kindness, for the man whose bread you eat, whose roof covers you?"

"Yes, aunt."

"Very well, then. Captain Coppinger has his bowl of porridge every morning. I suppose he was accustomed to it before he came into these parts, and he cannot breakfast without it. He says that our Cornish maids cannot make porridge properly, and I have been accustomed to see to it. Either it is lumpy, or it is watery, or it is saltless. Will you see to that?"

"Yes, aunt, willingly."

"You ought to know how to make porridge, as you are more than half Scottish."

"I certainly can make it. Dear papa always liked it."

"Then you will attend to that. If you are too high and too great a lady to put your hand to it yourself, you can see that the cook manages it aright. There is a new girl in now, who is a fool."

"I will make it myself. I will do all I can do."

"Then take the keys. Now that I go, you must be mistress of the house. But for your folly I might have been from here and in my own house, or rather in that given me for my use, Othello Cottage. I was to have gone there directly after your marriage. I had furnished it and made it comfortable, and then you took to your fantastic notions, and hung back, and refused to allow that you were married, and so I had to stick on here two months. Here, take the keys." Miss Trevisa almost flung them at her niece. "Now I have two thousand pounds of my own, and a house at S. Austell, it does not become me to be doing menial service. Take the keys. I will never have them back."

When Miss Trevisa was gone, and Judith was by herself, at night, Jamie being asleep, she was able to think over calmly what her aunt had said. She concerned herself not in the least relative to the promise her aunt had made of leaving her two thousand pounds were she submissive, and her threat of disinheriting her should she continue recalcitrant; but she did feel that there was truth in her aunt's words when she said that she, Judith, had placed herself in a wrong position, but it was a wrong position into which she had been forced, she had not voluntarily entered it. She had, indeed, consented to become Coppinger's wife, but when she found that Coppinger had employed Jamie to give signals that might lead a vessel to its ruin, she could not go further to meet him. Although he had endeavoured to clear himself in her eyes, she did not believe him. She was convinced that he was guilty, though at moments she hoped, and tried to persuade herself, that he was not. Then came the matter of the diamonds. There again the gravest suspicion rested on him. Again he had endeavoured to exculpate himself, yet she could not believe that he was innocent. Till full confidence that he was blameless in these matters was restored, an insuperable wall divided them. Never would she belong to a man who was a wrecker, who belonged to that class of criminals her father had regarded with the utmost horror.

Before she retired to bed she picked up from under the fender the scrap of paper on which Oliver's message had been written. It had lain there unobserved where Coppinger had flung it. Now, as she tidied her room and arranged the fire rug, she observed it. She smoothed it out, folded it, and went to her workbox to replace it where it had been before.

She raised the lid, and was about to put the note among some other papers she had there—a letter of her mother's, a piece of her father's writing, some little accounts she had kept—when she was startled to see that the packet of arsenic Mr. Menaida had given her was missing.

She turned out the contents of her workbox. It was nowhere to be found, either there or in her drawers. Her aunt must have been prying into the box, have found and removed it, so Judith thought, and with this thought appeased her alarm. Perhaps, considering the danger of having arsenic about, Aunt Dionysia had done right in removing it. She had done wrong in doing so without speaking to Judith.

# CHAPTER XLVI
## A SECOND LIE

NEXT day, Miss Trevisa being gone, Judith had to attend to the work of the house. It was her manifest duty to do so. Hitherto she had shrunk from the responsibility, because she shrank from assuming a position in the house to which she refused to consider that she had a right. Judith was perfectly competent to manage an establishment; she had a clear head, a love of order, and a power of exacting obedience of servants without incessant reproof. Moreover, she had that faculty, possessed by few, of directing others in their work, so that each moved along his or her own line and fulfilled the allotted work with ease. She had managed her father's house, and managed it admirably. She knew that, as the King's Government must be carried on, so the routine of a household must be kept going. Judith had sufficient acquaintance also with servants to be aware that the wheel would stop or move spasmodically unless an authoritative hand were applied to it to keep it in even revolution. She knew also that whatever happened in a house—a birth, a death, a wedding, an uproar—the round of common duties must be discharged, the meals prepared, the bread baked, the milk skimmed, the beds made, the carpets swept, the furniture dusted, the windows opened, the blinds drawn down, the table laid, the silver and glass burnished. Nothing save a fire which gutted a house must interfere with all this routine. Miss Trevisa was one of those ladies who, in their own opinion, are condemned by Providence never to have good servants. A benign Providence sheds good domestics into every other house save that which she rules. She is born under a star which inexecrably sends the scum and dregs of servantdom under her sceptre. Miss Trevisa regarded a servant as a cat regards a mouse, a dog regards a fox, and a dolphin a flying-fish, as something to be run after, snapped at, clawed, leaped upon, worried perpetually. She was incapable of believing that there could be any good in a servant, that there was any other side to a domestic save a seamy side. She could make no allowance for ignorance, for weakness, for lightheartedness. A servant, in her eyes, must be a drudge, ever working, never speaking, smiling, taking a hand off the duster, without a mind above flue and tea-leaves, and unable to soar above a cobweb, with a temper perfect in endurance of daily, hourly fault-finding, nagging, grumbling, a mind unambitious also of commendation. Miss Trevisa held that every servant that a malign Providence had sent her was clumsy, insolent, slatternly, unmethodical, idle, wasteful, a gossip, a gadabout, a liar, a thief, was dainty, greedy, one of a cursed generation; and when, in the Psalms, David launched out in denunciation of the enemies of the Lord, Miss Trevisa, when she heard or read these psalms, thought of servantdom. Servants were referred to when David said, "Hide me from the insurrection of the wicked doers, who have wet their tongues like a sword, that they may privily shoot at him that is perfect"—i.e., Me, was Miss Trevisa's Comment. "They encourage themselves in mischief: and commune among themselves how they may lay snares, and say that no man shall see them." "And how," said Miss Trevisa, "can men be so blind as not to believe that the Bible is inspired when David hits the character of servants off to the life!"

And not the Psalms only, but the Prophets were full of servants' delinquencies. What were Tyre and Egypt but figures of servantdom shadowed before. What else did Isaiah lift up his testimony about, and Jeremiah lament over, but the iniquities of the kitchen and the servants' hall. Miss Trevisa read her Bible, and great comfort did it afford her, because it did denounce the servant maids so unsparingly, and prepared brimstone and outer darkness for them.

Now, Judith had seen and heard much of the way in which Miss Trevisa managed Captain Coppinger's house. Her room adjoined that of her aunt, and she knew that if her aunt were engaged on—it mattered not what absorbing work—embroidery, darning a stocking, reading a novel, saying her prayers, studying the cookery book—if a servant sneezed within a hundred yards, or upset a drop of water, or clanked a dust-pan, or clicked a door-handle, Miss Trevisa would be distracted from her work and rush out of her room, just as a spider darts from its recess, and would sweep down on the luckless servant to worry and abuse her.

Judith, knowing this, knew also that the day of Miss Trevisa's departure would be marked with white chalk, and lead to a general relaxation of discipline, to an inhaling of long breaths, and a general stretching, and taking of ease. It was necessary, therefore, that she should go round and see that the wheel was kept turning. To her surprise, on entering the hall, she found Captain Coppinger there.

"I beg your pardon," she said, "I thought you were out."

She looked at him, and was struck with his appearance, the clay-like colour of his face, the dark lines in it, the faded look in his eyes.

"Are you unwell?" she asked. "You really look ill."

"I am ill."

"Ill—what is the matter?"

"A burning in my throat. Cramps and pains—but what is that to you?"

"When did it come on?"

"But recently."

"Will you not have a doctor to see you?"

"A doctor!—no."

"Was the porridge as you liked it this morning? I made it."

"It was good enough."

"Would you like more now?"

"No."

"And to-morrow morning, will you have the same?"

"Yes—the same."

"I will make it again. Aunt said the new cook did not understand how to mix and boil it to your liking."

Coppinger nodded.

Judith remained standing and observing him. Some faces when touched by pain and sickness are softened and sweetened. The hand of suffering passes over the countenance, and brushes away all that is frivolous, sordid, vulgar; it gives dignity, purity, refinement, and shows what the inner soul might be were it not entangled and degraded by base association and pursuit. It is different with other faces, the hand of suffering films away the assumed expression of good nature, honesty, straightforwardness, and unmasks the evil inner man. The touch of pain had not improved the expression of Cruel Coppinger. It cannot, however, with justice be said that the gentler aspect of the man which Judith had at one time seen was an assumption. He was a man in whom there was a certain element of good, but it was mixed up with headlong wilfulness, utter selfishness and resolution to have his own way at any cost.

Judith could see now that his face was pain-struck, how much of evil there was in the soul, that had been disguised by a certain dash of masculine over-bearing, and brusqueness.

"What are you looking at?" asked Coppinger, glancing up.

"I was thinking," answered Judith.

"Of what?"

"Of you—of Wyvill, of the wreck on Doom Bar, of the jewels of Lady Knighton, and, last of all, of Jamie's maltreatment."

"And what of all that?" he said, in irritable scorn.

"That I need not say. I have drawn my own conclusions."

"You torment me, you—when I am ill? They call me cruel, but it is you who are cruel."

Judith did not wish to be drawn into discussion that must be fruitless. She said quietly, in altered tone. "Can I get you anything to comfort you?"

"No—go your way. This will pass. Besides, it is naught to you. Go; I would be left alone."

Judith obeyed, but she was uneasy. She had never seen Coppinger look as he looked now. It was other altogether after he had broken his arm. Other also when for a day he was crippled with bruises after the wreck. She looked into the hall several times during the day. In the afternoon he was easier, and went out; his mouth had been parched and burning, and he had been drinking milk. The empty glass was on the table. He would eat nothing at mid-day. He turned from food, and left the room for his own chamber.

Judith was anxious. She more than once endeavoured to draw Coppinger into conversation relative to himself, but he would not speak of what afflicted him. He was annoyed and ashamed at being out of his usual rude health. "It is naught," he said, "but a bilious attack, and will pass. Leave me alone."

She had been so busy all day that she had seen little of Jamie. He had taken advantage of Captain Coppinger not being about to give himself more licence to roam than he had of late, and to go with his donkey on the cliffs. Anyhow, Judith on this day did not have him hanging to her skirts. She was glad of it, for, though she loved him, he would have been an incumbrance when she was so busy.

The last thing at night she did was to go to Coppinger to inquire what he would take. He desired nothing but spirits and milk. He thought that a milkpunch would give him ease and make him sleep. That he was weak and had suffered pain she saw, and she was full of pity for him. But this she did not like to exhibit, partly because he might misunderstand her feelings, and partly because he seemed irritated at being unwell, and at loss of power; irritated at all events, at it being observed that he was not in his usual plenitude of strength and health.

That night the Atlantic was troubled, and the wind carried the billows against the cliffs in a succession of rhythmic roars that filled the air with sound, and made the earth quiver. Judith could not sleep; she listened to the thud of the water-heaps flung against the rocks. There was a clock on the stairs, and in her wakefulness she listened to the tick of the clock and the boom of the waves, now coming together, then one behind the other, now the wave-beat catching up the clock-tick, then falling in arrear, the ocean getting angry and making up its pace by a double beat. Moreover, flakes of foam were carried on the wind, and came like snow against her window that looked seaward, striking the glass, and adhering to it.

As Judith lay watchful in the night her mind again recurred to the packet of arsenic that had been abstracted from her workbox. It was inconsiderate of her to have left it there: she ought to have locked her box. But who could have supposed that any one would have gone to the box, raised the tray, and searched the contents of the compartment beneath? Judith had been unaccustomed to lock up anything, because she had never had any secrets to hide from any eye. She again considered the probability of her aunt having removed it, and then it occurred to her that perhaps Miss Trevisa might have supposed that she, Judith, in a fit of revolt against the wretchedness of her life, might be induced to take the poison herself and finish her miseries. "It was absurd if Aunt Dunes thought that," said Judith to herself; "she can little have known how my dear papa's teaching has sunk into my heart to suppose me capable of such a thing, and then to run away like a coward, and leave Jamie unprotected. It was too absurd."

Next morning Judith was in her room getting a large needle with which to hem a bit of carpet-edge that had been fraying for the last five years, and which no one had thought of putting a thread to, and so arresting the disintegration. Jamie was in the room. Judith said to him:—

"My dear, you have not been skinning and stuffing any birds lately, have you?"

"No, Ju."

"Because I have missed—but, Jamie, I hope you have not been at my workbox?"

"What about your workbox, Ju?"

She knew the boy so well that her suspicions were at once aroused by this answer. When he had nothing to hide he replied with a direct negative or affirmative, but when he had done what his conscience would not quite allow was right, he fell into equivocation and shuffled awkwardly.

"Jamie," said Judith, looking him straight in the face, "have you been to my box?"

"Only just looked in."

Then he ran to the window. "Oh, do see, Ju! how patched the glass is with foam!—and is it not dirty?"

"Jamie, come back! I want an answer."

He had opened the casement and put his hand out, and was wiping off the patches of froth.

"What a lot of it there is, Ju!"

"Come here instantly, Jamie, and shut the window."

The boy obeyed, creeping towards her sideways, with his head down.

"Jamie, did you lift the tray?"

"Only on one side, just a little bit."

"Did you take anything from under the tray?"

He did not answer immediately. She looked at him searchingly and in suspense. He never could endure this questioning look of hers, and he ran to her, put his arms round her waist, and, clasped to her side, hid his face in her gown.

"Only a little."

"A little what?"

"I don't know."

"Jamie, no lies. There was a blue paper there containing poison that you were not to have unless there were occasion for it—some bird-skin to be preserved and dressed with it. Now—did you take that?"

"Yes."

"Go and bring it back to me immediately."

"I can't."

"Why not? Where is it?"

The boy fidgeted, looked up in his sister's face to see what expression it bore, buried his head again, and said—

"Ju, he is rightly called Cruel. I hate him, and so do you—don't you, Ju? I have put the arsenic into his oatmeal, and we will get rid of him and be free and go away—it will be jolly!"

"Jamie!" with a cry of horror.

"He won't whip me and scold you any more."

"Jamie! Oh, my Lord, have pity on him! Have pity on us!"

She clasped her hands to her head, rushed from the room, and flew down the stairs.

But ten minutes before that Judith had given Coppinger his bowl of porridge. He had risen late that morning. He was better, he said, and he looked more himself than the preceding day. He was now seated at the table in the hall, and had poured the fresh milk into the bowl, had dipped the spoon, put some of the porridge to his mouth, tasted, and was looking curiously into the spoon, when the door was flung open, Judith entered, and without a word of explanation, caught the bowl from him and dashed it on the floor.

Coppinger looked at her with his boring dark eyes, intently, and said, "What is the meaning of this?"

"It is poisoned."

Judith was breathless. She drew back, relieved at having cast away the fatal mess.

Coppinger rose to his feet and glared at her across the table, leaning with his knuckles on the board. He did not speak for a moment, his face became livid, and his hands resting on the table shook as though he were shivering in an ague.

"There is arsenic in the porridge," gasped Judith. She had not had time to weigh what she should say, how explain her conduct; but one thought had held her —to save Coppinger's life whilst there was yet time. The Captain's dog, that had been lying at his master's feet, rose, went to the spilt porridge, and began to lap the milk and devour the paste. Neither Judith nor Coppinger regarded him.

"It was an accident!" faltered Judith.

"You lie!" said Coppinger, in thrilling tones. "You lie—you murderess! You sought to kill me."

Judith did not answer for a moment. She also was trembling. She had to resolve what course to pursue. She could not, she would not, betray her brother, and subject him to the worst brutality of treatment from the infuriated man whose life he had sought.

It were better for her to take the blame on herself.

"I made the porridge—I and no one else."

"You told me so yesterday." He maintained his composure marvellously, but he was stunned by the sudden discovery of treachery in the woman he had loved and worshipped.

"You maddened me by your treatment; but I did not desire that you should die. I repented and have saved your life."

As Judith spoke she felt as though the flesh of her face stiffened, and the skin became as parchment. She could hardly open her mouth to speak and stir her tongue.

"Go!" said Coppinger, pointing to the door. "Go, you and your brother. Othello Cottage is empty. Go, murderess, poisoner of your husband, there, and wait till you hear from me. Under one roof, to eat off one board, is henceforth impossible. Go!" He remained pointing, and a sulphurous fire flickered in his eyes.

Then the hound began to howl, threw itself down, its limbs were contracted, it foamed at the mouth, and howled again.

To the howlings of the poisoned and dying dog Judith and Jamie left Pentyre.

## CHAPTER XLVII
## FAST IN HIS HANDS

JUDITH and Jamie were together in Othello Cottage— banished from Pentyre with a dark and threatening shadow over them, this however gave the boy but little concern; he was delighted to be away from a house where he had been in incessant terror, and where he was under restraint; moreover, it was joy to him to be now where he need not meet Coppinger at every turn.

Judith forbade his going to Polzeath to see Uncle Zachie and Oliver Menaida, as she thought it advisable under the circumstances to keep themselves to themselves, and, above all, not to give further occasion for the suspicions and jealousy of Coppinger. This was to her, under the present condition of affairs, specially distressing, as she needed some counsel as to what she should do. Uncle Zachie at his best was a poor adviser, but on no account now would she appeal to his son. She was embarrassed and alarmed, and she had excuse for embarrassment and alarm. She had taken upon herself the attempt that had been made on the life of Coppinger, and he would, she supposed, believe her to be guilty.

What would he do? Would he proceed against her for attempted murder? If so the case against her was very complete. It could be shown that Mr. Menaida had given her this arsenic, that she had kept it by her in her workbox whilst at the Glaze, that she had been on the most unsatisfactory terms with Captain Coppinger, and that she had refused to complete her marriage with him by appending her signature to the register. She was now aware—and the thought made her feel sick at heart and faint— that her association with the Menaidas had been most injudicious, and had been capable of misinterpretation. It had been misinterpreted by Coppinger, and probably also by the gossips of Polzeath. It could be shown that a secret correspondence had been carried on between her and Oliver, which had been intercepted by her husband. This was followed immediately by the attempt to poison Coppinger. The arsenic had been given him in the porridge her own hands had mixed, and which had been touched by no one else. It was natural to conclude that she had deliberately purposed to destroy her husband that she might be free to marry Oliver Menaida.

If she were prosecuted on the criminal charge of attempted murder, the case could be made so conclusive against her that her conviction was certain.

Her only chances of escape lay in two directions— one, that she should tell the truth, and allow Jamie to suffer the consequences of what he had done, which would be prison or a lunatic asylum; the other was that she should continue to screen him and trust that Coppinger would not prosecute her. He might hesitate about proceeding with such a case, which would attract attention to himself, to his household, and lay bare to the public eye much that he would reasonably be supposed to wish to keep concealed. If, for instance, the case were brought into court, the story of the enforced marriage must come out, and that would rake up once more the mystery of the wreckers on Doom Bar, and of Lady Knighton's jewels. Coppinger might, and probably would, grasp at the other alternative; take advantage of the incompletion of the marriage, repudiate her, and let the matter of the poisoned porridge remain untouched.

The more Judith turned the matter over in her head the more sure she became that the best course, indeed the only one in which safety lay, was for her to continue to assume to herself the guilt of the attempt on Coppinger's life. He would see by her interference the second time, and prevention of his taking a second portion of the arsenic, that she did not really seek his life, but sought to force him through personal fear to drive her from his house, and break the bond by which he bound her to him. For the sake of this going back from a purpose of murder, or because he thought that she had never intended to do more than drive him to a separation by alarm for his own safety; for the sake of the old love he had borne her, he might forbear pressing this matter to its bitter consequences, and accept what she desired—their separation.

But if Judith allowed the truth to come out, then her husband would have no such compunction. It would be an opportunity for him to get rid of the boy he detested, and even if he did not have him consigned to gaol, then it would be only because he would send him to an asylum.

Judith went out on the cliffs. The sea was troubled far as the horizon, strewn with white horses shaking their manes, pawing and prancing in their gallop landward. There was no blue, no greenness in the ocean now. The dull tinctures of winter were in it. The Atlantic wore its scowl, was leaden, and impatient. The foam on the rocks was driven up in spouts into the air and carried over the downs, it caught in the thorn-bushes like flocks of wool, and was no cleaner. It lay with the thin, melting snow, and melted with it into a dirty slush. It plastered the face of Othello Cottage, as though in brutal insolence Ocean had been spitting at the house that was built of the wreck he had failed to gulp down, though he had chewed the life out of it. The foam rested in flakes on the rushes, where it hung and fluttered like tufts of cotton grass. It was dropped about by the wind for miles inland, as though the wind were running in a paper-chase. It was as though sky and sea were contending in a game of pelting the land, the one with snow, the other with foam, the one sweet, the other salt. Judith walked near the edge of the cliffs, where there was no snow, and looked out at the angry ocean. All without was cold, rugged, ruffled, wretched; and within her heart burned a fire of apprehension, distress, almost of despair.

All at once she came upon Mr. Desiderius Mules, walking in an opposite direction, engaged in wiping the foam flakes out of his eyes.

"Halloa! you here, Mrs. Coppinger!" exclaimed the rector. "Glad to see you. I'm not here, like S. Anthony, preaching to the fishes, because I am a practical man. In the first place, in such a disturbed sea the fishes would have enough to do to look after themselves, and would be ill-disposed to lend me an ear. In the next place, the wind is on shore, and they could not hear me were I to lift up my voice. So I don't waste words and overstrain my larynx. If the bishop were a mile, or a mile-and-a-half, inland, it might be different; he might admire my zeal. And what brings you here?"

"Oh, Mr. Mules!" exclaimed Judith, with a leap of hope in her heart—here was some one who might, if he would, be a help to her. She had indeed made up her own mind as to what was the safest road on which to set her feet, but she was timid, shrank from falsehood, and earnestly craved for some one to whom she could speak, and from whom she could obtain advice.

"Oh, Mr. Mules! will you give me some advice and assistance?"

"Advice by all means," said the rector. "I'll turn and walk your way; the froth is blown into my face and stings it. My skin is sensitive, so are my eyes. Upon my word, when I get home my face will be as salt as if I had flooded it with tears. Fancy me crying. What did you say you wanted—advice?"

"Advice and assistance."

"Advice you shall have, it is my profession to give it. I mix it with pepper and salt and serve it out in soup-plates every week—am ready with it every day, Mrs. Coppinger. I have buckets of it at your disposal, bring your tureen and I'll tip in as much of the broth as you want, and may you like it. As to assistance, that is another matter. Pecuniary assistance I never give. I am unable to do so. My principles stand in the way.. I have set up a high standard for myself and I stick to it. I never render pecuniary assistance to any one, as it demoralizes the receiver. I hope and trust it was not pecuniary assistance you wanted."

"No, Mr. Mules; not that, only guidance."

"Oh, guidance! I'm your sign-post; where do you want to go?"

"It is this, sir. I have given poison to Mr. Coppinger."

"Mercy on me!"

The rector jumped back, and turned much the tinge of the foam plasters that were on his face.

"That is to say, I gave him arsenic mixed with his porridge the day before yesterday, and it made him very ill. Yesterday—"

"Hush, hush!" said Mr. Mules, "no more of this. This is ghastly. Let us say it is hallucination on your part. You are either not right in your head or are very wicked. If you please, don't come nearer to me. I can hear you quite well, hear a great deal more than pleases me. You ask my advice, and I give it: Sign the register, that will set me square, and put me in an unassailable position with the public, and also, secondarily, it will be to your advantage. You are now a nondescript, and a nondescript is objectionable. If you please—you will excuse me—I should prefer not standing between you and the cliff. There is no knowing what a person who confesses to poisoning her husband might do. If it be a case of lunacy—well, more reason that I should use precautions. My life is valuable. Come, there is only one thing you can do to make me comfortable, sign the register."

"You will not mention what I have told you to any one?"

"Save and defend us! I speak of it—I! Come, come, be rational. Sign the register and set my mind at ease. That is all I want and ask for, and then I wash my hands of you."

Then away went Mr. Desiderius Mules, with the wind catching his coat-tails, twisting them, throwing them up against his back, parting them, and driving them one on each side of them, taking and curling them and sending them between his legs.

Judith stood mournfully looking after him. The sign-post, as he had called himself, was flying from the traveller whom it was his duty to direct.

Then a hand was laid on her arm. She started, turned and saw Oliver Menaida, flushed with rapid walking and with the fresh air he had encountered.

"I have come to see you," he said, "come to offer my father's and my assistance. We have just heard—"

"What?"

"That Captain Coppinger has turned you and Jamie out of his house."

"Have you heard any reason assigned?"

"Because—so it is said—he had beaten the boy, and you were incensed, angry words passed, and it ended in a rupture."

"That, then, is the common explanation."

"Every one is talking about it. Every one says that. And now, what will you do?"

"Thank you. Jamie and I are at Othello Cottage, where we are comfortable. My aunt had furnished it intending to reside in it herself. As for our food, we receive that from the Glaze."

"But this cannot continue."

"It must continue for a while."

"And then?"

"The future is not open to my eyes."

"Judith, that has taken place at length which I have been long expecting."

"What do you mean?"

"This miserable condition of affairs has reached its climax, and there has been a turn."

Judith sighed. "It has taken a turn indeed."

"Now Captain Coppinger has been brought to his senses, and he sees that your resolve is not to be shaken, and he releases you, or you have released yourself from the thraldom you have been in. I do not suppose the popular account of the matter is true wholly." "It is not at all true."

"That matters not. The fact remains that you are out of Pentyre Glaze and your own mistress. The snare is broken and you are delivered."

Again Judith sighed, and she shook her head despondingly.

"You are free," persisted Oliver. "Just consider. You were hurried through a marriage when insensible, and when you came to consciousness you did what was the only thing you could do—you absolutely refused your signature that would validate what had taken place. That was conclusive. That ceremony was as worthless as this sea-foam that blows by. No court in the world would hold that you were bound by it. The consent, the free consent, of each party in such a convention is essential. As to your being at Pentyre, nothing against that can be alleged; Miss Trevisa was your aunt, and constituted your guardian by your father. Your place was by her. To her you went when my father's house was no longer at your service through my return. At Pentyre you remained as long as Miss Trevisa was there. She went, and at once you left the house."

"You do not understand."

"Excuse me, I think I do. But no matter as to details. When your aunt went, you went also—as was proper under the circumstances. We have heard, I do not know whether it be true, that your aunt has come in for a good property."

"For a little something."

"Then shall you go to her and reside with her?"

"No; she will not have Jamie and me."

"So we supposed. Now, my father has a proposal to make. The firm to which I belong has been good enough to take me into partnership, esteeming my services far higher than they deserve, and I am to live at Oporto and act for them there. As my income will now be far larger than my humble requirements, I have resolved to allow my dear father sufficient for him to live upon comfortably where he wills, and he has elected to follow me and take up his abode in Portugal. Now, what he has commissioned me to say is—Will you go with him? Will you continue to regard him as Uncle Zachie, and be to him as his dear little niece, and keep house for him in the sunny southern land?"

Judith's eyes filled with tears.

"And Jamie is included in the invitation. He is to come also, and help my father to stuff the birds of Portugal. A new ornithological field is opening before him, he says, and he must have help in it."

"I cannot," said Judith, in a low tone, with her head sunk on her breast. "I cannot leave here till Captain Coppinger gives me leave."

"But, surely, you are no longer bound to him?"

"He holds me faster than before."

"I cannot understand this."

"No; because you do not know all."

"Tell me the whole truth. Let me help you. Let my father help you. You little know how we both have our hearts in your service."

"Well, I will tell you."

But she hesitated and trembled. She fixed her eyes on the wild, foaming, leaden sea, and pressed her bosom with both hands.

"I poisoned him."

"Judith!"

"It is true. I gave him arsenic, once; that your father had let me have for Jamie. If he had taken it the second time, when I offered it him in his bowl of porridge, he would be dead now. Do you see—he holds me in his hands, and I cannot stir. I could not escape till I know what he intends to do with me. Now go—leave me to my fate."

"Judith—it is not true! Though I hear this from your lips, I will not believe it. No; you need my father's, you need my help more than ever." He put her hand to his lips. "It is white—innocent. I know it, in spite of your words."

## CHAPTER XLVIII
## TWO ALTERNATIVES

WHEN Judith returned to Othello Cottage, she was surprised to see a man promenading around it, flattening his nose at the window, so as to bring his eyes against the glass, then, finding that the breath from his nostrils dimmed the pane, wiping the glass and again flattening his nose. At first he held his hands on the window ledge, but being incommoded by the refraction of the light, put the open hands against the pane, one on each side of his face. Having satisfied himself at one casement, he went to another, and made the same desperate efforts to see in at that.

Judith coming up to the door, and putting the key in, disturbed him. He started, turned, and with a nose much like putty, but rapidly purpling with returned circulation, disclosed the features of Mr. Scantlebray senior.

"Ah, ha!" said that gentleman, in no way disconcerted; "here I have you, after having been looking for my orphing charmer in every direction but the right one. With your favour I will come inside and have a chat."

"Excuse me," said Judith, "but I do not desire to admit visitors."

"But I am an exception. I'm the man who should have looked after your interests, and would have done it a deal better than others. And so there has been a rumpus, eh? What about?"

"I really beg your pardon, Mr. Scantlebray, but I am engaged and cannot ask you to enter, nor delay conversing with you on the doorstep."

"Oh, Jimminy! don't consider me. I'll stand on the doorstep and talk with you inside. Don't consider me; go on with what you have to do, and let me amuse you. It must be dull and solitary here, but I will enliven you, though I have not my brother's gifts. Now, Obadiah is a man with a genius for entertaining people. He missed his way when he started in life; he would have made a comic actor. Bless your simple heart, had that man appeared on the boards he would have brought the house down."

"I have no doubt whatever he missed his way when he took to keeping an asylum," said Judith.

"We have all our gifts," said Scantlebray. "Mine is architecture; and 'pon my honour as a gentleman, I do admire the structure of Othello Cottage, uncommon. You won't object to my pulling out my tape and taking the plan of the edifice, will you?"

"The house belongs to Captain Coppinger; consult him."

"My dear orphing, not a bit. I'm not on the best terms with that gent. There lies a tract of ruffled water between us. Not that I have given him cause for offence, but that he is not sweet upon me. He took off my hands the management of your affairs in the valuation business, and let me tell you—between me and you and that post yonder—" he walked in and laid his hand on a beam—"that he mismanaged it confoundedly. He is your husband, I am well aware, and I ought not to say this to you. He took the job into his hands because he had an eye to you, I knew that well enough. But he hadn't the gift—the faculty. Now I have made all that sort of thing my speciality. How many rooms have you in this house? What does that door lead to?"

"Really, Mr. Scantlebray, you must excuse me; I am busy."

"Oh, yes—vastly busy. Walking on the cliffs, eh? Alone, eh? Well, 'mum' is the word. Come, make me your friend, and tell me all about it. How came you here? There are all kinds of stories afloat about the quarrel between you and your husband, and he is an Eolus, a blustering Boreas, all the winds in one box. Not surprised. He blew up a gale against me once. Domestic felicity is a fable of the poets. Home is a region of cyclones, tornadoes, hurricanes—what you like —anything but a Pacific Ocean. Now, you won't mind my throwing an eye round this house, will you? A scientific eye. Architecture is my passion."

"Mr. Scantlebray, that is my bedroom; I forbid your touching the handle. Excuse me—but I must request you to leave me in peace."

"My dear creature," said Scantlebray, "scientific thirst before all. It is unslakable save by the acquisition of what it desires. The structure of this house, as well as its object, has always been a puzzle to me. So your aunt was to have lived here—the divine, the fascinating Dionysia, as I remember her years ago. It wasn't built for the lovely Dionysia, was it? No. Then for what object was it built? And why so long untenanted? These are nuts for you to crack?"

"I do not trouble myself about these questions. I must pray you to depart."

"In half the twinkle of an eye," said Scantlebray. Then he seated himself. "Come, you haven't a super-abundance of friends; make me one, and unburden your soul to me. What is it all about? Why are you here? What has caused this squabble? I have a brother a solicitor at Bodmin. Let me dot down the items, and we'll get a case out of it. Trust me as a friend, and I'll have you righted. I hear Miss Trevisa has come in for a fortune. Be a good girl, set your back against her and show fight."

"I will thank you to leave the house," said Judith, haughtily. "A moment ago you made reference to your honour as a gentleman. I must appeal to that same honour which you pride yourself on possessing, and by virtue of that request you to depart."

"I'll go, I'll go. But, my dear child, why are you in such a hurry to get rid of me? Are you expecting some one? It is an odd thing, but as I came along I was overtaken by Mr. Oliver Menaida, making his way to the downs—to look at the sea, which is rough, and inhale the breeze of the ocean, of course. At one time, I am informed, you made daily visits to Polzeath, daily visits whilst Captain Coppinger was on the sea; since his return, I am informed, these visits have been discontinued. Is it possible that, instead of your visiting Mr. Oliver, Mr. Oliver is now visiting you—here, in this cottage."

A sudden slash across the back and shoulders made Mr. Scantlebray jump and bound aside. Coppinger had entered, and was armed with a stout walking-stick.

"What brings you here?" he asked.

"I came to pay my respects to the grass widow," sneered Scantlebray, as he sidled to the door and bolted, but not till, with a face full of malignity, he had shaken his fist at Coppinger behind his back.

"What brings this man here?" asked the Captain.

"Impertinence—nothing else," answered Judith.

"What was that he said about Oliver Menaida?"

"His insolence will not bear reporting."

"You are right. He is a cur, and deserves to be kicked, not spoken to or spoken of. I heed him not. There is in him a grudge against me. He thought at one time that I would have taken his daughter. Do you recall speaking to me once about the girl that you supposed was a fit mate for me? I laughed. I thought you had heard the chatter about Polly Scantlebray and me. A bold, fine girl, full of blood as a cherry is full of juice—one of the stock, but with better looks than the men, yet with the assurance, the effrontery, of her father. A girl to laugh and talk with, not to take to one's heart. I care for Polly Scantlebray! Not I! That man has never forgiven me the disappointment because I did not take her. I never intended to. I despised her. Now you know all. Now you see why he hates me. I do not care. I am his match. But I will not have him insolent to you. What did he say?"

It was a relief to Judith that Captain Coppinger had not heard the words that Mr. Scantlebray had used. They would have inflamed his jealousy and fired him into fury against the speaker.

"He told me that he had been passed on his way hither by Mr. Oliver Menaida coming to the cliffs to inhale the sea air and look at the angry ocean."

Captain Coppinger was satisfied, or pretended to be so. He went to the door and shut it, but not till he had gone outside and looked round to see—so Judith thought—whether Oliver Menaida were coming that way quite as much as to satisfy himself that Mr. Scantlebray was not lurking round a corner listening.

No! Oliver Menaida would not come there. Of that Judith was quite sure. He had the delicacy of mind and the good sense not to risk her reputation by approaching Othello Cottage. When he had made that offer to her she had known that his own heart spoke, but he had veiled its speech, and had made the offer as from his father, and in such a way as not to offend her. Only when she had accused herself of attempted murder did he break through his reserve, to show her his rooted confidence in her innocence, in spite of her confession.

When the door was fast, Coppinger came over to Judith, and standing at a little distance from her, said— "Judith—look at me."

She raised her eyes to him. He was pale and his face lined, but he had recovered greatly since that day when she had seen him suffering from the effects of the poison.

"Judith," said he, "I know all."

"What do you know?"

"You did not poison me."

"I mixed and prepared the bowl for you."

"Yes—but the poison had been put into the oatmeal before, not by you, not with your knowledge."

She was silent. She was no adept at lying. She could not invent another falsehood to convince him of her guilt.

"I know how it all came about," pursued Captain Coppinger. "The cook, Jane, has told me. Jamie came into the kitchen with a blue paper in his hand, asked for the oatmeal, and put in the contents of the paper so openly as not in the least to arouse suspicion. Not till I was taken ill and made inquiries did the woman connect his act with what followed. I have found the blue paper, and on it is written, in Mr. Menaida's handwriting, which I know: 'Arsenic. Poison: for Jamie, only to be used for the dressing of bird-skins, and a limited amount to be served to him at a time.' Now I am satisfied, because I know your character, and because I saw innocence in your manner when you came down to me on the second occasion —and dashed the bowl from my lips—I saw then that you were innocent."

Judith said nothing. Her eyes rested on the ground.

"I had angered that fool of a boy. I had beaten him. In a fit of sullen revenge, and without calculating either how best to do it, or what the consequences would be, he went to the place where he knew the arsenic was— Mr. Menaida had impressed on him the danger of playing with the poison—and he abstracted it. But he had not the wit or cunning generally present in idiots—"

"He is no idiot," said Judith.

"No, in fools," said Coppinger, "to put the poison into the oatmeal secretly when no one was in the kitchen. He asked the cook for the meal, and mingled the contents of the paper with it so openly as to disarm suspicion."

He paused for Judith to speak, but she did not. He went on—

"Then you, in utter guilelessness, prepared my breakfast for me, as instructed by Mrs. Trevisa. Next morning you did the same, but were either suspicious of evil through missing the paper from your cabinet, or drawer, or wherever you kept it, or else Jamie confessed to you what he had done. Thereupon you rushed to me, to save me from taking another portion. I do not know that I would have taken it—I had formed a half-suspicion from the burning sensation in my throat, and from what I saw in the spoon—but there was no doubt in my mind after the first discovery that you were guiltless. I sought the whole matter out, as far as I was able. Jamie is guilty—not you."

213

"And—," said Judith, drawing a long breath—"what about Jamie?"

"There are two alternatives," said Coppinger. "The boy is dangerous. Never again shall he come under my roof."

"No—," spoke Judith—"no, he must not go to the Glaze again. Let him remain here with me. I will take care of him that he does mischief to no one. He would never have hurt you had not you hurt him. Forgive him, because he was aggravated to it by the unjust and cruel treatment he received."

"The boy is a mischievous idiot," said Coppinger.

"He must not be allowed to be at large."

"What, then, are your alternatives?"

"In the first place, I propose to send him back to that establishment whence he should never have been released—to Scantlebray's asylum."

"No—no—no!" gasped Judith. "You do not know what that place is. I do. I got into it. I saw how Jamie had been treated."

"He cannot be treated too severely. He is dangerous. You refuse this alternative?"

"Yes—indeed I do."

"Very well. Then I put the matter in the hands of justice, and he is proceeded against, and convicted of having attempted my life with poison. To gaol he will go."

It was as Judith had feared. There were but two destinations for Jamie—her dear, dear brother—the son of that blameless father—gaol or an asylum.

"Oh, no!—no—no! not that!" cried Judith.

"One or the other, and I give you six hours to choose," said Coppinger. Then he went to the door, opened it and stood looking seaward. Suddenly he started. "Hah! The Black Prince!" He turned in the door and said to Judith, "One hour after sunset come to Pentyre Glaze. Come alone, and tell me your decision. I will wait for that."

# CHAPTER XLIX
# NOTHING LIKE GROG

THE Black Prince had been observed by Oliver Menaida. He did not know for certain that the vessel he saw in the offing was the smuggler's ship, but he suspected it, as he knew that Coppinger was in daily expectation of her arrival. He brought his father to the cliffs, and the old man at once identified her.

Oliver considered what was to be done. A feint was to be made at a point lower down the coast, so as to attract the coastguard in that direction, whereas she was to run for Pentyre as soon as night fell, with all lights hidden, and to discharge her cargo in the little cove.

Oliver knew pretty well who were confederate with Coppinger or were in his employ. His father was able to furnish him with a good deal of information, not perhaps very well authenticated, all resting on gossip. He resolved to have a look at these men, and observe whether they were making preparations to assist Coppinger in clearing the Black Prince the moment she arrived off the cove. But he found that he had not far to look. They were drawn to the cliffs one after another to observe the distant vessel.

Oliver now made his way to the coastguard station, and to reach it went round by Wadebridge, and this he did because he wished to avoid being noticed going to the Preventive Station across the estuary at the Doom Bar above S. Enodoc. On reaching his destination, he was shown into an ante-room, where he had to wait some minutes, because the captain happened to be engaged. He had plenty to occupy his mind. There was that mysterious confession of Judith that she had tried to poison the man who persisted in considering himself as her husband, in spite of her resistance, and who was holding her in a condition of bondage in his house. Oliver did not for a moment believe that she had intentionally sought his life. He had seen enough of her to gauge her character, and he knew that she was incapable of committing a crime. That she might have given poison in ignorance and by accident was possible. How this had happened it was in vain for him to attempt to conjecture; he could, however, quite believe that an innocent and sensitive conscience like that of Judith might feel the pangs of self-reproach when hurt had come to Coppinger through her negligence.

Oliver could also believe that the smuggler captain attributed her act to an evil motive. He was not the man to believe in guilelessness; and when he found that he had been partly poisoned by the woman whom he daily tortured almost to madness, he would at once conclude that a premeditated attempt had been made on his life. What course would he pursue? Would he make this wretched business public, and bring a criminal action against the unfortunate and unhappy girl who was linked to him against her will?

Oliver saw that, if he could obtain Coppinger's arrest on some such a charge as smuggling, he might prevent this scandal, and save Judith from much humiliation and misery. He was, therefore, most desirous to effect the capture of Coppinger at once, and flagrante delicto.

As he waited in the ante-room a harsh voice within was audible which he recognized as that of Mr. Scantlebray. Presently the door was half opened, and he heard the coastguard captain say—

"I trust you rewarded the fellow for his information. You may apply to me—"

"Oh, royally, royally."

"And for furnishing you with the code of signals?"

"Imperially—imperially."

"That is well—never underpay in these matters."

"Do not fear! I emptied my pockets. And as to the information you have received through me—rely on it as you would on the Bank of England."

"You have been deceived and befooled," said Oliver, unable to resist the chance of delivering a slap at a man for whom he entertained a peculiar aversion, having heard much concerning him from his father.

"What do you mean?"

"That the shilling you gave the clerk for his information, and the half-crown for his signal-table, were worth what you got—the information was false, and was intended to mislead."

Scantlebray coloured purple.

"What do you know? You know nothing. You are in league with them."

"Take care what you say," said Oliver.

"I maintain," said Scantlebray, somewhat cowed by his demeanour, "that what I have said to the captain here is something of which you know nothing, and which is of importance for him to know."

"And I maintain that you have been hoodwinked," answered Oliver. "But it matters not. The event will prove which of us is on the right track."

"Yes," laughed Scantlebray, "so be it. And let me bet you, captain, and you, Mr. Oliver Menaida, that I am on the scent of something else. I believe I know where Coppinger keeps his stores, and—but you shall see, and Captain Cruel also—ha—ha!"

Rubbing his hands, he went out.

Then Oliver begged a word with the Preventive captain, and told him what he had overheard, and also that he knew where was the cave in which the smugglers had their boat and to which they ran the cargo first, before removing it to their inland stores.

"I'm not so certain the Black Prince dare venture nigh the coast to-night," said the captain, "because of the sea and the on-shore wind. But the glass is rising, and the wind may change. Then she'll risk it for certain. Now, look you here. I can't go with you myself to-night, because I must be here; and I can only let you have six men."

"That will suffice."

"Under Wyvill. I cannot, of course, put them under you, but Wyvill shall command. He bears a grudge against Coppinger, and will be rejoiced to have the chance of paying it out. But, mind you, it is possible that the Black Prince dare not run in, because of the weather, at Pentyre Cove; she may run somewhere else, either down the coast or higher up. Coppinger has other ovens than one. You know the term. His store places are ovens. We can't find them, but we know that there are several of them along the coast, just as there are a score of landing places. When one is watched, then another is used, and that is how we are thrown out. There are plenty of folk interested in defrauding the revenue in every parish between Hartland and Lands End, and let the Black Prince or any other smuggling vessel appear where she will, there she has ready helpers to shore her cargo and convey it to the ovens. When we appear, it is signalled at once to the vessel, and she runs away, up or down the coast, and discharges somewhere else before we can reach the point. Now, I do not say that what you tell me is not true, and that it is not Coppinger's intent to land the goods in the Pentyre Cove, but if we are smelt, or if the wind or sea forbid a landing there, away goes the Black Prince and runs her cargo somewhere else. That is why I cannot accompany you, nor can I send you with more than half a dozen men. I must be on the look out, and I must be prepared in the event of her coming suddenly back and attempting to land her goods at Porthleze, or Constantine, or Harlyn. What you shall do is—remain here with me till near dusk, and then you shall have a boat and my men and get round Pentyre, and you shall take possession of that cave. You shall take with you provisions for twenty-four hours. If the Black Prince intends to make that bay and discharge there, then she will wait her opportunity. If she cannot to-night, she will to-morrow night. Now, seize every man who comes into that cave, and don't let him out. You see?"

"Perfectly."

"Very well. Wyvill shall be in command, and you shall be the guide, and I will speak to him to pay proper attention to what you recommend. You see?"

"Exactly."

"Very well—now we shall have something to eat and to drink, which is better, and drink that is worth the drinking, which is best of all. Here is some cognac; it was run goods that we captured and confiscated. Look at it. I wish there were artificial light and you would see, it is liquid amber—a liqueur. When you've tasted that, 'Ah-ha!' you will say, 'glad I lived to this moment.' There is all the difference, my boy, between your best cognac and common brandy. The one, the condensed sunshine in the queen of fruit sublimed to an essence; the other, coarse, raw fire—all the difference that there is between a princess of blood-royal and a gipsy wench. Drink and do not fear. This is not the stuff to smoke the head and clog the stomach."

When Oliver Menaida finally started, he left the first officer of the coastguard, in spite of his assurances, somewhat smoky in brain, and not in the condition to form the clearest estimate of what should be done in a contingency. The boat was laden with provisions for twenty-four hours, and placed under the command of Wyvill.

The crew had not rowed far before one of them sang out, "Gearge!"

"Aye, aye, mate!" responded Wyvill.

"I say, Gearge. Be us a going round Pentyre?"

"I reckon we be."

"And wet to the marrow-bone we shall be."

"I reckon we shall."

Then a pause in the conversation. Presently from another—"George!"

"Aye, aye, Will!"

"I say, Gearge! Where be the spirits to? There's a keg o' water, but sure alive the spirits be forgotten."

"Bless my body!" exclaimed Wyvill, "I reckon you're right. Here's a go."

"It will never do for us to be twenty-four hours wi' salt water outside of us and fresh wi'in," said Will. "What's a hat wi'out a head in it, or boots wi'out feet in 'em, or a man wi'out spirits in his in'ar'd parts?"

"Dear alive! 'Tis a nuisance," said Wyvill. "Who's been the idiot to forget the spirits?"

"Gearge!"

"Aye, aye, Samson!"

"I say, Gearge! Hadn't us better run over to the Rock, and get a little anker there?"

"I reckon it wouldn't be amiss, mate," responded Wyvill.

To Oliver's astonishment and annoyance, the boat was turned to run across to a little tavern, at what was called "The Rock."

He remonstrated. This was injudicious and unnecessary.

"Onnecessary!" said Wyvill. "Why, you don't suppose firearms will go off wi'out a charge? It's the same wi' men. What's the good of a human being unless he be loaded—and what's his proper load but a drop o' spirits?"

Then one of the rowers sang out— "Water drinkers are dull asses When they're met together, Milk is meet for infancy, Ladies like to sip Bohea, Not such stuff for you and me, When we're met together."

Oliver was not surprised that so few captures were effected on the coast, when those set to watch it loved so dearly the very goods they were to watch against being imported untaxed.

On reaching the shore, the man Samson and another were left in charge of the boat, whilst Wyvill, Will, and the rest went up to the Rock Inn to have a glass for the good of the house, and to lade themselves with an anker of brandy, which during their wait in the cave was to be distributed among them. Oliver thought it well to go to the tavern as well. He was impatient, and thought they would dawdle there, and perhaps take more than the nip to which they professed themselves content to limit themselves. Pentyre Point had to be rounded in rough water, and they must be primed to enable them to round Pentyre. "You see," said Wyvill, who seemed to suppose that some sort of an explanation of his conduct was due. "When ropes be dry they be terrible slack. Wet 'em, and they are taut. It is the same wi' men's muscles. We've Pentyre Point to get round. Very strainin' to the arms, and I reckon it couldn't be done unless we wetted the muscles. That's reason. That's convincin'."

At the Rock Tavern the Preventive men found the clerk of S. Enodoc, with his hands in his pockets, on the settle, his legs stretched out before him considering one of his knees that was threadbare, and trying to make up his mind whether the trouser would hold out another day without a thread being run through the thin portion, and whether if a day, then perhaps two days, and if perchance for two days, then for three. But if for three, then why not for four? And if for four, then possibly for five. Anyhow, as far as he could judge, there was no immediate call for him to have the right knee of his trouser repaired that day.

The sexton-clerk looked up when the party entered, and greeted them each man by name, and a conversation ensued relative to the weather. Each described his own impressions as to what the weather had been, and his anticipations as to what it would be.

"And how's your missus?"

"Middlin', and yours?"

"Same, thanky'. A little troubled wi' the rheumatics."

"Tell her to take a lump o' sugar wi' five drops o' turpentine."

"I will, thanky',—" and so on for half an hour, at the end of which time the party thought it time to rise, wipe their mouths, shoulder the anker, and return to the boat. No sooner were they in it, and had thrust off from shore, and prepared to make a second start, than Oliver touched Wyvill and said, pointing to the land, "Look yonder."

"What?"

"There is that clerk. Running, actually running."

"I reckon he be."

"And in the direction of Pentyre."

"So he be, I reckon."

"And what do you think of that?"

"Nothing," answered Wyvill, confusedly. "Why should I? He can't say nothing about where we be going. Not a word of that was said whilst us was there. I don't put no store on his running."

"I do," said Oliver, unable to smother his annoyance. "This folly will spoil our game."

Wyvill muttered, "I reckon I'm head of the concarn, and not you."

Oliver deemed it advisable, as the words were said low, to pretend that he did not hear them.

The wind had somewhat abated, but the sea was running furiously round Pentyre. Happily the tide was going out, so that tide and wind were conflicting, and this enabled the rowers to get round Pentyre, between the Point and the Newland Isle, that broke the force of the seas. But when past the shelter of Newland, doubling a spur of Pentyre that ran to the north, the rowers had to use their utmost endeavours, and had not their muscles been moistened, they might possibly had declared it impossible to proceed. It was advisable to run into the cove just after dark, and before the turn of the tide, as, in the event of the Black Prince attempting to land her cargo there, it would be made with the flow of the tide, and in the darkness.

The cove was reached, and found to be deserted. Oliver showed the way, and the boat was driven up on the shingle, and conveyed into the Smugglers' Cave behind the rock curtain. No one was there. Evidently, from the preparations made, the smugglers were ready for the run of the cargo that night.

"Now," said Will, one of the Preventive men, "us hev 'a laboured uncommon. What say you, mates? Does us desarve a drop of refreshment, or does us not? Every man as does his dooty by his country and his king should be paid for't is my doctrine. What do y' say, Gearge? Sarve out the grog?"

"I reckon—yes—sarve out the grog. There's nothing like grog—I think it was Solomon said that, and he was the wisest of men."

"For sure he made a song about it," said one of the coastguard. "It begins— 'A plague of those musty old lubbers   Who tell us to fast and to think, And patient fall in with life's rubbers,   With nothing but water to drink.'"

"To be sure," responded Wyvill, "Never was a truer word said than when Solomon was called the wisest o' men."

# CHAPTER L
## PLAYING FORFEITS

"Here am I once more," said Mr. Scantlebray, walking into Othello Cottage, with a rap at the door, but without waiting for an invitation to enter. "Come back like the golden summer, but at a quicker rate. How are you all? I left you rather curtly—without having had time to pay my proper congé."

Judith and Jamie were sitting over the fire. No candle had been lighted, for, though a good many things had been brought over to Othello Cottage for their use, candles had been forgotten, and Judith did not desire to ask for more than was furnished her, certainly not to go to the Glaze for the things needed. They had a fire, but not one that blazed. It was of drift-wood, that smouldered and would not flame, and as it burnt emitted a peculiar odour.

Jamie was in good spirits, he chattered and laughed, and Judith made pretence that she listened; but her mind was absent, she had cares that had demands on every faculty of her mind. Moreover, now and then her thoughts drifted off to a picture that busy fancy painted and dangled before them—of Portugal, with its woods of oranges, golden among the burnished leaves, and its vines hung with purple grapes—with its glowing sun, its blue glittering sea—and, above all, she mused on the rest from fears, the cessation from troubles which would have ensued, had there been a chance for her to accept the offer made, and to have left the Cornish coast for ever.

Looking into the glowing ashes, listening to her thoughts as they spoke, and seeming to attend to the prattle of the boy, Judith was surprised by the entry of Mr. Scantlebray.

"There—disengaged, that is capital," said the agent. "The very thing I hoped. And now we can have a talk. You have never understood that I was your sincere friend. You have turned from me and looked elsewhere, and now you suffer for it. But I am like all the best metal—strong and bright to the last—and see—I have come to you now, to forewarn you, because I thought that if it came on you all at once, there would be trouble and bother."

"Thank you, Mr. Scantlebray. It is true that we are not busy just now, but it does not follow that we are disposed for a talk. It is growing dark, and we shall lock up the cottage and go to bed."

"Oh, I will not detain you long. Besides, I'll take the wish out of your heart for bed in one jiffy. Look here—read this. Do you know the handwriting?"

He held out a letter. Judith reluctantly took it. She had risen; she had not asked Scantlebray to take a seat.

"Yes," she said, "that is the writing of Captain Coppinger."

"A good bold hand," said the agent; "and see, here is his seal, with his motto Thorough. You know that?"

"Yes; it is his seal."

"Now read it."

Judith knelt at the hearth.

"Blow, blow the fire up, my beauty!" called Scantlebray to Jamie. "Don't you see that your sister wants light, and is running the risk of blinding her sweet pretty eyes."

Jamie puffed vigorously, and sent out sparks snapping and blinking, and brought the wood to a white glow, by which Judith was able to decipher the letter.

It was a formal order from Cruel Coppinger to Mr. Obadiah Scantlebray to remove James Trevisa that evening after dark from Othello Cottage to his idiot asylum, to remain there in custody till further notice. Judith remained kneeling with her eyes on the letter after she had read it. She was considering. It was clear to her that directly after leaving her Captain Coppinger had formed his own resolve, either impatient of waiting the six hours he had allowed her, or because he thought the alternative of the asylum the only one that could be accepted by her; and it was one that would content himself, as the only one that avoided exposure of a scandal. But there were other asylums than that of Scantlebray, and others were presumably better managed, and those in charge less severe in their dealings. She had considered this as she looked into the fire. But a new idea had also at the same time lightened in her mind, and she had a third alternative to propose.

She had been waiting for the moment when to go to the Glaze and see Coppinger, and just at the moment when she was about to send Jamie to bed and leave the house, Scantlebray came in.

"Now, then," said the agent, "what do you think of me? That I am a real friend?"

"I thank you for having told me this," answered Judith. "And now I will go to Pentyre. I beg that you will not allow my brother to be conveyed away during my absence. Wait till I return. Perhaps Captain Coppinger may not insist on the removal at once. If you are a real friend, as you profess, you will do this for me."

"I will do it willingly. That I am a real friend I have shown you by my conduct. I have come beforehand to break news to you which might have been too great and too overwhelming had it come on you suddenly. My brother and a man or two will be here in an hour. Go by all means to Captain Cruel, but—" Scantlebray winked an eye—"I don't myself think you will prevail with him."

"I will thank you to remain here for half an hour with Jamie," said Judith, coldly. "And to stay all proceedings till my return. If I succeed—well. If not, then only a few minutes have been lost. I have that to say to Captain Coppinger which may, and I trust will, lead him to withdraw that order."

"Rely on me. I am a rock on which you may build," said Scantlebray. "I will do my best to entertain your brother, though, alas! I have not the abilities of Obadiah, who is a genius, and can keep folks hour by hour going from one roar of laughter into another."

No sooner was Judith gone than Scantlebray put his tongue into one side of his cheek, clicked, pointed over his shoulder with his thumb, and seated himself opposite Jamie, on the stool beside the fire, which had been vacated by Judith. Jamie had understood nothing of the conversation that had taken place; his name had not been mentioned, and consequently his attention had not been drawn to it, away from some chestnuts he had found, or which had been given to him, that he was baking in the ashes on the hearth.

"Fond of hunting, eh?" asked Scantlebray, stretching his legs, and rubbing his hands. "You are like me —like to be in at the death. What do you suppose I have in my pocket? Why, a fox with a fiery tail. Shall we run him to earth? Shall we make an end of him? Tally-ho! Tally-oh! here he is. Oh, sly reynard, I have you by the ears." And forth from the tail pocket of his coat Scantlebray produced a bottle of brandy. "What say you, Corporal? shall we drink his blood? Bring me a couple of glasses, and I'll pour out his gore."

"I haven't any," said Jamie; "Ju and I have two mugs, that is all."

"And they will do famously. Here goes—off with the mask!" and with a blow he knocked away the head and cork of the bottle. "No more running away for you my beauty, except down our throats. Mugs! That is famous. Come, shall we play at army and navy, and the forfeit be a drink of reynard's blood?"

Jamie pricked up his ears; he was always ready for a game of play.

"Look here," said Scantlebray. "You are in the military, I am in the nautical line. Each must address the other by some title in accordance with the profession each professes, and the forfeit of failure is a pull at the bottle. What do you say? I will begin. Set the bottle there between us. Now then, Sergeant, they tell me your aunt has come in for a fortune. How much? What is the figure, eh?"

"I don't know," responded Jamie, and was at once caught up with "Forfeit! forfeit!"

"Oh, by Jimminy, there am I too in the same box. Take your swig, Commander, and pass to me."

"But what am I to call you?" asked the puzzle-headed boy.

"Mate, or captain, or boatswain, or admiral."

"I can't remember all that."

"That will do. Always say mate, whatever you ask or answer. Do you understand, General?"

"Yes."

"Forfeit! Forfeit!—you should have said, 'Yes, mate.'" Mr. Scantlebray put his hands to his sides and laughed.

"Oh, Jimminy! there am I again. The instructor as bad as the pupil. I'm a bad fellow as instructor, that I am, Field-Marshal. So—your Aunt Dionysia has come in for some thousands of pounds; how many do you think? Have you heard?"

"I think I've heard—"

"Mate! Mate!"

"I think I've heard, Mate."

"Now, how many do you remember to have heard named? Was it five thousand? That is what I heard named—eh, Captain?"

"Oh, more than that," said Jamie, in his small mind, catching at a chance of talking big, "a great lot more than that."

"What, ten thousand?"

"I dare say—yes, I think so."

"Forfeit! forfeit! pull again, Centurion."

"Yes, mate; I'm sure."

"Ten thousand—why at five per cent that's a nice little sum for you and Ju to look forward to when the old hull springs a leak and goes to the bottom."

"Yes," answered Jamie, vaguely. He could not look beyond the day; moreover, he did not understand the figurative speech of his comrade.

"Forfeit again, general! but I'll forgive you this time, or you'll get so drunk you'll not be able to answer me a question. Bless my legs and arms! on that pretty little sum one could afford oneself a new tie every Sunday. You will prove a beau and buck indeed some day, Captain of thousands! And then you won't live in this little hole. By the way, I hear old Dunes Trevisa, I beg pardon, Field-Marshal Sir James, I mean your much-respected aunt, Miss Trevisa, has got a charming box down by S. Austell. You'll ask me down for the shooting, won't you, Commander-in-chief?"

"Yes, I will," answered Jamie.

"And you'll give me the best bedroom, and will have choice dinners, and the best old tawny port, eh?"

"Yes, to be sure," said the boy, flattered.

"Mate! mate! forfeit! and I suppose you'll keep a hunter?"

"I shall have two—three," said Jamie.

"And if I were you I'd keep a pack of fox-hounds."

"I will."

"That's for the winter. And other hounds for the summer."

"I am sure I will, and wear a red coat."

"Famous; but—there I spare you this time—you forfeited again."

"No; I won't be spared," protested the boy.

"As for a wretched little hole like this Othello Cottage—" said Scantlebray. "But, by the by, you have never shown me over the house. How many rooms are there in it, Generalissimo of His Majesty's Forces?"

"There's my bedroom, there," said Jamie.

"Yes; and that door leads to your sister's?"

"Yes. And there's the kitchen."

"And upstairs?"

"There's no upstairs."

"Now, you are very clever, clever. By Ginger, you must be to be Commander-in-chief, but upon my word, I can't believe that. No upstairs? There must be upstairs."

"No, there's not."

"But, by Jimminy! with such a roof as this house has got, and a little round window in the gable, there must be an upstairs."

"No, there's not."

"How do you make that out?"

"Because there are no stairs at all." Then Jamie jumped up, but rolled on one side; the brandy he had drunk had made him unsteady. "I'll show you, mate—mate—yes, mate. There, three times now will do for times I haven't said it. There—in my room. The floor is rolling; it won't stay steady. There are cramps in the wall—no stairs, and so you get up to where it all is."

"All what is?"

"Forfeit! forfeit!" shouted Jamie. "Say general or something military. I don't know; Ju won't let me go up there; but there's tobacco, for one thing."

"Where's a candle, Corporal?"

"There is none. We have no light but the fire. Then Jamie dropped back on his stool, unable to keep his legs.

"I am more provident than you. I have a lantern outside, unlighted, as I thought I might need it on my return. The nights close in very fast and very dark now, eh, Commander?"

Mr. Scantlebray went outside the cottage, looked about him, specially directing his eyes towards the Glaze. Then he chuckled and said—

"Sent Miss Judith on a wild goose chase, have I? Ah! ha! Captain Coppinger! I'll have a little entertainment for you to-night. The Preventives will snatch your goods at Porth-leze or Constantine, and here—behind your back—I'll attend to your store of tobacco and whatever else I may find."

Then he returned, and going to the fire, extracted the candle from the lantern, and lighted it at a burning log.

"Halloa, Captain of thousands! Going to sleep? There's the bottle. You must make up forfeits. You've been dishonest, I fear, and not paid half. That door did you say?"

But Jamie was past understanding a question, and Mr. Scantlebray could find out for himself now what he wanted to know. That this house had been used by Coppinger as a store for some of the smuggled cargoes he had long suspected, but he had never been able to obtain any evidence which would justify the coastguard in applying to the justices for a search warrant. Now he would be able to look about it at his leisure whilst Judith was absent. He did not suppose Coppinger was at the Glaze. He assumed that an attempt would be made, as the clerk of S. Enodoc had informed him, to land the cargo of the Black Prince to the west of the estuary of the Camel, and he supposed that Coppinger would be there to superintend. He had used the letter sent to his brother to induce the girl to go to Pentyre, and so leave the cottage clear for him to search it.

Now, holding the candle, he entered the bedroom of Jamie, and soon perceived the cramps the boy had spoken of, that served in place of stairs. Above was a door into the attic, whitewashed over, like the walls. Mr. Scantlebray climbed, thrust open the door, and crept into the garret.

"Ha, ha!" said the valuer. "So, so, Captain! I have come on one of your lairs at last. And I reckon I will make it warm for you. But, by Ginger, it is a pity I can't remove some of what is here."

He prowled about in the roomy loft, searching every corner. There were a few small kegs of spirit, but the stores were mostly of tobacco.

In about ten minutes Mr. Scantlebray reappeared in the room where was Jamie. He was without his candle. The poor boy, overcome by what he had drunk, had fallen on the floor, and was in a tipsy sleep. Scantlebray went to him.

"Come along with me," he said. "Come, there is no time to be lost. Come, you fool!"

He shook him, but Jamie would not be roused; he kicked and struck out with his fists.

"You won't come? I'll make you."

Then Scantlebray caught the boy by the shoulders to drag him to the door. The child began to struggle and resist.

"Oh, I'm not concerned for you, fool," said Scantlebray. "If you like to stay and take your chance—- My brother will be here to carry you off presently. Will you come?"

Scantlebray caught the boy by the feet and tried to drag him, but Jamie clung to the table legs.

Scantlebray uttered an oath. "Stay, you fool, and be smothered! The world will get on very well without you." And he strode forth from the cottage.

## CHAPTER LI
## SURRENDER

SCANTLEBRAY was mistaken. Coppinger had not crossed the estuary of the Camel. He was at Pentyre Glaze awaiting the time when the tide suited for landing the cargo of the Black Prince. In the kitchen were a number of men having their supper, and drinking, waiting also for the proper moment when to issue forth.

At the turn of the tide the Black Prince would approach in the gathering darkness, and would come as near in as she dare venture. The wind had fallen, but the sea was running, and with the tide setting in, she would approach the cove.

Judith hastened towards the Glaze. Darkness had set in, but in the north were auroral lights, first a great white halo, then rays that shot up to the zenith, and then a mackerel sky of rosy light. The growl and mutter of the sea filled the air with threat, like an angry multitude surging on with blood and destruction in their hearts.

The flicker overhead gave Judith light for her course, the snow had melted except in ditches and under hedges, and there it glared red or white in response to the changing luminous tinges of the heavens. When she reached the house she at once entered the hall; there Coppinger was awaiting her. He knew she would come to him when her mind was made up on the alternatives he had offered her, and he believed he knew pretty surely which she would choose. It was because he expected her that he had not suffered the men, collected for the work of this night, to invade the hall.

"You are here," he said. He was seated by the fire. He looked up, but did not rise. "Almost too late."

"Almost, maybe—but not altogether," answered Judith. "And yet it seems unnecessary, as you have already acted without awaiting my decision."

"What makes you say that?"

"I have been shown your letter."

"Oh! Obadiah Scantlebray is premature."

"He is not at Othello Cottage yet. His brother came beforehand to prepare me."

"How considerate of your feelings!" sneered Captain Cruel; "I would not have expected that of Scantlebray."

"You have not awaited my decision," said Judith.

"That is true," answered Coppinger, carelessly. "I knew you would shrink from the exposure, the disgrace, of publication of what has occurred here—I knew you so well, that I could reckon beforehand on what you would elect."

"But, why to Scantlebray? Are there not other asylums?"

"Yes; so long as that boy is placed where he can do no mischief, I care not."

"Then, if that be so, I have another proposal to make."

"What is that?" Coppinger stood up.

"If you have any regard for my feelings, any care for my happiness, you will grant my request."

"Let me hear it."

"Mr. Menaida is going to Portugal."

"What!" —in a tone of concentrated rage— "Oliver?"

"Oliver and his father. But the proposal concerns the father."

"Go on." Coppinger strode once across the room, then back again. "Go on," he said, savagely.

"Old Mr. Menaida offers to take Jamie with him. He intends to settle at Oporto, near his son, who has been appointed to a good situation there. He will gladly undertake the charge of Jamie. Let Jamie go with them. There he can do no harm."

"What, go—without you? Did they not want you to go also?"

Judith hesitated and flushed. There was a single tallow candle on the table. Coppinger took it up, snuffed it, and held the flame to her face, to study its expression.

"I thought so," he said, and put down the light again.

"Jamie is useful to Mr. Menaida," pleaded Judith, in some confusion, and with a voice of tremulous apology. "He stuffs birds so beautifully, and Uncle Zachie—I mean Mr. Menaida—has set his heart on making a collection of the Spanish and Portuguese birds."

"Oh, yes; he understands the properties of arsenic," said Coppinger, with a scoff.

Judith's eyes fell. Captain Cruel's tone was not reassuring.

"You say that you care not where Jamie be, so long as he is where he cannot hurt you," said Judith.

"I did not say that," answered Coppinger. "I said that he must be placed where he can injure no one."

"He can injure no one if he is with Mr. Menaida, who will well watch him, and keep him employed."

Coppinger laughed bitterly. "And you? Will you be satisfied to have the idolized brother with the deep seas rolling between you?"

"I must endure it; it is the least of evils."

"But you would be pining to have wings and fly over the sea to him."

"If I have not wings, I cannot go."

"Now hearken," said Coppinger. He clenched his fist and laid it on the table. "I know very well what this means. Oliver Menaida is at the bottom of this. It is not the fool Jamie who is wanted in Portugal, but the clever Judith. They have offered to take the boy, that through him they may attract you, unless"—his voice thrilled—"they have already dared to propose that you should go with them."

Judith was silent. Coppinger clenched his second hand and laid that also on the table.

"I swear to Heaven," said he," that if I and that Oliver Menaida meet again, it is for the last time for one or other of us. We have met twice already. It is an understood thing between us, when we meet again, one wets his boots in the other's blood. Do you hear? The world will not hold us to any longer. Portugal may be far off, but it is too near Cornwall for me."

Judith made no answer. She looked fixedly into the gloomy eyes of Coppinger, and said—

"You have strange thoughts. Suppose, if you will, that the invitation included me, I could not have accepted it."

"Why not? You refuse to regard yourself as married—and, if unmarried, you are free—and, if free, ready to elope with—-"

He would not utter the name, in his quivering fury.

"I pray you," said Judith, offended, "do not insult me."

"I—insult you? It is a daily insult to me to be treated as I have been. It is driving me mad."

"But, do you not see," urged Judith; "You have offered me two alternatives, and I ask for a third; yours are gaol or an asylum; mine is exile. Both yours are to me intolerable. Conceive of my state were Jamie either in gaol or with Mr. Scantlebray! In gaol—and I should be thinking of him all day and all night, in his prison garb, tramping the tread-mill, beaten, driven on, associated with the vilest of men, an indelible stain put not on him only, but on the name of our dear, dear father. Do you think I could bear that? Or take the other alternative. I know the Scantlebrays. I would have the thoughts of Jamie distressed, frightened, solitary, ill-treated, ever before me. I had it for a few hours once, and it drove me frantic. It would make me mad in a week. I know that I could not endure it. Either alternative would madden or kill me. And I offer another—if he were in exile, I could at least think of him as happy, among the orange groves, in the vineyards, among kind friends, happy, innocent—at worst, forgetting me. That I could bear. But the other—no, not for a week—they would be torture insufferable."

She spoke full of feverish vehemence, with her hands outspread before her.

"And this smiling vision of Jamie happy in Portugal would draw your heart from me."

"You never had my heart," said Judith.

Coppinger clenched his teeth. "I will hear no more of this," said he.

Then Judith threw herself on her knees, and caught him and held him, lifting her entreating face towards his.

"I have undergone it—for some hours. I know it will madden or kill me. I cannot—I cannot—I cannot." She could scarce breathe; she spoke in gasps.

"You cannot what?" he asked, sullenly.

"I cannot live on the terms you offer. You take from me even the very wish to live. Take away the arsenic from me, lest in madness I give it to myself. Take me far inland from these cliffs, lest in my madness I throw myself over—I could not bear it. Will nothing move you?"

"Nothing." He stood before her, his feet apart, his arms folded, his chin on his breast, looking into her uplifted, imploring face. "Yes—one thing. One thing only." He paused, raking her face with his eyes. "Yes—one thing. Be mine wholly—unconditionally. Then I will consent. Be mine; add your name where it is wanting. Resume your ring—and Jamie shall go with the Menaidas. Now, choose."

He drew back. Judith remained kneeling, upright, on the floor with arms extended; she had heard, and at first hardly comprehended him. Then she staggered to her feet.

"Well," said Coppinger, "what answer do you make?"

Still she could not speak. She went to the table with uncertain steps. There was a wooden form by it. She seated herself on this, placed her arms on the table-board, joining her hands, and laid her head, face downwards, between them on the table.

Coppinger remained where he was, watching and waiting. He knew what her action implied—that she was to be left alone with her thoughts, to form her resolve undisturbed.

He remained, accordingly, motionless, but with his eyes fixed on the golden hair, that flickered in the dim light of the one candle. The wick had a great fungus in it—so large and glowing that in another moment it would fall, and fall on Judith's hand. Coppinger saw this, and he thrust forth his arm to snuff the candle with his fingers, but his hand shook, and the light was extinguished. It mattered not. There were glowing coals on the hearth, and through the window flared and throbbed the auroral lights.

A step sounded outside. Then a hand was on the door. Coppinger at once strode across the hall, and arrested the intruder from entering.

"Who is that?"

"Hender Pendarvis"—the clerk of S. Enodoc. "I have som'ut partickler I must say."

Coppinger looked at Judith; she lay motionless, her head between her arms, on the board. He partly opened the door, and stepped forth into the porch.

When he had heard what the clerk of S. Enodoc had to say, he answered with an order—

"Round to the kitchen, bid the men arm, and go by the beach."

He returned into the hall, went to the fireplace, and took down a pair of pistols, tried them, that they were charged, and thrust them into his belt. Next he went up to Judith, and laid his hand on her shoulder.

"Time presses," he said; "I have to be off. Your answer."

She looked up. The board was studded with drops of water. She had not wept; these stains were not her tears, they were the sweat of anguish off her brow that had run over the board.

"Well, Judith, your answer."

"I accept."

"Unreservedly?"

"Unreservedly."

"Stay," said he. He spoke low, in distinctly articulated sentences. "Let there be no holding back between us—you shall know all. You have wondered concerning the death of Wyvill—I know you have asked questions about it. I killed him."

He paused.

"You heard of the wreckers on that vessel cast on Doom Bar. I was their leader."

Again he paused.

"You thought I had sent Jamie out with a light to mislead the vessel. You thought right. I did have her drawn to her destruction—and by your brother."

He paused again. He saw Judith's hand twitch that was the only sign of emotion in her.

"And Lady Knighton's jewels. I took them off her—it was I who tore her ear."

Again a stillness. The sky outside shone in at the window, a lurid red. From the kitchen could be heard the voice of a man singing.

"Now you know all," said Coppinger. "I would not have you take me finally, fully, unreservedly without knowing the truth. Give me your resolve."

She slightly lifted her hands; she looked steadily into his face with a stony expression in hers.

"What is it?"

"I cannot help myself—unreservedly yours."

Then he caught her to him, pressed her to his heart, and kissed her wet face— wet as though she had plunged it into the sea.

"To-morrow," said he—"to-morrow shall be our true wedding."

And he dashed out of the house.

# CHAPTER LII
## TO JUDITH

IN THE smugglers' cave were Oliver Menaida and the party of Preventive men, not under his charge, but under that of Wyvill. This man, though zealous in the execution of his duty, and not averse, should the opportunity offer, of paying off a debt in full with a bullet, instead of committing his adversary to the more lenient hands of the law, shared in that failing, if it were a failing, of being unable to do anything without being primed with spirits, a failing that was common at that period to coastguards and smugglers alike. The latter had to be primed in order to run a cargo, and the former must be in like condition to catch them at it. It was thought, not unjustly, that the magistrates before whom, if caught, the smugglers were brought, needed priming in order to ripen their intellects for pronouncing judgment. But it was not often that a capture was effected. When it was, priming was allowed for the due solemnization of the fact by the captors; failure always entitled them to priming in order to sustain their disappointment with fortitude. Wyvill had lost a brother in the cause, and his feelings often overcame him when he considered his loss, and their poignancy had to be slaked with the usual priming. It served, as its advocates alleged, as a great stimulant to courage; but it served also, as its deprecators asserted, as a solvent to discipline.

Now that the party were in possession of the den of their adversaries, such a success needed, in their eyes, commemoration. They were likely, speedily, to have a tussle with the smugglers, and to prepare themselves for that required the priming of their nerves and sinews. They had had a sharp struggle with the sea in rounding Pentyre Point, and their unstrung muscles and joints demanded screwing up again by the same means.

The Black Prince had been discerned through the falling darkness drawing shorewards with the rising tide; but it was certain that for another hour or two the men would have to wait before she dropped anchor, and before those ashore came down to the unloading.

A lantern was lighted, and the cave was explored. Certainly Coppinger's men from the land would arrive before the boats from the Black Prince, and it was determined to at once arrest them, and then await the contingent in the boats, and fall on them as they landed. The party was small, it consisted of but seven men, and it was advisable to deal with the smugglers piecemeal.

The men, having leisure, brought out their food, and tapped the keg they had procured at the Rock. It was satisfactory to them that the Black Prince was apparently bent on discharging her cargo that night and in that place, thus, they would not have to wait in the cave twenty-four hours, and not, after all, be disappointed.

"All your pistols charged?" asked Wyvill.

"Aye, aye, sir."

"Then take your suppers whilst you may. We shall have hot work presently. Should a step be heard below, throw a bit o' sailcloth over the lantern, Samson."

Oliver was neither hungry nor thirsty. He had both eaten and drunk sufficient when at the station. He therefore left the men to make their collation, prime their spirits, pluck up their courage, screw up their nerves, polish their wits, all with the same instrument, and descended the slope of shingle, stooped under the brow of rock that divided the lower from the upper cave, and made his way to the entrance, and thence out over the sands of the cove. He knew that the shore could be reached only by the donkey path, or by the dangerous track down the chimney—a track he had not discovered till he had made a third exploration of the cave. Down this tortuous and perilous descent he was convinced the smugglers would not come. It was, he saw, but rarely used, and designed as a way of escape only on an emergency. A too frequent employment of this path would have led to a treading of the turf on the cliff above, and to a marking of the line of descent, that would have attracted the attention of the curious, and revealed to the explorer the place of retreat.

Oliver, therefore, went forward towards the point where the donkey path reached the sands, deeming it advisable that a watch should be kept on this point, so that his party might be forewarned in time of the approach of the smugglers.

There was much light in the sky, a phantastic, mysterious glow, as though some great conflagration were taking place, and the clouds overhead reflected its flicker. There passed throbs of shadow from side to side, and, as Oliver looked, he could almost believe that the light he saw proceeded from a great bonfire, such as was kindled on the Cornish moors on Midsummer's Eve, and that the shadows were produced by men and women dancing round the flames and momentarily intercepting the light.

Then ensued a change—the rose hue vanished suddenly, and in its place shot up three broad ribands of silver light, and so bright and clear was the light that the edge of the cliff against it was cut as sharp as a black silhouette on white paper, and he could see every bush of gorse there, and a sheep—a solitary sheep.

Suddenly he was startled by seeing a man before him, coming over the sand.

"Who goes there?"

"What, Oliver! I have found you!" The answer was in his father's voice. "Oh, well, I got fidgeted, and I thought I would come and see if you had arrived."

"For Heaven's sake! you have told no one of our plans?"

"I—bless you, boy!—not I. You know you told me yourself, before going to the station, what you intended, and I was troubled and anxious, and I came to see how things were turning out. The Black Prince is coming in; she will anchor shortly. She can't come beyond the point yonder. I was sure you would be here. How many have you brought with you?"

"But six."

"Too few. However, now I am with you, that makes eight."

"I wish you had not come, father."

"My boy, I did not come only on your account. I have my poor little Ju so near my heart, that I long to put out if only a finger to liberate her from that ruffian, whom, by the way, I have challenged."

"Yes; but I have stepped in as your substitute. I shall, I trust, try conclusions with Coppinger to-night. Come with me to the cave I told you of. We will send a man to keep gaurd at the foot of the donkey path."

Oliver led the way; the sands reflected the illumination of the sky, and the foam that swept up the beach had a rosy tinge. The waves hissed as they rushed up the shore, as though impatient at men speaking and not listening to the voice of the ocean, that should subdue all human tongues, and command mute attention. And yet that roar is inarticulate, it is like the foaming fury of the dumb, that strives with noise and gesticulation to explain the thoughts that are working within.

In the cave it was dark, and Oliver lighted a piece of touchwood as a means of observing the shelving ground and taking his direction till he passed under the brow of rock and entered the upper cavern.

After a short scramble, the dim, yellow glow of light from this inner recess was visible, when Oliver extinguished his touchwood and pushed on, guided by this light.

On entering the upper cave he was surprised to find the guards lying about asleep and snoring. He went at once to Wyvill, seized him by the arm and shook him, but none of his efforts could rouse him. He lay as a log, or as one stunned.

"Father, help me with the others," said Oliver, in great concern.

Mr. Menaida went from one to the other, spoke to each, shook him, held the lantern to his eyes, he raised their heads, when he let go his hold they fell back.

"What is the meaning of this?" asked Oliver.

"Humph!" said old Menaida, "I'll tell you what this means: there is a rogue among them, and their drink has been drugged with deadly-nightshade. You might be sure of this—that among six coastguards one would be in the pay of Coppinger. Which is it? Whoever it is he is pretending to be as dead drunk and stupefied as the others, and which is the man, Noll?"

"I cannot tell. This keg of brandy was got at the Rock Inn."

"It was got there, and there drugged, but by one of this company. Who is it?"

"Yes," said Oliver, waxing wrathful, "and what is more, notice was sent to Coppinger to be on his guard. I saw the sexton going in the direction of Pentyre."

"That man is a rascal!"

"And now we shall not encounter Coppinger. He will be warned, and not come."

"Trust him to come. He has heard of this. He will come, and murder them all, as he did Wyvill."

Oliver felt as though a frost had fallen on him.

"Hah!" said old Menaida. "Never trust any one in this neighbourhood; you cannot tell who is not in the pay or under the control of Coppinger, from the magistrate on the bench to the huckster who goes round the country. Among these six men one is a spy and a traitor. Which it is we cannot tell. There is nothing else to be done but to bind them all, hand and foot. There is plenty of cord here."

"Plenty. But surely not Wyvill."

"Wyvill and all. How can you say that he is not the man who has done it?. Many a fellow has carried his brother in his pocket. What if he has been bought?"

Old Menaida was right. He had not lived so many years in the midst of smugglers without having learned something of their ways. His advice must be taken, for the danger was imminent. If, as he supposed, full information had been sent to Captain Cruel, then he and his men would be upon them shortly.

Oliver hastily brought together all the cord of a suitable thickness he could find, and the old father raised and held each Preventive man, whilst Oliver firmly bound him hand and foot. As he did not know which was shamming sleep he must bind all. Of the six, five were wholly unconscious what was being done to them, and the sixth thought it advisable to pretend to be as the rest, for he was quite aware that neither Oliver nor his father would scruple to silence him effectually did he show signs of animation.

When all were made fast, old Menaida said—

"Now, Noll, my boy, are you armed?"

"No, father. When I went from home I expected to return. I did not know I should want weapons. But these fellows have their pistols and cutlasses."

"Try the pistols. There, take that of the man Wyvill. Are you sure they are loaded?"

"I know they are."

"Well, try."

Oliver took Wyvill's pistol, and put in the ramrod.

"Oh yes, it is loaded."

"Make sure. Draw the loading. You don't know what it is to have to do with Coppinger."

Oliver drew the charge, and then, as is usual, when the powder has been removed, blew down the barrel. Then he observed that there was a choke somewhere. He took the pistol to the lantern, opened the side of the lantern, and examined it. The touch-hole was plugged with wax.

"Humph!" said Mr. Menaida, "the man who drugged the liquor waxed the touch-holes of the pistols. Try the rest."

Oliver did not now trouble himself to draw the charges, he cocked each man's pistol, and drew the trigger. Not one would discharge. All had been treated in like manner.

Oliver thought for a moment what was to be done. He dared not leave the sleeping men unprotected, and he and his father alone were insufficient to defend them.

"Father," said he, "there is but one thing that can be done now: you must go at once, fly to the nearest farm-houses and collect men, and, if possible, hold the donkey path before Coppinger and his men arrive. If you are too late, pursue them. I will choke the narrow entrance, and will light a fire. Perhaps they may be afraid when they see a blaze here, and may hold off. Anyhow, I can defend this place for a while. But I don't expect that they will attack it."

Mr. Menaida at once saw that his son's judgment was right, and he hurried out of the cave, Oliver holding the light to assist him to descend, and then he made his way over the sands to the path, and up that to the downs.

No sooner was he gone than Oliver collected what wood and straw were there, sailcloth, oilcloth, everything that was combustible, and piled them up into a heap, then applied the candle to them, and produced a flame. The wood was damp, and did not burn freely, but he was able to awake a good fire, that filled the cavern with light. He trusted that when the smugglers saw that their den was in the possession of the enemy they would not risk the attempt to enter and recover it. They might not, they probably did not, know to what condition the holders of the cave were reduced.

The light of the fire roused countless bats that had made the roof of the cave their resting-place, and they flew wildly to and fro with whirr of wings and shrill screams.

Oliver set to work with all haste to heap stones so as to choke the entrance from the lower cave, by which he anticipated that the smugglers would enter, should they resolve on so desperate a course. But, owing to the rapid inclination, the pebbles yielded, and what he piled up rolled down. He then, with great effort, got the boat thrust down to the opening, and by main force drew it partly across. It was not possible for him completely to block the entrance, but by planting the boat athwart it, he could prevent several men from entering at once, and whoever did enter must scramble over the bulwarks of the boat.

All this took some time, and he was thus engaged, when his attention was suddenly arrested by the click of a pistol brought to the cock. He looked hastily about him, and saw Coppinger, who, unobserved, had descended by the chimney, and now by the light of the fire was taking deliberate aim at him. Oliver drew back behind a rock.

"You coward!" shouted Captain Cruel. "Come out and be shot."

"I am no coward," answered Oliver. "Let us meet with equal arms; I have a cutlass." He had taken one from the side of one of a sleep-drunk coastguard.

"I prefer to shoot you down as a dog," said Coppinger.

Then, holding his pistol levelled in the direction of Oliver, he approached the sleeping men. Oliver saw at once his object—he would liberate the confederate. He stepped out from behind the rock, and immediately the pistol was discharged. A bat fell at the feet of Oliver. Had not that bat at the moment whizzed past his head and received the ball in its soft and yielding body, the young man would have fallen shot through the head.

Coppinger uttered a curse and put his hand to his belt and drew forth the second pistol. But Oliver sprang forward, and with a sweep of his cutlass caught him on the wrist with the blade as he was about to touch the trigger. The pistol fell from his hand, and a rush of blood overflowed the back of the hand.

Coppinger remained for one minute motionless. So did Oliver, who did not again raise his cutlass.

But at that moment a harsh voice was heard crying, "There he is, my men, at him; beat his brains out. A guinea for the first man who knocks him over," and from the further side of the boat illumined by the glare from the fire, were seen the faces of Mr. Scantlebray, his brother, and several men, who began to scramble over the obstruction.

Then, and then only in his life, did Coppinger's heart fail him. His right hand was powerless, the sharp blade had severed the tendons, and blood was flowing from his wrist in streams. One pistol was discharged, the other had fallen. In a minute he would be in the hands of his deadly enemies.

He turned and fled. The light from the fire, the illumined smoke, rose through the chimney, and by that he could run up the familiar track, reach the platform in the face of the cliff, thence make his way by the path up which he had formerly borne Judith. He did not hesitate, he fled, and Oliver, also without hesitation, pursued him. As he went up the narrow track, his feet trod in and were stained with the blood that had fallen from Coppinger's wounded arm, but he did not notice it—he was unaware of it till the morrow.

Coppinger reached the summit of the cliffs. His feet were on the down. He ran at once in the direction of Othello Cottage. His only chance of safety lay there. There he could hide in the attic, and Judith would never betray him. In his desperate condition, wounded, his blood flowing from him in streams, hunted by his foes, that one thought was in him—Judith—he must go to Judith. She would never betray him, she would be hacked to death rather than give him up. To Judith as his last refuge!

## CHAPTER LIII
## IN THE SMOKE

JUDITH left Pentyre Glaze when she had somewhat recovered herself after the interview with Coppinger and her surrender. She had fought a brave battle, but had been defeated and must lay down her arms. Resistance was no longer possible, if Jamie was to be saved from a miserable fate. Now, by the sacrifice of herself, she had assured to him a future of calm and innocent happiness. She knew that with Uncle Zachie and Oliver he would be cared for, kindly treated, and employed. Uncle Zachie himself was not to be trusted; whatever he might promise, his good nature was greater than his judgment. But she had confidence in Oliver, who would prove a check on the over-indulgence which his father would allow. But Jamie would forget her. His light and unretentive mind was not one to harbour deep feeling. He would forget her when on board ship, in his pleasure at running about the vessel, chattering with the sailors; and would only think of her if he wanted aught, or was ill. Rapidly the recollection of her, love for her, would die out of his mind and heart, and as it died out of his, her thought and love for him would deepen and become more fixed, for she would have no one, nothing in the world, to think of and love save her twin brother.

She walked on, in the dark winter night, lighted only by the auroral glow overhead, and was conscious of a smell of tobacco-smoke, that so persistently seemed to follow her, that she was forced to notice it. She became uneasy, thinking that some one was walking behind the hedge with a pipe, watching her, perhaps waiting to spring out upon her, when distant from the house where her cries for help might be heard.

She stood still. The smell was strong. She climbed the hedge on one side and looked over; as far as she could discern in the red glimmer from the flushed sky, there was no one there. She listened, she could hear no step. She walked hastily on to a gate in the hedge on the opposite side, and went through that. The smell of burning tobacco was as strong there. Judith turned in the lane and walked back in the direction of the house. The smell pursued her. It was strange. Could she carry the odour in her clothes? She turned again, and resumed her walk towards Othello Cottage. Now she was distinctly aware that the scent came to her on the wind. Her perplexity on this subject served as a diversion of her mind from her own troubles.

She emerged upon the downs, and made her way across them towards the cottage, that lay in a dip, not to be observed except by one close to it. The wind when it brushed up from the sea was odourless.

Presently she came in sight of Othello Cottage, and in spite of the darkness could see that a strange, dense white fog surrounded it, especially the roof, which seemed to be wearing a white wig. In a moment she understood what this signified. Othello Cottage was on fire, and the stores of tobacco in the attic were burning. Judith ran. Her own troubles were forgotten in her alarm for Jamie. No fire as yet had broken through the roof.

She reached the door, which was open. Mr. Scantlebray in leaving had not shut the door, so as to allow the boy to crawl out, should he recover sufficient intelligence to see that he was in danger.

It is probable that Scantlebray senior would have made further efforts to save Jamie, but that he believed he would meet with his brother and two or three men he was bringing with him near the house, and then it would be easy unitedly to drag the boy forth. He did, indeed, meet with Obadiah, but also, at the same time, with Uncle Zachie Menaida, and a small party of farm labourers and when he heard that Mr. Menaida desired help to secure Coppinger and the smugglers, he thought no more of the boy, and joined heartily in the attempt to rescue the Preventive men, and take Coppinger.

Through the open door dashed Judith, crying out to Jamie, whom she could not see. There was a dense white cloud in the room, let down from above and curling out at the top of the door, whence it issued as steam from a boiler. It was impossible to breathe in this fog of tobacco smoke, and Judith knew that if she allowed it to surround her, she would be stupefied. She therefore stopped and entered, calling Jamie. Although the thick matrass of white smoke had not as yet descended to the floor, and that it left comparatively clear air beneath it—the indraught from the door, yet the odour of the burning tobacco impregnated the atmosphere. Here and there curls of smoke descended, dropped capriciously from the bed of vapour above, and wantonly played about.

Judith saw her brother lying at full length near the fire. Scantlebray had drawn him partly to the door, but he had rolled back to his former position near the hearth, perhaps from feeling the cold wind that blew in on him.

There was no time to be lost. Judith knew that flame must burst forth directly— directly the burning tobacco had charred through the rafters and flooring of the attic, and allowed the fresh air from below to rush in, and, acting as a bellows, blow the whole mass of glowing tobacco into flame. It was obvious that the fire had originated above, in the attic. There was nothing burning in the room, and the smoke drove downward in strips, through the joints of the boards overhead.

"Jamie! come, come with me!" She shook the boy, she knelt by him and raised him on her knee. He was stupefied with cognac, and with the fumes of the burning tobacco he had inhaled.

She must drag him forth. He was no longer half conscious as he had been when Mr. Scantlebray made the same attempt; the power to resist was now gone from him.

Judith was delicately made, and was not strong, but she put her arms under the shoulders of Jamie, and, herself on her knees, dragged him along the floor. He was as heavy as a corpse. She drew him a little way, and desisted, overcome, panting, giddy, faint. But time must not be lost. Every moment was precious. Judith knew that overhead, in the loft, was something that would not smoulder and glow, but burst into furious flame—spirits. Not, indeed, many kegs, but there were some. When this became ignited, their escape would be impossible. She drew Jamie further up, she was behind him. She thrust him forward as she moved on, upon her knees, driving him a step further at every advance. It was slow and laborious work. She could not maintain this effort for long, and fell forwards on her hands, and he fell also, at the same time, on the floor.

Then she heard a sound, a roar, an angry growl. The shock of the fall, and striking his head against the slate pavement, roused Jamie momentarily, and he also heard the noise.

"Ju! the roar of the sea!"

"A sea of fire, Jamie! Oh, do push to the door."

He raised himself on his hands, looked vacantly round, and fell again into stupid unconsciousness. Now, still on her knees, but with a brain becoming bewildered with the fumes, she crept to his head, placed herself between him and the door, and, holding his shoulders, dragged him towards her, she moving backwards.

Even thus she could make but little way with him; his boot-tops caught in the edge of a slate slab, ill-fitted in the floor, and held him, so that she could not pull him to her with the addition of the resistance thus caused. Then an idea struck her. Staggering to her feet, holding her breath, she plunged in the direction of the window, beat it open, and panted in the inrush of pure air. With this new current wafted in behind her she returned amidst the smoke, and for a moment it dissipated the density of the cloud about her. The window had faced the wind, and the rush of air through it was more strong than that which entered by the door. And yet this expedient did not answer as she had expected, for the column of strong cold air pouring in from a higher level threw the cloud into confusion, stirred it up, as it were, and lessened the space of uninvaded atmosphere below the descending bed of vapour.

Again she went to Jamie. The roar overhead had increased, some vent had been found, and the attic was in full flagrance. Now, drawing a long breath at the door near the level of the ground, she returned to her brother, and disengaged his foot from the slate, then dragged, then thrust, sometimes at his head, sometimes at his side; then again she had her arms round him, and swung herself forward to the right knee sideways, then brought up the other knee, and swung herself with the dead weight in her arms again to the right, and thus was able to work her way nearer to the door, and, as she got nearer to the door, the air was clearer, and she was able to breathe freer.

At length she laid hold of the jamp with one hand, and with the other she caught the lappet of the boy's coat, and, assisted by the support she had gained, was able to drag him over the doorstep.

At that moment past her rushed a man. She looked, saw, and knew Coppinger. As he rushed past, the blood squirting from his maimed right hand fell on the girl, lying prostrate at the jamb to which she had clung.

And now within, a red light appeared, glowing through the mist as a fiery eye; not only so, but every now and then a fiery rain descended. The burning tobacco had consumed the boards, and was falling through in red masses.

Judith had but just brought her brother into safety, or comparative safety, and now another, Coppinger, had plunged into the burning cottage, rushed to almost certain death. She cried to him as well as she could with her short breath. She could not leave him within. Why had he run there? She saw on her dress the blood that had fallen from him. She went outside the hut and dragged Jamie forth, and laid him on the grass. Then, without hesitation, inhaling all the pure air she could, she darted once more into the burning cottage. Her eyes were stung with the smoke, but she pushed on, and found Coppinger under the open window, fallen on the floor, his back and head against the wall, his arms at his side, and the blood streaming over the slate pavement from his right gashed wrist. Accident or instinct—it could not have been judgment —had carried him to the only spot in the room where pure air was to be found, and there it descended like a rushing waterfall, blowing about the prostrate man's wild, long hair.

"Judith!" said he, looking at her, and he raised his left hand. "Judith, this is the end."

"Oh, Captain Coppinger, do come out! The house is burning. Quick, or it will be too late."

"It is too late for me," he said. "I am wounded." He held up his half-severed hand. "I gave this to you, and you rejected it."

"Come—oh, do come—or you and I will be burnt!"

In the inrushing sweep of air both were clear of the smoke and could breathe.

He shook his head. "I am followed. I will not be taken. I am no good now—without my right hand. I will not go to gaol."

She caught his arm, and, tearing the kerchief from her neck, bound it round and round where the veins were severed.

"It is in vain," he said. "I have lost most of my blood. Ju!"—he held her with his left hand—"Ju, if you live, swear to me—swear you will sign the register."

She was looking into his face—it was ghastly, partly through loss of blood, partly because lighted by the glare of the burning tobacco that dropped from above. Then a sense of vast pity came surging over her along with the thought of how he had loved her. Into her burning eyes tears came.

"Judith," he said, "I made my confession to you—I told you my sins. Give me also my release. Say you forgive me."

She had forgotten her peril, forgotten about the fire that was above and around, as she looked at his eyes, and, holding the maimed right arm, felt the hot blood welling through her kerchief and running over her hand.

"I pray you! oh, I pray you, come outside. There is still time."

Again he shook his head. "My time is up. I do not want to live. I have not your love. I could never win it—and if I went outside I should be captured, and sent to prison. Will you give me my absolution?"

"What do you mean?" And in her trembling concern for him, in the intensity of her pity, sorrow, care for him, she drew his wounded hand to her, and pressed it against her heaving bosom.

"What I mean is—can you forgive me?"

"Indeed—indeed I do."

"What—all I have done?"

"All."

She saw only a dying man before her, a man who might be saved if he would, but would not, because her love was everything to him, and that he never, never could gain. Would she make no concession to him? Could she not draw a few steps nearer? As she looked into his face, and held his bleeding arm to her bosom, pity overpowered her—pity, when she saw how strong had been this wild and wicked man's love. Now she truly realized its depth, its intensity, and its tenderness alternating with stormy blasts of passion, as he wavered between hope and fear, and the despair that was his when he knew he must lose her.

Then she stooped, and the tears streaming over her face, she kissed him on his brow and then on his lips, and then drew back, still holding his maimed hand, with both of hers crossed over it, to her heaving bosom. Kneeling, she had her eyes on his, and his were on hers—steady, searching, but with a gentle light in them. And, as she thus looked, she became unconscious, and sank, still holding his hand, on the floor.

At that instant, through the smoke and raining masses of burning tobacco, plunged Oliver Menaida. He saw Judith, bent, caught her in his arms, and rushed back through the door.

A moment after and he was at the entrance again, to plunge through and rescue his wounded adversary, but the moment when this could be done was past. There was an explosion above, followed by a fall as of a sheet of blue light, a curtain of fire through the mist of white smoke. No living man could pass that. Oliver went round to the window, and strove to enter by that way. The man who had taken refuge there was still in the same position, but he had torn the kerchief of Judith from the bleeding arm, and he held it to his mouth, looking with fixed eyes into the falling red and blue fires and the swirling flocks of white smoke.

There were iron bars at the window. Oliver tore at these to displace them.

"Coppinger!" he shouted, "stand up—help me to break these bars!"

But Coppinger would not move, or possibly the power was gone from him. The bars were firmly set. They had been placed in the windows by Coppinger's orders, and under his own supervision, to secure Othello Cottage, his store place, against invasion by the inquisitive.

At length Oliver succeeded in wrenching one bar away, and now a gap was made through which he might reach Coppinger, and draw him forth through the window. He was scrambling in when the Captain staggered to his feet.

"Let me alone," said he. "You have won what I have lost. Let me alone. I am defeated."

Then he stepped into the mass of smoke and falling liquid blue fire and dropping masses of red glowing tobacco. A moment more and the whole of the attic floor, with all the burning contents of the garret, fell in.

## CHAPTER LIV
## SQUAB PIE

NEXT morning, at an early hour, Judith, attended by Mr. Zachary Menaida, appeared at the rectory of S. Enodoc. She was deadly pale, but there was decision in her face. She asked to see Mr. Desiderius Mules in his study, and was shown into what had, in her father's days, been the pantry.

Mr. Menaida had a puzzled look in his watery eyes. He had been up all night; and indeed it had been a night in which few in the neighbourhood had slept, excepting Mr. Mules, who knew nothing of what had happened. The smugglers, alarmed by the fire at Othello Cottage, and by the party collected by Mr. Menaida to guard the descent to the beach, had not ventured to force their way to the cave. The Black Prince, finding that no signal was made from the ledge above the cave, suspected mischief, heaved anchor, and bore away.

The stupefied members of the Preventive service were conveyed to the nearest cottages, and there left to recover. As for Othello Cottage, it was a blazing and smoking mass of fire, and till late on the following day could not be searched. There was no fire-engine anywhere near, nor would a fire-engine have availed to save either the building or its contents.

When Mr. Mules appeared, Judith said, in a quiet but firm tone, "I have come to sign the register. Mr. Menaida is here. I do it willingly, and with no constraint."

"Thank you. This is most considerate to my feelings. I wish all my flock would obey my advice as you are now doing," said the rector, and produced the book, which Judith signed with trembling hand.

Mr. Desiderius was quite ignorant of the events of the night. He had no idea that at that time Captain Coppinger was dead.

It was not till some days later that Judith understood why, at the last moment, with death before his eyes, Coppinger had urged on her this ratification of her marriage. It was not till his will was found that she understood his meaning. He had left to her, as his wife, everything that he possessed. No one knew of any relatives that he had, for no one knew whence he came. No one ever appeared to put in a claim against the widow.

On the second day, the remains of the burnt cottage were cleared away, and then the body of Cruel Coppinger was found, fearfully charred, and disfigured past recognition. There were but two persons who knew that this blackened corpse belonged to the long-dreaded Captain, and these were Judith and Oliver. When the burnt body was cleared from the charred fragments of clothing that were about it, one article was discovered uninjured. About his throat Coppinger had worn a silk handkerchief, and this, as well as the collar of his coat, had preserved his neck and the upper portion of his chest from injury such as had befallen the rest of his person. And when the burnt kerchief was removed, and the singed cloth of the coat-collar, there was discovered round the throat a narrow black band, and sewn into this band one golden thread of hair encircling the neck.

Are our readers acquainted with that local delicacy entitled, in Cornwall and Devon, Squab Pie? To enlighten the ignorant, it shall be described. First, however, we premise that of squab pies there are two sorts, Devonian squab and Cornish squab. The Cornish squab differs from the Devonian squab in one particular; that shall be specified presently.

How to make a Squab Pie:—Take ½lb. of veal, cut into nice square pieces, and put a layer of them at the bottom of a pie-dish. Sprinkle over these a portion of herbs, spices, seasoning, lemon-peel, and the yolks of eggs cut in slices; cut ¼lb. of boiled ham very thin, and put in a layer of this. Take ½lb. of mutton cut into nice pieces, and put a layer of them on top of the veal. Sprinkle as before with herbs and spices.

Take ½lb. beef, cut into nice pieces, and put a layer of them on the top of the mutton. Sprinkle as before with herbs and spices. Cut up half a dozen apples very fine, also half a dozen onions, mix, and proceed to ram the onions and apples into every perceivable crevice. Take half a dozen pilchards, remove the bones, chop up, and strew the whole pie with pilchards. Then fill up with clotted cream, till the pie-dish will hold no more. [For Cornish Squab:—Add, treated in like manner, a cormorant.] Proceed to lay a puff-paste on the edge of the dish. Then insert a tablespoon and stir the contents till your arm aches. Cover with crust, or ornament it with leaves, brush it over with the yolk of an egg, and bake in a well-heated oven for one or one and a half hours, or longer, should the pie be very large [two, in the case of a Cornish Squab, and the cormorant very tough].

In one word, a squab pie is a scrap pie. So is the final chapter of a three-volume novel. It is made up, from the first word to the last, of scraps of all kinds, toothsome and the reverse.

Now let the reader observe—he has been already supplied with scraps. He has learned the result of Mr. Menaida's collecting men to assist him against the smugglers; also of his expedition along with Judith to the rectory of S. Enodoc; also he has heard the provisions of Captain Coppinger's will, also that this will was not contested. He has also heard of the recovery of the Captain's body from the burnt cottage.

Is not this a collection of scraps cut very small? But there are more, of a different character, with which this chapter will be made up, before the piecrust closes over it with a flourishing "Finis" to ornament it.

Mr. Scantlebray had lost his wife, who had been an ailing woman for some years, and, being a widower, cast about his eyes for a second wife, after the way of widowers. There was not the excuse of a young family needing a prudent housewife to manage the children, for Mr. Scantlebray had only one daughter, who had been allotted by her father and by popular opinion to Captain Coppinger, but had failed to secure him. Mr. Scantlebray, though an active man, had not amassed much money, and if he could add to his comforts, provide himself with good eating and good drinking, by marrying a woman with money, he was not averse to so doing. Now, Mr. Scantlebray had lent a ready ear to the voice of rumour which made Miss Dionysia Trevisa the heiress who had come in for all the leavings of that rich old spinster, Miss Ceely, of S. Austell, and Mr. Scantlebray gave credit to this rumour, and, acting on it, proposed to, and was accepted by Miss Dionysia.

Now when, after marriage, Mr. Scantlebray found out that the sweet creature he had taken to his side was worth under a quarter of the sum he had set down at the lowest figure at which he could endure her, and when the late Miss Trevisa, now the second Mrs. Scantlebray, learned from her husband's lips that he had married her only for her money, and not for her good looks or for any good quality she was supposed to be endowed with, the reader, knowing something of the characters of these two persons, may conjecture, if he please, what sort of scenes ensued daily between them; and it may be safely asserted that the bitterest enemies of either could not have desired for each a more unenviable lot than was theirs.

Very shortly after the death of Captain Coppinger, Judith and Jamie left Bristol in a vessel, with Uncle Zachie, bound for Lisbon. Oliver Menaida had gone to Oporto before, to make arrangements for his father. It was settled that Judith and her brother should live with the old man, and that the girl should keep house for him. Oliver would occupy his old quarters that belonged to the firm in which he was a partner.

It is a strange thing—but after the loss of Coppinger, Judith's mind reverted much to him; she thought long and tenderly of his consideration for her, his patience with her, his forbearance, his gentleness towards her, and of his intense and enduring love. His violence she forgot, and she put down the crimes he had committed to evil association, or to an irregulated, undisciplined conscience, excusable in a measure in one who had not the advantages she had enjoyed of growing up under the eye of a blameless, honourable, and right-minded father.

In the Consistory Court of Canterbury is a book of the marriages performed at the Oporto factory by the English chaplain resident there. It begins in the year 1788, and ends in 1807. The author has searched this volume in vain for a marriage between Oliver Menaida and Judith Coppinger. If such a marriage did take place, it must have been after 1807, but the book of register of marriages later than this date is not to be found in the Consistory Court.

Were they married?

On inquiry at S. Enodoc no information has been obtained, for neither Judith nor the Menaidas had any relatives there with whom they communicated. If Mrs. Scantlebray ever heard, she said nothing, or—at all events—nothing she said concerning them has been remembered.

Were they ever married?

That question the reader must decide as he likes.

# OTHER CORNISH BOOKS YOU MAY LIKE

**OUR COVE:**
*Victorian Life in a Cornish Fishing Village*
J HENRY HARRIS
ISBN 1846850517

**IN A CORNISH LOOKING GLASS**
J HENRY HARRIS
ISBN 1846851815

**DEEP DOWN:**
*A Tale Of The Cornish Mines*
R.M. BALLANTYNE
ISBN 1905363168

**TALES OF A TIN MINE**
SILAS K HOCKING
ISBN 1846850347

❖

*And for Children of all ages:*

**CLEMO THE CORNISH CAT**
ROSALIND FRANKLIN
1905363087

*Clemo is a very friendly ginger cat who lives in a little village on Bodmin Moor. Clemo's love for Cornish pasties takes him on an amazing adventure one day — all the way across the moor to the sea! In this thoroughly Cornish tale we also meet some of Clemo's friends: Denzil Dog, Jethro Seagull, Petroc Pony, Demelza Buzzard & Jago Fox.*

**BODRICK AND THE MAGIC PETALS**
ROSALIND FRANKLIN
ISBN 1846850207

*Bodrick, the Beast of Bodmin Moor is very lonely.
He meets the Cornish Piskies one midsummer night
on the moor and learns a valuable lesson about overcoming his
shyness and making friends.*

**Orderable from any good bookstore
or online retailer or direct from our website:
WWW.DIGGORYPRESS.COM**

Printed in the United Kingdom
by Lightning Source UK Ltd.
129029UK00001B/127/A